W9-ARG-778

# PRAISE FOR GABRIELA HOUSTON

"A lyrical tale of mothers and daughters, the lies we tell ourselves and the choking strictures of petty society. Gabriela Houston's twist on Slavic folklore offers readers a mediation on the power, beauty and danger of the natural world, seen through the eyes of a rich cast of characters whose behaviour is all too manifestly human, despite their sometimes supernatural nature. Captivating, provocative and poignant – not to be missed."

David Wragg, author of *The Black Hawks*

"A fabulous fairytale, beautifully written, full of very human darkness and not-so-human heart. There is magic and joy here, as well as struggle and sacrifice, with characters and a very personal story you won't be able to stop thinking about long after the tale is told."

Dan Hanks, author of *Captain Moxley and the Embers of the Empire*

"Houston deftly handles both characterization and pacing as she creates a realistic, enchanting fairy tale with real-world themes."

Ginger Smith, author of *The Rush's Edge*

"Prose that scintillates, characters that captivate, and a world that is at once enchanting in its magic, horrifying in its realism, and vice-versa. Houston has gifted us with a folktale that is both mythically resonant and all too human."

Tyler Hayes, author of *The Imaginary Corpse*

"Houston is able to mark the significance of daily events, highlight her characters, and comment on humanity's capacity for othering. This intimate fantasy offers a heartfelt reflection on what it means to be human that is sure to please."

Publishers Weekly

"*The Second Bell*, Gabriela D. Houston's debut novel, is a coming-of-age tale set in a lavishly detailed backdrop drawn from the writer's native Slavic mythology... The second bell of this novel may be an echo of the second heartbeat of the striga, but the first bell that rings out clear and loud throughout tolls a folkloric tale of female solidarity, sacrifice and love."

*Tracy Fahey*, author of *The Girl in the Fort* and *New Music For Old Rituals*

"Gabriela's Houston's debut novel *The Second Bell* is a captivating tale about the depths humans, and others, will go to hate, to love, to hurt or to help as they struggle between love and duty. A moving and complex mother-daughter pair, Miriat and Salka ask the eternal questions of what exactly a parent owes a child and vice versa. A fresh and provocative spin on the Slavic Stiga mythology, *The Second Bell* is a smart and complex journey into the meaning of family, community, nature and possibility. A gripping read and full of heart."

*Soniah Kamal*, award-winning author of *Unmarriageable*

*Gabriela Houston*

# THE SECOND BELL

**ANGRY
ROBOT**

ANGRY ROBOT
An imprint of Watkins Media Ltd

Unit 11, Shepperton House
89-93 Shepperton Road
London N1 3DF
UK

*angryrobotbooks.com*
*twitter.com/angryrobotbooks*
Follow Your Heart

An Angry Robot paperback original, 2021

Copyright © Gabriela Houston 2021

Edited by Eleanor Teasdale and Gemma Creffield
Cover by Glen Wilkins

All rights reserved. Gabriela Houston asserts the moral right to be identified as the author of this work. A catalogue record for this book is available from the British Library.

This novel is entirely a work of fiction. Names, characters, places, and incidents are the products of the author's imagination or are used fictitiously. Any resemblance to actual events, locales, organizations or persons, living or dead, is entirely coincidental.

Sales of this book without a front cover may be unauthorized. If this book is coverless, it may have been reported to the publisher as "unsold and destroyed" and neither the author nor the publisher may have received payment for it.

Angry Robot and the Angry Robot icon are registered trademarks of Watkins Media Ltd.

ISBN 978 0 85766 890 5
Ebook ISBN 978 0 85766 891 2

Printed and bound in the United Kingdom by TJ Books

9 8 7 6 5 4 3 2 1

MIX
Paper from
responsible sources
FSC
www.fsc.org   FSC® C013056

*To my beloved daughters Scarlett and Sienna*

*Salka held her arms steady before her. Her wet nightgown clung to her body, which got smaller with each heartbeat. She shivered as the shadow wrapped itself tight around her. It teased and pulled apart her defenses, greedily sucking at the meagre resources of her body.*

*She tried not to watch her arms as the fat moved under the skin like maggots, and was pried away from her, followed by her work-toughened muscles. It hurt a little, but she wouldn't watch. It was only energy to energy, she thought as a thin line of blood trickled down her nose and over her lips.*

*The shadow's tendril caressed her face and took even that.*

*Bell, bell, second bell,*
*Such a thirst as it can't quell,*
*it will burn and it will drown*
*First you drive it out of town.*

– The Heyne Mountains nursery rhyme

# CHAPTER 1

*Clang*

A slender hand hit the table, the iron rings on the fingers ringing out as they touched the wood. There were no words spoken after that. Everyone knew that Miriat had made her decision and no amount of talking would change it. The women crowded in the small room watched sullenly as Miriat took off her rings and bronze bracelets one by one. She made a point of lifting each item for everyone to see before putting them on a small pile in the middle of the table. You could only take the clothes on your back when you made the choice to go to the strigas' nest.

Miriat approached a narrow bed in the corner of the room and picked up a small, warm bundle. She pressed it to her chest. A cry came from inside the folds of the fabric, and a woman in the corner spat with disgust. Miriat ignored her and walked past with her head held high.

She paused only for a moment, just as her foot was about to pass the threshold. A young man stood outside the door, his hands fidgeting as if he was cold, though he stood in the still-warm autumn sun. His dark eyes watched her impassively, and perhaps Miriat was the only one who could notice the furrow on his forehead and the twitch in the corner of his lips. He said nothing though, and she replied with a silence of her own. Without breaking eye contact, he undid the clasp on his woolen cloak and wrapped it around Miriat's shoulders, his hands pausing for a brief moment as they brushed past her arms. Some of those back in the house muttered disapprovingly. Moments earlier they'd been family and friends, comforting and coaxing, drawing a vision of a life filled with joy and love. If she would only relent. If she would only let them take her child away. Now they begrudged her even the comfort of a warm cloak.

Miriat took a deep breath and stepped out, leaving her life behind.

She walked down the road, trying not to look at the people watching her go.

Aurek the baker, who had hoped to woo Miriat when she was but a girl, now spat at the sight of her and drew his wife closer to his chest. Gniev, the old shopkeeper who had a soft spot for children and would sometimes give them a chewy sweet or two from the big jar on one of the shop's shelves while their mothers weren't looking, twisted his amiable face and shouted an obscenity that Miriat would never have accused him of knowing.

She pulled the cloak closer around her little bundle as the wind blew. A rotten apple flew through the air and splattered in front of her on the stones, its juices spraying the hem of her long skirt. She looked at the crowd. It could have been anyone. Any of the women who, only a few days ago, would spend long hours chatting with her companionably, on the long daily walk bringing the men's lunches to the mine. Any of the men who drank with her husband to celebrate her pregnancy, or who patted him on the back after they married. Their faces, so familiar, and yet now so strange, like a nightmare that puts the face of a dragon on your child's head to frighten and confuse you. *This cannot be real.* She jutted out her chin with a defiance she didn't feel.

As was custom, the whole town had gathered to see her go. Three Dolas came down from the mountains in the morning to see the law was obeyed, and they stood now, silent, at the edge of the crowd. Their ceremonial cloaks had hoods drawn across their faces, so nothing but their unsmiling lips were visible. She was grateful for their presence. They were there for her safety as well.

*Save the tears for later.* She gritted her teeth.

A woman, a skilled pastry maker who'd made the cake to celebrate Miriat's wedding, and would accept no coin for it, ran in front of her and swung her arms wide. Miriat only had a moment to turn her back on the woman, protecting the baby as a bucketful of kitchen waste was emptied onto her back. The crowd whooped and laughed as the half-decomposed potato peel and bits of rotten onions and chicken bones slipped down Miriat's hair, the pungent juices trickling down her neck and under her collar.

"Rot to rot, striga," the woman said, nodding with satisfaction.

Miriat yearned to hit the woman, or else to throw the betrayed sisterhood in her face. But a glance at the crowd froze her mid-word. They hungered for a reaction. Any excuse to tear her to pieces. If Miriat hit the woman now, then all the Dolas of Prissan wouldn't be able to help her.

Miriat straightened her shoulders. "As you say," she said, turning away from the woman. As she continued down the road, Miriat's arms tensed, though she prayed none could see it. They would sniff out her fear, even under the stink of the rotting food caked in her hair.

Miriat left the town and walked down the muddy path leading towards the forest through the terraced fields. The last of the year's crops had been harvested, and the ground looked bare.

At the end of the road, just at the edge of the tree line, stood a small hunched-up figure of a woman. Miriat's heart sank, but she walked on.

"Are you planning on talking me out of it?" Miriat asked. There was no defiance in her voice, only resignation.

"No."

The older woman pulled the shawl lower over her forehead. She leaned on her walking stick, which some kind hand had decorated with a crude carving of twirling leaves. White, unseeing eyes turned towards Miriat.

"I won't ask you if it's worth it, either. Only you can answer that."

"It's worth it. It's worth it for me," Miriat said.

"Then there is your answer." The woman pulled out a pouch from the depths of her apron and proceeded to fill a small pipe. The two stood quietly for a time as she lit it and took the first two puffs. She coughed and said, quietly, "You could have other babies though. Later."

"Yes, but not this one," Miriat said.

"No, not this one," the woman replied, her voice making it clear that in her opinion that wouldn't be an altogether bad thing. "You can't come back, you understand."

"Good. I don't want to."

"Not even if it dies." The woman brushed the greying hair out of her face. "You're leaving forever. And the forest will never release you."

"And what would you have done?" Miriat asked. "If it were you in my place, what would you have done?"

The older woman puffed on the pipe and, as she exhaled, a circle of smoke wafted above their heads briefly, before dissipating into the air. She nodded. "You'd better be off then."

Miriat hesitated and leaned towards the old woman, planting a kiss on her cheek. "Goodbye, Mama."

Miriat pulled her child closer to her chest and walked towards the forest, never once looking back.

There was only one town in the Heyne Mountains. It was an ancient collection of houses and farms held together by law, tradition, and a single road. The houses were small but warm, built to withstand the winter cold. Most of the doors were painted pale blue, both to ward off evil, and to please the eye. The landscape was cold and unforgiving, and it bred a cold people. And sometimes it also bred strigas.

Sometimes in Heyne Town, a child was born with two hearts. Though no one knew why, everyone knew what was to be done about it. After each birth, a Dola midwife would put a hollowed-out horn to the baby's chest, place her ear to the narrow point, and listen. Most of the time the steady beating of a single heart would bring a smile to her face and reassure the anxious mother. But sometimes the baby's eyes would watch the midwife carefully, as the little thud-thud of a double heartbeat sealed the infant's fate.

The Dola would then take the child to the edge of the forest, tie a bit of red leather around its wrist and leave it there, never looking back. The family would mourn the child, burying their grief and shame in an empty grave.

But once in a while, a mother would refuse to let go of the child. And if no reasoning could convince her otherwise, she'd join her baby in its exile. The two of them would then seek a different life in the striga village high up in the mountains, never to return.


Miriat looked around her. The trees domed above her head swayed, their trunks creaking like a rusty hinge. She held her baby closer still and kissed its forehead. A happy little sigh rewarded her, before the baby's face screwed up with a threat of an imminent cry. "Oh no, little one, no no, hush, sweetling…"

She rocked the baby from side to side as she walked towards where the forest path led westward. The air was cold and felt wet, chilling her in each breath she took. The soft whispers of the forest did nothing to alleviate Miriat's fears. She knew nothing about how she might reach the strigas, whom she'd been taught all her life to avoid and fear. And would they accept her, or just tear her baby from her arms? She shivered. She would not let that happen. She would face them all if she had to.

The baby's screams pierced the air. Miriat sat down underneath a tall oak and put it to her breast. The baby's mouth screwed up in anger as its little arms flailed about her mother's chest.

"You should probably learn to keep it quiet," a high-pitched voice said from somewhere behind Miriat, sending her into a panic. She whipped her head around but saw nothing. Only the leaves moved in the breeze. "I could hear you from the other side of the Hope Tree," the voice continued, "and you're in the bear country now, you know."

"Where are you?" Miriat said, fighting to keep her voice level. "Show yourself. I have no fear of you."

A young girl of no more than twelve slid down the very tree Miriat was sitting under. She had dark eyes and dark hair with a hint of red. She jumped off a low branch and landed next to Miriat. For a moment, it seemed like two girls were standing side by side. But then Miriat blinked and there was just one.

"I'm Maladia," the girl said, eyeing the baby in Miriat's arms. "Can I see?" She reached out one hand towards the child.

Miriat stiffened and pulled the baby closer.

Maladia chuckled. "What, you scared of the big bad stigoi? You think I'm going to gobble you up? You're one of us now, better get used to it." She cocked her head to the side and waited.

Miriat resented the barb. Still, the girl was right. She unwrapped the baby, exposing its small face.

Maladia put two fingers on the baby's neck. Miriat sucked in a sharp breath as she fought the urge to push the girl away.

"A striga, sure enough," the girl said after a while. She turned her attention to Miriat's clothes. "You do realize it's almost winter, right? You didn't think to bring anything else with you?" Miriat only shook her head.

Maladia shrugged her shoulders. "It's your bum to freeze off, I guess. Some girls hide extra blankets around the edge of the forest before they're due. Just in case... you know."

Miriat looked down miserably. So stupid. She knew some girls took precautions, but in the past months the worry just seemed so distant; Miriat refused to even consider her firstborn might be born a striga.

Maladia took pity on her. "Let's look around. I bet there's some long-forgotten blanket tied to a tree somewhere. We can take the time and look for a bit."

Miriat tried to smile.

"So, what's the baby's name then?" Maladia asked as they walked along the treeline.

"Salka," Miriat said. "I named her Salka."

"Are we getting close? I need to feed her," Miriat said, as she and Maladia walked between the pine trees. They'd been walking for most of the day, and Miriat had to stop often. The walking was both painful and exhausting so soon after the birth, but she didn't complain, even though her impatient guide kept racing ahead, visibly bored with their slow pace. Salka began squirming in the cold, in spite of the woolen blanket Miriat had eventually found in the branches of a tree.

The girl laughed and smacked her forehead. "Right. Sorry! The critter must be starving. Here, sit down." Maladia skipped over to an old string bark aspen, growing solitary between a pile of large boulders. She looked encouragingly towards Miriat, who sat on the ground with a grunt.

Suddenly, a blue egg fell from the tree's branches, bounced off a moss-covered rock with a faint crack, rolled down and bumped against Miriat's boot. For a moment, the baby stopped crying, and Miriat and Maladia both looked on as a featherless creature squeaked weakly from inside the broken shell. To their surprise, it had survived the fall, the cold air waking it as it strove to free itself from what remained of the egg.

"A cuckoo hatchling must have pushed the poor thing out of the nest," Maladia said, looking up at the branches. "I've never seen a chick survive a fall like that. Must be an omen," she said, turning to Miriat. She cocked her head to the side and said, "It won't survive though. It'd be a mercy to kill it."

She stood without a smile and for a chilling moment, Miriat wasn't sure if Maladia was talking about the bird.

Miriat reached out to the chick and picked it up, and cradled it gently within the palm of her hand. The creature hopped and turned its open beak towards Miriat. At that moment, Salka stirred again, and looked at her mother.

"It will die anyway," Maladia said again, watching Miriat with interest.

"No, it won't," Miriat said. "There is enough of me for them both."

After Salka had been fed, and a grub had been dropped down the hungry chick's mouth, the three continued their slow climb towards the striga village. Maladia offered to carry Salka once, but the look Miriat gave her taught her not to repeat the offer. So, she carried the chick instead, and allowed Miriat to stop frequently. As the day wore on, they finally came up to a large wooden gate, which, if looked at from any other direction but the one they were approaching from, would have seemed a mere scattering of twigs and dry logs.

Maladia knocked. A raspy voice from above said, "So they kicked another one out, did they?" They both looked up and a plump face looked back from between the branches of a large tree growing on the other side of the gate.

"Stop your chattering and open the gate, calf-brain! We're tired and cold! Have you no shame?" Maladia called out with a broad smile on her face.

"Not much, goat-voice, not much. Shame doesn't pay. And it doesn't satisfy curiosity, either," the child said, slipping down the tree. Moments later the tall gate swung open.

The new girl was pleasant-looking, roughly the same age as Maladia, with a cheerful wide face, and warm brown eyes. The girls embraced. Maladia's friend had more meat on her bones and a soft look which spoke of an easier life. No fewer than three leather pouches were tied to her belt, all painted with colorful patterns, and her tunic had a small picture of embroidered thistle around the collar. Her clothing made her seem familiar, though Miriat was sure she'd never seen her face before.

"Are you a striga?" Miriat asked, carefully.

"Hah!" Maladia laughed. "She's a Dola. Can't you tell by the airs she gives herself?" Maladia said, her skinny arms crossed. Her friend made a pretense of kicking her.

"Dola?" Confusion crossed Miriat's face "But... you're so young? All the Dolas I've ever seen were old women."

"Some of us are old, but we don't exactly leave our mothers' wombs that way." Dola said with a laugh which made her cheeks shake. "My work tends to be on the other side of the mountain, so you wouldn't have seen me in Heyne Town."

"Your work..." Miriat turned her head to the side. She couldn't help but feel skeptical.

"'Work' she calls it" Maladia scoffed. "Don't believe a word she says. She's barely an apprentice." The Dola gave her a dirty look.

"And what do they call you? I mean, what's your name?" Miriat asked. The lighthearted banter between the two girls raised her spirit a bit. There was comfort in the everyday.

"They're all called 'Dola,'" Maladia said, rolling her eyes. "And they all tell the future. Some with less competence than others..."

"'There is one fate and so one name is enough for those who read it,'" Dola said with mock solemnity. "Anyway, you're in luck. The West Stream Dola is inside, attending a sick child so she can see you after. Saves us a trip down and up the mountain!"

Miriat shifted uncomfortably, casting a look at the tall gate in front of them. She tried to peek over Dola's shoulder to catch a glimpse of her new home.

A shiver ran down Miriat's back as she saw two quiet figures, observing her from the open gate. A middle-aged woman stood there with her hand on a dark-eyed boy's head. The boy was looking at Miriat with unabashed curiosity, his very dark brown hair hanging low across his forehead. His mother's hand tenderly swept it to the side. The woman locked eyes with Miriat, but she didn't smile.

Instead, she just said, "If you're bringing a new striga with you, Maladia, don't you think you ought to report to me rather than just stand there gossiping?"

The two young girls squealed in surprise and looked towards their feet. "Yes, Alma. Sorry, Alma," Maladia said, and gestured to Miriat to follow her. Dola trailed close behind. She leaned forward and whispered, "Maybe after you meet Alma and have the West Stream Dola look over you, you and I can have a talk? I'm a good talker. And a game of chance, perhaps?"

"Don't," Maladia said, rolling her eyes. "She cheats."

"I do not!" Dola said, indignant. "Not my fault if I can predict the outcome."

"Right. Knowing the extra bones you keep stashed in your sleeves must help with the predicting." Maladia ignored her friend's less than convincing show of outrage and nodded towards Miriat, "Take my word for it: with a Dola, even when you win, you lose."

The first thing Miriat noticed were the goats.

They were everywhere: nibbling on drying clothes, unwillingly giving an insistent child a ride, and fouling up the path and the entries to the houses indiscriminately. They were all clearly well-tended, their long coats glossy from brushing. They gave the air a distinct sour milky aroma that made Miriat feel nauseous and very hungry at the same time.

She followed Maladia and the woman called Alma, cradling her daughter in her arms. She became aware of a pair of eyes staring at her intently. The boy she saw at the gate was trotting beside her, clearly trying to catch a glimpse of Salka. Miriat noticed the difficulty with which he walked, one of his feet seeming to give him pain, as it twisted inwards at an odd angle. As they walked through the village, they were watched by its inhabitants. One by one, the villagers all followed them in a small procession of solemn curiosity.

Miriat's heart sank as she looked around at what was to be her new home. Though she'd expected hardship, nothing had prepared her for the squalor and the poverty now surrounding her.

The houses in the village were little more than round huts, and Alma led them to the largest one. Miriat spotted a small, raised vegetable garden and a few goats tied to a pole. The goats stared at the women impassively as they entered.

Inside the hut, herbs and dried cheese necklaces hung from the ceiling, and there were a couple of elevated pallet beds with a space underneath each for the livestock. The house was surprisingly organized and clean, though the smoke from the fire burning in the middle of the room made Miriat feel light-headed.

Alma called for everyone else to come inside, and she waited for the villagers to take their places along the walls before she spoke. Miriat looked at those around her, and a shiver ran down her spine as she saw a few once-familiar faces. She felt like she had crossed into the afterlife, with the ghosts of her past about to stand in judgement of her.

"So," Alma said, sitting down in a leather-covered wooden chair. "Sit yourself down and tell me why I should let you stay." The striga leader leaned back and steepled her fingers in front of her face. Alma had the lean wiry frame of someone who habitually worked harder and ate less than was good for them. Her face was pleasant enough to look at, though there were hard lines around her mouth and between her thin eyebrows, lines that spoke of hard choices made and much pain endured.

Miriat wasn't sure what was expected of her. She turned towards Maladia, but the girl avoided her eyes and busied herself stroking the bare head of the hatchling in her hand.

"What's that? Give me this!" the dark-eyed boy demanded, with all the greed and tact of toddlerhood.

"Leave it!" Maladia said sharply, doing her best to shake the boy off as he pulled on her sleeve. "It's Miriat's! She found it and it's hers!"

"Oh, indeed?" Alma chuckled, her sharp eyes taking everything in. "Looks to me like that bird will be dead soon. So, townswoman," she turned towards Miriat. "You have nothing to say for yourself?"

"You know why I'm here," Miriat said, inwardly berating herself for the quiver in her voice. "My daughter was born a striga. And I couldn't let them take her from me. So, I came here. To join you."

"Have you now?" Alma raised her eyebrows. "Oh, how very brave of you." A few of the strigas in the room sniggered.

"So, tell me now, girl. What else is there to recommend you to us than the minimum of a mother's feeling?" Alma raised her hand and the room fell silent again. "You haven't abandoned your child, which is all very well, but why should we take you on? As you see, we have plenty of mouths to feed as it is."

Miriat looked around. The men and women lining the walls were watching her. The room felt oppressive, the air was thick with the smell of these people, with the shadows dancing strangely on the walls.

"I have nowhere else to go," she whispered, her head down. *They will send us away,* she thought, *they will send us away to starve in the woods.* The courage of the morning had now left her, and hot tears fill her eyes. She wiped them with the back of her hand. "I don't know what I need to do for my daughter, but you do. I've no kin now, no friends to help or shelter me. So, I've come here. And if it's my blood and flesh you want as payment, you may have it. But my child won't survive Heyne winter unless you take us in."

"Your 'blood and flesh'?" a man standing in the corner scoffed. "Because what else would dirty stigois want, right?" Miriat shrunk as he used the word. "Who do you think we are, girl?" The other strigas in the room tensed. Clearly the taint of the word had power over them still, even in their own home.

"Mordat, show some manners." Alma looked upon the man fondly, though her words silenced him. "Our guest seems unaware of our customs. Which is not her fault, I'm sure," she added, though she gave Miriat a look as if to note that last point was yet to be decided. "Girl, we have no designs on your life. You'll find no striga here who'd follow the dark impulses of their second heart."

The strigas in the room all nodded and made small gestures by their chests, as if to ward off evil.

Alma rubbed her temple and paused before announcing, "You can stay." The crowd of strigas visibly relaxed, with some smiles exchanged shyly across the room. Alma raised her finger. "But one thing must be made clear. You're no hero. How many children have you seen left at the forest's edge? How many women did you see make that lonely journey into the night, with never so much as a 'fare thee well'? What did you do then, what did you say?" She paused, allowing her words to sink in, but expecting no reply. "I'm sure there are some among us who could answer that for you, if they so wished." Miriat shrunk within herself. Alma sighed and said, not unkindly, "But you have given your child a chance, and so we can do no less." She continued, "I see the chick in Maladia's hand. See it survives." Alma looked Miriat in the eyes and gave a curt nod. "That will be the right thing to do."

Miriat was ushered into a small hut no larger than her tool shed back in Heyne Town, with the young Dola she'd met by the wall trailing behind her. The woman referred to as the West Stream Dola was waiting for her inside and gestured towards an elevated straw and moss mattress, positioned by the back wall of the tiny room. "Come in, come in," she said with a smile as Miriat sat down.

"Pass me my bag, child," the older woman said to the younger Dola. The midwife rummaged through it and took out a small glass phial. She pulled out the cork with her teeth and poured a few drops into her palm. She passed the phial back to her young apprentice, without looking in her direction and rubbed her palms together. A sharp smell filled the room. Though not unpleasant, it was strong enough to make Miriat's eyes water.

"I see you've met my young friend here." The West Stream Dola pointed to the young girl who winked at Miriat. "She will observe, if you don't mind. I need to check the state of you."

Miriat nodded and allowed the older woman to place her hands on her stomach. "Not much more than two or three days since the little one came, I'd say," the old midwife said, gently kneading Miriat's flesh with her plump fingers. She shook her head. "Their love didn't hold out long enough for you to heal, did it?"

"They hoped mine wouldn't either," Miriat said, looking squarely into the old Dola's face.

The older woman nodded and placed a reassuring hand on Miriat's shoulder. "Well, you're safe now, at least. Though I'll have a talk with my fellow Dolas. The Heyne Town folk seem more and more impatient with their own. I'm not sure we'll be able to achieve much with the council, but perhaps the next time they throw a young mother out, they will wait for her wounds to heal at least. Lean back for me please."

Miriat couldn't help but feel reassured by the old midwife's quietly competent demeanor. It brought a sense of normality to the day which had been anything but. The young Dola gently took Salka from Miriat's arms so that she could lie down. The West Stream Dola hitched up Miriat's skirt and waved at her apprentice to watch what she was doing.

"This hut is not much, but at least it's a dry place to sleep," the old woman said. She noticed Miriat's expression. "It's nothing to what you had, I know..." Clearly nobody had lived in this hut for a long time, and the mud walls were crumbling, revealing the support branches underneath. The door was a half-rotten animal skin, stretched out and hooked on the sides of the doorframe to keep out the cold. But there was a lit fire pit in the middle of the room, with a stack of wood and peat for fuel in the corner. While Miriat was being interrogated by Alma, somebody had hung half a dozen or so of the cheese necklaces she'd seen before from the ceiling. Their dried squares glistened white in the firelight. In the corner there was a single clay pot with a roughly carved wooden spoon, and a single cup and a bowl, similarly fashioned out of wood. The floor had been swept and some kind hand had sought to fill the holes in the walls with moss. Either the hut had been kept ready or, more likely, the villagers knew Alma wouldn't turn Miriat away and, while their leader was putting her through the wringer, they had furnished her with the basic necessities quietly, without ceremony. Something stuck in Miriat's throat. Those people, strangers to her, would not allow their first kindness to be a debt.

"It's more than I expected," she said.

The midwife nodded with approval. "I'm glad you feel so. I had told Alma to prepare for your arrival. The bones told me you'd be coming, and a young mother needs a safe place to sleep." She watched Miriat carefully. "And to mourn, I suppose."

Miriat realized she was crying. She wiped the tears with the side of her hand, not trusting herself to speak.

The old Dola finished her examination. She pulled out a couple of sealed clay jars from her bag and put them on the mattress. "For your wounds and the bruising," she said.

Miriat's eyes opened wide. "But I have nothing to pay you with..."

"When you do, you'll pay me." The old woman raised her hand. "You will have to rely on others' help in the coming months. And in time, you will repay it. Make sure you do so. The strigas look after each other... to a point. But they will watch you too. Just because you can't see the tally, doesn't mean it's not kept.

"Now, for your child, make sure to keep her warm," the midwife said, gently passing the infant from her apprentice back to her mother's arms. "The child will learn to control the other heart in time, but you must stay vigilant as well. An infant cannot be expected to have any self-control. You must give the other heart no reason to assert itself."

The old woman smiled at Miriat and left the hut. Her young apprentice lingered for a moment and surprised Miriat with a quick hug before, she too, left.

Miriat looked around her new home. Salka gave a content sigh, wriggling in her mother's arms.

"We can make this work," Miriat said, smiling at Salka. "I can make this work."

# CHAPTER 2

*19 years later*

Salka listened to the steady rhythm of her feet pounding the ground. The cool autumn sun was barely filtering through the trees to the moss-covered ground. Above Salka, her falcon Munu screeched. She couldn't see him, so she just followed the sound, slowing down as the wet roots became a slippery tangle under her feet. It wouldn't do to slip and make a noise.

She paused to tighten the scarf tied around her head, keeping her black curls out of her eyes. Her hand rummaged blindly in her leather bag till it found the cord of her sling.

The loud rumbling in her belly sent a reminder of the missed breakfast, still carefully wrapped in her bag. She ignored it. If she didn't catch anything today, the small acorn-flour and hog-fat patty would have to last her till tomorrow. Miriat always made sure to set aside food for her daughter, no matter how barren their stores, but it'd been a long while since Salka had wisened up to the fact her bowl was often filled with her mother's dinner. Neither of them ever mentioned it, both making secret efforts to trick the other into satisfying their hunger first.

She leaned forward, her hands hovering over a freshly-nibbled sapling top. A tuft of soft grey fur blew onto a dry branch. The rabbits of the Heyne Mountains were changing their summer coats and left behind a trail a skilled hunter had no trouble following.

Salka liked to hunt on this side of the mountain; the softer ground was the preferred spot for the small game to dig burrows in. She grinned as a small grey-white rabbit's ears peeked from above the bilberry plants.

*There you are!* Salka placed one of her smooth-edged stream stones into the sling and rolled her shoulders. Her wrist moved in a well-practiced arch and the sling cord whistled above her head. The rabbit stood up on its hind legs, its ears pricking up at the noise. Round and round the sling pouch zoomed till Salka released the tab and let the stone fly.

It hit the rabbit with a dull thud. The animal swayed for a moment, as if it didn't quite realize it was already dead. It crumpled to the ground, a light patch among the red-green undergrowth.

Salka exhaled and whistled on her fingers. Munu dived through the sky and lifted up the rabbit, before dropping it at Salka's feet. The falcon then landed on Salka's shoulder and trilled as she petted his head. "Well, done, Munu!" She lifted up the rabbit and put it inside the bag. She scratched the bird's neck as he nibbled her fingers. "What do you think of taking the scenic route back? What's that? You'd love to?" She leaned her ear towards Munu, her teeth bared in a grin. "Your wish is my command!"

She whistled again as she made her way westward towards the wide ravine, where the now dry bed spoke of a long-forgotten river. The side of the ravine was steep, with fewer trees and wide beds of wild-roses. When she was a child, Salka used to come here in the summer to weave herself sweet-smelling crowns. She'd pretend she was a princess from one of her mother's stories, or else an enchantress, who could stand by the edge of the ravine's bank with her arms stretched wide, ready for the wind spirits to carry her to her palace beyond the Heyne Mountains.

Now she only came here for the tart rose hips, dotting the bare branches. Fantasies and stories didn't fill an empty stomach.

Salka squinted, unused to the bright light unfiltered by the domed branches of the pine trees. She was barely a step from the edge of the ravine, but the rose hips here were the richest red, ripened by the sun, away from the thick forest canopy.

She worked quickly, picking rosehips with one hand, the other holding her pack. Her finger slid across a thorny branch, imbedding a few needle-sharp thorns in her delicate flesh. "Ouch!" Salka's hand flew to her mouth, spilling the precious fruits onto the ground.

Salka darted forward, her hand trying to grasp the rose hips before they rolled off the edge.

Munu screeched a shrill warning as Salka's ankle twisted inward on a wet root. She fell, slipping off the edge, her hand grasping wildly at the roots and branches.

Salka didn't need to look down to know the sheer stony surface of the cliff with hard rocks awaiting her at the bottom. Her pulse quickened, and a sob of terror escaped her chest.

She saw a dark shape pool under her fingertips, digging into the ground, pulling her upwards.

*No!* A wave of disgust hit her, more powerful than her fear. She heard the rush of blood in her ears as her striga heart beat out the promise of help. She bit her lip till it bled, trying to slow her breathing in spite of the terror which sent rivulets of cold sweat down her back. The shadow withdrew as the striga heart in Salka's chest slowed down, its powers pushed back.

As the shadow tendrils receded from the ground, Salka's body slipped a little further back. She yelped in fear and pushed at the cliff's side with her feet, desperate for a foothold.

Her hand shot up and, in desperation, grabbed the thick twisting stem of the wild rose bush. The sharp thorns tore into Salka's palm, as she pulled herself up, sobbing, back onto the ground.

She lay on her back for a while, pulling the thorns out of her hand with her teeth. She'd done it, but a shiver of fear ran through her. She almost let go, almost. Salka closed her eyes for a moment. She'd tell nobody how close she'd come to breaking the law. She'd keep it quiet in her chest, the blasphemy of it. Revulsion shook her shoulders.

She'd be back on her way to the village soon. And then she'd forget this happened. She tried in vain to calm herself, with each breath feeling her striga heart batter at her defenses.

# CHAPTER 3

Miriat stretched her back, which ached after a morning of dyeing the goat-wool floss she had earmarked for her daughter's new cloak. She inspected her fingers, turned bright green by nettle dye. She sighed and looked around, waving as she caught sight of her friend carrying a pail of water into the hut next to hers. Trina, Maladia's mother, was a small, dark woman with a ready smile and wide brown eyes. A large wine stain bloomed on her cheek, which had been a great source of disappointment in her youth, but, to those who loved her, it was as insignificant as last year's snow.

"Do you need help with that water, Trina?" Miriat asked, torn between hoping for a resounding "no" and wishing for a reason to interrupt her own tedious work. The wool could be left in the water a while longer. The color would be all the richer for it, Miriat decided.

"I'm all right, but your company's always welcome. I'm making stew, and if you have anything to throw in, we can all eat it tonight." Trina made a nod towards Miriat's little plot of onions. Those were Miriat's pride and joy, their big round heads with a near translucent white skin the envy of the village.

"I can spare an onion or two." Miriat laughed and moved her stool next to her friend's door as Trina brought out a plump rabbit.

"Four can feast on this one," the woman said with pride. Maladia was a skilled hunter, both with a sling and with ingenious traps of her own design. When Salka was a child she was forever following the older striga, hanging on her every word with rapt interest.

"But I'm sure it can stretch to five," a cheerful voice interrupted as Dola dropped a small sack of potatoes in front of Miriat and then sat down heavily on Maladia's stool, which creaked a warning. Miriat shot Trina an amused look, as experience had taught her there would be scarcely more in the sack to satisfy Dola's own, considerable appetite.

"Why is it that your gifts of prophecy seem to only extend to other people's mealtimes?" Miriat asked, raising one eyebrow as she worked with her stone knife to remove the rabbit skin.

"We can't choose which parts of destiny are revealed to us," Dola said with a grin, shifting her bottom to find a more comfortable position. The perfect peach of a woman, Maladia's friend had grown both in size and good humor in the eighteen years since Miriat had come to the village. She was no longer the precocious child who first welcomed Miriat at the gates, but a confident woman, more than aware of the effect her pretty round face had on the young men in the village. Dola now stroked her rounded belly, which Miriat suspected carried more than just her last meal. But the young woman said nothing of it, and so Miriat didn't either.

"So, are we to expect my daughter this evening as well, or has she lost her way in the forest with Markus again? The way her sense of direction has been playing tricks on her lately, we might soon be in need of your midwifery skills. And I hope that there is more in this sack than a few wrinkled potatoes," Trina said, picking up the sack with a sigh. Though she would never turn a friend away, Dola could stretch the boundaries of Trina's generosity at times.

"Oh, Maladia was supposed to meet me here, but she –" Dola stopped abruptly, and her usually cheerful face hardened as she pointed over Miriat's shoulder. "Why is everyone running towards Alma's house?"


Alma sat in her chair surrounded by the villagers, her face betraying little emotion. A young man stood inside the circle, a mop of blonde hair covering his forehead, his eyes fixed on the ground.

"It's Markus..." Miriat said to Trina, caught behind taller shoulders. "I see Maladia too."

"Oh no..." Trina said.

A tall woman with long greying hair and a hooked nose which seemed to almost touch her upper lip shushed everyone and shot Miriat a disapproving look. Many strigas in the village felt there were some aspects of striga life from which the non-striga mothers should be excluded. Miriat ignored her.

Alma drummed her fingers on the armrest of her seat. "We've been called here today because of an accusation brought against one of us." A murmur rolled through the crowd. Alma waited for it to die down before continuing. "Kalina, come here, girl."

A young woman walked to the middle of the room. She stood straight in front of Alma, with her eyes modestly down, though Miriat noticed a small triumphant gaze cast at the aghast crowd. Kalina fidgeted as she awaited Alma's questions. Her eyes darted this way and that, and a little defiant smile stretched her lips when faced with the naked hostility of the villagers. Most called her "Pike" behind her back, for they'd say she was much like the toothy fish, likely to snatch your catch from the line and ruin your day.

Mordat, Trina's and Miriat's friend, spotted them from across the room. He moved closer to Trina and wordlessly placed a comforting hand on her shoulder. Trina shook it off. What comfort could there be in such a moment.

"That snake! She's been after Markus for as long as I can remember!" Trina said, shaking her head. "If she's Markus' accuser, I know what to think!"

Miriat looked at her friend briefly but kept quiet. There were many uncharitable things one could say of Kalina, with some justification, but she was not known to be a liar. Miriat cast her eyes about to see if Salka was there. She breathed a sigh of relief when her eyes didn't find her. For once she was glad of her daughter's tardiness. Salka's loyalty to her friend wouldn't let her sit through these proceedings quietly, and Miriat expected she'd have her hands full trying to restrain Trina.

"Tell us what you saw, and know you will be heard," Alma said with some ceremony.

"I was bringing my billy goat from its seclusion at the Old Teeth Hill for the mating season, and I came across Maladia and Markus in the woods," Kalina said, fiddling with the end of her woven belt.

"'Came across'! Hah! The little sneak was spying on us!" Maladia said with a snarl. Kalina shot her a hateful look, before lowering her eyes again.

Alma stood up and stared Maladia down. "You won't speak again unless I say so. You will not interrupt the proceedings here, or you will be removed from them." Alma turned back to Kalina. "How is it that neither Markus nor Maladia heard you approaching?"

Kalina shifted uncomfortably, "I took the bell off the billy goat's neck."

Alma raised an eyebrow. "And what did you see?" There were no sniggers or laughter from the crowd. The air was heavy with worry. None of the strigas wanted to witness this, and yet they couldn't look away.

"He was following his heart... the other one," Kalina said with so much relish that most everyone, Alma included, felt their stomachs pinch tight with disgust.

The striga leader raised her hand to quiet the room, as it erupted in a cacophony of angry cries and murmurs of disbelief. "How so?" she asked. Miriat noticed those standing nearest to Markus seemed to shrink back from him. Markus had not yet been convicted of anything, but the accusation alone was enough.

"Maladia's leg seemed broken. She must have fallen off a tree, gathering winter nuts most like." Kalina sniffed, "Not that she would ever offer to share any, I just saw them spilling out of the sack by her–"

"Remember where you are, Kalina," Alma said, the corner of her mouth twitching with barely concealed irritation. "Your petty grievances have no place here."

Kalina looked towards the floor, chastened. "I saw her on the ground, her leg twisted at a strange angle. There was a bone jutting out and her blood was flowing quickly. Bright and gushing in little streams. I was just about to come and help her, but something stopped me…"

"The something being her nasty nature and glee at my daughter's pain, no doubt," Trina said through clenched teeth.

For a moment Alma's eyes fixed on Trina's, and there was a shadow of sadness in the striga leader's face, though it disappeared so quickly, one could miss it entirely. Miriat put her arm around her friend's shoulder and squeezed her hard.

"…I saw Markus kneeling by Maladia. He put his hand on her chest. He wasn't trying to bandage the leg or even stop the bleeding. He was very still and quiet, but I saw his shadow move strangely above his head… And then it happened…

"The grass around them turned black and withered. It touched the nut tree next to them, and it dried, bark peeling and falling off in chunks. A bird fell off the tree, and I saw a squirrel too, trying to scamper away, though it didn't make it. Its body shriveled up just like the grass and it fell to the ground." Kalina shivered.

"Then Maladia's leg was fine again. I didn't know what they'd do to me if they saw me, so I left. I was running for my life, I was so scared. Once a striga turns into a stigoi, you never know…" she finished.

"Thank you, Kalina," Alma said in a voice that was anything but grateful. "Markus, step forward."

Markus stepped closer to Alma, his pale hair covering his downcast eyes.

"Do you deny it?"

Markus glanced at Maladia, his mouth in a grimace.

"Did you hear the question?"

"Yes, I heard your question." Markus looked up at Alma. Miriat took in a sharp breath, squeezing Trina's shoulder. Markus was always a soft-spoken lad, and gentle, too gentle even, for the hard life he led.

"Do you deny it?" Alma repeated the question, as if she'd heard nothing.

"That I'm a stigoi? Yes. But that I healed Maladia? Why would I deny it? The blood and the rip on her trousers would give me away if I tried."

"Then the law is clear." Alma stood up.

"The law that *you* make!" Maladia rushed towards Alma, pointing an accusatory finger at their leader. Alma looked at her calmly, and in her eyes, Miriat saw the compassion that Maladia was blind to.

"This is not your trial, Maladia, and I will have you removed if you can't control yourself."

"It might as well be!" The young woman took Markus by the hand. He tried to gently push her away, mouthing a quiet protestation, but Maladia would have none of it.

Alma nodded and stood up from her chair. "So be it. Markus, in following your heart you have drawn on a power that must always be kept in check. You have opened the floodgates that, if unguarded, could put our very survival in jeopardy. But you did so out of love, and I cannot fault you for that."

Alma closed her eyes and took a breath. "You will leave the safety of our community and the Heyne Mountains. You will never again be welcomed into our homes. You will not be offered aid or refuge. Should you defy me and return, your striga heart will be burnt out."

A collective gasp of breath and, for a heartbeat, the hut fell completely silent.

"You must leave within the hour," Alma continued. "I advise you to say your goodbyes." Alma closed her eyes and sunk back into her chair. The room erupted in loud cries, some cheering, others protesting the verdict. Trina pushed towards her daughter, who stood stone-faced by Markus.

"Markus, I'm so sorry…" Trina squeezed his hand, and at the same time, she gently pushed her own daughter away. Miriat could see her friend's desperation, as Trina tried to form and cement two parties to the goodbye: herself and her daughter on one side, and Markus on the other, the two parties divided by a handshake and a goodbye. To a lesser man, this might have seemed like the most profound ingratitude, but Markus understood. He shifted away from Maladia and smiled at Trina. "Take care of her for me," he said, and turned away.

Maladia made an outraged sound and pushed past her mother. "Oh no, you don't! I need nobody to take care of me, and you're not leaving without me!" She grabbed his limp hand and squeezed it. Markus kept looking at the floor, his hair obscuring his face. He nodded and pulled Maladia into his arms.

They walked out of Alma's house. The crowd parted before them, disgust and pity both marking the villagers' faces.

Trina and Miriat followed close behind them in a daze.

Markus lived in a tidy little hut not far from Trina's. Maladia helped him collect the few things they could carry while Trina dug out what was left in their garden. She used a flat stone to break the earth and pulled out what few potatoes there were. She cut the sprouts off their long stalks, carefully placing their green heads onto a square piece of fabric before tying the ends and placing the bundle inside Maladia's basket. Miriat tried to help, but Trina waved her away. "It's the last thing I'm allowed to do for my daughter. Let me." Miriat didn't insist. Instead, she went into Trina's house, and collected a few items for Maladia. The young striga seemed determined not to leave Markus alone, in case he tried to slip away without her.

Dola stayed on the outside of it all. A dozen times she reached out to help Maladia pack an item, and a dozen times she brought her hands back to her chest, as if such an act would make all this real and hasten her friend's departure. Miriat felt for her. Like her, Dola had no family except for the friendships she'd built.

Miriat gently put her arm around Dola and turned to Maladia and Markus. "Since the packing seems finished, we should feed you," she said, trying to keep her voice calm. "Come and have some stew before you leave."

She pulled Dola along, and they all walked to her house in a sad procession. Maladia walked holding both her mother's and

Markus' hands, though the path was narrow. The other strigas watched them from their own huts, either not daring or not willing to approach. Maladia and Markus had lived their entire lives within the village walls, but not a soul seemed willing to bid them goodbye. Even Trina seemed to shrink from Markus anytime he walked closer to her, and, noticing this, he kept his distance.

Miriat gave Maladia and Markus a generous portion. Nobody else ate anything. Trina sat by Maladia, one hand stroking her back. She watched her daughter eat and would pass her a cup of hot water before Maladia knew to even reach for it.

Dola sat on the ground and emptied one of her pouches, gazing intensely at the small, polished bones as if they could provide her with some solace. She selected one from the pile and dipped the end of it in the ashes under the pot. She took it out and blew on it before shuffling closer to Maladia and drawing ash patterns on the young striga's cheek.

"What are you doing?" Maladia looked towards her friend, somewhat startled. Dola didn't answer at first, stepping back to inspect her work. She cast her bones again and walked up to Maladia's other side.

"This is little enough protection, but it's all I can do for you, and it's something at least," she said. "Something's more than nothing, and I can't bear to give you nothing. I won't be there when the little one comes." Tears stood in her eyes, and she wiped them impatiently with her sleeve. Maladia stiffened and the startled Dola realized her mistake. Her hand flew to her mouth. She looked to Trina and back. "I thought you'd told her! You said you would!"

"I was going to…" Maladia tucked her hair behind her ear and turned to Trina, who sat motionless, her eyes as round as the moon. "At first, I waited until I was sure this one would stick. And then all this happened…" Maladia said, her eyes cast down.

"No," Trina said, standing up. She walked up closer to Markus, though not close enough for her shadow to reach his. "You can't really mean to take her with you. Not like this."

"It's my decision," Maladia said. She looked to Miriat for support.

"She's right, Trina. You can't keep her," Miriat said in a voice so quiet it barely reached their ears.

"I can't? So who has the right, if not me?" Trina's face turned red. "Markus is a stigoi now." She turned to Markus, "I'm sorry, child, but it's true. I'm thankful for what you did for my daughter, but how can you take care of her baby? How can you teach it to control its other heart, all the while letting your own feast on your soul?"

Markus sat very still, the steaming bowl of food in his lap. He half-turned to Maladia as if to say something. But he just continued sitting in silence, with a plaintive look on his face. He had used up what defiance he had in him at the trial. Maladia watched him quietly for a moment. She could see Trina's shoulders start to relax, letting herself believe she'd won. That her child and grandchild would indeed stay.

Trina's relief turned to horror as Maladia exhaled slowly, her shadow rippling on the ground, reaching its dark hand towards Markus' stigoi. The two shadows merged in an embrace.

Trina took a step back and Miriat nearly fell off her stool. It was the greatest of blasphemies – the second bell ringing for no other purpose than to hear its own music.

There was nothing left to be said after that. Trina just sat on the ground, empty-eyed, as Maladia approached her and kissed her cheek.

"Sorry, Mama. I love you, Mama," Maladia said. Then she walked away, never letting go of Markus' hand.

Once the two left, and she couldn't hear their footsteps anymore, Trina slid off the stool and seemed to fold into herself. A low wail escaped her throat.

"I didn't stop her, Miriat! Why couldn't I stop her?"

Miriat knelt by Trina and wrapped her arms around her. "She made her choice, Trina. Could your grandmother have stopped your own mother all those years ago?"

"She will die out there. Her baby will die. You know what they do to strigas when they find them. And they *will* find them. You saw his shadow! And you know how Maladia is! She's never careful, she never hides, she never..." Trina sobbed uncontrollably, supported by her friend.

Dola knelt by Trina and said, "She'll be all right. I can see she'll be all right." She let Trina hold her hand gratefully and exchanged a look with Miriat, sharing in the comfort of the lie.

# CHAPTER 4

Dran walked through the forest as quickly as his clubfoot allowed him. He tripped over a stone and winced at the pain, steadying himself by grabbing onto a tree. He took a breath and continued the hobbled half-walk, half-run. Soon Markus and Maladia would be too far for him to catch up to, and he would miss his chance.

A trickle of sweat ran down his forehead and he wiped it with the back of his hand. Dran had grown up to be a handsome, if a wiry young man, and he enjoyed the attentions of most of the young female strigas in the village. He had a narrow face with dark eyes often called soulful by those inclined to see them that way.

His foot hurt now, a steady familiar ache which he knew would soon turn into a sharp stabbing pain that would travel from his ankle right up to his groin. But he pressed on. Soon there would be no pain at all and no shame either.

He looked up. It was already getting dark, and in the Heyne Mountains it was a stupid time to be out, but it couldn't be helped. He stopped suddenly when a light flickered between the trees. Dran tried to approach quietly but his foot made it impossible to control his gait entirely. A twig snapped underfoot, and a familiar voice spoke behind him, "Turn around and put your palms up so I can see them, or I will crack your head open."

"It's me, Markus," Dran said, turning around with a smile.

"Dran! What are you doing?" Markus lowered the branch he was holding. "You know you're not supposed to be here! It's nearly night."

"Is that Dran? What are you doing here? Did my mother send you?" Maladia came out from behind Markus, her lips pursed into a thin line.

"No," Dran said. "But I'm cold and tired. If you let me sit by your fire, I'll tell you everything."

"Come then," Maladia nodded. Markus seemed uncertain and he tried to pull Maladia aside, but she shook him off. "What else can they do to us?" She shrugged her shoulders. Dran pretended not to notice the exchange and had already made himself comfortable at the fireside, stretching his leg. He winced as he did so and wrapped his coat closer around his shoulders as the evening wind beat against his back.

Maladia and Markus positioned themselves on the opposite side of the fire, with the bright flames dancing between them.

"So? What do you want?" Markus asked.

Dran stiffened. As Alma's only son, he was usually spoken to more kindly than this, but now wasn't the time to show temper.

Markus' pale blue eyes seemed darker by the fire, and his usually friendly, open face was clouded with worry. He tensed his broad shoulders, and Dran noticed how the gentle giant had placed his hand on Maladia's leg, shifting his shoulder ever so slightly in front of her, as if he would hide her behind his powerful frame.

"I'm sorry about what happened," Dran said. "I'm still your friend, you know. You don't need to act so suspicious."

Markus took a moment to reply. "No, Dran. We were neighbors, but we've never been friends. We've barely exchanged five words together in your whole life. And now you show up here, after your mother banished us. So again: what do you want?"

Dran's expression barely changed, though his eyes grew cold.

"I'm sorry you feel that way. My mother sent me." Dran softened his tone, "But if you don't care to hear what I have to say, it's no skin off my back." He moved as if he were about to get up.

Maladia raised her hand in alarm. "Wait! He didn't mean it." She shot a warning look at Markus, who leaned back and crossed his arms. Maladia continued, "We're tired and worried is all. We'll hear whatever message you bring."

Dran made his face into a perfect mask of indifference as he turned to Markus. "Is that so?" he asked.

"Aye," Markus said. His eyes never left Dran's face. Dran waited for a moment, and Markus sighed. "I'm sorry."

"Well, no harm no foul." Dran smiled broadly. "I even brought some tea. Sweet and warming." He passed a tall rod-reed flask to Maladia. She obligingly took a sip and passed the bottle to Markus who sniffed at it but then took a generous swig. The shadow behind Markus rose up ever so slightly. Dran shivered. The first time in his life facing a transformed striga shadow, a true stigoi, rattled him more than he cared to admit.

"My mother knows the punishment she dealt might be a bit extreme, and she's willing to reconsider. Markus broke the law, that's true…" he said. He paused, letting it sink in. Maladia had a hopeful look on her face. Encouraging. "…But in the end, he did so with good cause, and Alma believes that should count for something." Maladia was smiling now, though Markus' face was still. Dran took a breath.

"Then again, we all know that this wasn't some one-off transgression, but the reward of long and grueling practice. Practice which bore a *permanent* sort of fruit, I believe." It was a wild gamble on Dran's part, but it paid off as Maladia's hand rose protectively to her belly. It lingered there briefly before falling to her side, confirming his suspicions. He felt relief roll over him like a wave. Markus looked away, his hands rolled into a fist in his lap.

"But you wouldn't try such a delicate healing without being certain, would you? And that kind of a skill leaves a dark mark on a striga's heart. The other heart, I mean. My mother knew all that."

Maladia looked down, but Markus turned his eyes to Dran, his expression carefully blank. "What do you want, Dran? We're yet to hear your mother's offer."

Dran tensed under Markus' steady gaze. The words he had practiced on the way now stuck in his throat. He knew there was no helping it, but looking at Markus' honest face made this painful. Dran steeled himself. "My mother would be willing to let you come back, to live in a hut on the edges of the village so your child can grow up in the safety of our community–" Maladia's eyes brightened, "–but at a price. Your new skill, Markus…" Dran took a slow breath and placed his hands on his knees to steady them before speaking. "You must do again, what you did before. If you heal my leg, Markus, untwist it, make it whole, I swear to you, you will have your place in the village. And, as you'd be performing the healing while not technically a member of the village, it'll carry no punishment under our laws."

Maladia smiled broadly. "But that's wonderful! He can do it. Markus can do it." She moved towards Markus, who kept sitting there stone-faced. "You can do it safely, and one more healing won't change anything. Then we can go back. Our baby will be safe among our people. It's a good offer." There was a moment of silence, while Markus peered into the flames. But Dran wasn't watching Markus. He was staring at the shadow looming above their heads. He could swear that, for a moment, he could see the shadow's glowing eyes, staring at him, before it merged with the darkness of the forest.

"Well?" Dran asked.

"And how will your mother explain it to the other strigas?" Markus asked, his expression stony. "How our unbreakable laws can be set aside for the sake of her son?" He looked at Dran, and his face changed with a slow anger, burning steady and hot, which always comes as a surprise in a gentle man. He took Maladia's hand, and said quietly, as if to soften the blow. "This is no offer from Alma. The old lady won't have us back, not even for her precious son. She'd never break our laws. This is Dran's idea, and it is not for our sake, not for the sake of our child, but his own." Markus rose to his feet. "And I won't plunge deeper into the darkness for a liar and a cheat."

For his part, Dran remained seated, his expression frozen.

"Oh…" Maladia looked at Dran with hope already dying in her eyes. "I thought better of you, Dran…"

"Did you?" Dran said with a snarl, surprising even himself. "You thought so well of me and yet you didn't think to offer help? You could have made me whole at any time, Markus, but you hoarded your powers. Selfish. A true stigoi to the core. If I lied to you it was no more than you deserve." Dran felt the threat of tears sting his eyes and he struggled to calm himself. "Good Markus, kind Markus, and all the while you could have helped, but you didn't. I could have helped you keep this hidden, helped protect you."

"There's nothing wrong with you except that you're a spoiled brat and always have been!" Markus towered over the still seated Dran. "You have the position, the looks, half the girls in the village throwing themselves at you – but you always want more, more! And how would you have disguised the healing? Every step would have betrayed you!" Markus shook his head as if shaking off the last strands of sympathy.

"Leave. Now," Markus said. "If I see you again, I'll kill you for this."

"I'm sorry you feel that way," Dran said. He stood up, dusted his trousers in a casual way, and, with a quick movement, threw a small handful of powder into the flames. The fire leapt up and stinging fumes enveloped Markus and Maladia.

Dran remained still, safely upwind of the smoke as the couple coughed and spluttered.

"I didn't want to do this. If you'd been kinder, I wouldn't have had to."

Markus tried to step towards Dran, who avoided him easily. "Don't worry Markus, it's not poison. Just tanner's bark. The smoke, mixed with the sorrow root tea I gave you, can knock a man off his feet, as I understand."

Markus fell heavily, and his breath steadied to a raspy pace.

Dran smiled and caught Maladia, just as she was about to fall to the ground. "Shh, sleep now. It won't hurt you. You know I'd never hurt you."

He eased Maladia to the ground, and, just for a moment, felt the grasp of shadowy arms around his neck, before they too fell away.

Dran sat himself next to Markus and looked into the face of the shadow hanging over him.

"Hello," he said. He felt a strange thrill as he saw a shape of a face staring back at him. Here he was, talking to a creature that should not be.

"I think you can help me," he said. "And then you'll be free. That's what you want, isn't it? To break free of his control?" He reached out with his hand and waited. After a moment the shadow's hand met his and Dran stifled a cry. The flames of the fire leapt up, pulled on by Markus' stigoi, and poured through Dran like molten gold.

"Where have you been?" Alma asked without turning. Her hand went up and down as she stitched a patch onto an old pair of trousers. "I can smell the rain on you. You should change."

"I went for a walk, mother. There's little enough to do here otherwise, wouldn't you say?" Dran said. He pulled off his sodden boots with some effort and began to take his shirt off as the rain battered the roof of their house.

"No, I wouldn't. There are plenty enough chores for those willing to be useful," Alma said, biting the end off the thread.

"Well, let them do their chores then. I would hardly want to stand in the way of the obliging." He sat down on his bed and groaned.

"What's the matter? Is it your foot?" Alma pushed herself up from her seat by the fire. It'd been a long day and she was tired down to her soul. But the thought of her son's discomfort roused her. "I have a fresh batch of nettle ointment. It will warm the muscles and ease the pain," she said, reaching for a clay pot on the table. She moved towards Dran and touched his foot gently. She gasped as she saw the charred flesh on the side of his ankle. He hastily moved his leg away and covered it with a blanket.

"What's happened, Dran? Who did this?!"

"It's nothing, mother. I stepped into some embers by accident.

Now I need to sleep, and you do too. Please, just leave me be." He lay on his bed and turned towards the wall. A small sob escaped him, but Alma knew better than to acknowledge it. Dran would not thank her for recognizing his pain. Alma sat by the fire for a long while, a pot of ointment still in her hand. She listened to her son breathing, the sound of it soothing her as it always had. The flames lit up her face, as she stared at the wall above her son's head, her eyes fixed not on him, but on the shadows dancing above.

# CHAPTER 5

A drop of water fell on Salka's eyelid. She opened her eyes and looked toward the ceiling. The roof, battered by the night's storm, gave a soggy cry for help. Instead of turning over and going back to sleep, she got up and pulled on her second dirtiest trousers and tunic, followed by her old cloak. At this point the cloak was little more than a collection of darned spots held together by the faintest hint of the original woolen thread, but her mother wouldn't dream of getting rid of the damned thing. Miriat had a sentimental streak which so far hadn't manifested in her daughter. Salka looked longingly at the new cloth dripping in the corner.

She glanced over at her mother's sleeping face and briefly considered planting a kiss on the uncharacteristically unfurrowed eyebrows, but thought better of it. A morning adventure had a much better chance of starting if the chores didn't get in the way. She rubbed her palm, still a little swollen and sore after she'd pulled out the rose thorns embedded in it.

Salka stroked Munu's head, but quickly withdrew her hand as the falcon snapped at her fingers. "Shhh…" She put her finger to her lips to signal that, firstly, her fingers served a function other than that of a chewing toy, and, secondly, a shriek would end their escapade prematurely. He stretched out his wings and hopped off his perch above Salka's bed. He flew out of the house as Salka held the leather curtain opened for him.

She snuck out of the house and crept between the striga huts until she arrived at the west gate. Her companions were already waiting, so engrossed in a whispered conversation that they barely noticed Salka's arrival.

"A change of plans!" her friend Emila announced, pulling Salka aside. She spoke in feverish whispers. "We're going to Heyne Town." Emila could barely contain her excitement and the last was said in a voice so high-pitched she covered her mouth in embarrassment. Dran only chuckled and nodded.

"I thought you wanted to go to the Narrow Pass…" Salka said, shifting her weight. Not wanting to lose face, she added, "You told me it'd be crazy to venture there."

Emila shook her head, which she knew made her hair fly rather attractively about her face. "I think *you* were the one saying that. In any case, I want to go now."

"Come on, Salka, it'll be good for you. Adventures usually are," Dran added, with a broad smile.

"Except for when they aren't." Salka put her hand on her hip. "You know what they'll do to us if they find us?"

Every young striga grew up with the knowledge that the banishment from Heyne Town was considered clemency. Before the Dolas struck the agreement with the Heyne council all those years ago, infant strigas ended up at the bottom of the cliff as often as in the forest. There would be no mercy for a grown striga found in the town.

A shiver went down Salka's spine and she could feel the comforting warmth of her other heart's shadow slither up her back. She tensed her jaw and swatted it away, hoping her friends didn't notice.

"They won't catch us! Dran knows the trick of it, you know," Emila said, pointing to Dran. "He's been many times! He stole a chicken the last time he was there! Count the chickens in Alma's yard if you don't believe me."

Dran nodded.

Salka had to admit it was an impressive feat. She thought of how a laying hen could improve her mother's life. An egg each morning for Miriat's breakfast. Salka imagined her mother's surprise and how pleased she would be.

"How did you do it? I'm not saying I'll go with you, mind," she asked, though in her head she was already cooking up a breakfast of onion and eggs for her mother. Her proud offering. She wondered if her mother used to breakfast on eggs every day before she was forced to leave what Salka imagined as a life of endless comfort.

"Nothing to it," Dran said, shrugging his shoulders.

Salka put her hands on her hips. "Be specific," she said.

"All right, look," Dran sighed and rolled his eyes for Emila's benefit. She obliged with a giggle. "All the men leave at first light to work in the mine. Those who don't will be warming their bones by their fires this late in the year and all the women leave at midday to carry food to their men. The town is practically abandoned for near two hours every day. There's a path I know we can take, hidden from view. It's easy pickings from then on if you're fast."

Salka mulled it over. Miriat would be glad of a chicken, that was for sure and certain. But she would also be furious to know her daughter had gone where she had been explicitly forbidden to go.

"I'll do it," Salka said quickly and immediately felt guilty. She straightened her back. She wouldn't let Miriat dictate where she could and couldn't go.

They moved quietly, with Dran leading the way. He seemed to move more awkwardly than usual, but Salka supposed it was the storm of last night making his leg hurt.

"What were you two talking about before?" Salka asked in a whisper, giving Emila's arm a quick squeeze. "He stood awfully close, I thought..." She smiled and cast a sideways glance at her friend.

"Don't tease! I can't tell you anyway. It's a secret," Emila said, though she blushed with pleasure. She kept an even pace, though Salka noticed with some amusement that Emila's shadow rose up and fell with emotion. She nudged her friend, who immediately brought her heart under control and murmured a quick apology.

"A secret *you* can keep? Well, that's a first," Salka said.

Emila ignored the jibe. She was a little out of breath and called out to Dran to stop for a moment. She looked imploringly at Salka, who didn't bother sitting down, not even for solidarity's sake. Now that she'd agreed to the adventure, she was impatient to get there.

"How do you two manage to walk so fast! I can barely keep up!" Emila sat on a tree stump and stretched her legs in front of her. She glanced around "Where's Munu? I haven't seen him today."

"Oh, he's around," Salka said. "Never more than a whistle away. Watch." She put two fingers in her mouth and whistled loudly. An acorn fell down and bounced off Emila's head. "He's in a good mood." Salka grinned as Emila shot her an annoyed look.

"Why you keep that fleabag around I will never understand. His hunting days are behind him. And he seems to be getting meaner every day," Dran said, looking at the trees.

"Sort of like you, then," Salka shot back, and then covered her mouth. "I'm sorry, I didn't mean…"

"I know what you meant," Dran said. He looked away and shrugged his arms. "Are you both ready to go?"

Emila gave Salka a reproachful look and rushed forward to walk alongside Dran. She tried to take his arm, but he shook her off, so she just trotted beside him. Salka followed miserably after. She idly grabbed the fluffy tops of the tall yellowed grasses growing between the exposed slate they walked on. It was slippery and wet after the night's rain, and soon Salka's boots were sodden through. Still, she enjoyed the cold morning air, even if the walk suddenly held a lot less appeal. She whistled softly and Munu flew down and sat himself on her shoulder, as was his custom. Salka hoped that Emila would look back at her, but her friend was too engrossed in a conversation with Dran to pay her much attention.

Emila laughed at something he said and cast a furtive look backwards. Salka blushed and felt suddenly self-conscious in her ugly cloak and her short hair which the moisture of the mountain air had curled tighter, forming a halo around her head.

She woke up before the roosters for this? To be sneered at by her best friend? Her face darkened with anger and she jutted out her chin defiantly.

They walked for a few hours, till Dran stopped and turned to Emila and Salka with a grin stretching his handsome face. He made a wide sweeping motion. "We're here!"

Salka looked around. Instead of the tall pines which surrounded the striga village, the forest here was lush with vegetation. The changing autumn leaves colored the canopy above their heads with fiery reds and yellows.

"I've never been so far this side of the mountains," Salka said, gently touching the snow-white bark of the tree next to her.

"Well, it's high time if you ask me!" Dran said. "You have to live a little!"

He smiled at Salka, and Emila followed his lead, taking Salka's arm again. Salka felt her heart swell with the gratitude of the forgiven.

They came to the edge of the forest. A large, gnarled tree rose before them. It seemed out of place there, and yet strangely beautiful. Small wooden tags hung from its branches, each covered in carved writing. Most of them were old, with a deep cut across the markings. The breeze moved the branches, causing the tags to rattle against each other. It sent shivers down Salka's back.

Her mouth hung open. "What is it?" she said finally.

"It's the Hope Tree." Dran put his hand against the tree's mossy bark. "It tells us when to come and collect the striga babies born in the town."

"Maladia's mentioned it before... But nobody really wants to talk about it," Salka said, gently touching one of the markers. "Why is it called the Hope Tree?" She'd often seen Maladia and some of the other young strigas make the journey here, but she'd never been asked to go with them. She more than suspected her mother had something to do with that.

"I suppose the humans hope the baby will not be a striga and if it turns out to be one... Well, they hope it survives anyway..." Emila said. Dran raised his eyebrows, surprised at the uncharacteristic insight.

"The markers tell us when the baby is due. We usually send someone to camp out here for a bit, just in case it's one of ours." Dran took one of the tags down. "See, the ones that have a cross carved through are the old ones. That's how we keep track. It would be impossible to have someone stationed so far out of the village permanently."

"What if the baby comes early?" Emila asked, her eyes wide.

"We wait for a time before and after. There are few we miss," Dran said, and casually threw an old tag into the bushes. Salka wondered if the tag represented a baby saved or one that didn't need saving. One who'd been welcomed with joy; wrapped in a warm soft blanket, placed lovingly in a freshly carved crib. With parents and grandparents leaning over with smiles on their faces.

There was none of that for Salka and Miriat. Salka clenched her jaw. The townsfolk should count themselves lucky if all she did was steal a chicken.

They walked in silence again until they could see fields through the trees.

Salka had never wandered this close to the town. She felt a thrill as she exchanged a smile with Emila. But her smile fell when she thought of Maladia. "Do you think they're safe? Markus and Maladia, I mean?"

Dran turned to her sharply, as if stricken. "Why would you ask that?" As soon as the words left his lips he turned away, a blush spreading across his face.

It was Salka's turn to be surprised. "Maladia was a friend. Do you not wonder..."

"No, I don't," Dran said. He paused for a moment and then turned back to her with a nod. An apology of sorts, she thought. He added, "It's just there's no point in wondering and worrying and thinking about them. They're gone. Markus did a terrible thing and we had to let them go. We're all sad, Salka, but we have to go on. And I say the best way to do it is to forget them entirely."

Salka was about to say that the forgetting would not come so easily to Trina, except Emila pulled on her sleeve and pointed ahead.

"Look!" Emila said. "You can see the tops of the houses from here. Look how even they are, like teeth. Just one next to the other!"

Salka nodded, and they moved in a single file towards the town.

There were some terraced fields between the town and the forest, filled with hardy crops that could survive the unpredictable weather. There were small twisted purple potatoes, barley and oats growing in patches among the stones. The slate mines southeast of the town were the real bread and butter of the Heyne Mountain folk.

It was coming up on lunchtime and soon the miners' wives and children would be making the trek down with warm food in their baskets. It was a ritual which had started before, when the Heyne Town was a Heyne Village, and it had continued while the population grew as a way of remaining connected to the old ways. Dran knew this, of course, when he proposed the trip.

Salka looked at him as he was explaining all this, and then she glanced at Emila, who was near giddy with anticipation.

Dran knew so much about the town and their customs, he almost made it sound like home, though he was born in the striga village. He was the fourth generation of strigas in his line, and – his mother hoped – the second leader once she was gone. Alma announced she was pregnant one day during an assembly and then moved on to the matters of land allocation, herding duties, and shearing rotations. Nobody had ever dared ask about the father, and nobody even cared much who he was, from what Salka understood.

As if he could sense her thoughts, Dran looked at her, his even eyebrows furrowed quizzically. "We have to be quick, you understand? In and out. If you get caught, we leave you," Dran said with a smile which didn't quite reach his eyes.

"Dra-an!" Emila smacked him playfully on the shoulder. "She'll think you're serious!"

Salka turned red. Just as she opened her mouth, Dran said, "I hope she does, Emila. And you best believe it too. You mess up and get caught, you're on your own. There'll be nothing we can do. Now, we've got to make a move, we don't have a whole day." He pulled his hood low over his face and told them to follow. Salka, still smarting from Emila's comment, pushed ahead, letting her shoulder knock against Emila's side. She was rewarded with an annoyed look. Munu jumped up and flew over their heads, a black outline against the grey sky.

They walked fast, moving from boulder to boulder, trying to keep as low to the ground as possible. Salka thought Emila looked quite comical, her head bobbing forward and backwards like a chicken being chased around the coop. When they got behind an elevated bit of ground Salka poked Emila's arm and imitated a chicken gait. Emila tried to keep a severe expression but finally burst into giggles.

"Shut up!" Dran said. "You want to get the whole town on our heads? Be quiet or go back!"

Stifling their giggles, Emila and Salka said, "Sorry, Dran." They smiled at each other and followed him downhill.

It was easier to keep hidden once they reached the edge of town. There were small barns and outhouses to sneak behind. But it was also scarier, in a way Salka didn't think it would be. She had heard what the townsfolk did to a captured striga, and though she suspected at least half of it was made up, the other half was decidedly more risk than she was prepared to take.

But it was too late to turn back, especially without something to show for it.

"Dran," Salka said, "where are we going now? These people have chickens, I can hear them through the fence. Let's just grab a couple and we can go back."

"I want more than a chicken," he said without looking at her.

They kept moving through the quiet. Emila scrunched up her

nose, and her shadow seemed to crawl into her in disgust. "God, it reeks!" she said. And it did. In the village there was the comforting, ever-present smell of goats, but for all that, the air was still crisp and tasted fresh the way only mountain air can. Heyne Town was large enough that all the smells a large number of people can produce crowded and oppressed the nostrils of anyone who wandered in.

They were in the center of the town now, hunched together behind a shop with barrels of what smelled like salted fish on one side and an open space on the other. They made sure to stick to the west side of town, in case someone coming back from the mines should see them.

"Right, we meet here when the sun moves above that peak," Dran pointed towards a distant mountain. "It will be easier for us to go separately, rather than try to sneak through together. Keep your hoods over your faces. If somebody sees you, keep your wits about you, and don't run; they might take you for a local. Always keep to the dark side of the street and keep your shadows in the dark too. The townsfolk might not listen in to every stranger's heartbeat, but they would certainly notice your shadows."

Dran went first. After a moment, Emila gave Salka a hug and said quickly, "I'll try and get you something pretty." And then she was off.

Salka waited for a moment, trying to steady her breath. The wooden wall of the shop felt oddly soothing to her. She stretched out her arm and watched her hand until it stopped shaking. She looked around. She'd only have the one chance to pick a direction. Heyne Town might not be rich, but it looked the very picture of opulence to someone brought up in the striga village. The straight, two-story houses with their barns fascinated Salka. Keeping livestock in a separate building made very little sense to her: losing all that heat and the comfort of the warm bodies was unthinkable.

Pulling the hood of her worn-out cloak over her face, she looked at the street between the houses, the smoothed-out cobblestones and the painted front doors. They all seemed terribly beautiful.

That someone would paint their doors pale blue was an act of unimaginable extravagance. To have a door was luxury enough; to have a blue door was as far away from her world as the moon itself. She envied the inhabitants with all the savage strength of her heart. Anger rose up to the surface again, warming her chest and tightening her hands into fists. How dare those cold, cruel people have such loveliness in their lives while her mother's house had nothing but some old skins by the entrance to keep out the winter cold?

Looking west, she saw a house on top of a small hill, sixty or so yards away from the shop, surrounded by coniferous hedges. There was no smoke coming through the chimney.

She decided to slide down the side of the elevated path and walk in its shadow as Darn had suggested. She sniffed and wiped her nose absent mindedly with her sleeve. It was getting colder. She walked quickly and scaled the wooden steps wedged into the side of the hill. She crept up to the window of the house and looked inside.

The neatly swept floor and the rough wooden table looked promising. Anyone with a table like that would be sure to have things to put on it. Not just a chicken or two but likely a whole coop! Salka crept around the side of the wall and looked through the other window. She jumped as something wet touched her hand; a black and white lamb looked up at her and pressed its nose to the pocket of her trousers. "I have nothing for you. Go! Shoo!" Salka pushed the greedy face away, but the lamb was undeterred. It was very young, and Salka wondered briefly why a farmer would let a lamb be born so far into the autumn.

Munu landed noisily on the roof on the house and turned his head to the side. He then swept down toward Salka, grabbing her cloak, and started to pull on it.

"Ouch! What's gotten into you? Munu, let go!" She froze as she heard what Munu must have seen from the roof. The townsfolk were back. There was shouting and calling out, and a horrifying certitude crept up Salka's back in a shiver.

"Oh no…" she said. They must have seen Emila and Dran. She had to run. But she wasn't going to leave empty-handed. She looked around her and met eyes with the black-and-white lamb which was watching her with the uncommitted curiosity typical of its kind. Making a quick decision, Salka took off her cloak and, with one swift movement, she swept the lamb up into it, hoisting it onto her back. She broke into a run, sliding down the hill and scraping her knees on the sharp stones. The cries were getting closer.

"I saw one of them! It went into Rodik's house! Quick, don't let it escape!"

Salka wondered briefly who Rodik was and whether it was Emila or Dran they had seen. She climbed back up the path toward the shop where she started, and was relieved to see Emila and Dran there, the latter panting heavily, leaning against the barrels.

"Good, you're back! We have to get out of here… What the hell is that?!" Dran said, bristling. "That fucking thing will give us away!"

The lamb on Salka's back was indeed making rather pitiful noises as it squirmed to get out of the makeshift sling. "No, it's all right, let's go!" Salka shifted her position uncomfortably. "Emila, you go first!" Her friend, face drained of color, nodded curtly and moved fast along the side of the houses towards the field.

Dran was listening to the noises of the townsfolk approaching with his back glued to the wall. "All right, we've got to go. They're going house by house searching for us," he said. "Follow me."

They walked the narrow path, the houses on their left, and a steep hill on the right. Dran moved as quickly as he could, though Salka noticed his foot was clearly causing him pain now. The lamb on her back kicked and she lost her footing, nearly tumbling down. She let out a cry.

Dran turned around in a fury. "I told you to shut that thing up! They'll find us!" He suddenly grabbed the lamb on Salka's back, pulling at it with a force which made Salka spin. He swung it against the wall and with a savage blow broke the creature's neck.

The bones cracked with a sickening noise and the lamb let out a squeal.

They stood over the lamb's small body, twitching on the ground. Salka saw Dran's face blanch with the horror of what he'd just done.

"No! What did you just...?" Salka grabbed the lamb and pushed Dran away.

"I'm sorry, I..." He raised his hands as Salka lunged at him, her fist drawn back, cradling the lamb in her left arm. Dran ducked a blow meant for his face, and the sudden movement made Salka lose her footing. "Watch out!" Dran, panic written all over his face, tried to catch her, and missed. She fell on her stomach and slid down the hill to the untilled rocky ground some six yards below the path.

She looked up and saw Dran's face, looking down at her with his arm still outstretched. They stared at each other for a moment as the voices were getting louder. He grabbed handfuls of his hair as if he would tear it out, and shut his eyes tight. "I'm sorry," he said looking away. Then he turned around and ran.

Salka watched incredulously as he hobbled away as quickly as he could manage. But there was no time to think on that. The angry shouts were getting nearer, and she was painfully exposed. She looked around and spotted a string of four houses, each with a small vegetable patch in front. There was a large barn to the side, large enough to be shared by all the four households. She made for it as fast as she could, the lamb hanging limp on her back. She stifled her tears. The poor creature was dead because of her. What had possessed her to take it? Leaving empty-handed would have been preferable to this sorry result. She pushed the barn door open and slid inside. She could hear the noise of people turning their houses upside down looking for thieves. Looking for her.

She looked around for a hiding place. There were no good ones. The barn held several, rather poorly-fed, cows and sheep along with two farm horses. Below the rafters lay bales of hay on an elevated platform, and there were tools hanging on the wall. She sat down behind a crate of apples, each one carefully wrapped in hay. She'd only seen an apple once before, when Dola brought them a small basket one year.

Salka took the lamb off her back and gently put it in her lap. A sudden fluttering of the animal's eyelid gave Salka a start. The poor creature wasn't dead after all! But it *was* dying, and in pain, and she didn't know how to help it. "I'm so sorry..." she said, tears welling up in her eyes. She wondered where Munu was; she needed him now. Her fingers stroked the lamb's head and along its small neck. The lamb's eye looked at her intensely as it struggled for breath.

"We're done for, you and I," she said. Her own death was inevitable. There was nowhere to go, nowhere to hide. The voices outside were getting closer. She could feel her own two hearts, beating so loudly they were ringing in her ears. Were the people outside deaf that they couldn't hear them? She held the lamb in her arms and listened to the three heartbeats, one slowing, and two beating so fast.

It suddenly felt so hot, unbearably so. She tugged at her scarf and pulled her jumper off, the lamb in her lap staring at her silently. Salka started sweating and, as the anger inside her burned, she could feel her fingertips tingle. She looked at the lamb and took a breath. She touched the animal's neck again, where Dran's blow had broken the bone. She felt for the wrongness and sought to right it. She drew a breath and the chill turned to heat inside her lungs. So hot. So hot it was unbearable, so much heat she would never be able to hold it inside. And so she didn't.

The lamb took a sharp breath, as the heat worked its way through its body, pushing and pulling, savagely and without remorse. Salka's jaw slackened, her expression blank. She felt nothing but the surge of heat rushing through her body. She wanted to shake it off; she wanted to rip her own skin off to stop feeling it. But it continued to steadily flow. She felt that if she could only let go, she could make the whole world burn.

She held on, letting a mere trickle pour out around her. And then, all at once, it was over. The lamb in her lap wriggled out, reveling in the departure of pain. Salka opened her eyes. As she breathed out, a cloud of steam rose from her lips. Frost had painted a pattern on the wooden planks of the barn walls and her eyelashes were coated in ice.

With a start, she became aware of another's presence. A large man was standing next to her, watching her in silence. He had broad shoulders used to hard labor and a worn face that might have been handsome once. He held a miner's pickaxe in his hand. It would have taken him less than a moment to crush Salka's skull.

But the man wasn't looking at her. He was looking at her worn-out, patched-up cloak in which she still held the lamb. Without meeting her eyes, he turned around and called out, "Nobody here!" and left.

Salka sat very still, cradling the lamb in her arms. It could have been a trick, a ruse to get her to leave the safety of the barn. But the hours passed and nobody came for her.

When the night fell, she crawled out of the barn, the lamb asleep in the cocoon of her cloak. It seemed comfortable with her now, as if she had not made the clearest possible display of the evil lurking inside her. Salka looked down at its face and a pang of guilt and shame shot through her chest.

She walked along the path to the fields, stopping to listen every few yards. A sound of footsteps on the main road stopped her in her tracks and she clung to the wall. A narrow path joined the main road to where she was, and she judged it safer to wait till the unseen traveler had gone rather than make a dash and risk discovery. The sound ceased and she peeked out down the alley.

A Dola stood there, staring into the darkness. The woman carried a staff with her pouches tied to its head, and with the other hand she held an oil lamp, the orange glow illuminating her face. Salka didn't know her. She was much too finely dressed to attend the striga village, clearly favoring those who could pay for her services in more than skeins of wool and the occasional meal around an open fire. The woman wore a thick woolen skirt, richly embroidered, and a fine leather bag hung across her shoulders.

The Dola paused and kept staring in silence. Salka reminded herself that the Dola couldn't possibly see her. Salka was too far for the light to reach her. And yet Salka was certain the Dola *had* seen her. After the longest time, Salka heard footsteps once more, this time growing fainter.

Once she was sure she was once more alone in the night, Salka moved quickly and managed to get across the field to the safety of the forest. As she reached the Hope Tree, she saw a fire burning between the trees. She walked up to the makeshift camp quietly, and stood there, watching Emila and Dran as they slept by the fire. Emila's eyebrows were furrowed and tears marked her face. Salka knelt beside the two and touched Emila on the shoulder. Her friend stirred but it was Dran who woke first.

"Salka! You're alive! Thank the gods!" He seemed genuinely happy, which would have pleased Salka had she not remembered the savagery of the blow he had inflicted on the lamb. He opened his arms as if he would hug her but one look from Salka made him lower them and look at his feet in embarrassment.

She shrugged. "No thanks to you."

Emila opened her eyes. "Salka! Salka, are you all right? I can't believe you're back! How did you get away? Dran said he saw you take a wrong turn and we were so sure you were captured!"

Salka cast a quick look at Dran, who had the decency to look ashamed.

Emila grabbed Salka by the shoulders and hugged her tight. "Oh… What is that on your back? A lamb? In the autumn!" She opened her eyes wide.

"Yes." Salka shifted uncomfortably. "I hid in the barn after I… 'took the wrong turn'… They didn't find me." She could feel Dran's eyes on her.

"The lamb!" he said suddenly. "I mean, it's lucky it wasn't hurt during the escape." He stroked its head gently and Salka pulled away.

"I think we should stay here for the night," Salka said, brushing hair from her face.

"Oh, but you must warm yourself!" Emila said suddenly. "Look at you, you're drenched from the marshes and you're not even wearing your cloak."

"I'm fine..." Salka said. And she really was. She felt perfectly warm and comfortable, in spite of her wet shoes and trousers.

"Nonsense," Emila decided. "Take your boots off and put them by the fire. They will be dry by the morning." She started fussing with the fire, blushing and roughly refusing Dran's half-hearted offer of help.

Salka wondered briefly what words of affection had passed between Emila and Dran when they thought she was dead. But she decided she didn't care. She just wanted to sleep. The lamb was bleating loudly now and nuzzled her tummy. "Oh, I'm sorry, I don't have anything for you," she said awkwardly.

"Here. We can boil this in water. It will have to suffice until we can get back and feed it properly," Dran said, unfastening a small pouch he had tied to his wide leather belt. "I'm not sure about lambs, but this would do well enough for a kid."

Salka took the pouch from his outstretched hand, avoiding his eyes. She moved closer to Emila, who was picking up hot stones from the fire using two sticks as tongs and gently putting them in her waterskin to heat the water. Salka could feel Dran staring at her back, and she wished she could disappear into the fire. She felt the flames would burn less than his gaze.

As she studiously avoided looking at him, Salka didn't notice Dran was hungrily staring at her shadow, as it moved and writhed on the ground. Every few heartbeats the dark shape would rise a finger's width above the wet soil, as if struggling to take form and sit next to Salka. Sometimes a dark hand would rise gently and rest on the lamb's head, leaving the slightest imprint on the soft wool, before melting back into the night.

# CHAPTER 6

Dola stared at the polished pebbles scattered on the floor. Each had a symbol on it, painted carefully by her own hands. Each Dola had a different set, with different symbols painted. The symbols were for each of them to dream up and interpret themselves and no Dola would touch another one's stones within her lifetime.

For the third time that night, Dola cast her stones, hoping for a different answer. She stretched out on her polished wooden floor and placed her fingers on her growing belly. She rested like that for a moment, trying to still her mind till all she felt was the rise and fall of her chest. It often worked to calm her, but not this time.

She knew what she had to do. And the worst thing was she knew she would not hesitate, not in this.

Dola turned to her side and wept, ashamed of her strength.

# CHAPTER 7

"Are you mad? Risking yourself like this?! And this animal you brought with you! It still needs its mother's milk; it can't be more than three weeks old. A spring lamb in the autumn... Did you bring it here to watch it die in the winter months? If only this wasn't our goat's first pregnancy..." Miriat was fuming. She seldom got angry but when she did, Salka knew to let her talk. Her mother's fury burned high and fast but she could already see Miriat turn her mind to the practicalities.

"Well, Trina's goat is pregnant but will still give milk for another two months or so. Though heaven knows if she'll accept a lamb for the nursing." Miriat rubbed her temples. "Spit and bile, girl, why don't use your head more. And your cloak! It's a rag now, with the new one still unfinished." A thought struck her then, and she made an impatient gesture at Salka. "Well, get out of these clothes and under a blanket. I won't have you catch your death of cold before you finish all the extra chores you'll be doing as punishment. And don't you think you will get away with this. I'll put you to work, make no mistake. I'd expect this of that empty-headed friend of yours, but not you, my girl!"

The last words made Salka pause, with her shirt half over her head.

"And why not me?" she asked. Her mother turned towards her with wide eyes, and Salka felt a shiver of fear run across her back. Her mother had never struck her, but Salka knew there were times when her anger had carried Miriat within a hair's breadth of it. Still, Salka couldn't feel shame without feeling anger also, so she pushed on. "Why should I not want to go and explore farther than a couple of hours' walk away from these gates?" *And from you*, were the unspoken words hanging between them.

Miriat looked at her hands, before letting them fall limp by her sides. "Because you could die, Salka. And I have given up my own self so you might live," she added, so quietly Salka barely heard her.

Salka changed her shirt, quickly, without once looking up. The room felt suffocating, even with the fire burning low. The peat and logs they used for fuel filled her lungs with smoke and her eyes with tears. "Well, maybe you shouldn't have," she said finally.

Miriat's tall frame swayed a little, as if she'd been struck. "That's a foolish thing to say. Go fetch the water now. After that, go to the eastern slopes and gather as much black persimmon as you can carry in a basket. I don't wish to lay eyes on you before nightfall. And ask your aunt Trina if we can impose on her and deprive her of some of the milk for the lamb. You were stupid enough to bring the creature into our house so try to make sure it doesn't die before we can have some use of it." Absentmindedly, she let the lamb sniff and nuzzle her hand. "Tell Trina you will do trap hunting for her over winter. I intended for you to do it in any case. Gods know she will feel the loss of Maladia in her belly as well as her heart once the cold hits. Now go."

Miriat sat down heavily on a stool and faced her loom. She stared at it blankly, as if not quite recognizing her own work. Miriat had positioned herself by the door so she would have the benefit of daylight without the fear of the rain should it fall without warning, as it often did in the mountains. Salka squeezed past her, keeping her eyes down. She hesitated by the door and quickly planted a kiss on her mother's cheek. Miriat nodded. She reached out without looking and squeezed her daughter's hand before waving her on her way.

Miriat was holding onto her anger. She knew once it abated she would have to face the terror she'd felt the entirety of the night Salka was gone. She ran her fingers across the half-finished cloth of Salka's new cloak in front of her, noting with satisfaction the even weave and the deep green of the wool. She closed her eyes briefly and turned her face to the sun, as it made its rare appearance between the autumn clouds. Her fingers touched the loom weights gently, causing them to knock against each other with a faint hollow noise. She exhaled and went back to work.

She knew she'd have to talk to Alma about the children's excursion and she dreaded it. While Alma was fair in most things, her boy could do no wrong in her eyes. But this time it was too serious. If a striga was caught in the town they would be summarily executed. She had never seen such an execution, but she'd heard stories. She could feel a cold sweat run between her shoulder blades just thinking of it. A striga would have the second heart cut out of their chest to prevent them from coming back as shadows to haunt the living.

It was a nasty way to die and Miriat couldn't understand what would possess Dran to drag himself and the two young girls into the path of such danger. She looked up briefly from her work and nodded at a neighbor passing by, her fingers never stopping their labor. It was a beautiful morning, probably one of the last ones before the winter came in earnest, but she could not calm herself enough to enjoy it. A shadow fell across her face and she looked up to see Emila's father standing between her and the sun.

"Good morning to you, Miriat. May I sit and speak with you a moment?"

She nodded curtly and gestured towards the other stool. He brought it up close and sat, wringing his hands. Miriat sighed and put her work down. Emila's father was a kind enough man, slow and precise in his movements. He had a very handsome face and wavy auburn hair, which his daughter inherited, and a sense of calm, which she did not. Miriat liked him, though he was not the cleverest of men, just as much as she disliked Emila's mother, with her constant complaining and her greedy disposition.

"I'm listening, Tolan," she said.

"About yesterday's business… Rida wished to speak to you of it, but I thought it might be best if I did instead." The poor man looked miserable for a moment and Miriat understood instantly that this had come at a great personal sacrifice to him.

"You see, we went to see Alma this morning. Rida was frantic with worry when the children were gone, and then fuming once Emila was discovered safe and sound. So, you understand, we meant to have a stern word with Alma about it. And well, I wondered what Salka had told you about their trip." Salka's lamb approached Tolan and optimistically stuck its nose into his pocket. He patted the animal's head. "I see your daughter brought something more than pretty ribbons and beads, at least," he said, almost smiling. "Though it was still hardly worth the risk."

"Yes," Miriat said. She was deathly curious about Tolan's talk with Alma, but she knew the man was not to be hurried. "Salka told me they all decided on this adventure together, though I blame Dran. He's the eldest and should know better. What did Emila say?"

Tolan nodded, more to his own thoughts than in response to what Miriat had said. He stroked the lamb's head and said, "Emila's story is much the same, though she did include a great deal of flowery descriptions of Dran's bravery and daring…" He made a face.

"Alma's story was different, I take it," Miriat said.

Tolan nodded. "The long and short of it is, she said it was Salka's fault. That Salka was the one who'd suggested it, daring Dran to take them. And when he refused, she set out on her own. Dran went along to keep her safe and Emila was not to be left behind." He shifted uncomfortably and avoided Miriat's eyes.

Miriat dropped the shuffle and looked at Tolan in open surprise. Her face twitched as she struggled to keep her voice level "I see. I wonder where she got a story like that."

"Alma said her son wouldn't dream of going to Heyne Town himself, and that Salka…" He looked down and petted the lamb again, more to calm his hands than anything else. "…Begging your pardon, Miriat, but she said Salka was jealous of Dran and Emila and wanted to impress Dran. She said she can read between the lines, you know." He spread out his arms as if to say he was not one to question his leader's intuition.

"That's quite a tale. And what did you and Rida say to that?" Miriat said calmly, though anger was building up inside of her. "Surely you see it for the nonsense it is?"

"Well, you know Rida. She dotes on Dran." Tolan shrugged his shoulders. "She said that it was just like Emila to try to hide her friend's guilt."

Miriat had her own thoughts on Emila's selflessness but kept her mouth shut, not trusting herself to speak.

"So, you see, Alma is saying that Salka put both her friends in danger and should be punished. And my Rida agrees."

"Punished?" Miriat stood up so fast she knocked over the loom. Tolan hurried to lift it off the ground while Miriat watched, her hands rolled into fists at her sides. "You would all pile the blame on Salka for the stupidity of your own children? Shame on you, Tolan! Salka acted stupidly but she is *my* daughter! Any punishment will be up to *me* to decide on! Not you, not Alma and *certainly* not that wife of yours!"

Tolan rubbed his forehead. "I agree with you, my daughter is silly enough for anything. And true, Dran is careless of others enough to risk bringing two girls with him. *But* one thing that boy is not careless with, is himself. And so, I can find no reason why he'd risk his own life for the sake of a silly adventure. He needs for nothing.

"As to Salka – I do beg your pardon, Miriat, I mean no harm – but there is a lot of sense in what Alma said. You know our daughters have been inseparable their entire lives. And I was glad of it to tell you the truth…" He stopped for a moment and ran his fingers through his hair. Tolan loved his daughter dearly, but he did not share his wife's blind belief in Emila's finer qualities. As some strigas went past he lowered his voice respectfully, "But Miriat, things have changed lately. They're both grown now and

Emila seems to have taken up with Dran... Well, you know, I have doubts, though Rida is encouraging it, if you can believe it."

Miriat could well believe it. Rida was the kind of woman who liked to think she made the best of any situation.

Tolan continued miserably, avoiding Miriat's gaze. "And in the last year or two Salka has grown more headstrong. And she... Well, Alma suggested that she might have a soft spot for Dran herself. He's handsome and charming enough. Stranger things have happened than friends squabbling over a boy. So, I was thinking perhaps Salka wanted to seem brave in front of Dran. And... that maybe she went too far this time."

Tolan's eyes lifted to see Miriat's hard expression. "I don't mean to say I agree with Alma. But perhaps... Perhaps Salka feels jealous? And that is only natural in a girl."

"Please," Miriat said through clenched teeth, "do tell me what is natural in *my* daughter."

"Miriat, I–"

"And you really believe Dran would follow Salka? In case he needed to save her? The great hero of the strigas, indeed!" Miriat felt her cheeks turn red. "You said yourself, Dran is not careless with himself. Why would he go after her? Or are you as blind as Rida? I thought better of you, Tolan."

Tolan reddened. "No young man wants to seem a coward in his girl's eyes, Miriat. Especially a young man who already feels he has so much to prove," Tolan spoke without anger, but his eyes were fixed on the ground, too ashamed to meet hers.

"My daughter has no interest in Dran. Of that I'm quite certain. She's the youngest of the three, so for them to allow her to take the blame... That's just..." She felt tears of anger well up in her eyes. But she would not cry. She wouldn't have her fury misunderstood.

"Still, Rida insists on a period of... Well, they all need some sort of punishment, and perhaps Salka and Emila should spend some time apart? Keep them busy and away from each other, so to speak."

"Oh, do not worry about that. I shall make certain that Salka does not have the opportunity to be a *bad influence* on your daughter's fine character any longer."

"That's not what I said, Miriat. Please understand... Rida..."

"Oh, I understand. I understand *very* well." She glared at him, making sure he was aware which one of the girls she thought would be worse off for the separation. "Now, excuse me. I intend to clear this up with Alma myself." Miriat picked up her loom and put it inside the house, then drew the leather curtain shut behind herself without so much as a good-bye.

Tolan stood up, disturbing the lamb in the process. It had made itself comfortable leaning against his leg and now jumped up in alarm. He stood there for a moment and then turned towards his own house, feeling he had badly mishandled the conversation. Then again, in the end, perhaps it would all be for the best. As he walked, his eyes met Salka's on the way back to the house. He looked down at his feet and walked on without acknowledging her.

Salka felt her heart sink as she pushed aside the curtain at the entrance. "Mother? I just saw Tolan. Did he come here to talk to you?"

Miriat was tidying the hut furiously, something she did whenever agitated. "Did you get Trina to agree to take on the lamb? Good. Now take the poor thing over there. It must be starving!"

Salka nodded and went to pick up the lamb, which was dozing off in the corner of the hut.

"One more thing," Miriat said, sitting down heavily. "Emila's parents decided that you two are not to spend any more time together. For now, at least." She wanted to look anywhere but at her daughter. She hated herself for that bit of cowardice and forced herself to meet Salka's eyes. "I know it must be hard on you. But it is not a fraction of the hardship you could have experienced had the townsfolk discovered you. Your adventure... Well. It was a dreadfully stupid thing to do. And there are consequences. Though I wish they were different."

Salka's lip trembled. She moved away from her mother, and without a word, left the house.

# CHAPTER 8

Dola took a deep breath before entering Alma's hut. She placed her hand on her belly, reaffirming her intent by feeling for the flutter of life inside. She wore a heavy coat that day, the one decorated with feathers around the hood and with small stones weighing down the hem. As she walked, she was followed by a clickety-clack of the stones hitting against each other. She pushed the door open without knocking. A Dola doesn't have to knock, not even on the door to a striga leader's house.

She found Alma sitting by the fire, the air smokier than usual. The heavy smell of peat scratched at her throat. Alma looked up at her visitor, the irritation written plain on her face, though she didn't go as far as voicing it. In one look she took in Dola's ceremonial cloak and somber expression.

"I welcome you, Dola. Let me heat some water so you may warm yourself." Alma's words were respectful, though her tone made it clear she resented the intrusion. She pointed to a reed-woven round seat next to her, and Dola sat down on it with some effort. She wondered if she'd be able to get up from it again with any dignity.

A silence fell between them. Alma raised her eyebrow.

Dola cleared her throat. "Your son and the two girls." She said nothing more for a moment.

Alma rubbed her forehead. "Yes. The matter is being dealt with. I've spoken with Dran, and Salka will be punished for her part in endangering them all. Though in truth I'm almost as angry at Dran and Emila as I am at the girl. They should have known better. Still, they managed to escape unnoticed."

"Is that so?" Dola let the words hang heavy in the air. Her fingers were picking idly at the edge of her seat. She straightened herself and folded the hands back in her lap.

"What do you mean? I'm in no mood for riddles and mysteries. Just tell me what you know." Alma looked at Dola from above the iron kettle she pulled out of the firepit with a hook. She folded a cloth several times before wrapping it around the kettle's handle to pour the boiled water into the prepared cup.

"A beautiful kettle," Dola observed.

Alma smiled. "My mother's grandmother brought it with her when she left the town. It's made countless cups of tea for us over the years."

Dola nodded. She was stalling, but there was no turning back now, no matter how much she wished for it. "Salka's been seen. By a Dola, who chose not to betray the strigas."

Alma let the kettle down so heavily a drop of hot water splashed onto her hand. Swearing loudly, she rose up. "She was seen? When? I knew nothing of it!" She picked out a jar from the shelf.

"Let me help," Dola said, shuffling closer to Alma. For a moment, Alma looked like she was about to refuse, but she held out her scalded hand. Dola opened the jar and spent a few moments gently patting a thin layer of ointment onto Alma's skin.

"Well?" The old striga was losing her patience.

Dola glanced up. When she decided Alma was just about rattled enough, she spoke again. "It's been discussed among the Dolas of the two Sister Mountains." In fact, there had been no such discussion at all, and Dola hoped Alma would not see the blush spreading across her face. "It was decided the strigas would not be considered in breach of the truce..." Alma held her breath. Dola let the full weight of her words sink in as well as the implicit threat they carried. "...But the girl must be made an example of to discourage others from any such adventures in the future."

Alma nodded as she considered Dola's words. "I take it the Dolas have decided among themselves already which punishment would be best suited?" There was no hiding the bitterness in words.

Dola nodded. She steeled herself before she spoke. There was no turning back now. She pushed the image of Miriat and Salka out of her mind. It couldn't be helped.

"Three months alone at the Windry Pass."

Alma leaned back in her seat, as if trying to create more space between herself and Dola. "You can't be serious?"

Dola straightened herself and said nothing. She knew she had to be more than the young woman Alma had known her whole life in that moment. She was a Dola and her authority could not be questioned.

"She'll die out there. Winter is nearly upon us," Alma said with a stricken expression. "You can't possibly ask me to send a young woman away in Heyne winter."

"And yet, that is exactly what's required to uphold the truce," Dola said.

Alma closed her eyes for a moment. "But..." She licked her lips, as if steeling herself to the unsavory thought which she felt she had to voice. "You know the other danger there. If I send her – alone – she might... Without her tribe's vigilance and support, she might listen to the other heart. You know it's true."

Dola nodded. "That is a risk we are aware of. But, ultimately, that is a question of how well the girl has been taught to control herself. Should she stray, that will be a matter for the strigas to address. But there is a larger issue at stake here." Dola looked Alma in the eyes. "We're aware your son has gone to the town too, Alma..." It was a cruel thing to do, Dola knew, but she let the unspoken warning sink into Alma's mind. "Yet only Salka has been seen. The truce has been broken, yet the Dolas choose to keep it secret so the peace might continue. But there is a price."

"And Salka will pay it," Alma said.

# CHAPTER 9

Miriat marched across the village with her head held high, though she could feel the eyes of all her neighbors on her back. Munu landed on her shoulder, startling her. It was a rare thing for him to accompany anyone except for Salka, and Miriat appreciated the simple comfort of his presence. There was a whisper behind her, and he swiveled his head, giving out a piercing shriek: as clear a threat as any animal ever uttered. Miriat stroked his head gently and wondered at how alike Salka and her bird were in their sudden fury. The falcon had an almost human intelligence about him.

She came to Alma's house and paused for a moment at its door. As a non-striga, she never felt entirely welcome, and this time was no different. But it was her daughter they were spreading lies about and she'd be damned if she let herself be cut out of the conversation. She ran her fingers across the string of wind chimes hanging from the roof to alert Alma to her arrival, and after a polite pause, she pushed open the door.

Alma was sitting on a rug with her legs crossed, grinding something in the mortar. The house was filled with a sharp aroma, and each movement of the pestle made a crunching sound. Her shadow hovered above her head, its fingers playing with the bunches of herbs hanging from the rafters. As Miriat entered the house, the shadow slithered down to the floor and took its place by Alma, so quickly that Miriat almost missed it. Alma's face remained unmoving.

"Can I help you, Miriat?" Alma asked in a weary voice. She didn't stop the grinding nor did she look up and the rudeness of it was not lost on her guest.

Miriat decided to be direct: "We need to discuss our children's trip to Heyne Town."

"Do we?" Alma raised one thin eyebrow. She carefully transferred the contents of her mortar into a clay pot, before getting up to put it on a shelf. "Well, you came to talk, so talk you must, I suppose. I expect you came here to offer an apology on behalf of your daughter?" She said this with a smirk indicating she expected nothing of the kind.

"Hardly." Miriat narrowed her eyes. "Tolan paid me a visit, blaming my girl for *our* children's lack of judgement. I came to clear that up."

"There is nothing to clear up. Salka put my son and Emila in the path of danger and I expect her to be punished accordingly. I intended to speak to you on this matter in any case."

"She is the youngest of the three! And you are telling me... what? That she dragged them all to the village by herself?" Miriat fumed, as Alma calmly watched her.

"Dran and Emila wanted to go see the Hope Tree. Once there, Salka sprang on them her ridiculous plan. When they objected, she went anyway – they had no choice but to follow her. Would you rather they had left her there, alone?"

"That's a lie!"

Alma turned to face her guest. Miriat was taller than her, but Alma seemed unperturbed, as she squared up to her threateningly.

"Be careful what you say, Miriat. Remember, you are not one of us. And you're here only because *I* allow it." Miriat was going to open her mouth but Alma stopped her with a raised finger. "Your child put mine at risk, girl. Don't forget that.

"Now however *you* choose to discipline your child, I will not intervene. But what she did has repercussions for more than just herself. Actions have consequences." Alma turned her face away from Miriat. She took a deep breath and Miriat could see the striga leader tense her shoulders before she spoke again. "She is to be stationed on the east side of the Windry Pass for the next three months."

"You can't be serious!" Miriat looked at Alma in shock.

Alma continued, ignoring the interruption. "She can stay in the hut we have there for the summer goatherds. She can hunt and trap in the woods. After that time, she might better appreciate the safety and comfort of our village."

"Are you trying to kill her? She's little more than a child!"

"She is a striga, and she must learn to abide by our laws. Because if she does not, the consequences will be both brutal and permanent," Alma said. She tried not to look at Miriat's stricken face, for fear of seeing her own shame reflected there. "And one more thing. You may not go with her, lest you wish to not come back at all. This is to be a taste of banishment, make no mistake. I won't soften the punishment for fear of wasting the lesson."

She raised her hand as Miriat tried to speak, cutting her off. Munu flapped his wings lifting off Miriat's shoulder for a moment. Alma's shadow moved quick as a lash and faced the bird, separating as it did so for a moment from the wall of the house. Its sudden fury matched Alma's.

"Did you think she would get a slap on the wrist?" Alma spat as she talked, her face turned red. "For dragging my son into danger? What did you imagine? Extra herding duties? Laundry? The girl *will* learn to follow our laws. As will you."

# CHAPTER 10

Salka walked up the forest path, the frosted moss giving way under her feet with a gentle crackling. Miriat had cried the whole night before Salka's departure, her hands working tirelessly to finish Salka's new cloak, as Salka pretended to sleep.

In truth, when Miriat told her of the banishment, Salka felt little aside from relief. She did wrong, very wrong, to heal the lamb. She knew that, but she was alone in the knowledge of what she'd done, she was certain. If Dran had suspected anything, he would have told his mother. If anyone found out...

But nobody did, and there was a little relief in that. She had to live with the burden, she alone. They looked at her as if she was still one of them: a good, decent striga leading a good, decent life. And the banishment felt like a way to atone, to wash off the stigoi blemish and start again.

Munu shrieked overhead, letting Salka know he was there. She shifted the strap of the heavy sack she carried her supplies in. There was dried fish and cured meat, and she had no doubt she'd be grateful for both in the coming weeks. Multiple cheese necklaces hung from her neck. Trina had generously shared her own supplies, as Miriat had only what she managed to barter for with the other strigas. It was a kindness that Trina could ill afford, but Miriat had accepted all gratefully, hoping it would be enough.

The cold air pinched Salka's cheeks and she felt the skin on her face tingle. She pulled her scarf a bit higher and wiped her eyes.

She felt a rush of shame for what her banishment would end up costing her mother, both in their saved rations and in the absence of Salka's help in the winter months.

Salka looked up. She was still close to the village, and the sparse canopy of the familiar pines allowed some rays from the cooling sun to bring a memory of warmth to her face. A shriek from Munu admonished her to keep up the pace. She inspected the moss on the trees' bark and corrected her course. To get to the pass she would have to travel down the Green Sister and then move along the path barely protruding off the side of a craggy cliff. There she would finally face the Grim Sister, the twin peak to the home of the strigas.

After a few hours of steady walking, she heard a rustle in the bushes some way ahead. She took her sling out of the bag, and picked up a small rock, weighing it briefly in her palm. A hare burst from the bushes. Munu swooped down with a piercing shriek, scaring the animal towards Salka and her sling.

She did not miss.

It was only early afternoon, but the grey sky predicted an early night. Munu landed on a branch next to her and hopped excitedly, awaiting his reward. He snorted angrily when he saw her stow their catch away. "You will have your share, Munu," Salka said with a smile. "You just have to wait till we set up camp." She tried to stroke his head, but he hopped away, clearly not in an affectionate mood.

As Salka started walking again he perched on her shoulder but was promptly shaken off. "Oh no, you don't!" she said. "I have enough to carry here without you weighing me down as well. Make yourself useful and fly ahead, check the road is safe."

He did so quickly, but not without a sharp peck on Salka's shoulder first.

Salka kept walking, enjoying the rhythm of it. She turned her toes slightly inwards as she'd been taught, spreading her weight more evenly and allowing her to walk sure-footed for longer. The scarf on her head fell briefly over her eyes and she pushed it up impatiently. It was a pleasant day despite the chill. She could be either scared or excited and she made a concerted effort for the latter, and allowed herself to enjoy the thrill of the adventure.

Suddenly she heard a piercing shriek and felt the air rush by her cheek as Munu swooped down next to her, so close he brushed against her face with the tip of his wing as he passed. With a gasp of surprise, she spun around and froze when she saw what Munu was after.

Barely five paces behind Salka stood a huge brown bear, its ears pricked up and its eyes fixed on her. This was not a bear startled by an unwary traveler. This was a hungry animal certain of the kill. It must have been stalking her for a while and she hadn't even noticed.

Munu's claws ripped across the bear's snout, provoking a roar which shook Salka out of her dazed state. She spun around and ran.

*Stupid, stupid, stupid.* She'd been brought up in bear country and yet she'd walked around, lost in her thoughts, without a care for what might have been waiting in the forest. Like some prey. Like some helpless thing that had no business being in the Heyne Mountains. Had no business being alive at all.

If Munu could distract the bear for long enough, perhaps she could get away. As she ran, Salka resisted the urge to look behind her, though she heard the bear's angry roars coupled with Munu's squawks. She reached into her pack and threw the hare they'd caught to the ground. A bear could out-run her, out-climb her, out-swim her. If she was lucky it might be satisfied with the hare and leave the larger prey be.

A stitch in her side slowed her down but she pushed through the pain. The trees whizzed past, the purply red of the evening woods, as she heard nothing but her breathing and the rhythmic jingling of the sack on her back.

She tripped on a high root and fell on her face. She scrambled up and leaned against a tree, panting, trying to listen for the bear over the ringing of own heartbeats. She pushed the hood of her cloak back as hot blood rushed into her cheeks and beads of perspiration began to form on her forehead. She was scared and thirsty and terrified for Munu.

There was nothing to do but press ahead. By her estimation, she'd been running in roughly the right direction and there should be a stream at some point soon. She'd approach the pass from the east instead of west. It would add to her journey, but there was no helping it. She sighed. Munu was still not back, and while she wanted to wait for him, that might also mean waiting for the bear.

Salka walked for a while longer. It was already mid-afternoon, with barely one hour of sunlight left. Setting up camp was preferable to walking in the dark, though she wished she could have put more distance between herself and the bear. She set her bag to the side and went looking for kindling. She wrapped a rope to her food pack and stashed all her provisions inside, including the cheese necklaces. Then she took a jar of herb ointment from her pocket and rubbed it on her clothes and on the outside of the food pack before hanging them off a nearby tree. The ointment, a gift from Trina, obscured the smell of the food, so that with a bit of luck even the bear's sensitive nostrils wouldn't be able to pick up its scent.

Then Salka found a bit of ground that was safely away from the trees, and prepared to build two fires. She set some extra wood in between the fires and ripped a strip of cloth from one of her two spare shirts to prepare a torch. She winced as the fabric ripped and thought of the time it took to make it, but should she need to move in the night, a torch would be of more use to her than spare clothing. She lit the first of the fires and paused for a moment, mesmerized by the flames.

In spite of the crisp autumn air, she felt cozy in her new cloak. She ran her fingers over its even weave and choked back the tears. For the first time she was truly alone.

She wrapped the cloak around her knees, for comfort as much as for the warmth. Her boots were wet, but she couldn't risk taking them off. She shuffled closer to the fire and put her feet as close to it as she could without scorching them. The grey hour loomed heavy as the evening crept on, the air sparkled with the chill of a winter that was not to be delayed for much longer. Just before the day finally gave up its struggle with the night, Salka rose up and set the second bonfire ablaze, hoping it would be enough. Fires were generally good at keeping the predators away, as long as you weren't so stupid as to cook meat over them.

Salka got little sleep that night, waking at every distant hoot, screech, and chirp. Every time she did, she added wood to the fire to keep the flames high and the shadows farther.

Dawn found her curled up in her cloak, with the sides of her face crusted over and puffy from tears. She sat up and rubbed her eyes. Half asleep, she brought her fingers to her lips to whistle, but there was no Munu to answer her. Her lip trembled, and she bit it hard before it drew another sob out of her.

She got up, unwillingly, as the cold of the morning pushed away the relative warmth of the inside of her cloak. She pulled her things down from the tree and tied a makeshift torch to the side of her bag. She pulled out a hard biscuit wrapped in cloth and nibbled on it as she walked, letting the chilly sun and the moss growing on the side of the trees guide her.

Another thirsty, tired day passed, and Salka felt a thrill when she finally heard the welcome sound of water ahead. She followed it and had a moment's hesitation as she saw the steep sides of the gorge through which the stream flowed, with barely enough space for her to descend to fill her waterskins. She sat down on the mossy ground and considered her options. Looking for an easier descent was possible, but it would take time and she was loathe to spend another night in the forest. Her best bet was to use the young trees to the side of the stream as a makeshift ladder. She put her pack and her cloak on the ground, slung the waterskin's strap across her back and made her way down to the stream.

After she climbed about an arm's distance down, a rustling made her look up. The bear's soot-black eyes looked down at her with interest. Salka froze.

The animal made an exploratory swipe at Salka with its paw. It was inches away from her head, and nearly slipped as the soft soil crumbled under its weight. It let out an annoyed groan. The bear was only a yard or so above her, but the steep side of the gorge combined with the bear's weight made it difficult for it to reach her.

She could see the deep gash across the bear's nose, courtesy of Munu's talons, though she felt no satisfaction. Munu was not here now and the first blood meant little in the Heyne Mountains. The fight was over drawing the last blood, and she wouldn't let it be hers.

She tried to lower herself farther, eliciting an outraged huff and a growl from the bear; a strange set of noises which sounded almost conversational. Like a request. A plea. If she'd only be reasonable, it wouldn't have to be hungry that night...

The bear reached down again, trying to catch Salka as if she were a fish swimming down the river. She ducked, narrowly avoiding the claws. Her foot felt for another tree root to step on, to lower her farther away from the bear. The animal growled, and gave another swipe, leaning forward to reach Salka's hand. She yelped as one of the long claws grazed her skin making her let go of her handhold, and lose her balance.

She tumbled down, the branches scratching her painfully on the way. She screamed when her back made contact with the icy stream. It was so cold she thought her hearts would stop as the clear water closed over her eyes.

The stream wasn't deep but the stones beneath were slippery, and it took a moment before Salka could find her footing. She crawled onto the other side of the stream, panting and spluttering loudly. She looked up and saw the bear staring at her.

"Go! Just go!" Salka tried to holler, but only a whisper came out.

As Salka clung to the side of the gorge, she watched helplessly as the bear tore through her possessions, gorging on the hard-won dried meats and cheeses inside the pack. After it was satisfied that nothing more of interest was to be found inside, it looked down again and watched Salka for a while. Eventually, either judging her too troublesome or the descent too difficult, the bear got up and wandered off in search of an easier meal.

It was a while before Salka managed to build up the courage to make her way back to what remained of her once neatly packed provisions. The bag was torn open, and there was little food left untouched. Her hands grown blue with the cold. Salka took her drenched shirt off, its rough fabric sticking to her skin. She took off the wet cheese necklaces and wrapped them in a dry cloth, carefully placing them inside the ripped pack. She took out both her spare shirts, and put the undamaged one on first, with the torn one on top, before wrapping her cloak over her shoulders. She looked around for some wood, but there was not much around. She had to make do with some pine boughs, which she judged too full of sap to burn well.

It took her a moment to find her flint box that had been thrown into the deep moss, and her teeth were chattering by the time she saw it. She carefully lit the fire and blew on the embers till the branches caught flame. Only then did she take off her sodden trousers and boots, trying to heat up her feet by the fire.

She looked back through what remained of her pack. The bear had left some of the salted fish, but the biscuits and the meat were gone. The animal was fat with the autumn's plenty and it must have judged her easy enough prey to even bother following her. Salka ran her fingers through her hair, the curls quickly crusting over with frost. She would have to rely on her traps far more than she had expected, and it was not easy hunting by the pass.

She huddled by the fire, trying to make herself small, and cried. She thought of the blankets her mother had bartered away for the biscuits and the meat cured over the short summer months. All gone. Something fell on her shoulder and made her look up. Her tear-wet eyes focused on Munu, sitting on a branch directly above her head.

"Munu!"

He cocked his head to the side and flew down onto her outstretched arm. The fear and the loneliness hit her like a wave and she sobbed for a long time, nuzzling her face in the bird's feathers. Munu let her hold him for a while, before he gently pushed at her shoulder with his beak. He hopped onto the ground and inspected Salka's bag. He gave out a disapproving snort and looked at Salka with annoyance, as if to reprimand her for losing both the rabbit and the meat. Salka started crying again, and he hopped towards her and sat in her lap. She pulled some pine boughs over them until she could barely see from between the branches and stayed dangerously close to the fire. She and Munu stayed like this for a long while, as the fire crackled and danced in front of them.

Salka fell into an uncomfortable, fitful sleep.

As the early morning light fell on Salka's face, she shifted, some of the boughs falling off in the process, letting in more of the cold air. She reached out and patted her trousers. They weren't completely dry, but damp wool would be better than nothing at all. Her shoes were another matter; she bit her lip as she pulled them onto her feet, the sodden leather squeaking over her skin.

Her stomach rumbled. Salka got up and looked around for some deadwood. Using her knife, she pried open a rotten tree trunk and picked up the termites inside. She chewed them slowly, ignoring the sickening crunch as she crushed them between her teeth. The insects and some dandelion roots made a less-than-satisfying meal, but she was grateful for even that much.

She walked for the better part of the day before she finally reached the Windry Pass. She had never been there before, and the sight impressed her in spite of her cold feet and empty belly. The pass was a natural rock bridge between the two Sister Mountains: the Green Sister and the Grim Sister, a giant that towered over the other mountains. The top was always covered in snow even as the summer warmed its lower slopes.

A windowless log hut with a moss-covered roof huddled against the rocks, just over a hundred yards or so from the bridge and the cliff. It was a sad dwelling, but Salka felt she had never seen one quite as welcoming. She rushed towards it, with Munu circling above her.

She gingerly opened the door, and a stream of dust fell from the ancient frame. Munu flew in first and hopped onto what must have been the sleeping nook of whoever had been here last. Although Alma said it was sometimes used during summer herding, clearly the warmer weather discouraged any upkeep efforts.

The bed was an elevated platform of wood, moss and animal skins, though most of what had once made it comfortable had since rotted away. There was a fireplace, instead of the fire pit Salka was used to, with a chimney of slate and mud. Salka picked through the old bedding for whatever could be used as kindling and set to work by the fireplace.

There was a terrible draft, and she knew she would have to make some quick, rudimentary repairs, before the winter set in properly. She took out the damp cheese necklaces and hung them on a wall by the fire. Then she picked up a seemingly functional bucket from the corner and went out to collect some snow for melting.

On the way back, she collected some moss and pine boughs, dragging them behind her with some effort. Once back inside she shoved the moss into the worst of the holes and settled herself on the branches. She put a small piece of dry fish in the water as it came to a boil, and flavored the broth with pine needles. Munu watched her skeptically.

Salka let him out to do his own hunting, and he vanished with a joyful screech.

She stretched out and covered herself with her cloak, watching her meal as it cooked on the fire. It was the most comfortable she'd been since she left her mother's house. She drifted off as she thought of the traps she would set the next day, and the small improvements she could make to the hut, while outside the snow began to fall.

# CHAPTER 11

Salka slept deeply that first night. In the absence of a window, she didn't wake until well into the mid-morning. Munu had returned in the night, his talons stained with blood, and she slept with her falcon at her side.

In the end, the impatient bird nipped at her leg, and so she dragged herself, groggy, from underneath the pine boughs. The rotten branches and wool did not make for a long-lasting fire, and the hut was cold when she woke up. Salka shivered, and regretted not bringing in more kindling the night before. She broke off a little of the cheese from one of the necklaces and soaked it in cold water. It would be a while before she could eat it, so she decided to go out to get acquainted with her new home.

She wrapped the cloak around her shoulders and opened the door, letting Munu fly out as she did so. She paused for a moment and closed the door again. Overnight, easily a foot worth of snow had piled up on the pass. Salka closed her eyes, trying not to panic. She had little food and no wood for the fire. She took a deep breath and opened the door again. She bent down and picked up a handful of snow. She closed her fist, and the wet snow stuck together. There was no helping it. She had to collect the kindling first before it was all soaked through. She sighed and walked towards the woods.

It was slow work, as she had to go back to the hut often, not being able to carry much at a time. The snow stuck to her shoes making her feel as if she was walking on two wet pillows. Her feet were soon too cold to continue, so she went back in and started a fire again. After a moment's thought, she pulled out some of the moss she had stuck in the wall gaps the day before and set it aside to stuff in her shoes the next time she had to go out. She set some supple green twigs she had cut down in the woods in front of her, looping and tying them into two large woven hoops. She looked at the finished product and smiled. They would do quite nicely as snowshoes.

A screech by the door announced the return of Munu. He hopped closer to Salka and proudly dropped what Salka suspected to be mouse intestines in front of her, before beginning his fastidious grooming ritual. The blood splattered around his chest suggested it was not the first capture of the day. Salka winced at the gruesome offering but tossed it in her pot anyway. She knew she should be grateful, even for that much, and she stroked Munu's head with affection

While her shoes were drying by the fire, Salka took some of the branches she had dragged into the hut and began to cut them to size. There would be fish in the stream, and she decided she would make up a trap for them before the day was done. She paused for a moment, then with a stick she drew a few lines in the dust on the floor. Maladia had explained to her a few times how to make an obstruction trap, but Salka, not known for her fondness for fish, never expected to actually have to make one. She understood the basic concept though, and was confident she could recreate it.

The ground snares were easy to make in comparison, and the meat would be easier to preserve, but there was little game in winter. She went through her possessions and picked out a cord, thinking she'd have to be sparing with it, as one of the two coils was lost when the bear rummaged through her bag. She would set three traps that evening. She put the sticks for the funnel trap and the cord in her bag and strapped the snowshoes onto her, now only slightly damp, shoes before stepping out.

Looking towards the bridge, it struck her how little of the

mountains she had seen before her banishment. She grew up in a village surrounded by tall pines, and the wide-open view of the mountains still had an aspect of novelty to it. She looked up the steep slope of the Grim Sister and wondered briefly what lay to the other side of the peak. A gust of wind blew some of the snow off the bridge and sent it swirling towards the cliff in the north. Salka walked up as close to the bridge as she dared and took a deep breath. She could see a path running far below. Even with the freshly fallen snow, you could make it out: a thread winding its way westward. Salka thought of the villages the path must lead to, and she wished she could see them for herself one day.

It struck her then that perhaps that had been Alma's intention: to tempt her to willingly leave the strigas, to chance it with the folk below. If she could only get far away from the mountains, to where people had never heard of strigas, she could finally explore what life could be. The thought gave her a small thrill, and a shiver went up her spine. If she chanced to look at the ground, she would see her shadow writhing and stretching as if it too wished to move beyond the forest to where the mountain range ended and the plains began.

A sudden thought chilled her. Salka had never before thought of a life outside of the community, and her shadow shrank instantly, leaving only the slightest impression on the fresh snow. She thought of her mother, awaiting her return. No, she would not be tempted.

She turned around and headed for the stream, setting up two snares on the way. Munu screeched above her head, searching for prey of his own and she smiled. It was a comfort to know he was there, but she could not rely on the food he might bring her.

Salka came upon the stream and looked for a part shallow enough to set her trap. She took her shoes and socks off and rolled up her trousers above her knees. She picked up a flat rock and carefully lowered herself into the stream. She gasped as the icy water made contact with her skin. She started digging the sticks into the river bed to create a vase-like trap for the fish to swim into. The sticks she brought, however, were neither long enough, nor sturdy enough for the depth and the hard gravelly belly of the stream. Swearing loudly, she climbed out, pulling her socks and shoes back on. She couldn't look for better materials before warming up, unless she wanted to risk frostbite. She walked back to the hut in a rotten mood, on the way adjusting one of the snares, already upset by a pile of snow freshly fallen off a tree.

Once inside, she made up a small fire and sat warming her feet. The day was more than half gone and she needed far more firewood than the few boughs she'd dragged in if she were to keep herself warm through the night. She had no axe, just a small hatchet. Salka weighed it in her hand for a moment, sighed, and walked outside again.

She picked a small tree growing near the hut. It was not much more than a sapling, but her unpracticed hands took a long time felling it. She dragged it towards the hut and tried splitting it against an old stump. Her fingers were sticky with sap by the time she hauled the wood inside, and stacked it against the wall. She moved closer to the fire and threw some of the smaller branches in. They were too green to burn efficiently, and the smoke made her eyes water. She peered towards the wood she'd chopped down and wondered briefly if freezing to death was preferable to choking on the smoke. She had seen some deadfall on her way from the stream, but it would take a great deal of work to drag it back. Not that she had anything better to do.

She moved her supplies closer and counted every bit of salted fish and every square of cheese. Even with strict rationing, she didn't have enough to last the month. She'd have to try again with the stream trap. Maybe she could set some traps for birds, though she'd always hated doing that. Even though Munu had no qualms about devouring his smaller brethren, she always felt guilty. He was sitting beside her now, his eyes watching her with mild interest.

The sap on her fingers with its pleasant, familiar scent, made her painfully homesick. She took a deep breath in and the shadow behind her moved almost imperceptibly, with ripples like the surface of a lake. A sensation of warmth tracing the line of her spine jolted her. She held her breath and tried to force the shadow down into the listless pool on the floor, as she'd always done before.

*A breath in, hold, a breath out,* like she'd been taught. She gasped. For the first time, the shadow pushed back.

It felt like the protest her lungs would make when she tried to hold her breath for too long. The discomfort was sudden and overpowered any desire to continue. She looked at her shadow, and she could see a small whirlpool of darkness within it, so faint she would have missed it if she wasn't looking for it. A ripple that showed her the shadow would not allow her to starve it again.

Salka stifled a sob. She'd been warned. Everyone knew what happened if you let your second heart take over. She had healed the lamb and poisoned herself in the process. She was tainted now, she knew that. How long before her other heart would silence that within her which was human? Till all that was left was the stigoi?

She reached out and touched one finger to the floor. There was no response. She quietened her breath and waited. She could feel it inside her, a taut string. If she plucked at it, she knew it would respond. She pulled herself away from the feeling inside, gently, a thief tiptoeing out of a looted house.

Food. She would think about food. One worry at a time, one form of doom a day.

She rubbed some soot on her hands, preferring them grubby to sticky. As she did so, a sudden thought occurred to her. She pulled the tin cup out from the corner and spread some sap around the sides and the bottom of it with a twig. She then pulled out some of the biscuit crumbs still sitting at the bottom of her sack and sprinkled them in generously. She took the cup outside, and set it close to the trees, where the snow fell thinly.

A few hours later Salka ran outside, and was rewarded with the sight of a small bird struggling inside the now overturned cup. Its feathers stuck to the sap as it desperately tried to free itself. It was a cruel way to kill, but starvation was a cruel way to die. Salka picked up the cup carefully and made her way back to the house.

Munu was sitting by the fire, and squawked loudly, clearly irritated at having been left indoors. The bird in Salka's hand grabbed his attention though and he hopped towards her cheerfully.

Salka reached towards the bird, meaning to break its neck quickly. The idea of cracking its bones made her shiver with revulsion and she hesitated for less than a heartbeat. As she did so, a dark shape shot past her hand and the bird was dead before her finger even touched it.

Its feathers were scorched, and a smell of cooked meat filled Salka's nostrils. She dropped the cup with a yelp, and stood there staring at her hands. Her shadow seemed to mirror her every movement as she turned towards it. She crumpled to the floor and hid her face inside her hands, rocking slightly.

She had felt no pull this time. There had been no warning. Nothing at all that would have alerted her to her striga heart releasing its shadow.

# CHAPTER 12

Alma looked at Dran, and she felt a small knot in the pit of her stomach.

She had noticed him slowing down over the past weeks, his movements becoming more deliberate and calculated, as if all energy was to be rationed. He did a good job of hiding his weakness at first, but the shaking hands gave him away soon enough.

Still, she said nothing. Experience had taught her that he was not to be questioned, no, not even by her. Unless he was ready to speak of it, any mention of whatever seemed set on consuming his strength and body would elicit a furious denial.

She had thought that he would approve of the temporary banishment of Salka, seeing as the girl had put him and Emila in such danger. And though at first, Alma had to admit to herself, she did harbor some small doubts about Emila's version of the story, she soon put them aside. The wisdom of the Dolas was not to be questioned and, after all, it was they who ordered Salka's banishment. If they did so, then her guilt must have been beyond any doubt. So why should she blame her son, when even the Dolas didn't?

But the rage of Dran's reaction to the news was unusual, even for him. And now, more than a month later, he still eyed her with anger. As if it was her who had dragged him to the town. As if it was her fault Salka was a silly little girl who had let herself be seen.

Any doubt Alma had felt at first about the banishment was soon put aside. She was a just leader after all, a famously reasonable one. Everyone knew that. She had always been known for her sound judgement. Hard but fair, that was her. And so, she had to trust herself. And if it protected the village, if it protected her son, then it was the right course. The mere thought of Dran being put in the path of danger was enough to make Alma's second heart beat faster, and her shadow billow like a black sail on some of those boats she had heard tales of but would never see.

Alma could of course sense that many in the village disapproved of her decision to send Salka away. But though the girl was young, to be sure, she was capable, and Alma couldn't put the whole tribe at risk for her sake alone. She felt a pang of regret at not being able to share her reasons with the other strigas. But the Dolas had given her the gift of their silence and she would not waste it by letting the others know how close her own son had come to risking their truce with the townspeople.

She sighed and rolled her shoulders. She supposed, once the three months were over, she might send two strigas to retrieve the girl so that the long trek through the snow might be made safer on the way back. Alma doubted that it would do much to improve Miriat's opinion of her, but it would be the right thing to do nonetheless and would make Alma feel better if nothing else.

Alma reached into one of her many jars and took out a pinch of dry herbs, before adding it to the pot over the fire. A little cassandra berry to increase strength and stamina couldn't hurt.

For a moment she thought back to Markus and Maladia. The thought came unbidden, as she watched her son's sleeping frame. If only Markus had not been discovered, maybe now he would be able to help Dran. She indulged the fantasy for a moment, imagining how the man would notice her son's strange illness and volunteer to treat him in secret.

But even if he had, would she have allowed it?

She looked down at her hands and shook her head. The stigoi touch would corrupt even as it healed, and she would not sentence her only son to become a monster. He would live his life as she did, in discipline and with dignity, and their second hearts would lie unfed, slumbering in their chests. Not even the chance of a healthy body was worth opening that door.

So she used what knowledge she had of medicinal mountain plants and hoped that, once the snow cleared and the sun warmed their bones again, Dran's strength would return. Some cassandra berries, and some Toran's Wort for the pain.

There was so much pain, and she could do so little to relieve it. She wiped her wet eyes with the back of her hand. She thought back to when Dran was small, and a smile briefly brightened up her face. He had so much determination from the first. He'd never let his foot stop him from doing anything he had set his mind to, be it racing or climbing a tree. She was so proud of him then, and she was proud of him now, even though she had learnt to be wary of his changeable moods and quick temper.

She would watch him sometimes, when he talked to the girls in the village. His handsome face would light up with that easy charming smile of his, and her heart would swell as she saw how others cared for and admired him. He would take over as the head of the village after she was gone, she had no doubt about it. The strength of his character and his determination would more than make up for the deficiencies of his body. She looked down at her own hand for a moment, and held it out in front of her. If she could only make his as steady. She reached into the jar and added another pinch of cassandra berry to the stew.

# CHAPTER 13

The first twenty days in the Windry Pass were hard for Salka, but the following ten were worse still. The food she had brought from home was rarely dipped into, but the pitifully small pile of it kept growing smaller. Salka told herself it was to be expected, as it took time to set up the traps and to find the parts of the freezing stream where the fish might be found, and in the meantime, she had to eat.

But as the night once more fell all too soon, catching her hungry and cold at a distance from the safety of her hut, Salka felt tears come unbidden to her eyes. She tried to force them back, a sign of shameful self-pity, but they glistened still on her long eyelashes, turning into tiny balls of ice as the cold gripped her. A sudden warmth spread over her shoulders and she knew it was her shadow's unbidden comfort.

She would shake it off, any moment she would. But she luxuriated in the warmth of it for half a breath too long. Finally, she pushed it away, though she felt the struggle of it more than before. In the first days of her arrival, she had waited for the taint of her striga heart to spread. She thought it would feel different and was vigilant for any signs she might be turning into a stigoi. But she noticed no change in herself, beyond the ease with which her shadow would leap to assist her if she relaxed in her resistance. But there were no changes in her desires or thoughts, not that she could tell at least. She had no desire to hurt or kill beyond satisfying the needs of her body.

She still resisted the shadow, of course, though she felt it push back now, in a way she never had before the lamb's healing. The bird was hatched, as it were, and it voiced its demands for a share of Salka's life, much like a fledgling would. She wondered if she resisted for long enough, if she could starve her striga heart and bring it back in line. She somehow doubted it and shivered with the shame of that knowledge.

She walked towards the hut, the moonlight reflected in the snow, though the path immediately in front of her always seemed a bit too dark. She tripped over a root and fell face-first into the snow, scattering all the branches she'd gathered that evening. She gasped as some of the snow fell behind her collar and melted into an icy trickle on her neck. She punched the root in frustration and yelped in pain. She leaned against a tall pine to stand up and pulled herself up, digging into its rough bark with her fingers.

She was cold, and there was no wood in the house. Remembering what Pike said, how Markus had drawn on the trees' life to heal Maladia, curiosity overtook her. She walked up to a smaller tree, barely taller than her, and placed her hand on it. It couldn't hurt, not any more than what she'd already done. And she was too cold to look for the scattered branches, which were barely enough to last her through the night.

She was alone, nobody would ever know.

She searched for the place inside her where she heard the humming of her second heart, and pulled on it.

Salka opened her eyes. Nothing happened. She held her breath and grabbed the sapling as hard as her icy fingers would let her. Nothing. She let go.

Frustrated, she sat in the snow and groaned. She was not a stigoi after all then. Much comfort it would be to her frozen corpse. A silent sob shook her back. She shouldn't cry. Tears would just freeze on her cheeks and hurt her as everything hurt in these mountains. Struggling to control her breath, Salka exhaled slowly to calm herself.

As she did so, she felt something quicken inside her chest. A small tendril wrapped itself around the sapling, digging into the soft bark. A sudden sensation of warmth wrapped itself around her shoulders like a warm cloak. She let herself sink into it and luxuriated in it as feeling returned to her freezing toes and fingers. There was a sound, no louder than a baby's breath, as needles began to fall from the sapling.

She reached with her gloved hand and picked up a needle. It was dry and brittle. She pulled on the trunk, which snapped with a sad little sound, as if it had been dead and dry for months. She looked at it with a mix of joy and regret. It had been a lush green thing only moments earlier. The cost of her warmth had been great. She grunted as she picked up the fallen tree. Though her hand closed with ease around the trunk, it was not as simple to drag it back. But she would be warm that night at least. She whispered a thanks, which felt proper and right to her, though she couldn't say to what or to whom she was grateful.

She looked towards the moon. She still felt no different than before, though she could breathe a bit more easy perhaps. No scales sprouted from her skin, no fangs grew in her mouth. There were no outward signs that there was anything different in her. But a resolve began to form inside Salka. A small but hard thing it was.

She would not be cold anymore if she could keep herself warm.

# CHAPTER 14

Miriat trudged through the ankle-deep snow, her day's meagre catch in her bag. All the animals seemed to have travelled down the mountains and away from the striga traps. Miriat had managed to catch a rabbit, so thin and so white she barely saw him in the snow. She was lucky to have that much, she knew. Most of her snares showed up empty these days, as they did for the others in the village.

She tried not to think about Salka and the deep snow covering the path between the village and the Windry Pass, separating them more effectively than even Alma's edict could.

She had turned down Trina's offer of company, as she often did these days. She had too much anger bubbling under her skin to enjoy anyone's presence. She was angry at Alma most of all. And at Dran and Emila for not standing up for Salka. And at Rida and Tolan for believing Alma's nonsense. And the entire village of whispers and gossip.

Miriat counted all of them in her mind: a litany of rage.

The sudden banishment of Salka caused much surprise in the village, and Miriat was shocked to find out how quickly the strigas jumped to the conclusion that Salka must have done more than just wander to the Heyne town to deserve it. Nobody dared suggest so to Miriat, of course, but the odd looks and the hushed tones of conversations abruptly finished the moment she was in sight spoke volumes.

When pressed, Trina confirmed Miriat's suspicions.

"They are sure Salka might have... Well... not *followed* her heart perhaps, but tainted herself in some way, for Alma to throw her out like that. And in the winter months too... I *told* them it wasn't true, but after what happened with Maladia and Markus... Their trust in me is strained too, I think." Trina shrugged. Though she did not trust herself to speak, Miriat squeezed her friend's arm in appreciation of her loyalty.

Now, with her snowshoe-clad feet moving soundlessly over the fresh powder, Miriat pondered the extent to which the situation had damaged Salka's standing in the village already. If she would only settle among them better and learn to curb her wild ways, she might find some happiness in the village life. There was no space for defiance anymore.

Miriat gritted her teeth, passing two strigas on the path. The pair were sisters, roughly Alma's age, ready always to jump at the smallest slight, real or perceived. Miriat thoroughly despised the two gossips.

They noticed Miriat as they walked and started moving towards her. Miriat nodded a hello and hesitated, before stopping and engaging in a conversation she had no appetite for. As much as she would have liked to scowl and move on, Miriat had work to do if she and Salka were to return to a semblance of normalcy again.

# CHAPTER 15

A dotterel stretched its wing out and ran its beak through its long feathers, smoothing and separating them. It didn't hurry, instead slowly inspecting each wing. Some fresh powder fell off the branch, dropping soundlessly to the ground, marking the snow like fingertips on linen sheets. The dotterel, finally satisfied, straightened its wings and then fell to the ground, struck dead with a small stone.

Salka came out from among the trees and hooked her sling over her belt before picking up the bird. She put it inside her pouch and scarcely noticed as a shadow hand moved to fasten the pouch's strings. Her face impassive, she walked to the hut, Munu circling above her head.

In the three months since he saw her shadow take the life of her captured bird, Munu had kept his distance. But in the last few days, Salka felt he was once more becoming comfortable with her, his intelligent eyes never leaving her shadow when they were in the hut.

Salka stretched out her hand and felt the tendrils of her shadow slither around her arm and pour into the ground like dark ink. She took a sharp breath as the taste of the snow and the smell of the frozen ground beneath it hit her senses. She could feel the trees around her, the slow, steady life flowing through their branches. She could even feel their song, too high-pitched for her ears to hear, yet conveying so much feeling and peace. She pulled herself back with some effort. After immersing herself in the world around her, going back to her own limited senses felt like willingly shutting herself in a cage.

In the end, her shadow would obey her, only occasionally shooting out a thin tendril into the ground, channeling a jolt of enhanced sensation towards Salka. She was getting used to the rebellious nature of her second heart.

She walked towards the hut as the evening stretched her shadow on the snow ahead of her. It had been a good day. In addition to the dotterel, she had three minnows from her funnel trap. She and Munu would sleep with full bellies that night. She looked up towards the cold winter sun and closed her eyes briefly, letting the fleeting warmth soak into her skin. She found that the cold didn't bother her so much these days. She barely even needed her cloak anymore, though she continued to wear it out of habit.

Munu flew down and settled himself on her bony shoulder and she shifted her weight in response. She gave Munu a scratch on the head. Their hut was already visible in the distance, but she was in no real hurry to go and sit in the half-light of burning pine boughs. That was the real punishment, she thought, the boredom of the long evenings and nights. She slept as much as she could, but a young body will assert its need for adventure and freedom. She had more than once gone out in the moonlight to sit, holding a torch, staring out into the distance, trying to count the lights of the houses she would never visit. On those nights she let her other heart reach out far into the distance, to see and feel the places she herself could not.

Her whole life she had been confined by the red-brown pines, her world had shrunken so that she couldn't feel completely relaxed without the branches domed above her head. Still, there was something in the discomfort of this open space that thrilled her. Here, at last, was something new and different, and strange, after a lifetime of safety and familiarity. She was too smart to attempt crossing the narrow snow-covered pass in winter, and yet, having explored everything within a day's walk on either side of it, she felt like a string was pulling on her chest, drawing her towards the looming Grim Sister, staring at her across the rock bridge.

Walking up to the pass, she watched the snow on the ground ahead of her. She held her breath for a moment and her shadow elongated. She exhaled and lifted her arm as her shadow stretched farther along the bridge. Salka put her arm down, but the shadow kept crawling even further. She kept her eyes open and slowed her breathing, listening to her heartbeats. Without her noticing, the snow around her feet began to melt.

A loud screech broke her focus, and she turned towards the hut where Munu circled above the roof, making distressed noises. She ran towards him as quickly as her worn-out snowshoes allowed, her knife drawn. Munu dove and a roar filled the air. Salka held her breath, but then she saw Munu rise again, his talons bloody and a chunk of fur in his beak, which he let fall, screeching triumphantly. A skinny grey wolf bounded out from behind the hut, and snapped its jaws, narrowly missing Munu.

The wolf's sides were sunken in, its fur matted. It looked old: old and ragged enough for the pack to have driven it away. The animal's desperation drove it to enter Salka's hut, and it would not hesitate to attack her.

As Munu kept the wolf's attention away from Salka, she slowly backed away towards the woods. The green of her cloak showed clearly against the snow, and she knew any sudden movement would be enough to alert the wolf to her presence.

The animal jumped into the air, trying to grasp the flying pestilence tearing chunks of fur out of its back. Salka moved steadily, but her makeshift snowshoes were not built for racing and she tripped, falling face-first into the snow.

The movement caught the wolf's attention. It spotted Salka and turned hungrily towards her. Munu shrieked in fury and swooped down, scratching the wolf's muzzle. The animal barely noticed the attack, its starving eyes fixed greedily on the lump of warm flesh that was awkwardly scrambling to reach the woods.

Salka looked towards the trees which now seemed as desperately distant as the houses beyond the mountains. One of the straps holding the snowshoes to her feet had loosened when she fell. She was terrified it might slip off her foot at any moment, but she didn't dare pause to fix it. The wolf was eyeing her with a slow and steady interest as it started circling her, cutting her off from the forest.

Salka shot a look towards the pass; there was little chance of the wolf following her there, but her chances of being able to cross the narrow path without slipping were just as slim. Still, it was the only way that did not lead straight to the wolf's stomach, and she retraced her steps towards the edge. The wolf, now sure of the kill, was still moving slowly, but if she made a sudden move it would charge.

With a sinking feeling, she realized it would be impossible to outrun it. She was barely ten yards from the bridge now, her back towards the cliff, and the wolf was quickly closing the distance between them. Its shoulders moved rhythmically, and its eyes shone as the sun moved lower behind the trees. The strap that held Salka's right snowshoe fixed to her foot slipped off and once again she tumbled into the snow. The wolf broke into a trot.

Salka scrambled to get up and half hobbled, half ran to the bridge. The wolf shifted its weight to its haunches and leapt to where Salka had stood just moments before. She screamed as the animal's jaws closed inches from her head. She fell backwards onto the bridge, nearly falling off it in the process.

The wind picked up again and sent a gust of powdery snow from the bridge: a wide glittering ribbon in the evening light. The wolf bared its teeth, a looming dark shape against the remains of the day. Salka let out a sob as she backed away from it.

Munu once again swooped down, talons first, but the wolf, with a sort of absent-minded nonchalance, caught the end of Munu's wing and shook its head, throwing the falcon into the snow. Munu landed to the right of the wolf and remained there motionless.

Salka screamed as the wolf leapt towards her, the large paws falling heavily on either side of her face, its jaws ready to tear into her throat. She stabbed blindly with her small knife. It nipped the wolf's thick winter coat harmlessly, and the bulk of the falling animal knocked the knife out of her hand, breaking her wrist with a dull crunch. The animal's breath was warm on her skin and it stank of the dried fish that it had pilfered from the hut. Salka thought of the time and effort it took her to catch and preserve that food, and a silent fury swelled in her chest.

Her hands pushed at the animal's neck, even as the wolf's jaws were closing around her shoulder. Salka shrieked as a white-hot pain shot through her body. A flood of heat hit her, and she kept screaming as the long fangs punctured her flesh. She opened her eyes wide and put her left hand on the side of the wolf's head. The pain and the fury inside her was released in an instant, and they hit the wolf with cruel precision. A dark arrow shot through the wolf's head. The animal opened its eyes wide and sat on its haunches, swaying gently in the wind, a look of surprise in its eyes. Then a gust of wind gave the last gentle push and it fell forward, pinning Salka to the bridge.

Salka looked up towards the sky, the blood gushing through the wound on her shoulder and pouring down her chest. A warmth spread through her body as her shadow enveloped her gently, lovingly, stretching itself over her body and the wolf heavy on her chest, enclosing them both in a dark cocoon.

# CHAPTER 16

Miriat pinned up her long brown hair and put the strap of her bag across her shoulder. Three months had passed, and she would not let Alma keep her daughter away for one more day.

Trina was already waiting by the entrance to her house. "I'm going with you," she said, before Miriat had the chance to open her mouth. Trina held out her hand and squeezed Miriat's arm. "I lost my daughter. Give me the joy of helping return yours to you." She smiled at Miriat, and one would be forgiven for thinking that there stood the same old good-natured Trina. But Miriat could see that her smile no longer extended to her eyes.

Trina had grown thinner and more secretive since her daughter left, often disappearing for several days at a time, wishing for nobody's company but her own. Even Dola who, even now, was approaching the two women with a bright smile, no longer found a warm welcome in Trina's house. Dola stopped at the door, panting from the exertion of the long walk, her hand resting on her pregnant belly. Miriat didn't know who the father was, and she dared not ask; to pry would be the height of impropriety. Dolas had a rather relaxed attitude to coupling and felt little need to regulate, or indeed pay attention to, the causality between it and parenthood.

"Good winter weather we're having today!" Dola said. "Oh, don't let me keep you... *too* long, that is," she added, as Miriat tried to take her at her word.

"You're in a hurry, of course," Dola continued, "but let me have a word with you both, while Trina makes a pot of tea, perhaps?"

"The fire has died down and the water is cold," Trina said, her arms crossed. Dola was used to pushing the boundaries of the acceptable, but Trina felt a spark of rebellion light up within her.

"Well, you better get started on the fire then," Dola replied with narrowed eyes, quashing Trina's defiance. "It was a long walk through the snow this morning and you would not let an expectant mother back out there without as much as a drop of tea to warm her bones?" Dola pulled one of Miriat's stools out by her door and beamed at Trina, who shot Miriat an apologetic look.

"I suppose it won't take too long, Miriat."

Miriat was itching to go and Dola's intervention irritated her. She moved to follow Trina to her house, but Dola wagged her finger at her and said, "Not you. I want to speak with you."

Miriat sighed and sat herself next to Dola. The snow was already melting in places, so wet and sticky it still clung to the shoes and the clothes. Miriat thought of how cold Salka must be and she turned towards Dola with barely disguised annoyance. "What is it?"

"Well, right to the point and no mistake. Aren't I glad I trekked all this morning to speak with you, with this belly weighing me down, and my feet all swollen and painful." Dola crossed her arms and jutted her chin out petulantly. She looked like an angry apple.

"I'm sorry, Dola." Miriat half-smiled. "But I'm anxious for my daughter and want to waste no time in going to her."

"And what do you think I came to you for – that piss Trina calls tea?" Dola said, leaning her head towards Miriat. "I came to talk to you about Salka. You will lead her into a trap, and you don't even know it."

"A trap? What are you talking about?" Miriat looked up.

"Your daughter, a sheltered young woman with few skills and little enough common sense, was sent alone to spend the Heyne winter in a rotting hut. Why do you think Alma did that?" Dola looked towards the village. "I will speak plainly. Your daughter must have used her other heart quite a bit to survive, no question about that. And Alma knew it."

"Salka wouldn't. She's not stupid."

"She's not. Which is why she would have done whatever it took to survive."

A loud curse came from Trina's house, announcing the precariously stacked pans and cups in her hut had performed their usual tumble onto one of her feet. Trina never quite managed to keep things in working order in her house.

Dola leaned towards Miriat and pressed a small pouch into her hand. "Alma is a good woman, by and large, but a vindictive one. And where her son is concerned, she's as blind as a bat. You know what happens when a striga begins to use her other heart's powers. Salka's shadow will betray her. And she *will* be banished for good."

Miriat took a slow breath to steady herself. She looked Dola in the eyes. "Maybe that won't be such a bad thing then. The village is less of a haven than I used to think, and I'm starting to wonder if it's less than my daughter deserves."

Dola pursed her lips, annoyed. "You think it's a joke? If you could just go anywhere with her, we wouldn't be sitting here outside of your ramshackle excuse for a house, surrounded by the stench of goats. Where will you take her? Where will she be safe? No. You have to stay here. Bide your time at least, till you can figure out what else you can do. Now this–" She pointed at the pouch in Miriat's hand, "–this is what made me freeze off my backside walking this morning. When you see Salka, give it to her in a drink. A pinch at a time, once a day. It will slow her other heart and deaden her shadow." Dola leaned in so close to Miriat, she could feel the warm cloud of her breath hit her face. "Make sure nobody finds out about her following her other heart. Not even Trina, if you can help it."

"Trina is a good, loyal friend and she loves Salka," Miriat said, looking blankly at the small pouch in her hand.

"Oh, of course she is. But she lost her daughter. It would not be a kindness to allow Trina to watch Salka get away with the very thing that cost Markus and Maladia their lives here," Dola said. "Now, hide the pouch, and let us speak no more of it. You need only give it to Salka for a month or so. It will make the other heart small and weak, like a leg after a bed rest, and she will be back to normal." Dola looked down to the ground and stroked her belly thoughtfully. "Yes, no more than a month, I'd say."

"How is it you have this?" Miriat held the pouch in her hand, weighing it. She eyed Dola thoughtfully. "How is it the Dolas have such power that we've never heard of? Alma is well known for her potions and powders. I've never heard her utter a word of anything which could still the other heart. If she did, what need would there be to banish Markus? What need would there be to punish anyone for the use of their striga heart?" She shook her head. "You've always been a true friend to us, Dola, but what is this gift you offer me, truly?"

Dola leaned back and tapped at her knee with her fingers. Miriat could see Dola's rising irritation but she'd be damned if she poisoned her daughter as some kind of experiment for the Dolas.

"I got this herb from the North," Dola said finally. "In the northernmost end of Prissan, there are no more strigas. At least, not the kind you can tell apart from the humans. This pouch contains a root they grow there. After Maladia..." Dola took a deep breath. "I couldn't help her. But when Salka was sent away... Well, I had it sent for. It will poison the striga heart. And it will hurt." She paused, making sure Miriat understood.

"Hurt?" Miriat looked up sharply. "Hurt how exactly?"

Dola shrugged her shoulders. "Nothing lethal." Seeing Miriat still hesitated she slapped her thigh with exasperation. "Not like the burning would anyway! Is that what you want to risk?" Dola laughed. "Do you want Salka left wasting away, her second heart burned out of her chest? Or else that she's left a drooling idiot, until she slowly starves to death? One month, Miriat! That's all I ask, that's all that's needed! And if a little of Salka's discomfort is all that is stopping you now, believe me, you'd crawl through fire and crushed glass to save her from the purification ceremony! She *must* continue with it. It will keep her hidden and safe." Dola spread out her palms as if to show there was nothing more she could hide.

Miriat watched her for a moment longer. Then she put the pouch away and nodded a curt thanks. Dola exhaled, and relaxed her shoulders. They both waited in silence until Trina appeared with three cups. One of them was missing a handle, and somehow the sight grabbed Miriat by the heart and filled her with a rush of affection mixed with guilt. Still, she saw the wisdom in Dola's words and so she kept quiet.

They finished their tea in silence, then Dola stood up, massaging her aching lower back. "Well, you mustn't dilly-dally any longer! It's a long journey to the pass, and you don't want to waste any more time chit-chatting and gossiping. Head on to Alma's and then you should be on your way. I have some business of my own to attend to, and can't spend the whole day with you two, as nice as the tea was." She shot them a parting smile and waddled off.

"That was odd. Even for her." Trina cast a look at Miriat, narrowing her eyes.

"I suppose awaiting her baby makes her more restless than most?" Miriat stood up. She once more slung her pack across her shoulder and straightened her cloak.

"Hmm…" Trina cocked her head to the side, watching Miriat. In the end, she only shrugged. "That doesn't surprise me in the least. That woman is 'more than most' in many things."

They walked briskly through the village, its inhabitants only just starting to light their morning fires and usher out livestock. Miriat and Trina stopped in front of Alma's door, the smoke above her house signaling she was already up and about. Alma had always been an early riser, and like many early risers mistook a natural inclination for virtue.

Miriat raised her hand, but the door swung open before she had the chance to knock. Alma's face showed little surprise at seeing Miriat. She stood in the doorway, barring the entry. Miriat couldn't help but notice that Dran did not share his mother's view on mornings, his loud snoring filling the house.

"You're going to collect your daughter. Good. Saves me the trouble of sending people," Alma said curtly, before Miriat had a chance to speak. "I suppose you'll be taking Trina with you. Very well, report to me when you get back." She hesitated. "I hope she's well. Bring her home safe, Miriat." Then the heavy door slammed in their faces.

They looked at each other confused. Trina shrugged off the inexplicable for the second time that morning and they started their long walk towards the pass.

# CHAPTER 17

Salka opened her eyes and saw nothing but darkness.

She wiggled her toes and fingers and was relieved to find that she could still feel them. Falling asleep in the snow in the Heyne Mountains rarely ended well.

Something was digging into her chest and she shifted uncomfortably. She lifted her arm and pushed at what felt like several tree branches off her chest. They made an odd rattling sound before sliding off the side of the stone bridge. Salka suddenly remembered where she was and froze with a knot in her stomach. She was nearly in the middle of a bridge not even a yard wide, lying on her back in the deep snow. One false move would send her tumbling down.

She tried sitting up without turning over and felt a small tingle in her shoulder. The pale morning light blinded her as her shadow slid down her face and uncovered her body, leaving her shivering in the cold. Keeping her body as still as possible, she looked around. She froze as she realized what had been weighing her down. The wolf's skull, clean of its flesh and gleaming white in the morning light, lay with a mirthless grin between Salka's feet. Some of the wolf's bones that hadn't fallen off the bridge lay in the snow, with not a trace of skin or meat on them. Salka's fingers touched her shoulder where the wolf's teeth tore her flesh. The skin was unbroken, though the deep rusty stains on Salka's ripped clothes proved it had not been a dream. Her right wrist, broken when she'd tried to stab at the wolf, was now whole again.

"Munu!" Salka called out suddenly and scrambled to get off the bridge on all fours as quickly and carefully as possible. Once on solid ground again, Salka ran to the now-empty spot where Munu had fallen the night before. A familiar screech welcomed her as the falcon landed in front of her. He nuzzled his beak in Salka's belly, and she stroked his soft feathers, crying in relief.

"Oh Munu! I saw the wolf's bones and I thought you'd be dead too! I don't know how..." A sob escaped her, and she hugged Munu, who accepted it with grace. She felt the warmth of her shadow as it reached out above her hand and ruffled Munu's feathers. To her surprise, Munu nuzzled its beak in the shadowy form.

"Let's get ready, Munu. I want to get out of here. I want to go back. Surely it's time to go back!" She offered Munu her shoulder and made her way to the hut. Her falcon, however, kept looking at Salka's shadow, a dark stain in the snow forming a large train, rippling and twisting behind her.

# CHAPTER 18

"So, are we going to talk about Dola's visit this morning?" Trina asked without looking at Miriat. They were both focused on keeping a steady pace through the snow, and halfway through the day they were both pink with exertion.

Miriat stared straight ahead without answering.

"You're right. Why would you confide in me? I'm only the best friend you have in this world." Trina reached a large rock and slumped against it. "I think it's time for a break. You take out the food and I'll do the talking."

Miriat longingly looked at the path ahead. She wanted nothing more than to keep walking and close the distance between herself and Salka.

"I know you want to keep going," Trina said, reading her thoughts. "But you won't get there any quicker if you collapse along the way. Now, eat." Trina ordered and gestured at the pack on Miriat's back.

"I'm sorry. I know you're right. But I can't muster an appetite," Miriat said, fumbling to untie the food pack. The string holding it together was tight and her fingers were cold.

"Here, let me do it." Trina reached out and took the bag from Miriat's hands. "I don't get as cold." She smiled at her friend and took out two coarse bread rolls. "So, are you ready to tell me yet what Dola said to you?"

Miriat said nothing.

"Fine, keep your secrets."

They ate their food in silence and watched the pale light on the red bark of the pines surrounding them.

"It's about Salka," Miriat said.

"Obviously," Trina said without missing a beat. "Nothing else could make you clam up like that. What about her? Is she safe? Did Dola have a vision or something?"

"Dola seemed worried she might not be safe when she comes back to the village."

"In what way?" Trina stopped eating and looked up at Miriat.

"Dola thinks Alma might be holding a grudge." Miriat chose to reveal some of the truth. "That in the end, she might be planning to get rid of Salka."

Trina finished her food and carefully picked out the crumbs from her coat and ate them. "I have no love for Alma. The bitch banished my daughter. But I don't think she would hurt yours any further. Salka's punishment has already been excessive, and there is little worry she will willingly spend any more time with Dran." Trina stood up and straightened her tunic. She then set her calm brown eyes on Miriat. "When you're ready, you can tell me the *real* reason you're worried."

Miriat hung her head.

The pair walked in silence for a few more hours Their shadows lengthened and they would have to stop soon and make camp, in spite of their desire to put as many miles behind them as possible.

Suddenly, Trina stopped with her hand up, signaling for Miriat to stay quiet. "Hide," the striga said, and they both scrambled to hide behind tall bushes. The snow weighed down the branches, providing excellent cover.

A falcon flew above them with a loud screech. Miriat's face brightened and she jumped out from behind the bushes. "Munu!" She reached out her arms greedily and the bird swooped down, landing on her forearm. "Munu, you sweet-feathered miracle! Where is my baby, where is she?" She stroked him affectionately.

"I'm here, Mama!" a small voice came from behind Miriat.

"Salka!" Miriat turned around and ran towards her daughter as Munu rose to the sky, startled. Miriat leapt towards Salka, and they both fell down into the snow, wrapping their arms closely around each other. "My heart, my precious, look at you! Oh gods, just look at you, you're skin and bone! Your beautiful face! Your cheekbones look like they're about to burst through the skin! But oh, you've grown!" Miriat laughed through the tears, her hands cupping Salka's face. Salka's eyes welled up and she threw her arms around her mother's neck. They both sat there crying for a while.

Trina stood quietly, watching them, at first with joy, then with horror, as the shadow behind Salka towered above mother and daughter, no longer merely a shape on the ground, but a live creature, tethered to Salka, but watching the scene independently.

"Miriat, if you get started on setting up camp, Salka and I will go to collect kindling," Trina said through gritted teeth.

Miriat looked at her in surprise and was about to object, but Trina raised her hand. "There is something I need to talk to her about. It's a striga matter."

Miriat opened her mouth, but Salka smiled at her. "It's all right, Mama, we will have plenty of time to talk later." She gave Miriat a kiss on the cheek and followed the sullen Trina.

Once Miriat was out of the earshot, Trina rounded on Salka. "You've been a very stupid girl," she said, gesturing at Salka's shadow.

"What?" Salka looked up at Trina sharply, but was softened when she saw tears in the older woman's eyes. So she just shrugged her shoulders and said, "I did what I had to. You'd do no different. Or you'd die. That was also an option."

They gathered firewood in silence. When Trina pushed back the hair from her face, Salka noticed there was more gray than brown in it these days. She felt a surge of affection for her mother's friend, who had suffered so much.

"Have you heard anything of Maladia?" Salka asked softly.

"No. I tried to look for them, even going as far as the village in the north-side slopes of the Grim Sister. No sign of them." Trina looked up as she heard Miriat approach. Salka saw the broad smile on her mother's face disappear when she noticed the dark shape looming behind her daughter.

Trina nodded. "That what you've been keeping from me? Did Dola tell you to? You realize that there is not a striga alive that could miss this? The village will burn her heart out of her chest if they see it."

Salka gasped in horror and Miriat unconsciously moved to stand between her daughter and Trina.

"Please, you think I want to do it?" Trina threw her arms in the air, outraged. "You think it would not hurt me too? I love your daughter, as well you know. And I love you too, though you clearly have less trust in me than I thought."

Miriat turned to her daughter with an ashen face. "What have you done?"

Salka looked to the ground. "I didn't *do* anything."

Miriat closed the space between them with a couple of long steps. "What have you *done?!*" She grabbed her daughter's arms and brought her face close to her daughter's.

Salka pushed her mother away. "What I had to! I didn't kill anybody. I didn't steal anything! I did nothing wrong!"

"Nothing wrong? Have you seen that thing?" Miriat pointed her finger at Salka's shadow, which shifted and moved between them. Trina clutched her chest with one hand and tried to pull Miriat away with the other. But Miriat shook off her friend as fury darkened her face. "And this... this *thing!* Look how it stands between us! A threat? Are you threatening me, child? *Me?*"

Salka looked stricken. Her shadow instantly melted into the ground and reappeared behind her once more. "I'm not threatening you. I was angry and it just shows my anger."

"*You* are angry?" Miriat grabbed her daughter's face between her hands again. "What of my anger? Of *my* fear for you? Good grace and omens, child, I'm disappointed. All I've taught you, all you've seen and been told, and you listened to none of it! Not one of my lessons made you pause before you did this to yourself?"

To that, at least, Salka had an answer. She didn't flinch this time, but set her eyes calmly on her mother's, their faces inches from each other. "None of your lessons were what made me survive out here. My other heart did. I did what I had to do. I lived."

Miriat took a step back, breathing heavily. Her hand twitched by her side as if she would strike Salka. Instead, she covered her eyes as tears rolled down her cheek.

Trina stepped forward, her eyes never leaving the dark shape by Salka's feet. "But what do we do? Miriat, do you have an answer? Sniping at her now won't help. Gods know I'm not sure anything will. But if Dola had an answer... Whatever she asked in return, it's worth it."

"She asked for nothing," Miriat said. She and Salka were eyeing each other, each seeming ready to pounce. "But she did give me this." She took the small pouch out of her pack. "This... can make it go away. Dola said it would."

"What is it?" Trina looked dubious. "No herb can calm a stigoi heart." She made as if to take the pouch from Miriat's hand, but Miriat held it tight to her chest.

"Dola said this will starve the other heart. Weaken it, slowly," Miriat said. She looked guilty, seeing Trina's hungry expression. "Dola said it's rare. Painful too..."

Trina looked at the pouch as if it were made of gold. "Then we must use it."

Salka looked down. "*Must* we?"

"Salka!" Trina looked appalled. "We all hear our other hearts, but what you've done... It changes you. It will make you into something you're not, something monstrous."

"I don't *feel* like a monster." Salka kept looking at her feet. She looked so much like a child in the moment, Miriat felt the urge to wrap her arms around her. She resisted it. "And you say it's painful? What will it do to me exactly?"

"What does it matter?" Trina shrugged her shoulders. "If it made your hair fall out of your skull and the teeth rot in your mouth, it'd be worth it! You're a hair's breadth from becoming a stigoi, Salka! Is there no shame in you?"

"I would have *died*," Salka said.

"And you might yet, if Alma sees that thing you carry around." Trina turned towards Miriat. "My daughter and Markus are likely dead. You know that. I suppose that's why Dola told you to hide this from me. Maybe she thought I'd resent her hoarding such treasure when it could have helped save my child. And maybe I do. But I love you both and if this can free Salka from this horror then she must take it."

Miriat looked up and remained motionless for a while. "It will dampen your powers, Salka. Deaden your other heart while you take it, so the change in you can remain undetected." She reached towards her daughter but Salka recoiled.

"And after I stop taking it? What will happen then?" Her daughter stood up straight, and with a pang of regret, Miriat truly understood the change in Salka. The months alone in the mountains had altered her daughter, and though there were still signs of the girl she used to be, there was no mistaking the strength of those long limbs and the determination of the dark eyes, which were now flashing angrily.

"Dola told me your heart will remain silent."

"As it is *supposed* to be then!" Trina said with an impatient wave of the hand. "I don't see the point of this conversation. She must take it, or the other heart will consume her. The strigas will not let one of their own turn into a monster. Markus was banished, but he was nowhere near as far down the road as your daughter has travelled. You haven't seen a striga have her heart burnt out, Miriat. I have. It's brutal. And unpredictable. Salka has a chance at a good life. A proper life."

Miriat stood motionless for a moment. She shivered and pulled her cloak closer to her body. She looked at her daughter and recognized the defiance in her. "It is a choice, Trina. But it's not mine or yours. It is Salka's."

Trina scoffed but she turned to Salka with a curt nod. "Well then?"

Salka slumped down onto a fallen log and looked to her mother. Something important just happened here, and she felt a sense of both gratitude and overwhelming dread. She looked at the shadow next to her, its companionable silence both a comfort and an unspoken threat. She reached out her hand, and only as she saw the sudden drop of her mother's shoulders did she realize Miriat had been holding her breath. "Give me the pouch. I'll do it."

Her mother put the small pouch in the palm of Salka's hand and smiled at her. But Salka couldn't return the smile.

"I'll attend the fire," Trina said, "and make some tea so you can take it." She turned around and walked off.

Miriat sat next to her daughter and put her arm around her. "Are you sure this is what you want?" she asked.

Salka sensed it was not a true question but a hope. So she gave the answer her mother wanted. "Yes, it's the right thing to do."

They sat there for a moment. "What's it like?" Miriat finally asked.

"What's what like?" Salka said, though she knew what her mother meant.

"Being a striga. Having two hearts, all of it." Her mother gestured towards Salka's shadow, though Salka noticed she never quite looked at it directly.

"It feels like… Losing it would be like losing an arm," she said. "Or ears. I don't know." She sighed. "I can ask you what it's like having your eyes, but you won't have an answer either. I was never without it. And it might feel and look different to you now, but it feels to me like it was always there. Just because you can see it now doesn't mean it wasn't with me before. I'm learning more about it, and as I learn, it changes. But my body's changing too, and you don't seem to mind that."

"Oh, I wouldn't say that, my love," Miriat said, forcing a smile onto her lips and pulling her daughter closer. "It is hard to watch you leave your childhood behind. But that part of growing up I can understand. The other part of it though… Following your other heart will change you in ways I understand to be wrong and frightful."

"Are they wrong and frightful because you don't understand them then?" Salka said, her finger tracing an invisible pattern on her knee. "The village keeps us safe, but it feels like we see ourselves like the humans do sometimes. I'm not stupid, I know the other heart can do terrifying things... But Mama, it saved me. I can't explain it, but it killed a wolf for me. I felt the wolf's teeth tearing my shoulder, and I should be dead, but I'm not. I'm healed. Not even healed. Whole. As if nothing had happened at all. And I didn't know I could do it. I could have gone on forever not knowing it. But now I do. It frightens me I will never be able to do it again."

Miriat didn't answer. She just held her daughter closer as they stood up and walked back to the fire where Trina was waiting. Munu was hopping on the ground by the fire, trying to gain access to Trina's pack. She shooed him away. When she saw them, Trina gestured for Salka to sit down. She poured a bit of hot water into a cup and passed it to Salka. Then she watched as Salka put a pinch of Dola's herb into the drink and brought it to her lips.

Miriat felt a pang of guilt and she raised her hand, as if to take the cup away from her daughter's lips, but then put it down again.

Salka drank the liquid. They all sat in silence for a moment. A flicker of pain went across Salka's face, but she didn't move. Miriat reached out and held her daughter's hand. Trina wasn't watching Salka's face; her eyes were fixed on the girl's shadow as it twisted and writhed on the ground next to her. Then it shrank and collapsed, till it was no different from Miriat's shadow, no different from Munu's. Until it was no more than an absence of light.

Salka's breathing slowed, and she looked up at her mother. "Mama? I'm cold."

Miriat quickly pulled out a blanket from her pack and wrapped it tightly around her daughter's shoulders.

"What does it feel like?" Trina asked after a moment.

"It feels like nothing," Salka said. "It feels like nothing at all."

# CHAPTER 19

Dran stared at the wall of his mother's hut, slowly stretching his legs on the floor rug, as he listened to the sounds outside. He would spend hours like that, inside, hiding from the villagers. He despised both his feeble body and his mother for witnessing his struggle. He had a lifetime of practice at hiding his weakness, and he felt certain that nobody in the village knew of the slow progression of the sickness that consumed his strength, but he would take no chances.

Since he'd attempted a healing using Markus' shadow, Dran felt sicker by the day. A sudden flash of memory made Dran turn towards the wall, as if he could hide from the image. The burn on his foot had seemed to heal for a while, but then Dran's horror grew as the darkness of the wound spread farther up his leg. The medicine he stole from Heyne Town proved no more effective than his mother's concoctions. In desperation, he had tried to repair the damage himself using his other heart, but the pain it caused him seemed only to speed up the illness that made his hands shake and his chest seize whenever he attempted to walk for more than an hour. He dared not try a healing again.

But today was a day of hope. Salka was to come back, and Salka was going to help him.

Dran hadn't yet forgiven Emila, whose stupid lie had caused Salka's banishment. To her own parents, she had imparted some of the truth. And yet, when faced with the owlish gaze of his own mother, she saw fit to concoct a lie that elevated him to the role of rescuer of idiots and planted the seeds of hatred inside of Alma. Emila now followed him around the village like a beaten dog, trying to soothe and coax him into reciprocating her insipid affection.

Dran got up from the floor with effort and slipped his feet into the neatly placed fur-lined shoes. He enjoyed the ease with which he could reach them, while at the same time resented his mother's wearisome efforts to organize and sort everything around him to assure his comfort. Even the way she folded his clothes he had discarded carelessly the previous night, served to remind him of his own weakness. He could feel no gratitude for it.

He rolled his shoulders. Salka would no doubt feel some resentment towards him, and he would have plenty of work to do if he wanted to earn back her trust. He thought back to the lamb she stole from Heyne Town and the first smile of the morning stretched his lips. He had been watching the animal over the previous three months as it defied everyone's expectations and grew in strength. There was no sign of injury, no blight of the kind he had been taught to anticipate as the inevitable result of a striga healing. The lamb grew in strength every day, only bleating loudly and running to hide behind its adoptive goat mother whenever it saw Dran.

That was no good. He wanted there to be nothing that could serve as a reminder to Salka of anything he might have done that was less than charming. This, of course, would prove difficult, as Salka was just returning from her banishment, for which she had every cause to blame him.

He gritted his teeth as he thought of the three long months of pain he'd had to endure because of Emila's desire to flatter. After his mother had decided to punish Salka, all his protestations were considered to be yet more proof of his noble nature. Dran could see his mother's unease at the hasty decision to send Salka away, and he had tried to reason with her. But Alma, who usually accommodated her son's requests, had put her foot down.

Dran stretched his neck and hobbled to the carefully polished piece of tin that served as his mirror. He combed his black hair, using a dab of goose grease to make it shine. He smiled at his reflection. He was still good looking enough to break a girl's heart. Or at the very least to bend her to his wishes.

By the time Dran left his mother's house, most of the strigas were already assembled close to the village well, which afforded some decent seating and an unparalleled view of the gate. There was a hum of excitement in the air. Alma's choice of punishment for Salka had been an unpopular one with everyone but Emila's mother, who now stood sullenly by her husband and gave curt replies to anyone foolish enough to accost her.

Emila stood close to her mother, her cheeks flushed. Dran's admirer had taken her friend's punishment hard, and Dran's subsequent indifference to her even harder. Dran noticed a plethora of food baskets carried by the villagers, with still-steaming buns wrapped in cloths: an overabundance of bounty meant to appease the group's common sense of guilt at having participated in banishing a young woman during winter.

Dran nodded at all he saw in a restrained, dignified way. He stood apart from everyone, avoiding all conversation. His hands shook more than usual this morning and he would not betray himself. The whole village had waited for the best part of the morning. It couldn't be helped, of course. No striga would miss Salka's homecoming or risk being the last to welcome her.

It was a crisp morning, but the spring could already be felt in the air and the sun's rays warmed the bones a bit better. Still, there was little chatter. Nobody would say what everyone feared: that Salka might not return, or that she'd return so changed she could not be welcomed back. It was always a risk that, when outside of the watchful eyes of the community, a young striga might do the easy thing. The stupid thing.

So they all waited.

Finally, a happy ululation reached them from the top of the stairs by the gate.

"They're coming! The three of them!"

The whole village held its breath as the gate opened, painfully slowly. A collective sigh was released as Miriat and Trina entered, their hands placed protectively on Salka's shoulders as she walked between them. The silence broke suddenly, and a wave of happy calls and laughter broke over the girl's head as the strigas saw her shadow, which followed her limply, as if it had never been animated by Salka's second heart.

Dran, away from the crowd, pursed his lips. It made no sense. *You can't unspoil milk.* The evidence of the lamb spoke for itself. He'd broken that animal's neck, he was certain of it. He could still hear the sickening cracking of the bone. He shivered slightly. Salka must have affected a healing of some kind. Her obvious guilt and the way her shadow moved when she met them in the forest, all showed she had followed her heart. He couldn't be wrong.

"There's something odd about this whole business," a querulous voice said close to him, mirroring his thoughts in a most unwelcome way. Kalina stood close to Dran, her arms crossed over her chest.

"You always think there is something odd, Pike. Just mind your business, will you?" he said.

Kalina reddened, "It's everyone's business to make sure the law is obeyed. I, for one, don't for one second believe she didn't follow her second heart in the last three months. Not even once?" Kalina waved dismissively in the direction of Salka and straightened herself up a bit, jutting her chest out. "How would she have survived Heyne winter on her own, without at least some assistance?"

"We would know if something had happened," Dran replied, but the conviction was melting away from his voice.

Kalina jutted out her chin. "I know I'm right. We all expected to see her a bit changed, within the acceptable limits, of course. But this…" Kalina shook her head. "She could be human! Something strange is going on."

Dran watched Kalina from under his lashes. It was no good to have the village busybody going around spreading rumors. Not before he got the chance to speak with Salka himself.

"The only strange thing I've noticed is your willingness to see the worst in others, Pike. Are you saying the only thing keeping *you* from following your heart is our presence?" he said to Kalina, startling her. Her eyes popped wide open and she reddened at his rebuke.

He turned away from her, letting the full force of his disapproval wash over her.

He walked towards Salka, forcing the others to make space. The last thing he wanted was to be simply one of a crowd.

"Welcome back," he said, smiling. "I'm so glad you're well."

"Are you?" Salka asked with a stony expression. Her blunt reply surprised him and he was left with his mouth hanging as she and her mother walked towards their house.


"Nothing's changed," Salka said when she entered her mother's hut.

"I thought you'd be glad of that!" Miriat laughed. "And here, look who's been waiting for you!" The lamb bleated in the corner of the room and came out to investigate. Upon seeing Salka, it gave a small jump and ran straight into her.

"Here you are!" Salka chuckled as it nearly threw her off her feet. "Did you miss me? I've been thinking, we'll have to give you a name." She smiled, petting the lamb's head. "How's 'Curious'? Sound good?" She was rewarded with a loud "mee" as Curious began investigating the contents of Salka's sack.

"Did it just go 'mee'?" Salka laughed, gently pushing the lamb's head away.

"The company you keep, I suppose," Miriat said. "Though I'm sure surprised it remembers you so well. You only had it for a couple of days before you left..." She trailed off and suddenly crumpled to the floor.

"Mama?" Salka touched her mother's arm, alarmed. Miriat responded by wrapping her arms around her daughter and squeezing her with force.

A sob rose from deep inside Miriat's chest. "I'm so sorry, sweetling. I couldn't stop it. I didn't protect you... I should have gone with you, no matter the consequences! And now this... This *thing...*" She left the sentence unfinished. She shook her head. "If I were there with you it never would have happened."

"You couldn't do anything..." Salka said. She could smell the herb oil in her mother's hair. She closed her eyes. "We'd have no place to go. You knew it then, and I know it now."

Miriat sniffed. "Well, never again." She put her forehead to her daughter's. "I will never again let you be separated from me."

# CHAPTER 20

Salka slept till well after midday. When she finally opened her eyes, it took her a moment to realize she was back in the village and no longer in the Windry Pass. Her bed covers felt luxuriously warm, and the familiar peat smell coming from the fire made her smile. Curious lay its head on the side of her bed and she stroked it, luxuriating the silkiness of its coat under her fingers.

Miriat came in with water. "You're up, good. There's food for you. I thought I'd let you sleep. Here." She picked up a bowl of cooked grains along with a steaming cup and brought them over to Salka. She put a pinch of Dola's powder in the liquid and stirred it well.

Miriat watched Salka drink it. Watched a bit too closely, Salka thought. Still, she supposed trust was in short supply these days. Her own fault. The warmth of the liquid spread over her body, and she would have been glad to go back under the covers, as a groggy, sleepy feeling reached her head and she could feel a slight throbbing in the back of her skull.

"You had visitors this morning, but I sent them away," Miriat said. "Emila and Dran made an appearance."

"Is everything settled between them then?" Salka asked, more for conversation's sake than out of any real interest. It seemed like something Emila would do – making a show of bringing her lover around.

"They came separately, actually." Miriat took the cup from Salka and cast a furtive glance inside it to check the entirety of the liquid was gone. "Dran was very insistent. Although that boy's insistent on everything he wants, to be sure, from the exact moment he thinks of it."

"Oh?" Salka raised her eyebrows. She blew on the spoonful of grains. It had a spot of honey in it, and she would relish every last drop.

"I didn't know you two were this close," Miriat said. She poured some water into the cup and swirled it around before pouring it outside.

"We're not." Salka bristled at her mother's implied meaning. But then, because the grains were delicious, she added, "Maybe he feels bad his mother banished me for his sake."

Miriat nodded. "Perhaps. Still, be wary of him. Alma's mad about that boy and I'd rather she didn't watch you *too* closely for the time being."

"You've nothing to worry about there." Salka rubbed her temples. "I think I might have breathed in too much smoke, my head's throbbing. I should probably get some air." She stood up and moved towards the door.

"Not too far!" Miriat said and reddened as Salka looked at her with one raised eyebrow. "What I meant was, we don't know how you might feel with the powder doing its work. It's safer if you stay close to the house for now. Think of the questions it would raise if you collapsed in full view of the village. No, sit outside if you like, but I have plenty for you to do right here." She pulled out a large bag from the corner. "This is all the wool we have left from last year. With you gone I had no time to prepare it. You can brush it and spin it. I have plenty of teasels for the carding." She dug into her stores with enthusiasm and pulled out several heads of dried teasel flowers with their hardened, spiky heads.

Salka groaned. She weighed the bag in her hands. "You want me to do it all? Now? But it will take an age…"

Miriat nodded, satisfied. "And by the time you're done, hopefully you won't have to take the powder anymore. No." She raised her hands to stop Salka's complaint. "I won't hear another word. Spring will be upon us soon enough and there will be more wool to prepare then." She took out a stool and a wool comb for Salka and slung her own pack over her shoulders.

"And where are you going?" Salka asked. "I'm to stay behind while you go for a wander?" She knew how petty she sounded, but the pain behind her eyes was making her testy.

Miriat skewed her head to the side. "I have snares and traps to check. Unless you'd rather have the wolves eat our supper?" She stroked her daughter's head with affection. "I will be back before evening. I'm so glad you're back."

Salka sat down heavily in front of their house. She saw Trina walking with a basket of peat for the fire and waved to her. Trina propped the heavy basket against her hip and smiled back before disappearing into her house. Salka sighed and pulled a large handful of tangled wool from the bag. It had already been cleaned with the grease carefully collected into a small clay pot Miriat kept for that purpose, but its knotted strands required plenty of work. Salka put a sheet of leather over her trousers and began teasing out the tangles from the wool. It was a tedious task, but one she was used to. She saw several strigas walk past her as the pale sun made its way across the sky, barely visible above the tall pines. Watching their shadows, she could see their constant struggle to grow and move, just as she could see their owners' small gestures of irritation and twitches of effort as their other hearts were once more beaten into submission. The outward signs of struggle were so small, so subtle. Only one yearning for them would notice.

"I see you've been put to work already."

She lifted her head and squinted against the sun. Dran stood next to her with a small basket of rose hips.

"You startled me," she said, looking down at the wool in her lap. Lost in her thoughts she had let the teasel head fall from her hand. She bent down to lift it up but Dran was faster. He handed it to her with a smile.

"Thank you," she said. *If I say nothing, he might go.* She watched him out of the corner of her eye, hoping he would get the message.

Instead, he pulled up another stool and sat next to her, uninvited.

She sucked in a breath at the affront and quickly looked around. "Is Emila with you this morning?" she asked, making it clear where her loyalties lay.

"No, just me today," Dran laughed, as if they were both in on some joke. "It's all done between me and Emila. I'm sure she will tell you all about it herself. Though, truth be told, there is not much to tell. Some things are not meant to last."

Salka raised her eyebrows in surprise. "I didn't know that. Though I can't say I'm sad about it," she said, then blushed violently, realizing Dran might have misunderstood her words.

She looked up and saw a wide smile spread across his face. She frowned. "I only meant you two were not well suited for each other," she said and looked back to her work. Her hands were getting cold, but her head was still throbbing and she was not willing to go back into the smoky house. If only Dran would leave her be. But he seemed happy to sit next to her in silence, as if his mother hadn't banished her three months ago. As if he hadn't stayed silent when he could have spoken up on her behalf.

"Are you here to tell me something?" she asked, willing him gone. Munu dropped down from the roof of her mother's house and landed heavily on her shoulder. She grunted and shook him off in annoyance. The falcon hopped onto the ground between her and Dran and looked Dran over carefully. All of a sudden, Munu made a distressed, piercing noise and pecked Dran's foot hard before flying off.

"Munu!" Salka dropped her work in surprise. If she was to keep clear of Alma, then having her bird attack Dran was probably not the best way to go about it. "I'm so sorry, are you hurt?" she asked.

Dran made a pained expression, "Well it stings, but I'm used to the pain well enough." He smiled and massaged his foot. Before Salka could react, he reached out and grasped her hand in his. "Thank you for caring," he said.

She pulled her hand free. "I *don't*." She could feel the hotness in her cheeks and was angry at her body's indiscretion. "What are you doing here?" she asked.

"I just came to talk. I missed you." He picked up the small basket of rosehip and offered it to Salka. She didn't reach for it and so he placed it down on the ground. He seemed not to notice her annoyance at being touched. "Here, I saved these for you. I know you like them." He stood up and bowed his head. "I can see you're busy, though. I will come again tomorrow. I can't wait to hear all your stories from the Windry Pass. It's been boring here without you." He smiled and headed off, leaving Salka with a confused expression on her face and a warm impression still on her hand.

# CHAPTER 21

Over the next few weeks, Salka slowly settled back into her old life. Her mother made sure to keep her daughter busy, though never out of sight. This grated on Salka who, though she understood her mother's wish to stay close, had grown used to the freedom of being on her own.

She kept her head down, mindful of her mother's warnings. She continued with her chores; small tasks her mother would go to great lengths to invent to keep her in the village. Before her banishment, Salka would have been happy enough to sit in the warmth and spin the soft yarn with a drop spindle while Emila sat next to her and spoke of her conquests and her plans. But Salka barely saw her old friend anymore; the physical distance which separated them over the winter months exposed the weakening of their bond. Still, Salka missed it sometimes, more for the comfort of it than anything to do with Emila's conversation.

Salka found the village strange and familiar at the same time, the change shocking her. Her life seemed so small now, confined by the wall of swaying pines. Salka missed the expanse of the sky and would sometimes creep out at night to look up and pretend she could still feel her other heart's connection to the world around her.

Dran had continued with his daily visits, a source of confusion and irritation to Miriat, but secretly a small comfort to Salka. Some strigas would exchange a word or two with her when passing through the village, but nobody sought her out, and nobody wished for a true conversation with her anymore. A few of the villagers had noticed Dran's unusual attentions and thought to coax a bashful explanation out of Salka. But she would only shrug her shoulders. He came and talked, and she let him. There was no more to it than that. She only wished Emila would believe her.

Her friend saw Dran once, sitting close to Salka, helping with her work. Emila just stood there for a while, an ashen expression on her face. When Salka noticed her and waved her over, Emila walked up to them and silently passed Salka a pastry, still warm under the wrapping cloth. "Here. My mother sends thanks for the onions." Then she turned to leave.

Salka stood up, flustered. "Wait, why not join us? We're just talking. Dran asked me about the fishing traps I used in the Windry Pass. He means to make some as well." She didn't want Emila to get the wrong idea. She didn't want Dran to get the wrong idea either. But Emila just nodded to her stiffly.

"Yes, Emila, do sit with us," Dran said. "I know how very interested you are in trapping."

Emila reddened. "Thank you, I have work to do." She turned around on her heel and left.

Salka sat back down. "You didn't have to say that!" She turned to him. "Why did you make fun of her? Now she'll think…"

"What?" He looked at her seriously, a faint smile lingering on his lips. "What will she think?"

She looked at him for a moment, the angry words ready to leap to her lips. But she said nothing. There was nothing here she cared about, she realized. Not the gossip, not Emila's anger, not even Dran's hopes and assumptions. She shrugged her shoulders.

"You miss it, don't you?" Dran asked, his elbows leaning against his thighs, his face just a bit too close to her.

"Being cold, hungry, and scared? Not really," Salka said. What right did he have to try and guess her thoughts? Worse, what right did he have to be correct?

"No. Being free, unwatched and unjudged."

Salka looked up at him sharply. "I don't need to fear anyone's judgement, Dran."

He laughed and raised his hands in a conciliatory gesture. "I didn't say *you* did specifically. But we are watched and judged here, all of us." He smiled and shrugged his shoulders as if to show the invisible weight on them. "I just want you to know I don't judge you. I wish you wouldn't judge me." He seemed sad at that and left without as much as a goodbye. Salka sat very still for a while, thinking how strange it was he could know so well what she managed to hide so completely from those who loved her.

The next morning Salka woke up in a foul mood, wanting nothing more than to go off into the forest alone, something she no longer felt she could do. She sat up in bed and rolled her shoulders, releasing some of the tension in her neck.

"I was thinking I might take the animals out of the gates today. They might get some proper eating on the southern slopes. They get more sun and the grass might have come up there already," she said.

"That is at least a couple of hours away," Miriat said in a querulous voice which grated on them both. "No. It's too far."

Salka looked up at her mother. She could see Miriat's fidgeting hands and her ashen face and she tried to keep her voice level. "And how does it look to the village that you keep me here all this time? If you mean to keep others from suspecting me, the best way to do it is to have me do what I would normally do."

Miriat sat down on her bed and watched her daughter. "Fine," she said after a while. "The animals deserve a decent meal as much as anyone, I suppose. I'll fix you something to eat first, and you can be on your way. Make sure you get home by nightfall though."

The house was barely warmer than the outside and Miriat set to making a fire, while Salka used the time to clear the floor and usher their goat and the lamb out. Though the animals kept the house warm enough, their waste made the air pungent. Salka carefully collected it. It would be used to fertilize the soil and was not to be wasted. She then raked out the stinking straw from the dirt floor and scrubbed it to lessen the smell of urine. By the time she was finished, her hands were red, and the house was cleaner than it had been in a while.

She had nothing else to do for a while so, as Miriat busied herself cooking, she went outside and sat on her small stool. She had no wish to walk around the village. She was initially relieved by the welcome she received when she first came back, but the noise tired her quickly after three months of quiet. She sighed and wrapped her cloak closer around her body. Ever since her mother had given her the powder to still her other heart, she felt cold, with a chill she could not shake off. Was this what it was like to be human? She leaned against the crooked wall of their house. She felt restless and tired at the same time. It felt odd to have someone else prepare your food, to make the fire. She closed her eyes and tried to enjoy the feeling. Somehow, she found it difficult. She opened her eyes again as the sounds of the village intruded on her thoughts.

The cold kept most people indoors, though as the weather improved, more hands turned to spring labor. The soil on the tiny fenced-off vegetable patches by the houses, no longer frozen solid, would be worked as the families squabbled affectionately over which crops to plant.

Most of the goats in the village were coming close to term and their heavy, pregnant bellies nearly touched the ground they walked on as they searched for a hint of grass in the snow. Miriat owned one doe, and for nearly half her crop of onions was given access to one of her neighbors' billies in the autumn so they could expect two kids that spring. Miriat had hoped to keep at least one this time, trading the other for food and supplies with Dolas, the only trading partners available to the strigas. It was a hard life, but Miriat never complained. Salka thought back to the tall wooden houses in Heyne Town, with their painted doors and wide tables. All the riches she'd left behind. What right did Salka have to complain now?

"Here, drink this." Miriat emerged from their house, carrying heavily spiced tea. Salka winced. Her mother kept her hand outstretched until Salka accepted the cup.

"You have to, my girl. Just a while longer."

Salka put the mug to her lips. The liquid tasted sweet with the honey and some other spices her mother had added in for taste. However, none of it could disguise the lingering bitterness, or offer relief from the pressure in her head every time she drank it. After the first day of drinking Dola's concoction, the headaches started. They were mild at first, though by the end of the second week the pain was enough to knock Salka off her feet.

It scared Miriat so much she even thought to stop Salka drinking it, but Trina advised against it. "If she's meant to be drinking it for a month for the dampening effect on her powers to last, then that's what she must do," Trina had said, with more edge in her voice than Miriat had ever heard from her. "I have never seen a striga with a shadow that's been allowed to flourish the way Salka's had. Whatever Dola's given you, Salka will need every last drop to keep her safe." Trina looked away then, ashamed of her own sharpness.

Salka accepted Trina's explanation and her mother's decision ungraciously but had no other ideas to offer. And so, she went on with her headaches and the awful, empty feeling. The pain was mitigated by her mother's herbs at least, but the dead feeling inside weighed her down even more than the oppressive atmosphere of the village.

"How does it feel?" Miriat asked once more. And once more, Salka replied, "Like nothing." She stood up and went to pack a few necessities for the day ahead.

"I know it's hard, love, but you will get used to this." Miriat sat motionless, watching her daughter as she picked up a staff and shoved a piece of hard bread in her pack. Salka rarely smiled since she'd come back from the banishment. Miriat felt her chest squeeze as she watched her daughter, her child and yet a child no more, as she moved with the deliberate air of somebody who wants to get as far away as possible.

"I suppose I will." Salka didn't even look up. Miriat bit her lip and wrapped a piece of smoked fish inside a waxed cloth.

"You know, you're old enough now... You might find comfort in motherhood in time..."

Salka held her breath for a moment and then gave a mirthless chuckle. "As you did?"

Miriat's mouth fell open. She stood up abruptly, overturning her loom. She crossed the distance between them in two steps and put her hands on Salka's shoulders. "Don't you ever think otherwise. I didn't expect for things to happen the way they did, but I bless every day I've had with you. It shames me you don't know it!"

Salka leaned into her mother, surprising Miriat. "I know it, mama. I'm sorry. I didn't mean it." She gave her mother a kiss on the cheek and headed out. Miriat stood by the entrance to their hut and watched Salka as she led the goat and the lamb down the path towards the village gate before picking up her work once more.


Salka felt her mother's eyes on her, but she didn't turn around. She had little energy to reassure Miriat. In truth, she didn't feel she could, in good conscience, reassure anybody. She was feeling her spirit drain away, and she strongly suspected it was more than just Dola's potion.

The other strigas were friendly once more, but something had shifted inside of Salka, and she felt too detached to engage with anybody. She was there but no longer there. She could not forget the great expanse that stretched before her at the Windry Pass. She was scared then, but she preferred it to the fear which tainted her every moment now, the fear of losing the connection to the world around her that she had felt in the mountains. If she had never known what it meant to truly follow her heart, she would have been content to walk through life like the other strigas in the village. Content to live a life that was a poor reflection of the lives of the townsfolk living down below.

Salka clicked her tongue and Munu swooped down and landed on her shoulder. Salka had thought that taking Dola's potion would make Munu more comfortable, but she had often found him looking at her shadow and cautiously try to peck and scratch at it with its talon, as if trying to revive a sick friend.

She ushered her goat through the gate and absent mindedly pet Curious. Salka smiled as the animal nuzzled her hand. The air smelled sweet as the snow melted on the slopes of the mountain and trickled down, revealing patches of moss.

She had to watch her step, and she almost fell once, after placing her foot incautiously on a frost-covered stone, which rolled away as soon as she put her weight on it. She cursed under her breath. If she twisted her ankle, her mother would make her stay in the village for a week and she would die of boredom. She surprised herself with the thought. The striga village had always been a home, a place of safety. She might have wanted to roam the forests around it, but she always knew she'd come back. Now the sight of its mud paths and crooked one-room houses brought her a deep sense of weariness.

Her mother said that Dola's potion would permanently dampen her powers, like a muscle that atrophied from long disuse. She had once seen one of their neighbor's legs after he broke it slipping down a slope. When they took the splinters off, his calf was shrunken and shriveled up, like an apple left too long in the sun. Was that what she was doing to her other heart? She stopped for a moment and put two fingers to her wrist. She closed her eyes and tried to listen. She could barely hear the other heartbeat. It felt as if she'd gouged her own eyes out. A new sense she was just discovering, sacrificed so she could stay in a place she no longer felt at home in. But Miriat had already left one home for her daughter, and she worked so hard to settle into the striga village. Salka couldn't bring herself to take it from her.

"Oh, come on!" Salka said, as her lamb happily bounced away from the pregnant goat, who watched with little interest as Curious stepped on a large stone and stretched its neck to try to reach a branch holding a single dead leaf. "Curious, come here!" Salka called out, and in that moment the stone moved. The lamb lost its footing and started rolling down the slope.

"Curious!" Salka yelled and ran towards the lamb, half running and half sliding. She reached the bleating lamb, and found it wedged against two forked spruces.

"Nice work taking care of your livestock." Salka looked up, and saw Kalina standing above, petting her goat as it kept trying to eat the end of her belt. "Your mother has the total of two animals, and you can't even herd them properly?"

Salka glared at her, and started looking for the best way back up the hill. She ushered the lamb to go in front, occasionally pushing it upwards whenever it started to slide.

"You could at least try to be useful!" Salka said through gritted teeth as she finally reached Kalina.

"Why, I'm making sure your other animal doesn't follow you down!" Kalina smiled, gesturing towards the doe, who was nibbling on lichen and didn't even bother looking up.

"Hope you didn't tire yourself out," Salka said, hoisting the lamb onto the path before pulling herself up. She took a moment to catch her breath, eyeing Kalina suspiciously. "Well? What do you want?"

Kalina hadn't spoken more than two words to her in her entire life, though Salka had heard and seen plenty to expect nothing good from the village's self-designated snitch and rule enforcer.

Kalina gave Salka her friendliest smile. "I haven't had a chance to speak with you since you came back from Windry Pass. I just *had* to ask how you managed to survive the ordeal!"

Salka raised an eyebrow. "Couldn't you have asked me in the village? You know, when everyone *else* was asking me the same question?" She once more started on the path, with Kalina joining her uninvited.

"Oh, I could have." Kalina continued smiling, less friendly now. "But I do suspect you would have given me the same story you did the others. And I think there's more to it."

"Well, there was a lot more snow than I described. And a great deal more soaked cheese," Salka said. She feigned flippancy, though the question rattled her.

Kalina made a noise but otherwise said nothing. They walked up to a narrow footbridge over a freezing stream. The water ran deep there and even though the thaw had not begun in earnest yet, the water was high, ice outlining its sides in smooth lines.

"You can trust me, you know," Kalina said. She reached out for the goat's lead to help it across and Salka gave it to her, reluctantly. She wanted nothing more than to turn around and leave, but after Maladia and Markus' banishment, she knew not to underestimate Kalina.

"I know you might not like me." Kalina looked up at Salka, her lips pressed tight together. She took a deep breath. "I'm not very likeable. But I care about our village. I care about our rules. They are there to help us lead a good life, a true life, separate from the poison of the striga curse. Now, I think you might have done something you shouldn't have. And maybe you need a friend, to help bring you back to where you ought to be." Kalina led the goat safely across the footbridge, with the lamb trotting right after. Then she came back and reached out to Salka with her hand. She waited patiently. Salka hesitated.

"I haven't broken any rules," she said finally. "I don't know why you think I have, but you can see the evidence right here." She pointed to her own shadow with a sweeping gesture.

"I can see *you*. Your other heart is so quiet, you could be mistaken for a human. There is no way you had that kind of restraint. That kind of discipline."

Kalina still stood at the footbridge with her hand reaching out in a friendly gesture. Salka grasped it for fear of offending the woman. She glanced down. Kalina's shadow lay flat on the ground, a dead thing, suppressed beyond any sign of vitality. Much could be said of Kalina but not that she didn't follow the rules herself.

Salka took a breath and tried a different tactic. "Have I done something to offend you? I don't understand what you want from me. I've accepted my punishment. I was banished. I went away,

I came back. Nothing happened in the Windry Pass. They were three hard, boring months, and I'd rather forget about them if at all possible." *Except that is a lie,* Salka thought. The memory of how it felt to be truly connected to the world around her, to feel the power surging through her veins, those memories were all that sustained her in her current half-lived state.

Kalina seemed to sense Salka's hesitation. She cocked her head to the side and scratched her cheek with her hand. "That's just the thing. I don't think it was as boring as you make it out. You see, I think you made things a bit easier on yourself. I think you followed your heart, and broke every rule that keeps us from turning into the monsters the humans think we are.

"Trust me, I understand. They all think they're different; that they won't let this curse change them. But it always, always does." Kalina stepped closer across the ice-covered footbridge. "And there's a price to be paid. We can see the transgressors straight off. The monster they become is out for all to see. But not with you."

Salka swallowed. Kalina's face was now so close to her own that she could see every pore on her skin. She forced herself to look back and meet Kalina's gaze. The freezing water rushed below them, nearly drowning out the sound of Kalina's voice. The woman's hand closed tightly around Salka's.

"Let me go." Salka tried to wriggle away.

Kalina gave a mirthless chuckle. All pretense of friendliness melted away. "You're a child. You have no strength in you. No meat on your bones to sustain you."

"I don't need meat for hunting. Not that *you* know what it takes to be a good trapper. Or a good *anything* really. Except a snitch maybe," Salka regretted the words as soon as they left her mouth.

Kalina gasped and hit Salka with the back of her free hand.

Salka called out in shock and flailed her arms, trying to catch her balance. She fell backwards and somersaulted down before landing in the freezing water. Munu shrieked and attacked Kalina, who batted him away. She leaned forward, her face white with horror at what she had just done.

"Grab the root! There! To your left!" Kalina screamed.

Salka flayed wildly, but missed the root, her hand scraping badly against a stone. The current pushed her farther and she tumbled down a small waterfall, crashing through the thin ice.

Kalina swore loudly and hurried off the footbridge and down the stream where she climbed a boulder overhanging the water. She took off her coat and waved it at Salka. "Grab it! I'll pull you out!"

She leaned as far as she could, and when Salka's hands closed around the thick fabric of the coat, Kalina heaved, sliding down the boulder. Salka crashed into the rock's side, but didn't let go of the coat.

They both fell back into the snow. Kalina grunted loudly as she turned on her side. She took one look at Salka and took off her sweater. She helped Salka pull off her freezing wet clothes that stuck to her chilled skin. Salka was so cold she could do nothing but accept the help, though her eyes were flashing angrily.

"Here, put it on," Kalina said, avoiding Salka's gaze. The long garment went down to Salka's knees. After a moment's thought, Kalina also wrapped her coat around Salka's frame. "No meat on you at all..." Kalina mumbled. "We need to get a fire going."

At that Salka jumped up and punched Kalina in the jaw, sending her reeling. "What was that?!"

Kalina seemed dazed for a moment and sat in the snow massaging her jaw. "I didn't mean to. I just... I thought you'd... But your shadow..."

"What about my shadow? You're so obsessed with it you tried to kill me? And did it come out? Did you see the big bad stigoi you were after?"

Kalina stood up, watching Salka sullenly. "You knew I'd save you."

"*Did* I?" Salka laughed, an angry, ugly sound. "How do you think Alma is going to react once she finds out you attacked another striga? Maybe you'll be the one banished this time. You can test out your theories firsthand!"

"I wouldn't do that, if I were you," Kalina said. She tried to appear calm, though Salka saw how her hands shook. "I don't know how you did it, but I was watching. Your shadow didn't even move. It's like you had your other heart burnt out."

"Are you worried you would be tempted if it were you?" Salka asked. "Or jealous that I'm better at keeping this under control than you are?" Munu flapped his wings in Kalina's face and shrieked with glee as she winced and took a step back. For the briefest moment, Salka felt a pang of regret at her words watching the pathetic figure in front of her. But then she remembered Maladia and she pursed her lips into a thin line.

Kalina stood her ground. "This means nothing. I will catch you using your powers. And then you will be out for good," she said, but her voice lacked conviction. "Here, use this. Or don't. See if I care." She took out her flint box and a hot amber fire-starter necklace off her neck and tossed it in Salka's lap. She turned around and trotted back to the village, shivering in the cold.

By the time Salka returned to the striga village she was blue from the cold. Her shoes were put out to dry by the fire as Miriat sat on a small stool making their evening meal. The nanny goat and Curious were already asleep under Salka's raised bed, and Munu was sitting on his perch grooming his tail feathers. They all sat in silence for a while. Miriat noticed Salka wearing another's clothes but she hadn't asked about it. She just sat opposite her daughter, and waited for an explanation.

Finally, Salka approached her mother. She knelt by Miriat's side and put her head in her mother's lap. Miriat, surprised, ran her fingers through her daughter's tight curls.

"I think they know, Mama," Salka said in the end.

Miriat's hand paused for a brief moment. "What do you mean? Who knows?" She could feel her own heart beating hard within her chest and she fancied it made more noise than the two hearts of any strigas she'd ever met.

"Pike. She followed me into the forest. She tried to provoke my striga heart. She pushed me into a stream to see if I would release it."

Miriat took in a sharp breath "Who? Kalina? Why would she…?

I will speak with her!" She tried to stand up but Salka pulled on her hand and shook her head.

"No. Who will believe us? She'll say I fell down and that she saved me. The rest will be seen as me trying to avenge Maladia and Markus. The whole village knew we were close."

Miriat shook with a quiet fury. Kalina had no right to do what she'd done and Miriat wanted nothing more than to confront her. A sudden thought occurred to her. "And did she?" Miriat asked. "I mean, Kalina. Did she... succeed?"

"No," Salka said. "That's dead and gone. But Mama..." She looked up at Miriat, "I don't think she's convinced. What will happen now? After all this, will they still burn my other heart out like Trina said?"

Miriat took a deep breath. "No. They can't see it, so they can't punish you for it. The burning is the last resort to purge out the stigoi only." She didn't add what they both thought. That perhaps that word described Salka now. "We still have enough powder for another week. By then your other heart should be so weakened that nobody will suspect a thing. I will have a word with Kalina. You need not worry. As long as you don't follow your heart, they can do nothing." Miriat drew her daughter to her chest.

Miriat searched back to the memory of when she met Kalina. When Miriat first arrived at the village, Kalina was still a small child. Kalina's mother had died when her daughter was barely three years old and no other family had stepped up to take her place. A solemn child, Kalina had fallen through the cracks and been taken care of by everybody and nobody, absorbed in an absent minded fashion by the structures of the village life, gradually shaped into their strictest defender. Miriat felt with a small pang of guilt that she herself had been so engrossed with her own baby, and the strange new home she'd brought them to, it had not even occurred to her to take an interest in this awkward lone child. But, she supposed, that was a done thing. You can't unspoil milk.

Salka's breath slowed down and she fell asleep, her head still in Miriat's lap, her eyelids flickering as she was swept up in some dream. When Salka was a child, Miriat would have scooped her up in her arms and put her on the bed, but now all she could do was ease her daughter to the ground and put a blanket over her. She looked at Salka's face and tucked one of the unruly curls behind her ear. She placed her own blanket on the floor next to Salka's and put her arms around her. Soon she too closed her eyes, and the comfort that mother and daughter drew from each other rose up like a living thing, filling the room and quieting their sleep.

# CHAPTER 22

Kalina coughed as a burst of smoke hit her face. She added a branch to the fire and took a step back before sitting down and holding her feet and hands to the flame. Her hut was very dark, but it kept her warm. Whoever had built it had first dug a round hole in the ground and then used the soil mixed with hay to fortify the walls. The resulting structure was unsightly, though comfortable. Kalina knew she was lucky to have it.

Her two goats snored under her bed. Some who remembered a life before joining the village would sometimes complain of the goat smell, but Kalina loved it. It was the smell of warmth and comfort. It was a smell of achievement and wealth. There was no other place in the whole of Prissan she'd rather be when the grey hour fell than on her bed, listening to the breathing of her does underneath her.

She slid off the bed and snuggled between her animals, as she sometimes did, taking in their milky scent and the warmth of their long coats.

She thought of that morning. She could feel the fire's heat on her face but knew the blush that spread across her cheeks had nothing to do with it. It was a stupid thing she had done. Salka made her angry, but that was no excuse.

Kalina hadn't meant to push her in, it was an accident. It was Salka's fault, really. She wouldn't listen. Kalina had meant to be kind, she wanted to help. She just wanted to know how Salka did it. How she managed to keep her other heart quiet. So easily, so effortlessly. If Salka had only confided in her, it would all have been different. Kalina would have helped her, and maybe then Salka would show her, teach her, how to make this so easy, so very easy.

Kalina felt loneliness rise inside her chest. She knew it was dangerous, of course. Sadness was dangerous; self-pity was dangerous. So she pushed them down, though her human heart felt like it would burst from the strain.

She was right about Salka, she knew she was. There was a pain in her chest which told her eloquently enough: if it'd been her thrown into an icy stream, she would not be able to hold back.

A deep shame made her shrink into herself. Salka couldn't have that kind of self-control. Not unless she was a stigoi, a true stigoi. She could hide it then, because she had the deep knowing of it. Yes, there was no other explanation.

Kalina dug her fingers into the soft tangles of her goat's fur. She would flush the stigoi out herself. She would do it for the village. She would do it for her home.

# CHAPTER 23

Dran timed his visits with Salka to coincide with Miriat's visits to her traps. He had a sneaking suspicion that Miriat wasn't all that keen on him. Which was fine for now – he'd win her over later. Once he was whole, she would see that her daughter truly couldn't do any better. The thought hit him hard and he sat back down on his bed. He ran his fingers through his hair. Could he truly consider continuing with Salka after she healed him?

No. Of course, no. She would be a stigoi. The healing would require it. Besides, she was a difficult girl. She showed no great partiality to him, not even after he'd spent so many days trying to win her over. He pursed his lips and rubbed his eyebrow in irritation. She *tolerated* him. But could he blame her? Lame, sickly creature that he was now, why would she show any interest in him if she never had before.

She smiled sometimes when he made a joke and she looked at him warmly when he helped her at one of the endlessly tedious tasks Miriat set her. But she hadn't once offered up her lips for a kiss or reached out for his hand.

His face darkened. *Maybe today I won't go. Maybe she will miss me if I don't go.* But the pain in his foot travelled along the dark tendrils of his spreading illness to remind him he had no time for coyness. He walked towards Salka's house with a frown. He heard a couple of old women giggle as they saw him pass, as they cooked and gossiped outside their homes.

"A lovers' quarrel…" he heard one of them whisper and he shot her a contemptuous look meant to chide her. But she only laughed in an open-hearted way and turned back to her friend.

This did nothing to improve his mood. He strode ahead, passing Trina's house. Salka was sitting outside, as she did most mornings, spinning wool. The drop spindle twirled fast, as she twisted the yarn into long even threads. She seemed tired, with her hair unbrushed and dark circles under her eyes. Dran's hearts dropped as he looked at her. Was she ill? He looked at her shadow, a dead thing at her feet. Was it possible she was pushing it down, making herself sick? Her constant headaches, which she tried to hide from him, caused him much worry. He told himself it was because she was no good to him sick and weak. But in truth, it moved him, this commonality between them, the weakness and the pride required to hide it.

She looked up as he approached and smiled. She moved as if to get up and accidentally dropped the spindle.

"Rats and fleas!" she swore under her breath.

He leaned down to pick up her spindle. "You seem less attentive to your work these days."

She rolled her eyes. "You try spending morning after morning watching a piece of wood spin. I swear, much more of this and I will turn stupider than a rabbit." She took the spindle from his hand with thanks. He smiled and felt a small pain inside his chest as his other heart tried to reassert itself. He pushed it down. Salka waited respectfully as he did so, a small courtesy all strigas gave one another, one he usually resented. He had enough weakness of his own to conceal without others patronizing his struggle. But he didn't mind so much with Salka somehow.

"You seem tired," he said.

"Thanks." Salka pulled out a bit of wool from the small cloud she kept in her left hand and attached it to the broken thread, sending the spindle twirling once more.

"No, I mean, are you well?"

She looked at him in silence for a moment, and while he respected it, it rankled him she should still be so cautious with him.

"I'm not, actually. Kalina seems determined to prove I'm a stigoi." She looked up at him, as if gauging his reaction.

This surprised him more than it should have. He had heard the woman that first day on Salka's return. He should have thought she might do more than voice her suspicions. "What did she do?" he asked.

"Oh, just tried to drown me," Salka said. She laughed at his shock. "Well, she threw me into a stream, hoping my shadow would leap to my defense. It didn't. So she pulled me out again."

"*Pike* did that?" Dran rubbed his forehead.

"Yes, she did." The voice behind him startled him. He stood up and faced the cold-eyed Miriat. "But perhaps you already knew it."

"Mama!" Salka turned bright red. "Dran had nothing to do with it, you know that!"

"Do I?" Miriat kept her expression blank. "All I know is this young man has paid you an unusual amount of attention since you came back. And Kalina would not have the gall to risk another striga's life if she wasn't given certain assurances…"

"You'd think any attention paid to me unusual." Salka shook with anger, throwing the spindle down angrily into the bag of wool. "You'd suspect anyone I spent time with who wasn't you."

Miriat's jaw tightened and she turned to Dran. "I think this is for me and my daughter to discuss. Please leave us."

Dran narrowed his eyes. "I don't know why you think so badly of me, Miriat. I have never given you cause to, I'm sure." He turned to Salka. "Let me know if I can do anything to help. I'm sure my mother had nothing to do with it, but I'll talk to her if you want me to. She won't lie to me."

"No. Don't. Thank you." Salka reached out and squeezed his hand. He stood there for a moment, dumbfounded, till a small cough from Miriat reminded him that he was unwelcome.

Miriat didn't speak again until she was certain Dran was out of earshot. She gestured, and Salka grudgingly followed her into the house. Miriat tied the leather panels across the door before she spoke again. The low orange light danced across her face as she strained against her anger.

"Are you insane?" she nearly hissed. "Have you a single thought for your future or your safety here?"

"You mean besides taking your poison every day and following every new rule that pops into your head?" Salka said through clenched teeth. "I've sat on this stool every day for weeks, brushing and spinning the wool. More wool than our nanny has produced in the last four years, by the way. You think I don't know you traded for it to keep me occupied? I'm not a child anymore, I don't need you to protect me!"

Curious approached her with a small whine and nibbled on her sleeve. She pushed its head away.

"Clearly you do!" Miriat made an impatient gesture. "The one time I agreed to you spending a day out of the village gates, look what happened! It's not for much longer, all you need is a bit more patience and then you'll be safe. And Dran could put it all at risk!"

Salka sucked in a breath. She straightened herself. Her mother's suspicion of Dran upset her more than she cared to admit. "A little more is a lot to ask when my head aches so much I can barely see most days. And *you* don't have to trust Dran. *I* do. He has no suspicions of me. Never once has he accused me of anything, or judged me. You think I don't see you check that I drink every last drop of this vile concoction you give me? Or that you watch my shadow more than you watch my face?"

Miriat turned away. "How can I trust you after what you did? You fed your other heart, in spite of all I've told you. In spite of all you've been taught. You see the spinning as a punishment, child? You should count yourself lucky. A small, safe life is the best that one can hope for in this world. The sooner you accept it, the sooner you'll find contentment. There is nothing more I hope for now, Salka." Miriat looked at her hands, all the fight gone out of her.

Salka wanted to tell her of the endless sky beyond the Windry Pass, and of the wild, joyful freedom of the other heart and the knowledge it brought her. But there were no words she could find to make her mother understand.

So they faced each other, each one staring at the gulf that opened between them.

Curious rammed into Salka's leg suddenly, nearly toppling her. She looked at it in surprise, started by its cry. A distressed bleating came from outside.

"Something's wrong" Miriat looked up sharply. "Where's the doe?"

"Still tied outside," Salka said, already on her way out of the door.

# CHAPTER 24

Salka's arms were bloodied up to the elbows. Their goat had been giving birth for the best part of an hour already, and the house was filled with a metallic smell. Miriat had her hands gently placed on the goat's belly, pressing and feeling her way around the twin kids inside. The doe's eyes were wide with terror and her breathing was shallow.

"The kids are not positioned right, but I can't correct it myself," Miriat said. "You must run to get Rida. She will know what to do." She brushed her hair out of her eyes. The room was warm, too warm, and they both had sweat running down their faces.

"She won't come if I ask for her," Salka said, her eyes down. "She wouldn't even look at me, not since I came back."

Miriat swore under her breath. "Well, then tell the petty bitch she can have one of the kids if she saves the doe!" Salka was taken aback. They needed those kids. They hadn't been able to afford the goating price for two years now, but the help in birthing was the one thing none of the community should charge for. Her trip to the Heyne Town continued to cost them. She nodded and left the house, pushing aside the heavy leathers of the door. She moved at a sprint and was soon at Emila's family's door. She knocked hard and waited, shivering. In her hurry she hadn't brought a cloak with her, and the Heyne nights were a cold affair.

The door opened, and Emila's face peeped out. Her hair was wet, and the room smelled of arrowroot. Rida had no use for waste

151

and used the same water to wash Emila's hair and the clothes.

"What are you doing?" Emila said. "You know you're not supposed to come here!"

"Who is it, child?" Rida's voice rose up. Salka could swear the woman never had a good-humored day in her life. Salka gave Emila a curt nod and pushed past her.

"It's me, Aunt Rida," she said.

Rida stiffened at seeing Salka. Tolan looked up from his chair and Salka imagined she saw a brief expression of sympathy running through his face.

"What do you want?" Rida said. She shot her husband a glance that threatened serious consequences at the slightest show of hospitality.

"Our goat's birthing. There is something wrong and we need your skills," Salka said. "Please," she added.

Rida smiled one of her less pleasant smiles and returned to washing her clothes. "I see. My daughter was in danger not so long ago, all because of you and your wild antics. And here you expect me to jump to your assistance the moment you ask?" She stared Salka down.

"My mother said you may have one of the kids if you can keep the doe alive," Salka said.

Rida threw the cloth she was washing down into the tub with a fury. The soapy water splashed onto the dirt floor. "I see. So now you and your mother seek to insult me!"

Salka looked to Tolan for assistance, but he had none to offer. "I didn't... I don't–" she sputtered.

"It is our *custom* and *law* to assist each other in such matters. As your mother would know, had she been a real striga. As *you* would know, had your mother raised you right!" She pointed a bony finger at Salka's face. "Yet you want to *bribe* me to help you? Well, I will show you that a real striga needs no bribes to use her skills when needed. Emila, my coat!"

Emila brought Rida her warm coat, which Rida took her time draping around her shoulders. She strode towards the door. As she opened it with one hand she paused for a moment. "Of course, should your mother wish to *thank me* for my assistance with a gift of a kid and – I don't know – a basket of onions or so, then, of course, I will accept. Emila, follow me. There will be skills to be learnt today." Rida strode forward like a queen, with Salka and Emila following meekly, both afraid to breathe too loudly, in case it should bring Rida's fury upon them.

When they reached Miriat's house, Rida stopped for a moment. "Salka, stay here. I don't wish to be disturbed by you. And make sure to keep that filthy bird away too, unless you want me to make him into soup. Emila, follow me." Emila gave Salka an embarrassed smile and followed her mother inside.

Rida's words made Salka realize that she hadn't seen Munu since the morning. She walked a little way and whistled on her fingers. There was no answer. The evening air made her shiver. Ever since she started taking Dola's potion, half the time she felt as if she'd been plunged neck-high into snow. It was odd to think that this was how humans must have felt the entire time. Cold and alone. She whistled again and again, but was met only with silence.

She walked among the small houses and huts used for keeping tools and food stores overwinter. Nobody bothered locking anything away. Thievery was reserved for humans, if occasion struck.

"Munu!" she called out. It was unlike him to not respond to her calls. Salka furrowed her eyebrows. Her falcon was getting old. Many small feathers around his beak were touched with silver, as if frost had drawn patterns on it with the smallest of brushes. One day soon, Salka knew, he would not answer her call. But it wouldn't be today.

A screech pierced the cold air, sending her running. It came from right behind the well. As she approached, a shape moved in the dark.

"I see I got your attention." Kalina leaned against the well, as if the wildly thrashing sack in her hand was nothing unusual.

Salka froze. She bared her teeth without realizing. "Let him go."

"Shan't." Kalina gave Salka a friendly smile. "Unless you tell me how you hid the pollution of your other heart. Otherwise, we'll see if your bird can swim." She held the sack over the well.

"Don't hurt him!" Salka raised her hands. "It was Alma who told my mother to save his life! She will punish you if you hurt him."

"Alma?" Kalina laughed. "She wouldn't hear a complaint from you now!"

"Why are you doing this?" Salka pleaded. She could hear Munu's muffled shrieks and her eyes filled with tears. She hated those tears, they were a poor way to express the rage she felt. She looked at Kalina's face and she craved her power back, so much that she could almost feel it surge through her body. Instead, all that she felt was the pounding in her head, getting worse every moment.

"Admit it," Kalina said. "You broke the law and followed your heart. Admit it! You're a stigoi."

The word of hatred hit Salka like a slap on the face and she could feel her cheeks begin to burn.

"I'm not. You look at my shadow! *Look* at it! If I was a stigoi, don't you think I would tear Munu from your hands right now? Don't you think I would hurt you for doing this?"

Kalina hesitated. But then her face hardened again. "I suppose we'll see. Catch!" Kalina threw the sack with Munu up in the air above the well.

Salka threw herself forward, but even as she ran, she knew she would never get to him in time. Tears streamed down her face, and she willed her shadow to leap forward, to catch Munu. But nothing came. The sack fell down, and in a moment, a muffled splash was heard in the square.

"No!" Salka yelled. She ran to the well and threw the bucket in. She turned the crank. It seemed an eternity before the bucket came back up, filled with water, but no Munu.

Salka's face was wet with tears, but she ignored them. Again, and again, she threw the bucket back in the water, and again and again it came back empty.

Kalina was standing to the side, watching Salka with a shocked face. Color leached from her skin as she watched Salka's increasingly frantic labor.

After the third time the bucket came up empty, Kalina seemed to come to a decision. She walked up to the crank and put her hands next to Salka's. She put her weight behind it, and the bucket whizzed up and down the well. Salka couldn't see Kalina. All she looked at was the crank, turning, turning. All she could see was the bucket coming back empty, again and again.

Kalina picked up a stone and threw it in the bucket to make it sink faster. This time, it came back up heavier. Salka screamed when she saw the sack come up. She threw herself at it and attempted to untie the string with her trembling wet hands. The knot was wet, and it held tight. Kalina walked up quietly, slipped out her skinning knife, and with one movement cut through the string.

The fabric fell off, and inside, unmoving, lay Munu. His wet feathers glistened in the moonlight. "No... Oh please, Munu... No, please..." Salka touched his beak gently and lifted him up. His head lolled back. Salka keened and held the body of her falcon to her chest.

Kalina stood a few steps away. "I was so certain – I was so sure you were using some trick – I was sure he wouldn't fall."

With a mad shriek, Salka threw herself at Kalina, surprising her. Kalina was heavier, but she was not prepared for the fury that overtook Salka. The girl thrashed, pulled and hit like a mad dog. She bit down hard on Kalina's shoulder. Kalina screamed and tried to push her away. Salka only chomped down harder. She ignored Kalina's fists pummeling her back and the hot blood that burst into her mouth. She ground her teeth and pulled, until a lump of flesh came off. She spat it out and turned around, wild-eyed, ready to attack again. A fist to the head knocked her off her feet.

Kalina kicked Salka in the stomach to keep her down. Blood was flowing freely from the woman's shoulder, and she was blinded by pain and helpless anger. She moved her leg back to kick

Salka again, as the girl lay on the ground clutching her stomach. But another's hand pulled Kalina away.

"No!" a voice called out. "You've done enough!" Kalina watched in disbelief as Dran strode up to the weeping Salka and, with some considerable effort, scooped her up in his arms.

"I saw what you did, Pike!" Dran yelled.

Kalina shrunk as he shouted, his handsome face contorted with anger.

"For no reason you, attacked her! You killed her animal. Make no mistake, striga, you *will* be punished for it."

Salka watched Dran through tear-stained eyes. He held her closer to his chest and she was comforted by the warmth of him. She was wrapped in his shadow and felt safe.

Kalina stood there stupidly, blood pouring down her tunic, looking wide-eyed at Dran. "But I... I didn't mean to–"

"Shut up!" Dran growled. "Get out of my sight. You don't have to use your powers to be a stigoi. You managed it all on your own by not using *either* of your hearts." Dran turned around and walked off towards a bench.

Kalina stood there for a moment, ignored, watching as Dran gently put Salka down, and pushed her hair out of her face. He took out his handkerchief and wiped away her tears and the blood staining her face.

Kalina turned around and staggered away.


Had Kalina looked up, she might have noticed Emila watching as Salka collapsed crying in Dran's arms. Watching, as Dran placed a kiss on her forehead. Emila waited until the pair left, Salka stopping only to pick up Munu's pitiful small body off the ground. Then, quite calmly, Emila drew up a bucket of water from the well as her mother had asked, and walked back towards Miriat's house. Once inside, she set the bucket down, and, ignoring her mother's questions, walked straight towards Alma's house.

# CHAPTER 25

"It's good you came," Miriat wrung her hands and gestured towards the house. "Salka says she will no longer take the potion. What if her shadow comes back?"

Dola nodded. "Did she say what happened?"

"No. She just sits there in silence. But Munu's gone. Something must have happened. I was hoping you might know..." She looked at Dola expectantly. She usually would not question Dola's timely appearances and would wait for her to volunteer what she had seen, but this time Miriat was desperate.

Dola shook her head. "I haven't seen what happened with my eyes or in a vision. But I thought something of this kind might happen. Perhaps even at Alma's behest," she added before walking towards Miriat's house. She pushed aside the leathers blocking the entrance and gestured to Miriat to stay outside.

Dola entered the small house and immediately saw the doe, nursing its twin kids. It was eyeing her with disinterest, chewing on the hay lovingly placed before it. The room was filled with the sickly-sweet smell of afterbirth and the kids, so small and soft, now scrambling for the teat as their patient, exhausted mother lay resting.

"The kids look healthy. It's a blessing. Your mother must be very pleased."

There was no reply.

"I hear a sad thing happened. Want to tell me about it?" Dola said.

"You're the Dola. You tell me," Salka said. She sat cross-legged on her bed, her tear-stained face rigid with anger.

Dola sighed and walked up to the bed. "Scooch over."

Salka didn't budge.

"You're not going to make a pregnant woman stand while you sit, are you?"

Salka moved to the side, her expression sullen.

"Now that we're finally *both* comfortable," Dola said, stroking her belly, "you can tell me all about it. I'm told Munu is not here and that bird never leaves your side, that much I know. Do you want to know what else I know?"

"No, but I bet you will tell me anyway," Salka said with a grimace. She was wedged into a corner, with Dola taking up most of her bed.

"Well, so I will. See, all of us have some small powers of premonition, it would seem." Dola gave a mirthless chuckle. "If that falcon of yours is gone, then he is gone for good. And if you want your powers back then it is to punish whatever or whoever took him."

Salka didn't reply. Her face, however, could hide nothing.

"Look here, I have some answers for you. Not all of them, but enough for now."

The girl looked up to meet Dola's serious gaze, and nodded.

"Now what I told your mama, that was what one might call a lie."

Salka's eyes widened. "What do you mean?"

"The moment you stop taking the potion, your powers will come back, and there will be no stemming them."

"I hope they do! I hope they come right out and strangle her! I hope they–"

"Listen to me! It's important." Dola reached out, causing Salka to flinch. But she only put her hand gently to Salka's face. "You've been having headaches, yes?"

Salka nodded.

"You can't stop the other heart for long, dear, it will always reassert itself. You are who you are and what you are is a striga. Your powers will be back, stronger than before and your shadow will be back to betray you. You must wait for the right moment to release it. And it cannot be in the village."

"So… Pike was right. I *am* a stigoi?" Salka's eyes filled with tears. She held her head between her hands as if it were ready to split in two.

Dola drew Salka to her chest. Dola smelled of leaves and cloves and Salka let herself be comforted.

"Now you listen to me," Dola spoke in a raspy voice. "Pike is a sad fool, who poisons herself to ward off her own soul, pushing her second heart down till she's able to think of nothing else.

"Stigoi is just a word for what folk fear you could become. The strigas took that word and threw all their own fear and shame at it until it became a monster they neither knew nor understood. You can use your other heart for ill *or* for good, just as a hand can strike as well as comfort a friend. You hold that knowledge inside you, you hold it close. But all the same…" Dola raised Salka's face and looked her in the eyes. "All the same, like I told you once before, it *does* change you. It has already changed you, in ways that cannot be undone. You must learn to handle it, the best you can. And you can't do it here."

Salka looked at Dola blankly. "Why didn't you just say that before? I could have left sooner. You didn't have to give me the potion at all! If I'd gone before, then Munu would still be alive!"

"But *you* wouldn't be." Dola looked back at Salka. "You can't control it as well as you think you can. Not yet. You couldn't hide it, and if you used it to defend yourself, you'd be as likely to kill your attacker as yourself. And I don't have you counted as a cold-blooded killer either. How would you live with yourself if you saw your shadow pull the life out of a man? Not being able to stop it? And it would happen, sooner or later. You wouldn't be safe anywhere in the Heyne Mountains. The humans would kill you on sight. And if the strigas got you… Tell me, girl, have you seen a striga have her other heart burnt out?"

Salka shook her head.

"The entire village gathers round and uses a tiny bit of their second hearts. The strigas that are deemed to have crossed the line into becoming stigois will have their second heart turned to ash inside their chests. Most of them survive, that much is true. They live, for a time, but a sad life it is indeed. They have no understanding, no feeling left in them. No strength. That's what would have happened to you. A kindness, strigas call it. Far better to be half a human than a stigoi."

"Markus was banished... Nobody hurt him."

Dola looked at Salka sadly and opened her mouth as if she was going to say something, then shut it again. "He was not like you, love. He only just began exploring his powers. His shadow was no greater than that of the older strigas. Even Alma's second heart is stronger than his was. But she is old and will not get much stronger before she dies. Markus was young. And the road he set upon would have eventually led him to where you are now."

Salka looked at the fire and gently stroked something lying in her lap with her thumb. It was a feather, woven into a necklace.

"Did you see it? My shadow, I mean? In your visions? How did you know how bad it was?"

Dola stroked her belly with her swollen hands. "My visions are my own, girl. I tell you what you need to know. Today I came down to the village to tell you that you won't be safe here for much longer. Keep taking the potion, for now, and get ready to leave. Stay here a day or two at the most. When the trouble comes, you don't want to be here to greet it. And when you're ready, come to my house."

"I've never been to your house," Salka said.

"A doubtful honor," Dola smiled. "Walk eastward, only turning north at the boulder marking the edge of the striga forest. I'll help you."

"What about my mother?" Salka asked.

Dola got up from the bed. The movement clearly caused her discomfort and she winced when her feet touched the ground. She rubbed her lower back and said, "You must decide for yourself, I think." She left the house and nodded briefly at Miriat, evading the questions Salka's mother would have likely showered her with, and turned towards home.

Dola leaned against a tree. It was a long walk to the striga village. Far too long for her heavy belly and the swollen legs which made every step torturous. She stroked her stomach and ground her teeth as shame threatened to temporarily overwhelm her. It would be worth it in the end. A sharp pain ran across her back and around her hips. She sucked in the cold air greedily, as if it could take the place of the pain.

She knew what had to be done. Shame was of no use to her now. No use at all.

# CHAPTER 26

Dran woke up early that morning, some sweet dream bringing a smile onto his face even before he shook the last of the sleep off. His first thought was of Salka: the way she had laced her fingers together behind his neck, and how warm her breath had felt on his collarbone as she leaned into him for comfort.

He'd felt strong then, for a moment. Strong and healthy – as he should have been. He could weep at the memory of it. But that was then, and today he was himself again. He gritted his teeth as pain shot up his leg.

It was not the time to ask her, it really wasn't. He could feel a knot of shame in his chest as he thought of what he needed from her. But it was not the time to delay either.

What if he asked her and she never again looked at him like she did yesterday?

When he opened the door, the crisp morning air brought blood to his cheeks. He thought about bringing a small gift for Salka, something to comfort her. He decided against it.

He walked towards Miriat's house, his leg dragging. He knew once he warmed up, it would work better again, but he struggled through the mornings. He saw Dola leaving Miriat's house, and he stepped into the shadow underneath the eaves of Trina's hut. Ever since Markus, he studiously avoided Dola, lest she looked at him with her witch eye and saw the truth of what he'd done. He thought himself well hidden, but as Dola passed him, she pierced him with a look that chilled him to the bone. *You know nothing,* he reassured himself as he matched her gaze with his own. But then she was gone, and he was left standing alone, waiting for Salka to come out of her house.

At long last she did, leading out her lamb for grazing. Dran looked around and walked up to her, his hands in his pockets to hide their shaking. "Good morning, Salka. How are you feeling?" he asked.

Salka looked up at him, as if she couldn't quite place him for a moment. "I'm well," she said, her eyes on the ground, as she walked past him.

Dran frowned. It was not the welcome he'd hoped for. "I was worried about you," he said, catching up with her. "Would it be all right if I accompanied you today?"

Salka looked at him askance, then blushed. The previous night she had allowed herself to be comforted by Dran. The morning saw her regretting her weakness. He scared and attracted her in equal measure. She ventured a look at his face again. It was handsome, for sure. His eyes slanted delicately, giving his face a cat-like aspect. In spite of the confidence he exuded, he was still new to manhood, and his chin had only the faintest shadow of a beard on it.

She looked down as he met her eyes. When he looked at her, she thought she saw a tenderness that went beyond the careless bluster and ostentatious flirtation he had displayed with Emila. He looked at her now and smiled sadly, as if her silence caused him physical discomfort.

Once they passed the gate, she said, "Thank you for your kindness yesterday." She felt she could talk freely only outside the village walls.

He nodded. "Losing a friend, that's a hard thing. Still..." He reached out and clasped Salka's hand, causing heat to rush all the way up her neck and to the roots of her black curls. "A new friend, though he can't replace one lost, can make things easier? Let me help, Salka. I hope you can learn to trust me."

Salka nodded and walked for a while holding his hand, not wishing to offend him. It felt cold to the touch. In the end, he drew his hand away, as if sensing her discomfort. She wanted to tell him about Dola's earlier visit, but she didn't dare. Even a heart as lonely as hers would not let itself be hurried too much. So instead she said, "What will happen now?"

"Well," Dran said. "We need to speak with my mother. Pike will be punished, though perhaps not as severely as she would have been, had you not nearly mauled her to death." Dran smiled good-humoredly.

Salka looked down. "I wish I had. I wish she was dead instead of Munu." As they walked, she kept looking down to the ground, as if she could find an answer in the browned, muddied pine needles. Suddenly, she became aware of Dran slowing down and looked up in alarm. "Are you well? Do you need to rest? I'm sorry, I didn't think…"

Dran shot her an angry look. Then his expression changed once more, as quick as a flash, so Salka thought she imagined it. "Yes. I suppose that would be nice. There is a small clearing close to here, if we leave the path and turn by the big tree over there." He pointed with his finger. "There's some decent grazing, your lamb won't be worse off for you not making the long hike to the eastern slopes."

Salka nodded. "Thank you."

The clearing was well hidden, with thick bushes growing on either side and big boulders at the edge of it, some flat-topped and easy to climb. "It's almost as if somebody made this," Salka said, sitting herself comfortably. "I've walked these woods my entire life and have never come across it."

"I found it as a small lad. A refuge of sorts, as there is just one path leading into it. I'm happy to share it with you, if you promise to keep it secret." He winked at Salka, and a small smile brightened her face.

"Can I ask you something?" she said, her fingers tracing the smooth surface of the stone they sat on. Curious grazed on the sparse grass below, methodically chewing through the spring vegetation.

Dran nodded.

"Are you not well?" she asked. "I'm sorry to mention it, only...
You've always been strong, even with your foot. And I noticed...
Your hands shook today."

Dran gave her a careful look. "I won't insult your intelligence
by pretending you're wrong. And I suppose talking to someone
about it might make the burden lighter as well." He lay back and
put his arms under his head. "I'm sick. And I will only get sicker.
My mother's herbs have brought no relief and I fear there is not
much anyone can do." He paused, weighing his options. He then
grabbed the neck of his tunic and pulled it down, revealing the
dark tendrils swirling in a horrific pattern on his chest.

Salka gasped and put her hands to her mouth. They sat in
silence for a moment.

"Markus could cure you if he were still here..." Salka said and
shot a glance at Dran, who tensed up. "I know it's forbidden," she
added quickly, and began fiddling with a piece of lichen growing
from a crack in the stone. "But surely your mother could sanction
it... A special dispensation..."

Dran gave a mirthless chuckle. "Oh no. My mother would do
nearly anything for me, but not that, never that. Her precious laws
are more precious than her son, it would seem." He looked at
Salka. "You can see how deeply the fear of stigois runs through
our village. Pike was poisoned with it enough to kill your bird, and
my mother is no different."

"And what do you think?" Salka asked.

"I think if another could help me, they'd have my thanks and
respect, not my condemnation."

"Even if it turned the striga helping you into a stigoi?" Salka
asked. She fidgeted, weaving her fingers together.

Dran noticed but pretended not to. Instead, he turned to face
Salka with his hand propping up his chin. "What is a stigoi but a
powerful striga? The humans want us to stay powerless and we
help them by tying our own hands."

"Why don't you use your own powers to do it then?" Salka
asked.

"I tried. I couldn't do it," he said. Not the whole truth, but a shameful enough part of it. He bit his lip, afraid of her reaction. She watched him for a moment. Then she reached out and squeezed his hand. She meant to pull it back, but he laced his fingers with hers and she could not withdraw. She reddened.

"I wish I could help you," she said simply.

"Can't you?" he asked. He looked towards the grazing animals and she followed his gaze towards the lamb.

She blanched.

He laughed. "Don't worry, I would never betray you. We're friends, aren't we?"

She nodded.

"Tell me, how are you managing to keep your powers down this way? Anyone would say your other heart was burned out of you. But your mind's too clear for that." He reached out and tucked a curl behind Salka's ear.

Salka played with the feather necklace. "I can't help you now," she finally said.

Dran's face fell. He moved away and stared at the forest. "Then I'm lost," he said.

"But…" Salka bit her lip, "I might be able to do something in the future. The close future."

Dran looked at her with interest.

"I can't say anymore. Not yet. But maybe soon…"

Dran smiled and brushed Salka's cheek with the tips of his fingers, contouring her jawline and stopping right under her chin. He gently tilted it upwards so she was facing him. He leaned forward and kissed her.

Salka stiffened at first and then, hesitantly, put her arms around his neck. She ran her fingers through his thick black hair and breathed in his scent as he pulled her closer in his arms.

Dran pulled away, finally, and smiled at her. "Don't worry, Salka, I will keep your secret if you keep mine. Your kindness… I don't deserve it. But thank you."

# CHAPTER 27

"I called you here to confirm a report I was given," Alma said, drumming her long fingers on the armrest of her chair.

Kalina stood sad and forlorn. Her hair was unbrushed and fell in greasy streaks down her puffed-up face. She'd been crying and looked close to tears now. A part of Alma wanted to comfort the girl, but the anger within her was so consuming that it was all she could do to control herself.

"What report?" Kalina asked. She shifted her weight and winced at the pulsating pain in her shoulder. She braced yourself and met Alma's cold stare.

"Show me your shoulder."

Kalina hung her head. There it was. After a lifetime of service, she had finally proven herself undeserving. She loosened the strap at her throat and waist. It took her a moment to disentangle herself, pulling on her clothes with one arm. Alma gasped. The inexpertly done dressing slid off Kalina's arm and revealed a jagged wound, crusted over with blood and pus.

"You should have come to me with this, child! It will fester if you don't treat it!" Alma said, shaking her head.

Kalina's eyes filled with tears. "Thank you, Alma, I know I don't deserve such kindness…"

"Nonsense!" Alma hit the armrest with her fist and got up to face Kalina. She cupped Kalina's face with her hands. "I admit I haven't always appreciated you, Kalina, but your compassion and kindness, though misplaced, are to be admired and praised. I'm ashamed to say I hadn't thought you capable of such selflessness. I won't forget it."

Kalina's mouth hung open. "I don't understand…"

Alma shook her head and walked towards her herb cabinet. "You can stop this now. I know the whole story. I just needed to see the wound to have it confirmed, for I could scarcely believe it. Truth be told, I didn't want to believe it." Alma pulled out a few clay jars and a mortar. "It surprised me, I admit – here, sit down over there – why you'd try to protect her. I thought, I truly thought the months in the Windry Pass would teach her caution and respect, but I was mistaken then as you were mistaken now in shielding her."

Kalina walked towards the stool in a daze. She was afraid to speak, lest she incriminate herself in some way. A knock on the door made her jump and turn sharply to the entrance.

"Come in, Emila," Alma called without looking up. The dark room was already filled with the smell of the herbs she was mixing. Normally, Kalina would have killed to witness the preparation of Alma's famous tonics and ointments, but today she could muster no interest.

Emila opened the door and slid in. Her auburn hair half covered her face, and she shot Kalina a look that warned her not to speak. "You called me, Alma."

"Yes. Tell Kalina what you told me."

Kalina watched with an open mouth as Emila bent her head and said, "Yes, Alma." She pulled the hair from her forehead and was fiddling with the edge of her scarf. Kalina focused her eyes on it, on its lovely green and yellow stripes, expertly woven by Rida. She was not willing to look Emila in the face, lest she betray herself somehow.

"Last night Salka called my mother to assist in the labor of Miriat's doe. I went with her to help. Salka was told to stay outside of her mother's house so she would not get in the way. It was a difficult birthing and overcrowding the room would not have made it easier."

Kalina couldn't help but think how much Emila looked like Rida in that moment, in spite of having inherited none of her mother's features.

"We needed water, and since Salka didn't come when called, I was asked to bring some from the well. As I got closer, I heard screaming." Emila coughed and shifted uncomfortably. She cast a furtive glance at Kalina. "I was surprised it didn't wake the whole village, it was so blood-curdling."

"Just straight to the point, please," Alma hurried her. She had no time for flowery descriptions. Kalina wondered briefly if it was because she could sense the falsehood in them and chose to ignore her instinct to get to the answer she wanted.

Emila stood confused for a moment, like a singer asked to skip a line of a well-known song. She blushed under Kalina's gaze and continued in halting tones: "I walked up, and I saw Salka, on top of Pi... *Kalina*, biting her shoulder. It looked like she would drink the blood, had she the time. She was interrupted by your own brave son, who tore Salka away from Kalina before she could kill her."

"And her shadow? Tell me again of her shadow, child. I know it must be hard for you. But speak true."

Emila had the decency to look embarrassed. "Salka's shadow seemed to feed on the blood from the ground. It grew till it stood from the ground, like a woman grown behind her."

"Did you see Salka's face then?" Alma asked. She gently placed the prepared salve on Kalina's wound with her finger. Kalina winced as the fingers touched her torn skin, but then felt a cooling sensation which numbed the pain quickly.

Emila coughed and looked down at her feet.

*You're lying, you're lying...* Kalina watched Emila's face in fascination. She didn't dare say a word. Emila met her eyes and a look of recognition passed between them. One, a liar out of spite, and one out of fear.

"Yes, Alma. She was no longer the Salka we knew before. She was a stigoi, I'm sure. Though I had not seen one before that evening."

"And there you have it," Alma said, gently placing a fresh dressing over Kalina's wound. "Now there are just two things here I cannot for the life of me understand. How does she manage to hide the corruption in her soul, and..." She looked into Kalina's eyes. "Why did you and my son try to protect her?"

Kalina was speechless, but, luckily, Alma didn't require a response.

"You know our laws better than most, Kalina. I know you understand their value, though they might at times seem hard and pitiless. Your kindness does you credit. To protect our young is an admirable goal, but we cannot protect them by letting a wolf roam freely among them. And that's what Salka is now. It is a sad thing we must accept, and I'm only sorry that it had to come to this..." she gestured towards Kalina's arm, "...to teach you that lesson. Thank you, Emila," Alma nodded towards her, "for doing the right thing. And for recognizing that Salka is Salka no more. A stigoi can never go back to being a striga, any more than I can bleed and birth again.

"And now, we shall have to move quickly to contain her. The stigois are the least powerful when the sun is high, as the darkness flees the light, always. So our traditions dictate. Tonight, we must prepare, swiftly, quietly. For in the morning the entire village must be ready."

"What's going to happen to her?" Kalina asked.

"We will save her, child. We will purify her. We will turn her stigoi heart to ash so that the girl within can live on." Alma stroked Kalina's cheek. "Don't fret, my girl. We don't do this in anger but out of love and out of duty. Our people depend on us to do the right thing. However painful it may be."

# CHAPTER 28

The evening clouds were blotting out the sun's last rays by the time Salka and Dran walked back into the village. Dran let his fingers run across her arm, as if by accident, just before they entered through the gate. A shiver ran down Salka's back.

"It's best we don't provoke my mother. Sooner or later, she learns of everything that happens inside the village walls." He smiled.

Salka traced the lines of his face with her eyes, before she turned away, biting her lip.

"You're thinking of Munu?" Dran asked.

She nodded. "I know most here don't think much of a bird, but he was so much more to me. He saved my life back there in the Pass, and I need to give him some justice. Will you... Will you speak to your mother for me?" She looked in Dran's eyes with such earnestness, he couldn't help but smile.

"For you? Yes, I will speak to her."

Salka seemed to accept that answer and nodded a goodbye as she led her lamb back through the village towards her mother's house. She passed Rida, and raised her hand in a greeting, but Rida just walked on, without so much as a glance in her direction.

Salka shrugged her shoulders and walked into her house, where Miriat was feverishly pulling out some old fabrics from their reed-woven chest. Two packs were lying on Miriat's bed, and she barely gave her daughter a glance as she walked in. Instead, she gestured towards the back of the room where they kept their dry foods.

"Take out anything we can carry. Oh, for gods' sake, make sure the entrance is sealed!" Miriat stood up and carefully tied the sides of the leather panels to the walls. "Where have you been gone so long?"

"What's going on?" Salka asked. She sat next to the doe and gently stroked the leg of one of the kids.

"We're getting banished, that's what," Miriat said, and, as if the words themselves were too much to bear she sat on the floor and hid her face in her hands.

Salka opened her mouth and closed it again. She slipped down to the floor and stared blankly at her mother. "So that's why Rida wouldn't look at me. But why? And how did you find out? There's been no trial."

"No, not yet. But there's one coming, and we must be prepared." Miriat nodded towards the entry to the house. "I'm not a fool and strigas are poor secret keepers. The entire village has been abuzz ever since this morning. Not a soul spoke to me the entire time you've been gone. No one so much as looked at me. And then your Aunt Trina came to me. They all know we're close, they wouldn't tell her a thing either. But she caught a snippet here and there and she's certain Alma means to banish you."

"But..." Salka hesitated. "They don't know about the potion, do they? My shadow hasn't betrayed me."

Miriat rubbed her forehead. "No. But I was afraid something like this might happen. Dran was paying you too much attention. I'm sure that put Alma on edge. And then the Kalina business. I don't know what she must have told Alma, but I will bet you anything she had something to do with it."

Salka didn't reply. Thinking about the ragged wound her teeth left in Kalina's flesh made her stomach drop. Attacking another striga was against the laws of the village, even if the second heart wasn't involved. And there would be few who'd think the loss of Munu a sufficient provocation.

Miriat slapped her thigh with an open hand. "They want us gone? Fine! But I will not let anybody throw me out of my own house without so much as warm clothes or food. I have worked for this! *All* of this!" She gestured around the room. "And it might not be much, but I'll take what I can. We'll have to throw it over the wall today. I won't run the risk of them not letting us come back to pack."

Salka was too stunned to speak for a moment. "It's not 'us', Mama..." she finally said. Miriat shot her a warning look, but Salka shook her head. "You don't have to do this for me. Not again." Her eyes filled with tears. "It's my fault, I don't want you to lose everything again, just because of me. I'm grown, mama, I can manage."

Miriat stared ahead for a moment then stood up and grabbed Salka's shoulders, bringing their faces close. "There is no me without you, daughter, do you understand? I wouldn't wish to stay in a place that doesn't want you. I couldn't."

A sob shook Salka's chest and she collapsed in her mother's arms. "I can't do this to you again, Mama! How can I do this to you..."

Miriat stroked her daughter's hair and pulled her closer to her chest. "I make the decisions for me. And I choose you, sweetling. I will *always* choose you."

When Salka finished crying, Miriat said, "Here, take these packs. Throw them over the western side of the fence. The eastern side is always guarded, and it won't add much to the journey to go around the village. There's a cart there. You can push against it to climb up. I have some preparations to do here."

Salka nodded and set out to do as she was told.

While Salka was gone, Miriat cleaned up the house and swept the floor for the final time. Even if she had to leave her house, she'd be damned if she left it in a mess. She gave the last of the winter carrots to the goat and stroked the head of one of the kids. "I'm sorry I won't be here to see your babies grow. Trina will take good care of you, though, you'll see," she said. The goat nuzzled its face under Miriat's armpit and chewed on her tunic, more out of affection than hunger.

"It's done, Mama," Salka said softly as she entered the house again.

"Good." Miriat wiped the tears hastily with her sleeve. "Here, I laid out the best clothes for you. You won't leave the village looking like a beggar. I will not give them the satisfaction."

Salka ran her fingers across the new woven tunic and the old, but lovingly patched-up leggings. "They're lovely, Mama."

"Well, yes. I made it when you were gone. At least I can give it to you now." Miriat sighed. "Put them all on. When they come for you, you must be ready."

Salka nodded and slipped into the prepared clothes. They fit her taller frame well. She was so used to having things too short and tight that she couldn't help smiling at how unconstricted she now felt.

"It might all turn out for the best," Miriat said finally. She looked at her daughter affectionately and kissed her forehead. "We will be together, and thanks to Dola, your shadow won't betray you now. We don't need to fear anymore, Salka. We don't need to hide. Nobody will know you're a striga when we leave the mountains." She smiled, stroking Salka's cheek with her thumb. "Now, let's sleep. We'll have to walk very far tomorrow." She lay on her narrow bed and stared at the low ceiling for a moment.

Salka's heart sank. Her mother didn't know. Well, of course she didn't. Salka hadn't told her about Dola's lie. That there would be no escaping from the striga heart. There would be no safety for them, no adventure. All she had to offer her mother was more of the same. More poverty, more hunger. Endless, endless fear.

"Where will we go?" Salka asked, willing her voice not to break. She wrapped herself in her warm blanket. She would indulge the fantasy a while longer. Just a moment more to imagine this golden new life for the two of them. It couldn't be, but she would at least have the memory of sharing in her mother's hope.

"The west road down the mountain is steep, far too steep, and water logged at this time of year to risk it with your headaches. But then your shadow doesn't look like a striga's," Miriat said. She made the effort to sound cheerful, though Salka noticed how her mother plucked at the loose ends of the blanket with her fingers. "So, the safest way for us might well be through the Heyne Town. After all, after nearly twenty years, who will know me there?" She turned to the wall and pulled her blanket right up to her neck. "Sleep now, if you can."

Salka waited for a long time, until she was certain of the steadiness of her mother's breathing. She slipped from under the covers, and rolled her blanket beneath them, should her mother wake in the night and glance towards her bed. She stood over her sleeping mother and reached out her hand. She let it hover above Miriat's shoulder, and then turned away. She wouldn't risk waking her to satisfy the childish desire for that last touch. She would not be so selfish.

Salka tiptoed to the door. She looked back for just a moment, and tried to take it all in. Tried to imprint on her memory the shape of the small hut she grew up in, the dirt floor and the mud walls, the animals sleeping warm in the corner, and of the outline of her sleeping mother's back.

She wouldn't cry. Salka balled her hands into fists, digging her nails into the flesh of her palm. Out of habit she reached out towards Munu's perch. She caught her breath when she remembered.

It wouldn't be wise to delay any longer. She walked out of the house and headed for the unguarded western side of the village, slipping quiet and unnoticed between the houses. She came up to the side of the fence and deftly climbed the cart she had previously pushed against it. On the second try, she managed to jump high enough to grasp the top of the fence and then pull herself up. She looked down the fence. It was too dark to tell where the tree roots and stones were, so she just had to hope she wouldn't break her leg coming down. She hung off the outside of the fence, took a deep breath, and let go.

The packs she had thrown over earlier thankfully cushioned her fall. She picked up one of them and headed out, taking the long route around the village eastward towards Dola's house, never once looking back.

# CHAPTER 29

"Pike's lying!" Dran threw his arms up in exasperation.

"It wasn't Kalina who told me, though her wounds spoke eloquently enough," Alma said. She was trying, and failing, to keep her voice level. "It was Emila who saw the whole thing. I heard the truth from Salka's closest friend. What do you say to that?"

"I say she's a liar also! A jealous liar. I was there, remember? I saw no stigoi! All I saw was a girl with a drowned bird." Dran was pacing up and down the house.

"Yes, you were there. Why didn't you come to me with this? Why are you protecting her? Have I taught you nothing?"

"I was going to tell you! I was going to tell you that Pike attacked Salka for no reason and paid for it!"

"Yes, so you tell me. And yes, Kalina has her faults. She's eager to find fault in others, gods know. But she lives and breathes to protect our village. She has proven this over years of loyalty and service. *You*, however, you have protected Salka once already, and nearly paid for it with your life! Tell me, what charms does this scrawny child possess to inspire such loyalty in you?"

Dran scoffed. "It's not about her! I want justice for her, as I would for any striga."

Alma cocked her head to the side. Dran blushed under his mother's skeptical gaze.

"Fine!" Dran raised his arms. "Fine, banish her! But don't burn her. She doesn't deserve that."

"That's true," Alma said, her shadow flowing behind her. "She doesn't deserve the *mercy* of a purification. She's betrayed us all by opening herself up to the filth and the poison of her other heart. She hasn't *earned* the right to have this curse lifted from her. But we must do it, nonetheless. No!" She raised her hand. "No more talk from you!" She took a couple breaths to steady herself. "I bear her no ill will, though I am angry at her deception. No, we *must* heal her. We must do it, for her sake, and for ours. Do you want to bring death to our doors? We exist only because we're *allowed* to exist. Because we keep each other in check. Can you imagine what would happen if a fully-transformed stigoi came down the mountains, and plagued the humans with her powers? Do you think they would allow us to continue as we are? Or would they come and murder us all for this confirmation of their worst fears?"

"You let Markus go."

"Markus was on the wrong path. A path which, if he lives, will eventually bring him ruin and death. But he'll be far away from us by then, and his shame will be his alone."

Dran hit the wall with his fist. "I won't allow it!"

"You won't *allow* it?" Alma said. Her eyes darkened with anger. "I give you license in most things. You are my son and heir, though you seem to forget now what you owe this village, what you owe *me*. When the morning comes and she is dragged out in front of the village and tied to a pole, you will do *nothing*." Alma's shadow pulsated with her anger. As she raised her voice it grew behind her, stifling out the fire. She raised her finger. "And when the purifying causes her to writhe in pain and call on you for help, you will do *nothing*. You will do your duty, even if I have to tie you alongside her. And you will not leave this house tonight." She snapped her fingers and two solemn-faced striga men entered through the door. "Just in case you thought to warn her." She smoothed her dress with her hands and strode out. "I will spend the night in meditation. If you find it difficult to rest, I suggest you do the same."

The heavy doors slammed shut behind her, leaving Dran in the darkness.

# CHAPTER 30

The skins covering the door were pulled aside so violently they tore. The morning light poured into the house, startling Miriat awake.

"Salka, you are called before Alma to receive her judgement," the man at the door said. Miriat looked up at him. His kind, heavily lined face was contorted with worry and puffy from a sleepless night. Mordat had always doted on Salka. The smell of some liquid courage on his breath suggested he did not relish his duty that morning.

*How cruel of Alma to send him for this task,* Miriat thought as she slid out from under her covers. She gave Mordat a small nod. He ignored her and looked away.

"Salka, it is time," she said softly, and walked up to her daughter's bed. She put her hand gently on the rolled-up covers. She knew before her hand touched the blanket that Salka was gone.

"Where is she?" Mordat sounded weary. "Miriat, you can't hide her."

"I didn't." All blood left Miriat's face. "She's gone."

"What's the holdup?" A young striga came in through the entrance. He stopped suddenly. "Where is she?"

Mordat sighed and rubbed his wide forehead with his hand. "A nasty business," he said and looked sadly at Miriat. "I'm sorry, lass," he said before turning to the young man in the door. "Dorni, sound the alarm. The stigoi's escaped. She can't have gone far. We'll get her."

"Wait, what?" Miriat stood up with a start. "What do you mean? She's not a stigoi. What are you talking about? You wanted to banish her, and she's gone, what more do you want?"

Mordat looked strangely at Miriat and said, "Follow me."

They walked together to the village square. All the strigas were gathered there, with the youngest fearfully holding on to their parents. In the middle of the square, right next to the well, stood a freshly erected pole, with a thick hemp rope lying in a coil next to it.

"No…" Miriat said. She stopped, but was nudged forward by Mordat. He held her arm and brought her in front of Alma, who sat like a queen in her high-backed chair. On her greying hair, she wore the judgement crown of woven reeds. Over her shoulders, she wore a dark cloak. It was long enough to hide her shadow within its folds. Behind her, with one arm resting on the back of his mother's chair stood Dran. Miriat looked at his face but he turned away rather than face her gaze.

"Where is the stigoi?" Alma asked. Her sharp eyes looked Miriat over. A mirthless smile twisted her lips. "I see you slept in your travel clothes. And yet your daughter is not with us. I take it she ran." She looked to Mordat for confirmation. He simply nodded.

"I suppose we must recover her. I will need volunteers. Three for each of the four paths leading out of the village. She can't be too far."

"I volunteer!" A voice rang through the village. Emila stepped forward.

Miriat looked at her, disbelief twisting her features. "Emila? Why? They want to burn her other heart out! And for what? She's your friend! She's always been kind to you!"

Emila's cheeks flushed. She had the decency to look ashamed, though the resentment in her eyes burned still. Rida put her hand on her daughter's shoulder and fixed her with a stony stare. Alma answered for her. "There are no more secrets, Miriat. We all know now how you sought to deceive us, though I admit I don't yet know how Salka managed to hide the truth from us. You have both deceived us, and Kalina paid the price for your arrogance and treachery."

"I don't understand!" Miriat nearly screamed. "She's not a stigoi. She didn't hurt anyone! She couldn't have! It's all a misunderstanding…"

"Is *this* a misunderstanding?" Alma gestured at Kalina who approached her with an ashen face. "Uncover your shoulder, girl."

Kalina hung her head, but obeyed. The entire village gasped as she peeled off the dressing to reveal the wound where Salka had bitten off a chunk of her flesh.

"Does *this* look like something a young woman would do, Miriat?" Alma rose from her seat. "Our laws are there to protect us. Thanks to them, this is only the second time I have had to carry out the cleansing." She approached Miriat and put a hand on her shoulder. Miriat recoiled and would have struck Alma, had Mordat not held down her arm. The old woman shook her head. "This is necessary, Miriat. Please believe me, I am not enjoying this. But Salka is no longer the daughter you once knew. There is no love, no humanity in a stigoi. They are wild yet crafty animals, who will devour you if you let them. By burning out her other heart we can return your daughter to you. Tell me where she is."

"She didn't do it." Miriat shook her head. "I know she didn't. She's not like you describe, she's barely more than a child…" Tears rose to Miriat's eyes, as Alma's grew colder.

"We will find her," she said. "There can be no escaping this."

"Alma, I found a pack of food and tools on the west side of the village!" A young girl ran up to Alma, dragging behind her Miriat's pack. Miriat's face fell.

Alma looked at Miriat and smiled. "You meant to travel west. That is wise. Trina!" she called out. Trina stepped forward, hesitantly. "Take three other strigas with you and go west. The other teams will search in the other directions. Make haste. She has the advantage, but she expected banishment. She won't be anticipating a pursuit." Trina stood there with her head down, not moving. Alma narrowed her eyes. "This is your chance to prove your loyalty, Trina. Unless you wish me to believe you were in on Miriat's deception?"

Trina opened her mouth and closed it again. She shot Miriat a look. The entire village around them seemed to be holding its breath.

"Answer me, Trina. Are we to understand Salka's treachery is yours as well? Is her blasphemy yours too?"

"No, Alma." Trina shook her head. She kept her eyes down, and a blush spread over her face, making the mark on her face a deeper shade of purple. She bowed and walked towards the west gate. Three more strigas picked out by Alma trailed behind.

Alma sighed and turned to Miriat. "I'm sorry it had to be done like this, Miriat. It's for her own good. I know in time you will see this."

"Don't count on it," Miriat said through clenched teeth. She would have torn Alma's throat out herself, had her arms not been held behind her.

Alma closed her eyes briefly and turned towards the crowd. "I'm afraid we have no choice but to wait now." She turned towards Miriat. "But we will not be thwarted. Salka puts us all in danger and I will not allow that, Miriat. She is too far gone for us to simply let her leave. It would break every truce the strigas have ever made. You will be kept under lock and key until we can recover her. We cannot have you running off to search for her yourself. Tolan!"

Tolan stepped forward, half pushed by his wife. He was looking down at his feet and a blush was spreading from his neck up to the roots of his auburn hair. Alma gestured towards Miriat. "My storeroom. You can bar the door and there are no windows for her to escape through. You will stay outside and guard her." She turned to Miriat and whispered, so that no other striga heard her. "I know your mother's instincts tell you to stop this, to spare your daughter the pain. I understand those instincts, but believe me, were it my own son, I would tie him up to that pole myself. It is love that guides us." Miriat only shot her a furious look. Alma sighed and gestured at Tolan to take Miriat away.

Tolan grabbed one of Miriat's arms. She struggled as he led her towards Alma's storeroom, but she might as well have struggled against an oak tree. "Tolan, please don't do this!" she pleaded. "You know Salka, you know this isn't her!" He hesitated for a moment.

"I'm sorry, Miriat," he said, pushing her inside the storeroom. Miriat rammed into the door with her entire weight, but it was already barred. She crumpled down to the floor and began to cry: a low wail which began in her chest and escaped as a heart-rending keen.

Outside the storeroom, Tolan slid to the ground. He closed his eyes and put his fists against his ears. "I'm so sorry..."

# CHAPTER 31

Salka walked at a steady pace. She dared not rest. The early morning light already began to filter through the trees and her mother would wake soon. She imagined the expression on Miriat's face when she realized Salka had left alone. The disbelief and the shock she would feel. Salka tortured herself with the image. Tears that streamed down her face in the first hours since she left had dried, but she could still feel their salty tracks on her cheeks. She did not rub them off. There was a small satisfaction in the discomfort, a sense that she deserved it.

Miriat would get over it, Salka reasoned with herself. Eventually, she'd realize it was for the best. She had already left one home for her daughter, she owed her nothing more. Salka sniffed. It was the right thing to do, she was certain. If one of them had to make the sacrifice she wouldn't let it be Miriat.

The forest was already buzzing with activity. Spring had finally arrived to the Heyne Mountains and the wet, cool air breathed life into the bushes and color into the moss and the hedges. The tiniest leaf buds covered the branches of rabbit-bushes: little humps of potential. The ground was wet, and a tiny trickle of water here and there showed the soaked soil would not take much more. The spring came high and fast this year and the snow topping the Green Sister mountain was melting far too quickly. Salka tried not to slip in the mud, which nearly pulled her boots off once or twice.

Salka stopped for a moment to catch her breath. She was lost.

The directions given to her by Dola were accurate, she was sure, but not exhaustive. They failed to mention that there were more boulders at the edge of the striga forest than there were fleas on a dog. And Salka had clearly picked the wrong one. She had been walking around for a few hours now, not daring to go back to the main path. The new tunic kept her warm, but it did nothing for the hunger in her belly.

She pulled open her pack and reached inside. Miriat had packed a great array of provisions, with a few onions right at the top. There was also some of her famously hard and stodgy flatbread, and Salka pulled out a piece of it now. She chewed on it slowly as she sat on her haunches leaning against the trunk of a tall pine. She rubbed her temples. She hadn't taken Dola's potion that morning, but the headache came nonetheless.

Flecks of light danced before her eyes and she felt a wave of nausea hit her. She turned to the side and threw up violently. She lifted herself with some effort and picked up a handful of melting snow to wipe her mouth. She then pulled out some moss and wiped a spatter of vomit off the top of her shoe. The morning was finally here, and the light only made the pain in Salka's head worse.

She picked up her pack and walked back down the path again. She would choose a different boulder this time and hope for luck.

As she got closer to the path, Salka heard some movement below her. She hid behind a thick juniper leaning against a pine. If it was her mother, would she stay hidden? Could she? She closed her eyes shut. She couldn't do it, she decided. She only had the strength to leave Miriat once. She lifted herself up with some effort and was about to call out when she heard a familiar voice rise in complaint.

"It's a waste of time. We all know she went west! Trina will be back and we will miss the burning for certain!" Rida said. One of them mumbled an objection. Salka broke out in cold sweat. *The burning.* So that was what they had in mind for her? But it was impossible. Nobody saw her use her powers. Nobody knew except... Dran? Could he have betrayed her? *No...* Salka's mouth twisted in pain. He needed her. She promised she would help him…

"She's not stupid enough to go down to the town again. I say we go back."

Salka could see Rida's face from between the juniper branches as the woman stood stubbornly in the middle of the path.

"Wait." This came from Mordat, who was looking at the ground. Salka's heart sank. He was an excellent tracker, and even though the snow was now mostly gone this low in the mountains, he would easily find her footprints in the wet moss.

"Oh, come off it!" Rida complained. "This side of the mountains is riddled with Dola homesteads. You think the girl is the only one capable of disturbing some leaves?"

Mordat ignored her. He walked up a little way to the right on the path. "No," he said. "But these footprints are fresh. You can stay here if you want. Me and Lesny will bring her down ourselves if she's up there."

"I never said I *wouldn't* go, did I?" Rida shook her head. "If you see a track, we'll follow it. I won't have it said that I shirk my duty. Though you can smell rain on the air, and we're as likely to be washed away in the downpour as we are to find her," she said the last under her breath, her voice just barely reaching Salka's ears.

Nonetheless, Rida joined the other two as they began climbing up the narrow forest path up the slope. Salka clung to the side of the tree. They were following the path she took herself an hour or so back. She was less than fifty yards to the east of it and if they continued up, they would soon see her. She pressed her back against the tree. The blinding pain once again pierced her head.

Salka bit her lip. Her back was now drenched in sweat. She couldn't stay hidden for much longer. She could hear Mordat's labored breath and Rida's continued complaining as from behind a screen. The thumping noise in her brain was getting louder. She closed her eyes and tried to push down another wave of nausea. They were getting closer, they would discover her. There was nowhere to hide; the bushes were too thin, the trees too far apart.

If she moved, they would see her. If she stayed, they would see her. Tears escaped from her eyes. She dug her fingers into the pine's hard bark. It cut the delicate skin around her nails, but she didn't notice.

"Can I help you, my fine friends?" a voice boomed across the forest, echoing between the rocks.

"Dola! You're up so early! I would have guessed you'd be warming by the fire for it looks like rain," Lesny said with a grin. Mordat shot him an angry look, which wiped the young man's smile away. It was a solemn business they were on, and he did not appreciate this lack of decorum.

"We're looking for Salka. Have you seen her?" Mordat asked.

"Well, that's rather abrupt," Dola said, stroking her stomach. "Not a 'Hello' or a 'How fare thee?' even. No, I haven't seen the girl. Not since last night anyway. Why?"

Mordat and Lesny looked at each other.

"When and where did you see her?" Lesny asked.

"Late in the night, handsome, in a vision of mine."

"You and your visions," Rida scoffed.

Dola gave her most innocent smile. "Well, if you feel that way, I suggest you be on your way following goat tracks. I won't waste any more of your time." She turned around and continued walking down the path.

Salka swallowed. Rida had already begun walking up the path. Another moment and she would be discovered.

"Wait!" Lesny called out. "Please, tell us!" He shot Rida an angry look. She shrugged her shoulders, but Salka noticed she paused.

"She's headed to the Windry Pass, my dears." Dola smiled. "And once she crosses the stone bridge you won't have another chance of finding her."

Mordat swore under his breath. "Rida, Lesny, we're going back. Thank you, Dola, for your counsel." He bowed his head and started climbing down towards the path. Above him, Salka held her breath.

"That's nonsense. You want to head all the way to the Windry Pass on her say so? She and Miriat are thick as thieves! I wouldn't believe a word she says. Salka is probably halfway down the west slopes already and we're going to be wasting even more time!"

"Shut up, Rida!" Lesny turned towards her with a growl. "You will not disrespect her! She's a Dola first!"

Rida blinked in surprise.

Mordat raised his eyebrow at Lesny who looked down with a blush already coloring his cheeks, but then he turned to Rida, "Lesny is right. Dolas are the keepers of the laws. It isn't your place to question her, Rida."

Rida, chastened, muttered an apology, and then followed Mordat, muttering under her breath.

"Thank you, Dola." Lesny said before following the other strigas. He hesitated. "I hope the birthing comes soon and comes easy."

Dola turned her head to the side. "Don't worry yourself about the matters of Dolas. I accept your good wishes."

Lesny looked like he was going to say more, but then he just nodded and walked back towards the striga village.

Dola watched them go and after what seemed like an eternity she said, "You can come out now." She looked up and waited as Salka made her way down the slope, gripping the protruding roots for balance.

"You're unwell," Dola said, more stating a fact than asking. "Follow me. You can't rest here." Dola made her best effort to walk briskly, but they still moved at a painfully slow pace. "I expected you sooner. I got worried when you dawdled."

Salka squinted at Dola, trying to pierce through the fog of pain and confusion. "What do you mean? How did you know I was coming today? Did you have a vision?"

"No," Dola said. "I met a… friend… on my way home yesterday. He was cutting down a tree for a pole. I persuaded him to tell me what it was for."

Salka couldn't help but smile. Dola had several "friends", many among the striga men in particular.

"You could have told my mother," Salka said. She leaned against a tree, fighting back a wave of nausea. The ringing in her ears was getting worse. The sweat-soaked clothes on her back stuck uncomfortably to her skin.

"If I'd showed my face in the village again that night, both you and your mother would have been apprehended immediately, tradition or no. Instead, I told the next striga I met to tell the others that you have been judged, and hoped that Miriat would put two and two together or that somebody would have the loyalty to tell her if she did not. Strigas are terrible gossips and for once that worked in our favor. Here, drink this." She uncorked her waterskin and stuck it under Salka's nose. Salka took a small sip and gagged at the bitter taste. She threw up again under a tree. She turned towards Dola. "What is that? That's not water!"

"Just a tea meant to settle your stomach. A great job it's done of that, clearly." Dola smiled. "In fairness, it was meant for me more than you."

"No, it's… better, really…" Salka said, still heaving.

"Are you done?" Dola asked. "Not to be unkind, but we need to make our way to my house. There is much to be getting on with." She once again began her slow climb up the path.

"Like what?" Salka said under her breath. She followed Dola miserably, trying to shield her eyes from the light. Dola didn't reply, instead focusing on what must have been a difficult walk. As she climbed, Dola would stop here and there, to touch the ground or to feel the rough bark of a pine, looking for signs Salka couldn't interpret.

After what seemed an eternity, they arrived at a small grove. It seemed so out of place wedged into the middle of a mountain forest, Salka stopped and gawked. The native pines had been cleared, and instead, there grew a wealth of smaller trees, still bare from winter.

"Are these fruit trees?" Salka asked, her eyes wide. "How did you manage to make them grow this high up?"

"I have my ways. Which are my grandmother's ways, to tell the truth. She used to say that it is best to be remembered by the green things we make grow. And so, every summer and autumn

I think of her, as I enjoy the apples from the orchard. But we best get inside. Lesny was right: there is rain coming. And it might not be safe outside when it does."

Dola led Salka among the trees to a crooked, steep-roofed house, which to Salka's eyes looked like an extravagant jewel, with glassed windows and a brick chimney. A small fence surrounded the house, and a vine twisted its way around it. A tiny enclosure to the side housed several chickens and geese, judging by the noise and the smell that lingered around it.

"I'll remember these if you ever come scrounging a lunch off of us again!" Salka said, pointing towards the hens. In spite of her headache, a small smile appeared on her lips, to then disappear almost instantly. Because, of course, there would be no more lunches together, with Miriat and Trina laughing while they prepared the ingredients for a stew. No more Maladia coming back from her traps with a rabbit or a wild bird strung over her shoulder. That was all gone now. Salka's eyes filled up with tears and she hung her head.

Dola put her hand on Salka's shoulder and nodded her head. "I know, my girl, I know. It will get easier in time. Come in now. You might not have enjoyed the fullness of my stores in the past, perhaps, but I am about to correct that."

"Dola!" Salka stood rigid, pointing at Dola's window. "Somebody's in your house! They found me!"

Dola smiled. "I think you best come on in," she said.

Salka looked at her uncomprehendingly, but she followed her nonetheless.

The inside of the house smelled of pinesap and rich food. Salka's stomach churned. There was precious little light filtering through the windows, and she blinked a couple of times as she looked at the woman seated in front of her, who now stood with some considerable effort.

"Salka, you're all right! I thought you'd never come! Shame on you for making Dola walk all that way," Maladia said, smiling broadly, though her eyes glistened wet in the blue-grey light.

"You have questions." Dola smiled at Salka, as she sat heavily in the other chair in the room. She pulled her shoe off by pulling on its heel with her toes. "Ask them." Dola grunted as the other shoe went flying across the floor. "Fire and rheumatism, but I'm tired out!" she said, leaning back. Salka kept standing by the open door, shocked frozen. Dola waved at her to come in. "Come on, all the heat's escaping through the door!"

Salka obeyed and walked up to Maladia, who stood in the middle of the floor waiting. Salka reached out and gently touched Maladia's protruding belly. "So…" she said.

"So." Maladia smiled. "Yes, a little one's coming, and soon."

"How did you…? And you're staying here…" Her head spun and she touched her forehead, as her knees buckled under her.

Maladia grabbed Salka's shoulders with a grunt. "I think you need rest, dear. There will be time enough for explanations soon." She led Salka by the hand to the one bed in the corner of the room and, as Salka laid down, Maladia gently put her hand over Salka's eyes. The sleep came immediately, soothing and smoothing the edges off the pain in Salka's head. She meant to hold on and stay awake, but consciousness slipped from her like a snuffed candle.

# CHAPTER 32

"Please, Tolan! Please! Just let me go!"

The small storeroom was nearly completely dark, the cracks in the door serving as the only source of light. Miriat clung to the door and let the tears fall freely. "Tolan, you know me, you know my daughter! You've known her since she was a baby."

Outside, Tolan sat with his back to the door, slunk to the ground. "I'm sorry, Miriat," he said. "It's the law and by gods, I wish it were otherwise. But if your daughter is a stigoi then she's a danger to all of us. And what of *my* daughter? If the folk from down the mountains come for us, do you think they will spare her?"

A quiet sob answered him.

"I wish we could avoid this, Miriat. I hold no bad feelings for you two, but I see no other way. It will not be pleasant, for sure, but your daughter will be treated gently." Tolan scratched his head and shifted uncomfortably. "It doesn't kill a striga, the burning. It will be hard at first, but your daughter will live. All will be forgiven. We'll take care of you both." Tolan looked up as a few heavy droplets of rain fell on his head.

A sudden activity in the village made him jump up. Lesny was running towards Alma's house. "Lesny, what news?" Tolan called out.

"We met Dola on the way. She said Salka's gone north to the Windry Pass! She's hoping to cross the stone bridge!" Lesny shouted before disappearing inside Alma's house. After a moment, Alma emerged.

"Lesny, you and your team need to head north; join the others. Make sure you spread out, there are at least two paths leading towards the Windry Pass and she might be on either. Here, take this with you." She put a small pouch inside of Lesny's hand. "Make sure you don't breathe in any of it. Put it to her nose and it will knock her out. And Lesny, if there is trouble…"

Tolan strained to hear the rest of the conversation, but he only saw color drain from Lesny's face. The young man shot Tolan a look and then turned away and walked off at a brisk pace.

"Lesny is a good boy," Tolan said, leaning against the door to the storeroom, though the words provided him with no more comfort than they did Miriat, he suspected. "He won't hurt her, Miriat."

Only silence answered him.

"Miriat?" Tolan put his eye to one of the cracks in the door but could see nothing. "Can you hear me, lass?" He listened at the door for a moment, but all was quiet. He cast a critical look over the storeroom. It was, in essence, a hole in the ground, with a small door at the front. It was excellent for keeping potatoes from sprouting but was not intended for live things. "Miriat, are you well?"

Nothing.

He stood there for a moment, then finally seemed to have arrived at a decision. He took the bolt off the door, and, slowly, opened it up. Miriat lay motionless on the ground, her hair covering her face.

"Oh, stigoi's breath…" Tolan rushed inside. He pulled Miriat up and tried fanning her with his big hand. "Come on, lass, suffocation's a stupid way to die, don't you do it, come on!" He never saw the jug of mead as it made a wide arc and connected with the side of his head. The jug cracked open, pouring the sweet liquid over both of them, mixing with the blood from the side of Tolan's head as he crumpled to the ground. Miriat pushed him off her and scrambled to the door. There was nobody outside.

Miriat snuck her way to the wall of the herb patch near Alma's house. She swore under her breath. The wall was too tall for her to scale. She looked around frantically. A crate was propped against the side of Alma's house. It was not very deep, and barely two elbows' wide. Miriat picked it up and put it on its side against the wall, ignoring the cold water pouring down her back. If she hopped on the crate, it could serve as a platform to scale the fence.

She gave herself some space and ran. She jumped and then jumped again, pushing off the crate, which fell with a loud crack. It gave her the lift she needed to grasp the top of the fence with her fingers. She could feel the splinters enter her skin, but she refused to let go. She used her legs to push against the fence, her feet slipping on the wet wood, scraping her knees badly in the process. She finally managed to hoist the top half of her body over the fence. Dizziness overcame her for a moment and she nearly lost balance before carefully putting her legs over to the other side.

"Miriat's escaping!" A cry reverberated through the village. Miriat looked up sharply, causing her to lose her balance. She fell heavily atop of holly bush lining the wall. The hard, thorny sides of the leaves scraped her skin and tore her tunic. It took her a moment before she could stand. Nothing was broken, but she would feel the bruises for a long time after.

Inside the village, she could hear loud yells as all the strigas remaining in the village became alerted to her absence. She didn't wait to listen. With a grunt, she sprinted off.

She'd heard that Dola had told Lesny Salka went north. But Miriat couldn't believe Dola would betray Salka. Not when she went to all that trouble to hide Salka's powers in the first place.

Could the strigas have been following the right trail? Miriat didn't dare stop running, though her feet slipped in the mud more than once. The soaked earth could take no more water, which streamed down the hill. No. Salka wouldn't go back to the Windry Pass. She wasn't stupid. She wouldn't travel north in her state, with the snowmelt pouring down the Sister Mountain. And Miriat didn't believe she'd chance the west path. The girl wanted to put as much distance as she could between herself and the village. There was only one road she could take.

Miriat ignored the pain in her side and increased the pace as she imagined she heard a call coming from behind her. She wished she had more to go on than speculation and blind faith in Dola's loyalty. She looked up, as if the thick canopy could provide her with answers. It seemed her daughter went east.

And so, after all these years, Miriat would go home.

# CHAPTER 33

The first thing Salka became aware of was the absence of pain. The relief was overwhelming. She was afraid to move, in case it was a temporary respite only. When she was certain the pain was really gone she stretched out her toes and fingers. A gentle tingling sensation ran through her body. The smell of freshly baked bread filled her nostrils and her stomach at once reasserted itself.

"You're awake," Maladia said. "You slept the whole day right through, you know. You might as well get up and come join us."

Salka opened her eyes and rolled out of the bed.

"How'd you know I wasn't asleep anymore?" Salka asked. She rubbed her eyes.

"Look behind you." Maladia pointed with her chin at the wall behind Salka. Salka turned around. On the bed next to her sat her shadow. It flowed and flickered in response to the dance of the fire in the hearth, but in all other respects, it was a being separate from Salka. It swung its feet off the bed but stopped when Salka looked at it with her mouth hanging open.

She looked back to Maladia, whose hands were holding two plates, one filled with fresh buns and the other with strips of roasted meats. An unheard-of feast.

"What you waiting for? Go and fill your stomach. There'll be plenty of time for introductions," Dola said, smiling as she came in through the front door, holding a basket with some winter carrots and ash-preserved tomatoes. "Here, let's put up a feast for our guest," she said, putting the bounty on the table.

Salka got up and walked up to her hosts. The shadow girl beside her jumped off the bed and walked next to her. Salka stopped abruptly, but the shadow girl didn't stop, and sat herself at the table, after touching the chair's shadow and pulling it up with her fingertips till it was solid enough for her to sit on. The shadow faced Salka expectantly and gestured towards the empty chair. Salka sat next to her and looked to Maladia, who pushed a mug of hot liquid towards her.

"Here, drink this," Maladia said.

Salka picked up the mug. "What is that?"

"Some tea and honey to help settle your stomach."

"No, I mean... *That*." Salka pointed at the shadow girl.

"Why, it's you, my dear young stigoi," Dola said with a wry smile as she sat heavily in her chair.

"Don't call me that!"

Maladia cocked her head to the side. "Well, that's what everyone else will be calling you. Best get used to it."

"It's so strange..." Salka reached out with her hand and touched the shadow girl's arm. It rippled gently, but the shape held. "It's so soft... Like a baby chick." Salka looked down and exclaimed in shock. "Look! It has its own shadow!" She pointed with a shaking finger.

"Well, yes," Dola sighed. "The laws of nature cannot be altered, not even for a striga. Look here, maybe *you* are not a stigoi, but *she* certainly is." She pointed at the shadow girl. "She's just freed from living in your shadow is all. But she is *you*, in a manner of speaking."

"What do you mean? Isn't that the same thing?" Salka reached out to touch the shadow girl's hand, but hesitated. The shadow just watched her silently, wisps of darkness flowing above her head. The sight fascinated and repulsed Salka at the same time.

"Well, to some folk it's the same thing or so close to the same as to make no difference. It's just a word really. But the power is real, as you well know by now," Maladia smiled, her hand stroking her belly.

Salka reached out again and this time her stigoi brushed her fingers against her, sending a gentle current of warmth through Salka's body. Salka gasped in surprise then immediately looked at her hand as if expecting there to be some mark to show where the stigoi had touched her.

"That was... strange," she said. "I never expected... I know it's wrong, but all I feel is warmth and..."

"Relief?" Maladia asked. "Like having a meal after years of starvation? Yes. And, Alma be damned, I don't feel shame for it anymore. And neither should you." Maladia's face darkened. She leaned back in her chair and tore off a piece of the bread roll.

Salka watched her for a moment. A thought occurred to her, "Is Markus' stigoi like mine now? I have a lot to learn, I imagine. Would he teach me? Where is he?" The words had no sooner left her mouth than she regretted them. Maladia's shoulders sagged and Salka knew the truth before she said a word.

"He's gone," Maladia said without looking up. Her eyes filled with tears.

"There will be time to talk of it, Salka. But that time is not now. You are both welcome to stay here as long as you wish," Dola said, putting a comforting hand on Maladia's shoulder. Maladia bit her lip and put her own hand on Dola's.

"But... Aren't you scared I will hurt you?" Salka shot her stigoi a nervous look. "That the stigoi will hurt you? I mean, if Alma saw this..."

"Well, Alma isn't here. No striga would dare accuse a Dola or invade her home. Do you wish me harm, dear?" Dola asked. She looked Salka straight in the eyes and, after a moment, Salka realized Dola was waiting for an answer. Salka shook her head.

"Good. Because it won't be long till I need your help." Dola smiled and shifted in her seat.

"Help with what?" Salka asked.

A few drops of rain hit the window. Dola furrowed her eyebrows and walked to the window.

"The first thunderstorm of the season, it would seem. A powerful one at that," Dola said, to no one in particular. Maladia walked up to her and put her arm around Dola's shoulders. They watched together as the wind picked up and behind the window the trees began to sway.

# CHAPTER 34

The evening cold was biting and, not for the first time, Miriat wished she had her warm cloak with her.

The Hope Tree with its gnarled branches loomed before her. The wind had picked up and the markers on the tree's branches clacked against each in a dissonant symphony that made Miriat's skin crawl. She wondered briefly if her own marker was still up there. She smiled mirthlessly as she walked past the tree. She had never expected to come back.

*Clever Salka,* Miriat thought. The strigas wouldn't expect it. Nobody would expect it. But with the potion still in her veins, Salka would be no different than any human her age. Not even the suspicious Heyne folk would know.

But would they know *her*?

Miriat hugged herself and squinted, as she looked across the jagged field to where the Heyne Town houses stood as they ever did. At the edge of the forest she paused and took a deep breath. The rain had now started to fall, great big gusts of wind carrying the raindrops in waves which broke over Miriat's body as she walked.

*The homecoming I deserve,* Miriat thought, hugging herself. She bit her lip.

She wasn't able to protect her daughter, and now she was running, once more with nothing, in the hope of catching up with Salka. If her daughter was even going this way.

She had no idea what she'd do once she came to the town. Her best bet was to pass through it unnoticed. She picked up the pace and ran, as thunder rumbled across the sky. The storm was coming and it would not be wise to get caught in it in the middle of a field.

Her long brown hair created rivers across her face and neck, with the rain following its coils and pouring down her chest and back in cold streams. She had to find shelter. The one good thing about the storm was that all the Heyne folk would be inside their homes, grateful for the warmth of their fires and the roofs over their heads. Even as she thought it, she felt a moment's regret for her small hut in the striga village. It was not much, gods knew it was barely anything, but it was hers. It was the home she'd fixed up and made her own, as the infant Salka cooed in the folds of her cloak, watching her mother work.

It was getting late now and the first step she'd taken in her home town in nineteen years was taken in the dark. She moved swiftly through the main street, hoping nobody would care to look out the windows, and if they did, that the security of their homes would override any curiosity they might feel about a lone woman out of place. The main road was a river of mud by now and she had to watch her step. She walked till she passed all the houses and then she took the winding road towards the mines. There would be shelter there, in one of the huts made for the storage of tools and for shelter during meal times. How often she had gone there, bringing warm lunch for her father and then her husband. Her big strong husband with his steady gaze and his warm arms, who turned out to be not quite as strong as she had imagined. There were no tears at that thought. There was no sadness, not anymore. Just an old echo of an ache in her chest.

Though much had changed and grown around it, she could follow this road with her eyes closed. Her teeth were now chattering in the cold. A gust of wind hit her from the side, enough to lose her footing. She slid and fell face-first into the mud. She sat up with a grunt and made an attempt at wiping it off with the edge of her drenched tunic.

"Are you well? What are you doing here, hen?" a kind voice asked her. She looked up and saw a man she didn't recognize. He was wearing an oiled leather coat against the rain and he looked at her like she was mad.

"I'm well, I thank you, I must be on my way," she managed to say through her chattering teeth.

"If you wish to die, that would be the quickest way to do it, for sure. The path down is not passable, with all the snow-melt water and the rain and the mud. And you with nothing on but a bit of homespun!" The stranger looked at Miriat with true concern. He was a good thirty years older than her and had a pleasant, friendly face. He smiled. "You can look at me all you like, child, once you're safe and dry inside my walls. My wife would never forgive me if I let you leave! Come now, you're quite safe, I assure you!"

Miriat looked down the path which looked more treacherous with each passing moment. She turned to the stranger and nodded. Better he think her slow than ungrateful.

"I thank you, yes," she said.

He led her to a small house on the edge of town, only a short distance from where she used to live. The well-tended garden in the front of the house and the good state of the barn next to it was the very image of domestic bliss to Miriat. She swallowed down her jealousy at seeing the smoke coming out from the chimney.

The door swung open and a broad face peeked out. "Abrik, I was deathly worried! I was about to call on the neighbor to go look for you!" Abrik smiled and nodded and ushered Miriat in. "My wife, Estancia. Estancia, here you see a stranger I picked up on the way home. I thought you might not find it amiss." He gave his astonished wife a kiss.

Like Abrik, she was a stranger to Miriat, but she was clearly no stranger to the Heyne ways, as she clutched her husband's arm. "Have you listened to her chest, husband? Who are you bringing to my house?"

Abrik looked at her with a smile. "I think a lady, even one as miserable and wet as this one, might object if a stranger chose to put his face to her chest uninvited. Still, her shadow looks to me fairly unremarkable, if that puts your mind at ease."

"I'm not a striga," Miriat interjected. Estancia gave her an appraising look for a moment and shot an angry glance at Abrik, though she seemed temporarily reassured.

"I just suppose I will have to take your word for it. You might as well come in and make yourself comfortable, as gods know there will be no leaving this house tonight. Take your shoes off. Abrik, make yourself useful and bring down a blanket or two and some of my old clothes from the colored chest."

She looked Miriat up and down. "It will all come short on you, but it's better than these wet rags. I will warm some water, you can wipe yourself clean at least." While Estancia busied herself by the stove, Miriat pulled off her wet clothes and wrapped herself in a blanket. She looked around the small house. Its clean wooden floors and a brick chimney seemed palatial after years of living in the squalor of the striga village.

She had almost forgotten what it was like to live not surrounded by the smell of goats. Her hand slid over the smooth wooden mantel. Good carpentry was just one more thing the strigas did without, and it made Miriat feel tired more than anything. There was so much that her daughter hadn't known in her life, and so much she did without realizing the lack of it. Miriat turned around, suddenly aware of Estancia's eyes fixed on her back.

"Here's some water to clean yourself with. I suppose you will be staying with us for supper. And I don't serve food to dirty folk."

She placed the bowl of steaming water down and placed a tiny sliver of soap next to it. Miriat lifted it to her nose and smelled pine oil. She closed her eyes in pleasure.

"My own recipe." Estancia nodded with satisfaction. "The best soap in these parts. I sell them to the fancier townsfolk, though gods know cleanliness isn't a priority for most of them."

"You're too hard on them, Stancy!" Abrik's voice came from upstairs.

"And you would do well not to listen in to other folk's conversations!" Estancia shot back, crossing her arms.

Miriat sank her hands in the hot water and felt the cold leave her fingertips. "Are you from around these parts?" she asked carefully, washing her face.

"With your Heyne accent you should know ours to not be local, I think." Estancia said, narrowing her eyes.

Miriat wasn't sure what to say.

"Oh, leave her be, woman! She's just being polite! No, we're not from around here, child!" Abrik called out from above. "I travel where my art takes me, you see, and my dear faithful wife comes along, with the greatest grace and forbearance."

Estancia rolled her eyes as if to say the latter was Abrik's wishful thinking. "We're from the westernmost edge of Prissan, a seaside town called Zamory. It's a proper town, not like this ramshackle village. My family has a very nice little clothing business there, but my husband took it upon himself to drag us to these gods-forsaken, striga-infested mountains."

Miriat wiped herself with a towel and put on one of Estancia's old shirts. Its sleeves barely brushed past her elbows, but she was glad for its warmth.

"So, what is your trade then?" she asked the ceiling.

"Well, you see, it's like that," a voice came through the floorboards. "I'm a painter by trade and a poet by nature, and there is precious little poetry to be found in a town which smells of fish and guts all year round. May I come down now?" Abrik asked. After Estancia grunted a reply he hurried down. "There are too many people in the west of our country, you see. Too much stink and dirt, not enough *life* as it was meant to be, in all of its simplicity and grace! Just the grind, grind, everlasting grind!"

"Not that you ever participated in the grind, grind, grind of anything much, I'd say." Estancia ushered Miriat into the chair in front of the fire and screwed up her face in disgust at the dirt and mud coloring the water in the bowl left by Miriat. She picked it up and walked off, leaving Abrik filling his pipe.

"Pay my lovely wife no mind. She has a heart of gold, but it is not lined with the poetry of life, I'm afraid." He shook his head in mock resignation. "Still, I would be lost without her, quite lost. And speaking of lost, would you like to tell me what you were doing tramping around the countryside in the greatest downpour of my long life?" He leaned forward as if to better hear. His intelligent blue eyes sparkled with interest.

Miriat felt uncomfortable beneath his piercing gaze, even more than under the scrutiny of his wife's questions. An answer was required, and silence would draw suspicion.

"I'm looking for my daughter," she said in the end. Some truth would carry her further than a lie, she thought. "We live on the other side of the Grim Sister and her trail led me to this town."

"Ah, say no more! A young girl, seeking adventure in the big city, no doubt? Following the dreams that lead as far from home as possible?" Abrik chuckled, to Miriat's relief. She nodded, allowing him to fill the gaps in her story. Estancia brought in two steaming bowls of stew. They were clearly in the habit of eating their food wherever they wished, rather than at the table and Miriat found she enjoyed their easy manner. She accepted the food gratefully. She furrowed her eyebrows, thinking on Salka and whether she had found a shelter that night.

"Don't you worry about your girl. Children are resourceful buggers." Abrik looked wistfully at the flames, leaning back in his chair. "I remember when I was a young man, so full of life and a desire to see anywhere that wasn't here, and to reach anything that wasn't 'now'."

"And do you find much trade in the mountains? I haven't heard of any painters making a living in these parts," Miriat said, eager to change the subject.

"Well, I won't lie, it's not an easy life. Still, I find a way to keep us comfortable enough. A small job here and there pays for the fine vittles Stancy treated us to this night," he said, emptying his pipe into the fire. "I suppose you better be getting some rest. There is a bench over there in the corner." He pointed. "I wager a good deal more comfortable than whatever you had planned for the night."

Estancia brought another blanket for Miriat, and bowed stiffly when thanked.

As her hosts retired upstairs, Miriat lay down on the hard bench. She knew she needed to sleep but couldn't help but think about Salka.

It would be a smart move to go through town. No striga pursuit could follow her here. But what if she misunderstood Dola? What if there was no message meant for her and she was just following her own wishful thinking? Miriat turned to face the wall and listened to the sounds of rain and thunder outside until sleep came.

# CHAPTER 35

The last of the striga search parties came in through the gates, drenched and covered in dirt, as the rain was battering their heads. Alma stood ankle-deep in mud watching them return. She pursed her lips when Emila shook her head silently – the last one through. The mood in the village was solemn. Though none of them relished the thought of punishing Salka, they would now likely have to face worse themselves.

"Don't celebrate," Alma said to her son as he smiled from the shadows of their doorframe, hiding from the rain. "She will be killed as soon as the humans see her. There is no safety for stigois outside these walls."

Dran only moved his head in a way that could mean both yes and no. He felt someone's eyes on him and turned to face Kalina, standing alone, watching him. She cut a sad figure that day, her hair unbrushed and her clothing hanging shapelessly on her, devoid of the small vanities she usually adorned it with. Dran rolled his eyes and walked back into the house without a word.

# CHAPTER 36

"It's fascinating..." Maladia said. She was watching Salka's shadow as Salka went about preparing a modest meal. Dola had no appetite and was lying on her side facing the wall. "What can you make it do?"

Salka looked at her surprised. She hovered her hand above the hot stove to check it was hot enough. Dola had a proper clay stove, the first Salka had ever seen, and she enjoyed preparing some flatbreads on a heated flat stone, once Maladia had shown her how to work it.

"What do you mean?" Salka said, though she knew perfectly well what Maladia meant. She still found talking about her stigoi awkward, as if voicing all she felt would finally bring upon her some dreadful punishment.

"Can you make it do things? Markus couldn't, not quite," Maladia said. She was leaning against the table, her hands propping up her head.

"Shouldn't you be resting?" Salka asked. She placed another bread on the stone and smiled as its creamy brown surface began to bubble in places. "I'll be done in a moment."

"Come now, you don't have to be shy with me, you know," Maladia laughed. She wagged her finger at Salka. "We're both outcasts now, you and I. The least we can do is embrace it."

"It's not so easy." The smell of the bread made Salka's stomach rumble. She looked out of the window at the wet forest. The chickens were squawking loudly at a distant thunder. Salka peeled the bread off the stone with a flat piece of wood and placed it on a plate made of real tin. She traced its outline with her finger. The wealth of the Dolas seemed to know no bounds.

"It's not supposed to be easy." Maladia shrugged her shoulders. "Do you know why Markus followed his other heart?" She raised her hand as Salka nodded. "It wasn't because of the accident. I was going to heal myself. For the sake of a baby I didn't seem able to carry. He caught me practicing. Made me promise I wouldn't do it anymore if he learnt how to instead. His revulsion was great, but he did it for me. He thought he was polluting himself for my sake." She leaned back in her seat and hugged herself, as if suddenly cold. Her shadow crept up over her shoulders, for warmth or comfort, Salka couldn't tell. Both, probably.

"Was it hard for him?" she asked. She put the final piece of bread on the plate and brought it to the table, sitting herself opposite Maladia.

"In a manner of speaking." Maladia shrugged her shoulders. "It took time and practice. He was like that with everything, Markus. Slow and steady." She smiled at some memory and stayed silent for a while.

Salka sighed and put her hands palm up on the table. She was surprised how easy it was, to reach into that place inside herself and let go. Her stigoi's hands rose from within her own palms, picked up the plate of bread and held it in front of Maladia's face.

Maladia chuckled. "That's little more than a trick. What else can you do?"

Salka cocked her head to the side. "Anything more and I'd need to feed it from somewhere. Why not try this yourself if you think it so easy?" She half expected Maladia to say no, but instead, the woman placed her hands on the table with their fingers wide apart and stared intently at the plate. Her shadow rose behind her, but its tendrils withered and broke before they reached the bread. Maladia groaned with frustration.

Salka couldn't help but laugh. "It takes practice. Not to worry, just starve in the mountains for three months and you'll catch up." She thought for a moment. "How long did it take Markus? Before he could heal you?"

Maladia took a sharp breath and fell silent.

"I'm sorry, we don't have to speak of it..." Salka said.

Maladia shook her head. "No. It's fine. In any case it was hard for him, but not how you might think. He hated his shadow. He starved it when he could, and near sickened himself in the attempt. He was ashamed of it. Until my child quickened inside me thanks to him. After that, the shame was gone. Still, he never meant to use it again. And he wouldn't have, if I hadn't broken my leg..." Maladia winced.

Salka reached out and put her hand to Maladia's elbow. "It wasn't your fault."

Maladia shook her off. "Of course it wasn't. It wasn't even Kalina's fault. *Or* Alma's. They thought he was a monster. As he did himself, in a way. But I never saw a monster. And believe me, I looked." She wiped a tear quickly with her sleeve. Salka looked away, pretending not to notice.

There was a moment of silence between them.

"What happened to him?" Salka asked finally.

Maladia stared at her for a moment. And then she told her.


"Do you disbelieve us, love?" Dola rubbed Salka's back, as the younger woman struggled to compose her breathing. "I know you and Dran... You were friends."

Salka shook her head. "No, it's..." She looked up at Maladia, a plaintive look in her face. "I'm sure it was an accident. I've seen Dran angry, he doesn't control it. But he's not cruel, I'm sure of it." She thought of how he held her after Munu's death, the comfort he offered. "He didn't mean to..." She was silenced by a look in Maladia's eyes.

"And do you think it matters? You think it matters to me, whether or not he *meant* to kill my man and orphan my child? I woke up to see Markus, my beautiful, kind Markus, reduced to a smoldering corpse. I don't care *why* Dran did it. The greedy little shit was stupid at the very least, and that cost us. And did he pay for his crime?" Maladia scoffed, turning to the wall. "No, of course not. Not Alma's precious baby, not the future leader of the Heyne strigas."

"I wouldn't be so certain of that..." Salka said, thinking of Dran's shaking hands and the tendrils of sickness spreading across his body.

# CHAPTER 37

A rough shove snapped Miriat awake.

"Well, look here, it wakes!"

She turned her sleep-bleary eyes towards the voice. Five men and women stood over her, with Estancia in the back, her lips pursed and her arms crossed. Abrik sat in his chair, his fingers drumming the side of the armrest.

Miriat sat up and looked at the faces of the people gathered. They were older, but she recognized each and every one. Her heart sank. "Aurek?"

A hand slapped her across the face. "It talks! But we know it shouldn't talk, should it? Strigas have no call to talk to decent folk. Now, we heard your little spawn ran off, didn't it? Don't worry, if it passes by, we'll be sure to give it a proper Heyne welcome." Aurek screwed up his face in anger. "You had your chance to run. You should've taken it." A hand on his shoulder made him pause.

"Aurek, don't give way to anger. Miriat will have to face her punishment soon enough."

Aurek snapped back, "She thought herself so special, so much better than us, to leave? Not so superior now, your majesty?" He pulled up Miriat by her shirt and pushed her against the wall as if she were no heavier than a rag doll. He stood looming over her, his face inches from hers. "No, no need, Tomlin." He raised his hand as the other man moved to pull him away. "I know the rules, same as anyone. Rope."

A mousy woman standing next to him, her face nearly covered with blond hair, silently passed him the rope without looking up. Miriat's heart skipped a beat. "Annie?"

The girl didn't look up. She stepped behind Tomlin, as Aurek roughly tied the rope around Miriat's wrists.

Miriat looked at Estancia, who stood with her face turned away. "Have I harmed you in some way that you would betray me? Did I ask to stay at your house? You brought me here, broke bread with me!"

"Don't blame her, love." Abrik filled his pipe. "She wasn't the one to call the hounds on you."

Miriat looked at him in shock.

"Bless you, girl, your eyes are as round as the moon right now. Don't be so surprised." He smiled amiably. "Poetry feeds the soul, but the coin the townsfolk pay to any who might capture errant strigas feeds the belly. There's been some thefts, I understand. Well, one man's loss is another man's opportunity, I always say. I could tell you were a woman out of place, soon as I laid eyes on you, child." He bowed his head solemnly and smiled, as if Miriat was a friendly neighbor come to lend him a cup of sugar.

Estancia shot Miriat an apologetic look.

Aurek pushed Miriat ahead of him, and they left the house, walking into the still-pouring rain.

They threw her inside the shop's cellar, on account of it being the only one with a lock on the outside. Miriat tried to struggle, but without much conviction. They had her now, and they were not going to let her run again. The last thing she saw before they locked the door was Aurek's face and it made her momentarily glad he was on the other side of the barred door.

She looked around her small prison and tears came unbidden to her eyes. There was an understanding that leaving Heyne Town for the striga village was a one-time offer only.

Miriat put her forehead against the cold wall. The cellar was meant to keep the food from spoiling and a chill ran up her back, as the precious warmth was already leaving her bones. Raised voices above made her creep up the narrow stair and put her ear to the door.

"Let me see her, Aurek!" There was a growl at the back of the voice, so familiar it made her heart pound.

"You know I can't do that."

"Why the hell not? You think I will carry her off? Or that she'll disappear in a puff of smoke?"

"Well, I have no reason to think that's your *plan*, seeing as you didn't go with her when you had your chance..." Aurek's voice was loaded with malice. "But we have no idea what powers she's picked up from the strigas. A stigoi's powers of persuasion can be rather impressive, so I hear."

"She's not a stigoi, you idiot! You can't catch it like a cold! All I want is talk to her, man. What if it were Kristin in her place?"

"Don't you wipe your mouth with her name! Kristin was a good woman! She did what your bitch should have, and didn't have the guts to!"

"Drowning herself and your baby in a well is not the work of a good woman; a mad one, maybe!" A loud crack and a grunt followed, with what sounded like a body landing heavily against the store's well-stocked shelves.

"Go."

"I'm sorry, Aurek, I shouldn't have–"

"Go!"

Miriat heard a slow sound of footsteps and the slamming of the door. She leaned her back against the cellar door and put her hand to her mouth, stifling a sob. Outside she heard a chair dragged across the floor towards the cellar. Somebody, presumably Aurek, sat in it heavily.

"You heard that, didn't you?" Aurek's voice came through the door.

"Yes." She didn't know what else to say. Would he be angered by her sympathy?

"Don't you be getting your hopes up that he'll come to your rescue now," Aurek said in a measured voice, his anger suppressed to a low rumble that threatened to escape at any moment.

"I don't. I didn't," she said. She paused. "I'm sorry about Kristin. She was always kind."

There was a moment of silence. So long that Miriat wondered if Aurek heard her at all.

"So she was," he said. "She was too good to unleash the monster she bore onto the world. And too gentle to let it die alone."

"They're not monsters…"

"I bet you think that. Much like a wolf thinks its fangs kind." Aurek gave a mirthless chuckle.

"Aurek… We used to be friends once."

"No," Aurek said. "I was friends with a decent girl, a dutiful daughter. And she's gone. Did you even ask after your ma? Did you even care how she died? Alone, leaning on the kindness of strangers."

Miriat closed her eyes, but that didn't stop tears from falling.

"See, I was never friends with you. I don't know you. Don't act like you know me." Aurek spat loudly and leaned against the back of the chair until the wood groaned under his weight.

# CHAPTER 38

"Salka, wake up!" Maladia shook Salka awake. The rain outside showed no signs of letting up. "It's time! You must go fetch a midwife. She lives half a mile up north. Hurry, Dola's not doing well!"

"Wait, who's not well?" Salka asked, still confused from her sleep.

"Dola. She's running a temperature and has barely moved since the birthing began. Go!" Maladia ushered Salka to the door, throwing her cloak at her. She periodically stopped and leaned against the wall, panting heavily.

"Are *you* all right?" Salka asked, confused.

"Of course not, you idiot, I'm about to drop this baby! Go!" Maladia said, screwing up her face with effort. "Half a mile north as the crow flies." Maladia saw Salka's conflicted face and pointed. "Go!"

Salka needed no further urging. She pulled on her shoes and ran outside. The rain and the wind battered her face and she looked up fearfully at the pines which swayed with loud cracking noise, threatening to fall and crush her at any moment. She walked as fast as she could but the mud and water pouring down the mountain made it hard to find good footing. All the while her stigoi moved effortlessly beside her, skipping and jumping as if she was running across a summer meadow.

"Good grace and omens, you're annoying," Salka said under her breath. The stigoi cocked her head to the side and reached out with her hand. Salka stopped for a moment and eyed it suspiciously. She reached out with her own hand and touched the shadowy fingers.

The world exploded in color. Without as much as a thought, Salka took half a step to the right, narrowly avoiding being hit by a falling branch. She took a deep breath and the water pouring down her face felt warm. She smiled and took another step, guided by the stigoi. She heard the whispers of the forest and felt the soil's warm surface, felt it give way and soften with the rain. She felt where the ground was firm and where it had become like gruel. Salka smiled and, holding her stigoi's hand, she ran.

She found the other Dola's house with little effort, but the smile on her face faded when she saw no smoke coming from the chimney. She came up to the door and knocked loudly, but she knew even then that the house was empty. She pushed the door open and called out.

No answer.

She walked back as quickly as she could and prayed that the midwife had somehow known she was needed.

She heard Dola and Maladia's screams before she saw their house. Her heart sank and she rushed in.

"Where is she?" Maladia turned to the door, her eyes wide and her stigoi standing beside her, cradling her head against her shadowy chest. Salka was shocked to see it so clearly, though it was not as solid as her own.

"She wasn't in the house. I'm sorry… It's just us…" Salka looked at the floor. She never felt so useless.

"Snap out of it, girl! We need you!" Maladia said through gritted teeth before her words turned into a long moan.

Salka stumbled forward. She looked back at her stigoi which had pushed her lightly and now stood with its arms crossed.

"Right." She picked up the kettle and put it on the fire which she was faintly aware was something one would do at a birthing, though she wasn't quite sure as to what one might do with the water once it boiled.

She walked over to Dola and Maladia who were both kneeling on either side of the same narrow bed. Maladia held Dola's hands and stared at her intently. Dola's face was pale and her breathing shallow.

When Salka approached them, Maladia grabbed her hand. "Listen!" she demanded.

Salka's stigoi put her shadowy hands on her shoulders. Salka closed her eyes and listened. She heard the sharp breaths of Maladia and Dola, the rain hitting the roof. She heard the creaky complaint of the old wooden walls of Dola's house and the whistling of the wind as it sought a way through the cracks in the door. Suddenly she opened her eyes wide. "Dola's heart! The baby's heart! Something's wrong, it's too fast!" she said, color draining from her face.

"Salka?" Dola whispered. Her eyes were unfocused, as if she couldn't quite recognize the woman in front of her. "Come. Here," she said with effort.

Salka came to her side and kneeled on the floor next to her. "How can I help? I don't know what to do…"

Dola's body went rigid, only to relax after a moment. A groan escaped her lips. "Cut it out," she said. "It's why you're here. Do it."

Salka recoiled. "I can't! I don't know how to! It'll kill you!"

"I'm dead if you don't," Dola said with effort. She reached out, but instead of holding Salka's hand she reached for her stigoi. And Salka understood what she was meant to do. She watched Dola for a moment, and pursed her lips. She nodded.

She walked up to the kitchen and, with a shaky hand, picked up a knife and a whetstone. With a slow, deliberate movement, she ran the blade alongside it. She took off her leather belt and ran the blade along that too, until it was so sharp it could cut a breath in two. She put the blade in a bowl and poured boiling water over it, breathing a half-forgotten, but earnestly meant prayer. All the while, her stigoi stood by her side, watching. Salka put the knife on a clean folded cloth and brought it onto the bed.

Dola reached out with a shaking finger to point at a small basket in the corner. Inside it, Salka found a needle and thread.

She threaded the needle and placed it on the cloth by the knife. She knelt by Dola's side. Dola's face was covered in sweat, and the long strands of her brown hair were stuck to her forehead.

"Can you lie down on the bed?" Salka asked.

Dola didn't respond, but, with effort, she lifted herself up and sat on the sweat-soaked mattress. In that moment, Maladia screamed in pain and grabbed Dola's hand. They locked eyes, breathing heavily, and so they remained, as Salka put her leather belt between Dola's teeth to bite down on.

She lifted Dola's nightshirt and raised the knife.

"Steady now," Maladia said, without taking her eyes off Dola, and Salka wasn't sure whether the young striga was talking to her or herself.

Dola lifted her finger and with it drew a line on her stomach where the cut should be. Salka put the knife to the quickly fading line made by Dola's fingernail and pressed. The sharp blade went in easily, followed by a trickle of blood. Salka's stigoi hovered over the two of them and descended on Dola, both embracing her and keeping her still. Salka bit her lip so hard her teeth broke the skin, as she forced herself to pull the knife horizontally across Dola's skin.

Dola's eyes widened and she groaned, but the stigoi kept her from thrashing about.

A hard ball rose in Salka's throat and her eyes watered as she pushed the knife through layers of fat and muscle till the pale whitish pink of the womb was revealed. She glanced at Maladia, but the older striga was now entirely engrossed in her own labor as she shifted to a crouching position and panted. Salka took a deep breath and cut.

The baby boy came out pale and quiet. Salka pulled him out and put him on Dola's chest. Even though he was tiny, no bigger than Salka's forearm, the woman was too weak to hold him, and he began sliding down as her arm fell limp to her side. Salka's stigoi was there in an instant, gently supporting the child, and bringing him back to Dola's breast.

A loud groan and a crashing sound came from the other side of the bed, where Maladia was on her knees, her face hidden in her folded arms.

Salka's hands shook as she removed the afterbirth and picked up a needle to sew the wound shut. A gasp from Maladia and a weak cry came from across the bed. Salka looked up to see Maladia holding her child to her chest. Their eyes met and Salka thought a smile, but it had no time to come to her lips. She began sewing up the wound, stitch by stitch.

"Salka!" Maladia called out. "Look!" Her eyes went wide with horror.

Dola's body convulsed, her eyes rolling back in her head. Salka's stigoi caught the baby before it rolled on the floor and placed it gently in Maladia's arms.

"Help her!" Maladia screamed, holding both the babies. She suddenly looked at Dola's child's face and her face twisted in horror. "Salka, it's not moving! Dola's baby's barely breathing! Help it!"

"I don't know how!" Salka struggled to keep Dola down. "You can do it. Markus must have showed you."

"I can't, Salka, I'd kill them if I tried it. My stigoi's not as strong as yours, and I'm spent after the birth. Why do you think you're here in the first place–" Maladia suddenly stopped, her face white.

Salka looked from Maladia to Dola and was struck by a sudden realization. "You knew about the Windry Pass... The potion..." Her expression hardened. "It's no matter. There will be time to explain later. Which you *will* do."

Salka placed her hand on Dola's chest. Her stigoi followed suit. Her eyes glistened wet in the half-light of the room. The blazing fire in the chimney went out like a blown-out candle and Dola's seizures stopped, her body soothed under the stigoi's dark hands.

"Put the baby on her chest," Salka ordered. She then placed her other hand on the baby's bluish skin. The stigoi behind her grew until the entire room was darkness. The air cooled rapidly. Maladia scrambled for a quilt, which she wrapped around herself and her newborn. Frost patterns formed on the windows, flowery forests climbed up the glass and spread to the walls as the rain kept battering the house.

"I can't..." Salka stood rigid, icicles forming on her lashes as her tears fell down. "The stigoi wants more... I'm scared it will take you to save Dola. I have nothing else I can take; I need to balance it."

Salka's hands grew cold and claw-like, while the bodies of her patients glowed in the darkness. A loud crack and a rumble shook the house as a lightning struck a pine somewhere close.

*Yes!* Salka beamed and looked up, her sight moving past the darkness of the room, past the roof and the canopy of the trees. Soft tendrils erupted from her stigoi and travelled high until at last, they found what they needed.

A hot red light filled the room, the electricity filling the air. Salka's curly hair escaped from under her scarf and surrounded her head like a lion's mane, each dark curl incandescent. Her skin began to glow, as the energy flowed through her. It was fast, much too fast. She had to redirect and shape it, rebuilding and mending.

Salka screamed.

And then it was over. Darkness once more filled the room. Not the darkness of a stigoi, but of a night in the Heyne Mountains. A once more familiar darkness that now enveloped them in comfort.

"Dola? Are you well? Speak to me!" Maladia crawled to the bed and grappled for her friend's hand in the darkness.

"I suppose I am," Dola said, as she reached out and squeezed Maladia's hand in turn. "And so is he," she said with a smile, even though tears were falling down her cheeks. Maladia put a finger inside the boy's hand and was rewarded with a little squeeze.

"And your little one?" Dola asked, her arm already outstretched to welcome Maladia's child.

"She's well. Strong." Maladia looked thoughtful, as she stroked the hair on her baby's head. Suddenly she straightened up. "Salka! Salka, where are you?" She crawled towards the dark shape, laying motionless on the floor. "Oh gods, Salka, what happened to you? Child, I'm so sorry!"

Maladia scooped up Salka in her arms as she slowly opened her eyes. Salka's lips felt parched and a searing pain ran through her back. Her clothes were gone, reduced to ashes. She winced as feeling returned to her hands. The skin on her palms was red and raw, layers of it burnt off by the lightning she wielded just moments ago. Raised welts snaked up her arms, like branches devoid of their leaves.

"Did you see it? Did you see what I did?" Salka asked, her voice sounding strange and raspy to her ears.

Maladia smiled through tears. "I did. You were magnificent, Salka. You were everything you were meant to be."

Salka smiled in return before her eyes rolled back and she passed out.

# CHAPTER 39

Alma stood in the rain, knee-deep in water, directing the panic-stricken strigas, as the rivers of mud flowed through their village. Her oiled leather coat gave some protection from the water, though the wind had blown the hood off her head. Her grey hair lashed around her face: a nest of snakes, biting and writhing.

They were evacuating, scrambling to gather their most treasured possessions. The snowmelt came fast, with the torrential storms hurrying on the flood that now threatened to carry away the entire village. Ropes were used to tie the livestock together to stop them being washed away.

"Lesny, what news?" Alma called out across the square. Lesny, drenched to the bone, waded through the ice-cold water until he stood face to face with his leader.

"The western path is flooded. The water was so fast it nearly took me with it. There is no way north either. I don't know the state of the Windry Pass, but the path towards it is blocked. An avalanche must have fallen once the caps shifted. It won't melt fast enough for us to go through."

"Don't wish for that, foolish boy!" Alma snapped at him. "If it melts too quickly, it will carry all of our homes with it. Never mind that. We'd never manage to get all across the bridge, not in this weather. The south is a cliff, the ways north and west are blocked. That leaves us with one route only." She strode off towards the center of the village and put an old horn to her lips. Its note rang over the caving roofs of the striga homes, mostly lost among the noise of the storm. "Strigas! We must march east! Gather your belongings! Keep your livestock close and your children closer. I will speak to the Dola elders. They will intercede on our behalf to beg a safe passage through Heyne Town." She held onto the pole for support, as a wooden crate floated past her. The water was now up to her waist. Her shadow enveloped her like a cloak. She shrugged it off impatiently the moment she felt its warmth.

"Lead the way, Alma!" Tolan called back, leaning on Rida. His head was wrapped in a dirty bandage, now threatening to slip down his face. Rida had a determined expression on her face as she pushed Emila forward. Like many villagers, the family had tied a long rope around each other's waists, binding them together. If one fell, they'd either be saved or their families would perish with them. It was the striga way. Alma nodded her approval.

She waded through to her house, where Dran stood shivering, his face drained of color, carrying a small pack on his back. Alma tied a rope to his waist and tied the other end under her arms. She had little hope to hold her son back, were he to be swept away, but wanted no hope for herself at all, were he to be lost.

She put her hand gently to Dran's cheek. "It's time, my love. You must make an effort." He nodded. The same determination she had always been so proud of shone through his dark eyes. "Here," she said. "Put this blanket over you. Wool will help keep you warm, even when wet." She held out her arm, and was half-surprised Dran took it. The old woman led her son through the gates of their home.

The strigas walked through the open gate. Most of the houses had been destroyed by the quick-flowing water, with pieces of wooden debris floating dangerously around the villagers. The terrified livestock added to the noise of the storm and the collapsing houses. The way through the forest was muddy, but it had been spared the worst of the flooding. Still, the path was treacherous, with some parts of the route washed away by the torrential rain.

A young child in her father's arms cried from the cold, and her shadow rose up to envelop her shoulders. Kalina looked up at it and opened her mouth as if to say something, but then just drew her coat closer over her own hunched shoulders. Alma noticed and narrowed her eyes. She walked up to the father carrying his child and exchanged a few tense words. The child turned her face away, but the shadow once more lifted itself from her back, exposing it to the elements.

They had been walking for three hours by the time they arrived at the clearing with the boulders marking the path towards the Dola houses, scattered as they were. The meadow was now only ankle-deep in water, making it the driest spot the strigas had seen since the day before.

The exhausted villagers did what they could to find a comfortable spot to await their leader's return, as Alma began the trek up the hill.

"No, Dran, you must stay," she said. She was mindful of Dran wanting to keep his feebleness a secret, but she was also exhausted from the long walk.

Dran objected weakly. She felt a lump in her throat as his eyes gleamed feverishly.

"I'll be back soon," she said, pushing a strand of wet hair off his face. He was too tired to bat her hand away. "Find shelter if you can." She turned towards the strigas. "If I'm not back before sundown, you must head towards the village on your own. Niev, you come with me," she said to a young striga with red curly hair.

"Go, son. Be safe." Niev's father struggled to smile and put his hand on his son's shoulder. "I'll be waiting with your mother, don't you worry." Niev nodded and walked behind Alma. Alma's body was used to hard work and she climbed with as much ease as the muddy path permitted.

"I've never been to a Dola house before," Niev said. He was clearly tired, but too proud to allow an old woman to outpace him. "Do they live much like us?"

"Their houses are richer, though they lack our community," Alma said. She disliked what she considered to be idle conversation, and pressed on, leaving Niev scrambling to keep up with her.

They reached Dola's house and Alma knocked on the door. She was welcomed by silence, though there was smoke coming from the chimney. She tried to peer through the windows, but they were dark, as if someone had painted them over with ash.

"It's Alma. Are you well? I'm here to solicit the help of your tribe." Alma paused and then added, "Please!" The word tasted odd on her lips.

After a long pause, the door shifted, and Dola's round face appeared.

"May we come in?" Alma asked, since Dola was blocking the entry.

Dola, her eyes bloodshot, didn't budge. "What is it you need?"

Alma bristled, and struggled to keep her voice level. "I need the help of your tribe, and your house is the closest to our village. We've been flooded, our houses destroyed. We need to cross the Heyne Town to escape the deluge, and we will need a Dola with us to make sure the humans don't attack us."

A gasp of horror, and Maladia stood by Dola's side. "Is my mama all right?" she asked, ignoring the wide-eyed shock from Alma and Niev.

"Maladia?" Alma looked from Dola to Maladia as if trying to understand what just happened.

"Maladia! You're well! Your ma's just fine, and she'll be so glad to know–" Niev caught Alma's eye and took a step back, shooting Maladia an apologetic look.

"I must say I never expected to see *you* again, child, much less in a house belonging to one of the Dolas," Alma said. She looked at Dola. "Do your elders know you're harboring a banished striga in your own home? Is Markus there as well?" She moved as if to push past them, but Maladia and Dola linked arms and stood in her way.

"Markus is not here," a weak voice came from inside the house. "But I'm sure you know that already."

Alma blanched and pushed past Dola. She looked around in

shock, noting the room's scorched walls. Her eyes then fell on the small figure in the rocking chair by the fire, cradling two babies in her arms. Alma stared at her for a moment without recognition. Salka sat very still, her skin pink and puffy, as if she'd slept too long in the sun. She kept her raw hands, palm outwards, on her lap, as if she were offering a gift. Quick as a whip, Alma turned to the door. "Niev! Come in here boy. We seem to have found our runaway."

Niev didn't move. "What did she mean? That thing she said of Markus?"

Alma shivered. She didn't want to hear what they had to say, she didn't need to hear it. There was work to be done and her village to save. Everything else could wait.

"Fine. The stigoi is a problem for another time. We need your help, woman. For the truce to hold we need the Dolas."

"What happened to Markus?" Niev asked again. His young face was drawn.

"Yes, Alma, don't you want to know?" Maladia said, her eyes dark. Dola put her hand on her friend's shoulder.

Alma straightened herself, "I don't know what you're talking about. You two were banished. What happened after was no business of mine or of any other decent striga's, for that matter." She sent Niev a look meant to chasten him. "Dola, there is a bond between our people. I ask you now to honor it." Dola's unsmiling face remained impassive. *She's really rather plain, after all.* Alma thought. How different she seemed when all friendship was gone from Dola's expression.

"You're the voice of justice for the strigas, Alma. Don't you want to hear what Maladia has to say?" Dola said.

*No, no I don't.* Alma felt her hands shaking, though the room was warm. She tucked her thumbs behind her belt to steady her hands against her body.

"If a crime has been committed it is my duty to hear it." The words came, the right words. She wanted to push them back down her own throat.

She saw Maladia's lips move. They moved for what seemed a long time, though she couldn't hear a word. Her ears were ringing, and her two hearts were beating too loud in her chest. She knew, of course. She knew ever since Dran came back with the burn on his leg. She knew every day since, as he sickened, poisoned by his second heart. She knew from how his hands shook and by his furtive, guilty look. She knew it all, and now everyone else would know as well. She could tell by Niev's expression, how it would go. She thought of Dran's smile, his dark eyes. So quiet, ever since he was a baby. He came to her late, her body near past the hope of a child. His dimpled hands closing around her finger, his satisfied little grunts as he fed.

She turned to Salka. "And you believe it?" The girl wouldn't believe that of her friend, and if she trusted in Dran then perhaps Alma was wrong herself. Perhaps Salka's faith and love could carry them both.

Salka's silent stare was answer enough.

"Niev. We will get no help here," she said. Alma was so weary. But her village was waiting. Her people trusted in her. She turned around and left Dola's house.

Dola nodded to Niev: "The West Stream Dola lives with her daughter not far from here. They are both known and respected in Heyne Town. They will help the strigas if they can. Go up the hill and then cross the stream at the two boulders. Good luck." And then she shut the door in Niev's face.

He nodded slightly, as if coming to a decision, and with barely a look at his leader he began north.

Alma followed him in silence for a while. She needed her breath to scale the steep hill in any case. They had no time to look for an easier ascent, they both knew it. But the truth hung heavily between them.

The path to the elder's house was washed away by the storm, and they had to rely on tree roots and trunks to pull themselves upwards each step of the way. Alma was tough, but her age was catching up with her. She leaned against a pine and closed her eyes for a moment, trying to catch her breath. The rain showed no signs of letting up, and the wind swayed the pines dangerously above their heads. If a tree or a branch were to fall on their heads, there would be no warning, only a quick death. She took a breath and once more pulled herself upwards as Niev stayed a little above her, watching her intently. He was always a chatty boy, with a story and a smile for everyone. Now he looked at her sullenly, as if she hadn't been present at his birth, as if she wasn't his leader, the only leader he had ever known.

She leaned against a tree again to steady herself. She caught Niev's eye. "They lied!" she said abruptly through gritted teeth, though the words rang false, even to her own ears.

"I suppose we will find out during the trial," he said, then turned away from her and continued up the hill.

Alma clutched her chest, suddenly colder than the rain pouring down her back. Dran would be tried. *She* would have to try him. And she would have to admit to the village that he had left the house on the night of Markus' banishment. That the burn on his leg appeared the same night. Her face twisted in despair. She followed Niev, until they came to the top of the cliff. To their left, where a traveler would normally find a welcome brook, torrential water poured down the mountainside.

"Be careful!" Niev said, reaching out to steady Alma, who tripped and almost fell.

She took a deep breath. "The house we need to go to is on the other side of this. There are ropes tied to the trees on either side, with an elevated bridge, but it will not be an easy pass." She pointed at what was little more than long tree planks, roughly planed, thrown across the water and resting on two large boulders. Above the makeshift bridge a rope was stretched taut at waist height for added security.

"Madness!" Niev said. "If we fall in the water, we're done for."

Alma looked at him steadily. "And if we fail, so are our people. Move."

Niev climbed on top of the boulder. He reached down and pulled Alma up.

"I will go first," Alma said, looking into the water swirling below them. "I am still your leader. I will lead while I can." Niev had the decency to look embarrassed, she noticed with some satisfaction. She then stepped onto the planks, holding tight onto the rope. It was far more difficult than she reckoned, and a couple of times she slipped and nearly fell into the water. She inched forward, barely daring to take a breath, as the wind pushed and pulled at her.

She finally reached the other side, climbing onto the boulder on her knees. She looked up with relief and then signaled for Niev to cross.

He walked slowly, holding on to the support rope with both arms, relying on it too much, swinging dangerously from side to side.

There was fear in the young man's eyes, and he bit his lip in concentration. Alma watched his excruciatingly slow progress, half hoping he would slip into the water.

He would tell the others about her son. She was sure he would. Chances were the strigas wouldn't even wait for a trial. They'd kill Dran there and then or leave him in the flooded woods, which would amount to the same thing. They wouldn't care about his guilt or innocence. They would not bother with justice. He would be punished, not just for what he might have done, but for their pain and fear of losing the only home most of them had ever known.

Niev slipped and Alma found herself holding her breath, willing him to fall. He lurched forward and found his footing again. Alma looked up and thought of Dran. Her beautiful son would never have been able to cross such a bridge. The life they led was hard, yet he never complained. She admired his courage and his strength, just as she loved him for his fragility. She closed her eyes. She understood how deep his desire for a healthy body ran. How could she blame him for trying to fight for it?

And yet, he strove to obey their laws, by not polluting himself with his powers. If he'd turned himself into a stigoi, he could have healed his flesh. But her son would never have debased himself in such a way.

And in the end what did he actually do? He asked Markus for help. Barely a thought's work for one already on the dark path, as Markus was. And what did the stigoi do? Maladia said herself, he turned Dran down. For spite, he would not heal her boy, not out of principle.

His death was an accident, Alma had no doubt of that. But the strigas would not care. They'd burn Dran from the inside, erasing all that made him whole.

She looked at Niev, and her hearts beat faster. The young man was now halfway across the bridge.

Evening was fast approaching, and the strigas would soon be on the move. There was little chance of them reaching another Dola homestead in time. She looked at the sky and pulled the hood off her head. The rain fell on her face and every drop strengthened her resolve. She exhaled and relaxed her shoulders. It felt so easy. Like shedding a weight you didn't know you were carrying. Creeping in from underneath her, her shadow rose up.

Its tendrils travelled down the bridge, beneath the planks, twisting and curving around the knots and the bits of rough wood. She felt every splinter, every crevice, as if she were running her fingers along it. A smile came upon her face. At the same time, a piercing shriek echoed across the mountains. Niev, pulled by Alma's stigoi, tumbled into the water.

She watched him impassively as he tried to swim to the bank, pieces of rock and floating branches cutting his arms as he sought for a handhold. The rush of the water pulled him under, again and again, until he was out of sight.

Alma stood there, watching for a while, luxuriating in the warmth and the comfort of her stigoi enveloping her shoulders. She felt no regret. Why should she, when Niev would have condemned Dran without a second thought? But there was more work to be done.

At the moment, the course of the river ran safely around the house where Dola harbored Maladia and Salka.

But was that entirely fair?

Was it fair for the traitors and the fugitives to warm their bones by the fire, while the law-abiding strigas faced danger and death in the town below? For Maladia to be safe, while she plotted Dran's downfall? Alma's face twisted with anger. Her eyes darkened as the years of resentment and pain and self-restraint were released in the dark wave beneath her. It grew and swelled until it enveloped the trees and the boulders around her, tearing and pulling. She closed her eyes, the release after so many years of denying herself was almost too much to bear.

She heard the tree roots groan as they were ripped from the ground and the splash of water, as one by one they fell in, and the boulders rolled. She reached out with her stigoi, and felt the water, its cold, slick surface, running, racing, finding the pathways through the forest as the river's course changed. It turned and twisted and jumped and rolled, as it found the way she meant for it.

Only one more boulder, that's all that was needed. Only one more and the river would go where she willed it to. Only one more, and Dran would be safe. She looked up and smiled, when the boulder she stood on shifted and rolled into the cold water.

She kept her eyes open, as the freezing waters closed above her head. She gasped at the cold and the water filled her mouth, pushing out bubbles of air. Her lungs hurt and she kicked at the water, even as her heavy cloak weighed her down. Her other heart beat hard in her chest, and she reached with her shadow out of the water, giving it the remaining energy of her lean body. The black tendrils shot out, her striga heart fighting for life, even as her human one had given up. But for years she had starved her other heart, kept it quiet, kept it small, kept it hungry. She had used the what strength she had to wreak her destruction and now there was none left to pull her out. The shadow thrashed and swirled in the water for a while longer, but soon it too faded and was gone under the current.

# CHAPTER 40

Salka rocked in the chair. She wore only a thin nightgown, too big and too long for her, making her look like a small child within its folds. But she didn't feel the cold. Maladia and Dola were both sitting on the bed, nursing their babies. Maladia, not having benefitted from Salka's healing, was trying to rest her eyes, with her daughter cradled in her arms.

"So," Dola said. "I expect you have questions."

"Do I?" Salka asked. She stared ahead with her back as straight as a bow-string.

"You saved me and my child, Salka. And I know it cost you." Dola looked down at her baby's face. She wrapped the blanket closer around him.

"Did you know?" Salka asked. Her hands rested in her lap. Her stigoi lay curled at her feet like a dog.

"Yes," Dola said. "I knew I would need you."

"One of your visions, I suppose?" Salka smiled bitterly.

"I didn't need a vision to know this pregnancy was going to kill me unless I sought help." Dola looked to the wall. Maladia reached out and squeezed Dola's hand.

"There isn't much money in visions, Salka. We're all midwives first." Dola looked weary. "But no midwife alive could help what ailed me."

"When did you decide it had to be me?" Salka asked.

"When you came back from the town. A blind man could see

the change in you. And, well, I'm no man, and no Dola can afford to be blind." Dola sighed. "I'm sorry I used you."

"I understand," Salka said. "I would have done the same." They sat still for a while.

"And Dran?" Salka began, but the words choked her. She thought of his smiling face. She put her fingertips to her lips. When Maladia told her what he'd done, she couldn't speak for a moment. Dran was so gentle with her, so considerate. She knew there was another side to him, she'd seen it. But she willed that knowledge away for the sake of friendly conversation and the feeling it gave her to be listened to, attended to. *To be desired,* she thought with shame.

Dola watched her carefully. "Did he approach you? For a healing?"

Salka started to shake her head and stopped as her eyes widened in realization. Yes, he had. She nodded, then hung her head low. "I'm sorry, Maladia. I didn't know, I didn't realize…"

The house was silent for a moment. "Nothing you could have done," Maladia waved away Salka's apology. "But there is still something we haven't discussed," she said from the bed, without opening her eyes. "Salka, want to do the honors?"

Dola stared at Salka.

"Your boy," Salka said. "He's a striga."

Dola's face fell. "No, that can't be!" She brought her ear to her son's chest and all was still for a moment. She lifted her head from his chest and watched his face.

"I didn't know," she said, her eyes filling with tears. "It's my job to know, and I didn't know."

"You don't live in Heyne Town, Dola. You'll be fine." Maladia placed a comforting hand on Dola's shoulder. "I'm here."

"You don't understand," Dola said, tracing the outline of her baby's cheek. "I can no longer *be* a Dola! Nobody will seek my skills after this. A Dola is not allowed to have a striga child, any more than a Heyne Town woman is. I will be banished."

"But…" Salka looked surprised. She rubbed her singed

eyebrows. "As long as I remember, you've been hanging around the striga village."

"Oh, that." Dola chuckled mirthlessly. "We go where we please, but the elders will cast me out, as soon as they discover him. As a Dola, I should have foreseen this. And *dealt* with it... Who will hire a midwife that birthed a striga?"

"So what will you do?" Maladia asked.

"What *can* I do?" Dola looked at the baby in her arms. "I will have to find myself another tribe, I suppose."

They sat in silence for a while, Maladia's arm wrapped around her friend.

Salka got up from her chair and walked up to the window, to give them a moment alone. There are some moments that are private.

The rain seemed to be letting up, so she opened the window slightly, and let her stigoi loose. Its tendrils ran across the windowsill and deep into the soft soil. She closed her eyes and let herself feel the sweet smell of the thawed ground and the plants releasing their aromas into the air. The stigoi snaked and danced among the fallen branches and dug into the ground, disturbing the moles and the earthworms. It went up the wind-snapped trees and tasted the fresh sap. It twirled around the raindrops as they fell, only to bounce up in their last brief dance before going back into the earth. She felt the tremors of the trees and the branches falling down, the distant roar of an overflowing spring, a roar that was suddenly less distant than before. She opened her eyes.

"Dola! Maladia!" she screamed. "We must go! Now!" She ignored their puzzled looks. She could feel the groan of the trees as water washed around them, pulling at their roots, as it searched for a path. It was too close, too fast.

"To the roof!" She picked up a couple of blankets from the bed, and looked exasperated for a moment before screaming at the motionless women, "Now!"

They listened, more because of Salka's stigoi's suddenly threatening presence, than because of her scream.

No sooner did they reach the top of the stairs than the water hit the house. It burst the door to splinters and lay waste to what only moments before had been a comfortable room. Dola unhooked the latch on the hatch door leading into the attic and they tumbled inside. The entire house groaned, like a large man struggling to stay upright.

"What do we do?" Dola screamed. "There are no windows here! We'll drown!"

"More likely we'll get washed away first," Maladia said. Her face was ashen, as she looked through the hatch to see the water level rising quickly.

"Not if you help me," Salka said. She walked up to the eaves and reached out to Maladia with her hand. Maladia nodded and gave her baby to Dola.

Salka and Maladia put a hand each on the roof between the support beams. "I haven't used it like this before." Maladia hesitated. "I could burn us."

"Not burn." Salka smiled. "You use what's on hand." She pointed at the hatch with her chin. "Listen to it. Feel the water's strength."

Maladia nodded and closed her eyes. Her stigoi reached down through the hatch with Salka's and at the same time pushed with a shadowy hand at the roof. The sudden burst of energy pierced a hole in the roof's planks, showering them in fine dust.

Maladia stared at it for a moment, her expression elated. She turned towards Dola and laughed, the sound of her voice merging with the thundering sounds of the water below. Salka and Maladia climbed through first so that Dola could pass them the babies. Then it took both of the stigois to pull Dola upwards, making her shoot up through the hole in the roof before she landed with a loud grunt.

"What now?" Dola asked massaging her bruised bottom. She looked below and her eyes widened. In the evening light, they saw the torrential water pour down the mountainside, washing away everything in its path. The house's strong walls were the only thing that kept it standing, though it was impossible to say for how long.

"It will wash away at the foundations and pretty soon the whole thing will collapse," Maladia said.

The house was now an island in the middle of a river. The water was battering its walls, washing away pieces of wood. There was no trace of the small orchard and the henhouse.

"My chickens!" Dola covered her mouth with her hands.

"We're next if we don't find a way off this roof," Salka said.

"If we could find a way to cross over to those trees, we'd be safe." Maladia nodded towards the large pine growing just outside of the water's reach.

"Is there a ladder here? Or something long enough to make into a bridge?" Salka asked.

Dola shook her head. "Of course not. Can you imagine me on a ladder?" And the image was so ridiculous, their situation so hopeless that all of them suddenly burst out laughing. Maladia sat down, cradling her baby as her laughter turned into a sob.

The silence that followed was interrupted by Salka, who screamed, "Look!" pointing at something in the dark.

Dola squinted. "A tree."

"It's floating down, it will be here in a moment. We can use it!" Salka shook Maladia's shoulder. "Give Dola your baby."

"What?" Maladia looked confused.

"Now! We don't have time!"

Dola reached out and picked up Maladia's daughter, who was wailing now.

"What do I do?" Maladia asked.

"Hold my hand. I will steer you." Salka reached out her hand.

The moment their skin touched, Maladia felt a sharp pull, like someone trying to yank out her hair and teeth all at once.

"Relax!" Salka snapped. "Let the strength of the water run through you! Don't block it or it will kill you!"

Maladia closed her eyes and tried to relax, but the pulling sensation didn't stop.

"Let it pour through you. You're a vehicle for it, not the destination." Salka gritted her teeth. "It's like unclenching your fists."

And suddenly, Maladia saw it. There was no stopping it. The power of the water rushing below them, the force of it moving through her. She could see its strength, but as if from a distance. If she tried to hold it, it would carry her with it.

Maladia's eyes went blank as her stigoi merged with Salka's. The two of them stood still and rigid as a shadow shot out of Salka's chest and flew down to where a large pine floated down the river. The combined stigois wrapped themselves around the trunk of the tree, shapeless, and lifted it up. There was a moment of resistance as the tree fought against the current. And then it rose up. Held by the two stigois, it landed heavily, bridging the gap between the roof and the bank.

Salka opened her eyes and smiled.

"Maladia!" Dola screamed as Maladia crumpled down.

Salka rushed to her side and lifted the striga's head.

"Wake up!"

"It was too much," Dola said. "She's just given birth. She has no strength for this."

"You need to cross." Salka stood up and picked up one of the blankets she picked up at the house. She tore at it with her teeth and ripped thick long strips. "Tie this around you. I intended that we'd each carry one, but you must hold them both."

"I'm not going to leave her!" Dola cried as Salka tied the long strip of fabric around her to provide support for the two newborns.

"I will take care of her. You will have to support them with one arm, and use the other for balance. It won't be easy, but you have to make it." Salka looked at her creation critically. The two infants were strapped tight to Dola's chest.

"Nothing has been easy so far. Why should this be different?" Dola said. She looked at the unconscious Maladia. "Bring her to me safely."

Salka nodded. She helped Dola climb on top of their makeshift bridge and watched her as she shuffled backward down the trunk.

Salka's stigoi snaked down the tree, shielding Dola from any sudden gusts of wind until she was safely on the ground.

"What am I going to do?" Salka said out loud, watching Maladia. Her words were carried by the wind. She suddenly felt very tired, and longed to lie down beside the older woman to rest, just for a moment.

The house groaned and the glass in the windows burst, the shards glistening in the moonlight as they were carried by the current. Salka turned Maladia onto her back, crouched between her legs, and then pulled on her arms till the unconscious woman was sitting up, leaning against Salka's back. She then snuck what remained of the blanket underneath Maladia's backside and pulled the ends under her arms to tie them behind her neck just as if she were carrying a goat on her back. Getting up proved to be more difficult, but Salka's stigoi pushed where she pulled, and she managed to stand upright. She didn't dare let her stigoi reach out to the water for strength again for fear it would wash them both away. Instead, she let it draw on her own reserves in slow miserly drips.

As the first of Salka's strength poured into her stigoi, Maladia's stigoi woke up, suddenly enveloping Salka. Climbing onto the fallen pine tree, Salka felt Maladia's stigoi search and prod, craving the strength that she needed in order to carry them both to safety. Salka's stigoi responded with outrage, rising like a lynx, growling and biting at the parasitic reach of Maladia's shadow. It took everything Salka had not to topple over into the water. Her cheeks sunk in, as the two battling shadows drained her body of what little fat she had left. The tree between the house and the bank seemed to stretch forever. Salka peered into the torrential water beneath her and the thought of how easy it would be to shed her burden rose, unbidden. As if sensing her thoughts, Maladia's shadow entwined itself closer around her, feeding her strength into Maladia's weakened body. Salka looked to the shore in despair and saw Dola standing there in the rain, cradling the two children in her arms. Salka bit her lip hard, letting a small trickle of blood drip down her chin. Her stigoi moved a soft tendril across her face and took even that. Nothing was to be wasted.

Salka continued the painstaking journey down. She wouldn't let them fall. Not even as the muscle under her skin melted away and she struggled for each breath.

When her feet finally touched the ground, she had no strength to pull herself upward. She fell sideways, tumbling with Maladia to the wet ground.

Dola's face loomed over her. "You've done well, Salka. You've done very well." Dola's hand stroked her cheek. Salka merely nodded and closed her eyes.

# CHAPTER 41

Dran moved slowly, his hand holding together the sides of his cloak, as each gust of wind threatened to pull them apart. He had no words for any of his companions and they were happy to leave him be, each striga wrapped up in their own grief.

Dran thought of his mother's house, of the village he grew up in. He didn't share the other strigas' sense of loss.

*Let it all wash away.*

There was nothing left, no hope, no pride.

The escape had exposed him, had exposed his weakness, his sickness to all. And in the end, it didn't matter. He didn't manage to keep Salka, and there could be no more hope, no more schemes. He'd likely be dead soon, whether or not they were granted passage by the Heyne folk. His mother wouldn't see it, at least. That was something.

They left as the evening light dimmed, just as Alma had instructed.

Dran observed the people who walked alongside him. None of them knew what he'd done, none of them would have even suspected. If he told them all now, they would probably shrug their shoulders and simply feel a bit less guilty about leaving him behind. He accidentally killed a banished stigoi. His darkest secret, and they wouldn't even care.

*But* she *would care.* He thought of her dark curls, and how she'd brush them aside when she was irritated. He pictured her face if he told her. She'd look at him with her dark eyes wide-open. Would she recoil from him? He liked to think she'd be compassionate. He'd tell her it was an accident. How it hurt him, how he paid for it every day since, as his other heart seeped poison into his body. Markus made him pay, and Dran's striga heart would consume him in the end. Salka would see it.

She'd be angry at first, of course she would be. But then she'd see he was just like her, only wanting to be free of weakness, free of the constraints of his own body. She'd forgive him.

A gust of wind nearly toppled him over. He leaned heavily on a tree, struggling for breath. Emila saw it and turned away, her face impassive. Mordat paused for a moment and offered him his hand.

*What's the point?* Dran thought, and almost didn't take it.

Almost.

# CHAPTER 42

The first person to see the flood water that rushed towards Heyne Town had no time to raise a cry. His body, carried by a branch that impaled him, was a message for the others. The warning rang from the bell tower towards the houses. The first rush of water in the distance looked like a shimmer until the rumbling current tore through the meadow, levelling the terraces, and tumbling towards the town.

Torik ran out of his house upon hearing the bell, and stood still for a moment, as he saw the first wave in the distance. The water and the mud combined, in a tsunami that ripped trees from the ground.

He ran down towards the shop, where Aurek stood, mouth open, in the doorway.

"Out of my way!" Torik screamed, pushing Aurek aside. Aurek looked at him strangely but didn't resist.

He ran to the back of the shop, flinging open the door to the cellar. For a moment he stood still, as Miriat's face stared back at him.

"Everyone, run!" Aurek yelled as water poured down the street. The flow of the water had slowed somewhat once it hit the first buildings, but the houses were not built to withstand a flood. Torik grabbed Miriat by the hand and pulled her out of the cellar.

"Shit! The bell tower's washed away!" Aurek screamed. Miriat looked into his face. Their eyes met, briefly, and then Aurek looked away. "Take her," he said, his voice breaking.

Torik turned to Miriat. "Our house is on the hill. You can make it. Go!" She nodded and ran away at speed. She was chilled to the bone, but one glance at the water made her dig into the reserves she didn't know she had. The town had changed since she'd left it, but she could find the route to her old house blindfolded. The townsfolk had by now all heard the alarm, and rushed out of their homes, searching for a safe haven. The water in the street was now more than knee-high, and pieces of debris floated quickly, hitting those too slow to move out of the way. When Miriat reached the house, there was already a fair number of people gathered there. Few paid her any attention, as she slunk by the side of the house, not daring to cross the threshold of what once was a happy home.

She bit her lip as she looked down the hill and towards the town. Water ravaged the small wooden houses, adding the timber of their walls to its deadly cargo. Miriat could swear she saw some bodies floating there as well and she closed her eyes. Best not to see, not to notice a familiar face in the cold water.

"My house!" somebody wailed, "My beautiful house! It's gone!" Kind hands on shoulders, a soft word of encouragement, arms supporting in grief. Miriat watched this all, unseen, and felt her eyes brim over with tears. She shrunk into herself, and watched the dark waters tear away pieces of what she once knew.

"A fantastic bit of living, isn't it?" a voice near her chuckled. She looked up into Abrik's eyes. Her own widened as he rubbed his hands together in glee, staring down as the town was ravaged. Estancia stood next to him, a small huddled figure. The woman looked briefly at Miriat and then turned away. She had the decency to look embarrassed at least, Miriat thought. She suddenly felt sorry for her, forced to watch her life float away while her husband looked on with a smile on his face.

"What's that over there?" A young girl pointed towards the line of the forest. To the east of the raging water, a column of lights appeared. Like fireflies reflected in a lake. The lights grew closer, in an orderly line.

"There's folk out there! They're coming towards the town."

"They'll get washed away in the mud."

Miriat squinted at where the forest met the fields. The torches lit up the night. Her eyes widened in horror. "Oh no…"

"Marvelous bit of living." Abrik chuckled, nodding to himself.


The town loomed in the distance. Mordat raised his hand to signal the strigas to stop. They were all drenched to the bone and tired, the humans among them faring the worst. Had they waited any longer for Alma they would have been washed away by the roaring river. As it was, they teetered on the edge of the narrow eastern ridge hanging above the terraced fields leading towards the town.

"The water has ripped through the town. We have to keep to the hill or risk being swept away," Trina said. She was panting heavily as she pulled on the rope in her hand. She was followed by an orderly line of goats and a lamb, trailing in the back.

Mordat nodded. He was not a natural leader and now felt out of his depth. Rida ceased her complaining a while back, which he felt was a bad sign. She struggled to move one leg in front of the other, leaning heavily on Emila. Niev's father looked stricken. He meant to stay back and wait for his son once the decision had been made to move the tribe forward, but the choice had been taken out of his hands by the surging waters.

Dran looked close to death and so everyone had looked to Mordat for leadership. Rest was impossible and moving forward was getting harder. He looked up to where Trina was pointing towards the small houses on the hill and chewed on his lip.

"We're likely to meet the entire town up there. We might be better served to find a dry spot in the field and try to set up camp," Tolan said to Mordat. In spite of his injury, he was carrying a kid goat on his shoulders. He didn't look like he could hold out much longer.

Rida scoffed behind him. "Dry? Where?" She made a broad gesture. "I'd rather face down the entire damned town than freeze here out of cowardice." Tolan looked down at his feet. They all knew she was right. But looking up at the lights on the hill, none of them was sure if the welcome they would receive would not be worse than the rushing water. Tolan looked at his daughter and sighed. Mordat put a hand on his shoulder to show he understood. He himself was carrying his youngest daughter on his shoulders and he shared Tolan's worries.

"Keep moving," Mordat said, quietly.

# CHAPTER 43

"Wake up, Salka, wake up." Dola patted Salka's cheeks. Salka grunted and opened her eyes.

"She's awake? Is she all right?" Maladia's high voice grated on Salka. Her mouth felt dry while the rest of her body was drenched.

"She's awake," Dola said. Her brown eyes were filled with affection and concern. Salka thought nobody, aside from her mother, had ever looked at her like that before.

"How bad is it?" she asked. Her voice came out as a croak, no louder than a whisper.

"Well, you're not ready to go courting, but you'll be just fine." Dola smiled. "Are you strong enough to sit up?"

Salka nodded without much conviction. She grabbed Dola's outstretched hand and gasped. The skin on her arm hung loose, with barely enough muscle left to wrap her fingers around Dola's hand. Instinctively, Salka raised her other hand to her face.

Dola grabbed it before Salka had the chance to investigate. "Don't," she said. "You need rest and food. And you'll soon get back to normal, I promise. For now, those of us without a striga heart will freeze if we don't find shelter."

Salka made an effort to sit up. Maladia, holding the two babies, was awake and smiled shyly.

"Glad to see you're well," Salka said with a grunt, as Dola helped her stand up.

Maladia looked down to the floor. "I'm so sorry. I don't know

246

how it happened. Our stigois touched and it seemed you healed me. I feel well now, whole... You saved me, Salka."

"But at a cost," Dola said. "I swear, I could see your body waste away, like water pouring out of a cracked bucket. I wasn't sure you'd make it down."

"Seems I have some learning left to do." Salka tried to smile. The look of pity on Dola's and Maladia's faces told her the attempt was not successful.

"The strigas spend so much energy suppressing their gifts, you are probably the most qualified to do the teaching right now," Maladia said with a strained smile.

"The babies! Look!" Salka pointed at the infants tied to Maladia's chest. The boy's stigoi was tightly wrapped around both of them.

"They've been like that ever since I came down from the roof. He keeps them both warm." Dola smiled. "Lean on me."

"Where are we going?" Salka asked.

"The closest Dola is on the other side of all this..." Dola gestured at the water raging past them. "The striga village is flooded, and not safe for either of you in any case. There's only one place we can go."

"Heyne Town," Salka's face fell.

Dola nodded as Maladia brought the children closer to her chest.

"The Heyne folk listen to the Dolas. I will protect you," Dola said. Her voice sounded certain, but her hands shook.

"I sure hope so. There is no hiding this." Salka smiled, as her stigoi rose beside her, so that Salka could lean on it as well.

# CHAPTER 44

The Heyne folk huddled by the walls of Torik's house. They continued looking out towards the slopes of the Green Sister, where torchlights still bobbed at a distance.

"They're getting closer," somebody in the crowd said. "They can't go through the main road. Look there, they're heading here!"

"Dolas, do you think?" an old woman asked, her voice shaking.

"Oh, I'm willing to bet somebody much more exciting than that..." Abrik winked at Miriat. She wanted to rip his face off.

"Look, Torik and Aurek are coming. Torik, what news?"

Miriat leaned in to hear what Torik had to say. He scanned the crowd until he locked eyes with her. His shoulders relaxed.

"The water level is dropping but not fast enough. Anyone living on the west side of town below Gurov's house will be lucky to have anything left of their home by the morning. The livestock is gone, save what managed to escape to higher ground." There were groans from some townsfolk, as they looked at the devastation.

"What about the mines?" a man in the crowd asked.

"Well, I'm not going down there to investigate. It's flooded, most like." Aurek crouched down. "At least the rain has stopped now."

"In all my years here, we've never had flooding like this. Something off about it, make no mistake," an aged man said from underneath the eaves of the house. Some folk mumbled an agreement.

Though the door of Torik's house was not locked, hardly anyone was inside. Not so much out of respect for Torik's privacy as because they all felt compelled to watch as their lives were swept away. To look away would have felt almost disrespectful, like leaving the deathbed of a loved one.

Hesitantly, Torik approached Miriat and sat next to her, leaning against the wall of the house they once shared.

"I saw our daughter," he said.

Miriat looked at him wide-eyed.

"Not now." He raised his arms up. "Months back. At least, I think it was our daughter," he said. "I recognized the cloak she wore."

Miriat pursed her lips and said nothing for a while. "She came here in the autumn. A silly childish adventure. I'm surprised you didn't have her captured."

Torik tensed up his shoulders. Miriat watched him from under her eyelashes.

But he only let out a sigh and hung his head. "I deserve that," he said. "And who knows, maybe I would have, had I not recognized her."

They sat in silence for a moment, Miriat's anger growing.

"Did you know she uses her powers? I saw her. It was terrifying. She sucked all the warmth and life straight out of the air." He shook his head. "If I'd told anybody they would have invaded your village, truce or not."

Miriat tensed. She didn't know. How many secrets had her daughter kept from her? She wasn't going to let Torik see it though. "So, she used her powers. And what terrible ill befell this place? Did she hurt someone?" she asked.

Torik hesitated for a moment. "She healed a lamb, I think. It lay as if dead in her arms and then, as soon as she was finished, the animal started wriggling."

"Terrible dark powers indeed then!" Miriat scoffed. She turned her face away from Torik, so he wouldn't see just how much his words had affected her.

"Nobody should have the power to do that," Torik said. "What if she meant for it to go the other way?"

Miriat didn't respond.

"They're coming up the hill!" Aurek called out. "They're not ours and they don't look like Dolas!"

The whisper of *strigas* rolled through the assembled townsfolk. Such a thing was unimaginable.

"They done it!" a young woman screamed. "Our town's never been flooded! And now this?"

"It's an invasion!" someone else chimed in.

Aurek noticed Miriat. His expression turned hard and he strode up to her. He reached out and grabbed her by the neck, lifting her up and slamming her against the wall of the house. Torik jumped up but was warned off by a look Aurek gave him. It was the first time the townsfolk really noticed Miriat's presence, and those who knew her spread the whispered word.

"Did you know? Are they coming for you? Did you make them destroy our town? Maybe you did it yourself?" Aurek grabbed the front of Miriat's shirt and ripped it open.

"Have you grown another heart while you were over there? Or has yours simply blackened?"

"Cut her open and we will find out!" A short woman waddled up to Aurek, pulling a paring knife from the pocket of her apron.

"No!" Torik punched Aurek, making him roll back into the dirt. Miriat fell to the ground, coughing. "Are you mad? It's Miriat, for gods' sake! There is not one ounce of magic in her! She wouldn't hurt us!"

"And why not? We threw her out, didn't we? She whelped a monster and kept it! What does that say of her?"

Torik took a step back, shielding Miriat. "It's a *flood*, Aurek. We live in the mountains; floods and avalanches happen. The strigas have no cause to hurt us now. Miriat least of all."

"Why? Because she loves you so?" the woman who had given Aurek the knife jeered. "Because she loved her mother? She left you both for the sake of the two-hearted demon she spawned.

The council lets the Dolas tell us how to go about our business and this is the result: the entire town's underwater. My house is gone. Look at it. Look at what your bitch has brought onto us," she spat.

"Aurek knows his duty. As do we." She made a sweeping gesture to include the gathered crowd. "Do *you*?"

"I won't let you hurt her," Torik said.

"Let?" Aurek said. He made a gesture and a couple of young men moved forward.

Torik leaned backwards and whispered, "When they attack, you run." She gave an almost imperceptible nod.

The two men lunged at Torik, who punched the first in the jaw. The loud crack of bone breaking rang in Miriat's ears as she ran.

"She's escaping!" somebody screamed. Miriat didn't dare look back. She rolled and slid down the other side of the hill, ankle-deep in soft mud.

"Got you!" Aurek's hand closed around Miriat's wrist. She turned and saw only madness in his eyes. Miriat spun around and bit his hand hard, till her mouth filled with the coppery taste of blood. Aurek screamed and slammed his other hand into Miriat's head, making her reel back. She regained her balance and turned to run again. Aurek took out the small knife. "You're not escaping from me tonight. Not after what you done."

"I didn't *do* anything." Miriat spat. Her chin was covered in Aurek's blood, which speckled her chest where Aurek had torn her shirt open.

"That what you think? It's because of you Kristin's dead."

Miriat's face blanched. "I never hurt Kristin. It breaks my heart she's gone but I had no part in it…"

"She would have followed *you*," Aurek said, his face red. "She saw you leave and thought she could do it too. She told me. She told me she wouldn't give up the baby, stigoi or not."

He stared at her through the rain and the realization of what he meant dawned on Miriat.

"Aurek… What have you done?"

Aurek didn't seem to hear her. "She asked me to go with her.

Do you get that? *Me!* To leave our life here, my bakery, my trade. To live in poverty, hunger and squalor with the other monsters in the forest. And for what? That worm she pushed out of her body?"

"You... You killed her..." Miriat said through gritted teeth. She felt a sudden urge to bite him again, wanted to tear his throat out.

"No." Aurek shook his head. As he talked he was edging closer to her. "Don't you see? It was you. The stigoi had to go. Fallen into the well, nobody would care. But it was *you*, in her head. You made her follow it. She wanted to fish it out, to save it. She jumped right in. Kristin died because of you."

"Aurek?" A voice made Aurek spin around. A dozen or so stone-faced townsfolk stood a little above him.

Aurek spun around. "She's here, Tomlin! Get her, boys!"

"I don't think so, Aurek," the man addressed as Tomlin said.

Aurek twisted his face. He turned around and charged at Miriat, swinging wildly with the knife. He slashed her lightly across her exposed chest. She screamed and stepped away. Her foot slipped in the mud and she fell back, landing on the soft ground. Aurek jumped forward, losing his balance. Miriat kicked out with both her feet making him fly over her head and roll downhill till he landed face down in the mud.

He lay there motionless. The townsfolk walked past Miriat, without as much as a glance in her direction. Tomlin grunted as he and another man rolled Aurek over.

"Broke his neck," Tomlin said. He stood up from the mud, with a strange expression on his face. "Leave him here for now. He don't deserve no special attention. We can bury him once all is back to normal."

They all walked past Miriat, just as if she wasn't there, heading back to the top of the hill. Tomlin paused for a moment, and without looking at her he tipped his hat, ever so slightly.

She stood there, shivering as they left. She looked towards the mines in the distance. The river of mud separated her from the world and her daughter, both. She sat down on the ground and buried her face in her hands. Large hot tears poured between her fingers.

She jumped up as someone sat heavily next to her. Torik looked at her sadly. "You never had cause to fear me in the past, lass, and you don't have one now." He rested his elbows on his bent knees and looked eastward.

Miriat stood there watching the swelling bruise under his eye and his split lip and felt a moment of sympathy. Then she thought of Salka and looked away. "What are you doing here? You should go back to your people."

"You're my people," Torik said, shrugging his shoulders.

Miriat growled, surprising herself at the sound. "Don't presume."

"You're right. I'm sorry." He closed his eyes, looking for the right words, which never came easily to him. "I have no claim."

"Damn right you don't," she said, looking away.

"In any case, the strigas are coming whether we wish them to or not. And the question is, do you want to be here when they arrive?" he asked. "I will abide by whatever you say."

"Oh, will you?" Miriat looked at him properly for the first time. His once black hair was greying at the temples. His muscles were hardened from years of hard labor and his face was lined from the harsh mountain sun. He looked tired and resigned.

The old Miriat would have wrapped her arms around his neck and tried to comfort him. But that Miriat was gone, she reminded herself. So she just looked away and sat back down in silence.

"I'm not the same as I was, Miriat. I have regrets," he said. "But you know, you never actually asked me, back then, to come with you. Ever since you give birth to her, it was you and her against everyone else. And you counted me among them." He gestured at the townsfolk up on the hill.

"Should I have asked? You wanted me to beg you to come with me?" Miriat stood up and tied a knot with the torn shirt ends to cover herself. She caught Torik looking at her. He blushed and turned away.

"I have no time for whatever is to come. I need to find *my* daughter," she said.

"I'll come with you." He raised his hands quickly. "I owe you that much. But we will leave in the morning. You stand a better chance of killing yourself than finding anyone in the dark. Let's hope your daughter had sense enough to find shelter. But you must wait till the morning. You can stay in the house. I'll make sure nobody bothers you."

She looked at him as if expecting a trick and then nodded reluctantly. "Will they let me go?" She pointed upwards, where the flood survivors stood.

"After what Aurek did... nobody will have any appetite for more bloodshed." He looked at Miriat strangely. "And I promise you if any blood is spilt tonight, it will not be yours."

He rose up and offered his hand to Miriat. She looked at it for a moment, then took it in her own.

# CHAPTER 45

Salka stopped again, gasping for breath. The nightgown she wore was falling off her skeletal frame, and she shivered in the cold, in spite of her stigoi's arm spread protectively over her shoulders. Maladia and Dola exchanged a worried look.

"You must make an effort, pet. We have no water, no food. We need to find you a shelter. You need to rest, and you can't do it here," Dola said.

"Leave me," Salka croaked. She leaned against a tree. "I can't walk anymore."

Maladia came up to her and took her by the shoulder. "You saved us all. More than once. You think I'm going to leave you here? I wouldn't be able to look my babies in the face if I did. Now, lean on me."

"You're carrying our children," Dola said. "Don't worry, I will carry her if I have to."

"But–"

Dola snapped. "Enough! You can't quieten your conscience by risking slipping and hurting the children you carry." She wiped her sweaty forehead. She looked up and saw Maladia's stricken expression so she added, more kindly, "We're both responsible, but none's more guilty than me. Let me carry the load."

Dola turned to Salka, and adjusted the drenched fabric on the girl's shoulders, uncertain whether it would be better to remove it entirely or keep it on Salka in spite of the water dripping off its seams. She set on the latter. "Are you able to put your arms around my neck? I will hold your legs and you can travel on my back, broad as it is." She made an effort to smile, but none were fooled by it. "Can your stigoi help?"

Salka nodded reluctantly. Even speaking seemed like terrible effort. Her stigoi spread out, growing legs like a spider, and moved to either side of Dola to help her carry Salka. Dola eyed the stigoi's disconcerting form and was momentarily glad there was nobody around them to witness it. She felt unsettled not so much because of the shape, but by how much fainter the stigoi itself looked, almost transparent in places. She said nothing though. It would do nobody any good to think on what couldn't be mended. It would take time and rest and food, and plenty of it, for Salka to survive this. And Dola had little confidence such luxuries were within their grasp.

Still, she walked on, wishing her burden greater. She could feel every bone in Salka's bony arms and legs, as the young girl barely had the strength to hold on. Dola listened intently to the raspy breath and willed herself to walk faster.

They had left the forest now, and they stopped in horror at the sight of the devastated town in front of them.

"Look! Over there!" Maladia pointed with her chin, both her hands holding the babies secure. "The lights!"

"The strigas!" Dola said, her mouth open. "Alma must have not returned to them, or else she didn't manage to reach the Dola elders!"

Maladia looked at her in alarm. "What do we do? If they see Salka, they'll kill her. They'll kill me too if they get the chance."

Dola felt Salka's stigoi wash away from her, her body feeling even colder once it left. "We're dead if we stay here," Dola said. "And I think the strigas will have other things on their minds right now." She looked Maladia in the eyes. A thread of understanding ran between them. They turned towards the hill which was now the only passage through the town, and walked on, both with a stony expression on their faces.

# CHAPTER 46

The Heyne townsfolk watched the strigas walking up the hill they stood on. They huddled together for comfort. Most of them had never seen a single striga out of its infancy, and to see a whole village of them put a face on their most ancient fear.

"They're coming!"

"You think they'll walk through here?" a somber looking woman asked as her young daughter clung to her knees.

"There's no other path open to them," Tomlin said. "We have to be prepared. Karam?"

A heavy-set man, maybe ten years older than Tomlin stepped out. "What?"

"Help the women and children hide in Torik's house. There will be tools and knives in the shed and the kitchen. We must defend ourselves if they attack."

"*If?*" Karam sneered. He did not appreciate Tomlin assuming the leader's mantle and he bristled at being ordered around. "They're strigas. I bet it's no accident the town has been flooded just as they seek to invade us!"

Tomlin cast a doubtful look at the ragged group making their way up the hill. An invasion seemed like somewhat of an exaggeration.

"And who's to say we'll be safe inside the house? You know what they can do," Annie grabbed his arm. "We all need to do what we can to protect ourselves." She looked at him expectantly.

They all stood waiting, watching the strigas approach.

When they were less than a stone's-throw away, the man leading them called out. "I am Mordat, son of Karina and Marek, once of Heyne Town. I ask for a safe passage for me and mine."

Karam grabbed Tomlin's arm. "The law is clear, Tomlin. No striga can go through Heyne Town and live. If you let them go, we will never be safe." Tomlin shook his arm free.

The wind howled above their heads and the rush of the water below scared Tomlin more than the ragged group in front of him. He raised his hands to signal they should wait and walked towards the rest of the townsfolk.

"This is a decision for all of you. What must we do?" He spread out his hands, asking for answers no one had. They all looked towards the haggard group a mere fifty or so steps below them.

"They will bring their curse onto us!" an old woman grumbled, pulling the shawl closer around her shoulders. She watched the strigas carefully, and there was no pity in her eyes. Many of the townsfolk seemed to agree with her, disgust clear in their faces.

One of the men, however, a widower Tomlin's father's age, took a step forward and fixed his gaze on a young woman standing a little way to the right of the man calling himself Mordat. She saw the older man looking and jutted her chin out defiantly. If she noticed the older man's high cheekbones and his wide jaw, so much like her own, she gave no sign of it.

"Maybe we can let them through?" The older man seemed surprised at his own words and looked down quickly.

"And let them drain us all? They'd pull the life out of us as soon as they come close!" the old woman who spoke previously hissed. She waddled over to Tomlin and jabbed her arthritic finger in his belly. "What you gonna do about it? You just gonna let them kill us all? What the water didn't manage, you will leave to the strigas to finish?" Tomlin was getting tired of her, but he was brought up to respect his elders, so he merely nodded.

"Go towards them," Annie said to Tomlin. "Block their passage. They can go down, there is still a path standing by the water. They can go that way."

Tomlin looked at the flood survivors and took his direction from their scared faces.

"Stay there!" he called out. He turned towards Karam and his teenage son, Pavel. "You two come with me. We need to direct them, so they can pass us by safely."

"Safely?" Karam spat. "Throw them in the water. No striga's been allowed to set foot in the town in generations and now we'll just escort them through like they're the king of Prissan?"

"There are children with them. Women. Some, I don't doubt, are human. You gonna let them all drown for the sake of your stubbornness?" Tomlin asked.

Karam pursed his lips but said nothing.

"Good," Tomlin said. "You and your son can help me make sure they don't come anywhere near our people. You want to make the demons desperate?"

Karam shook his head. He waved at his son, who had been watching the strigas with great interest.

They walked down to where the shivering strigas stood, some still lucky enough to be leading their livestock, some counting themselves lucky in only managing to keep their families whole. Tomlin noted their clothes, their rough-spun woolen tunics and their much-mended cloaks. A little boy, exhausted by the long march, was tied to the back of a large goat, his mother too weary to carry him. The strigas were quiet. Too tired to talk, too resigned to even fight for themselves anymore, he realized. He thought of how many townsfolk would relish this opportunity to rid the mountains of the striga scourge once and for all. He wondered briefly, once the water receded and the sun came out again, whether he would be judged wanting for his mercy.

"Well, have you decided yet if you're going to kill us? Because if not, I need to find my people shelter," Mordat said, barely suppressing a growl that sat deep in his throat. His wife put her hand on his shoulder, and he relaxed. A young girl sat on his shoulders, her small hands folded on top of her father's head. She watched Tomlin with unsettling eyes.

"You can go past, but not through the hill," Tomlin said.

"Are we meant to fly over then? Or swim, perhaps?" Rida stepped forward. Her anger had long passed any barriers of self-restraint and she looked as if she'd jump to Tomlin's throat. Mordat put his arm out in front of her and shot her a warning look.

"There's a path downhill that still looks secure. My two friends and I will escort you so there can be no suspicion of foul play."

"We need water and food," Mordat barked. "Or all your guiding will not save us."

"Ha!" Karam spat. He looked to Tomlin. "You hear that? What else do they want? Should I call my wife to bake them a cake perhaps? Some molasses for the little stigois?" He crossed his arms on his chest.

His son looked somewhat less certain. "Father, there's children there."

"Shut your mouth, boy! There're children up on the hill too, and they need feeding! You'd give our food to the demons?" He smacked Pavel over the head. The boy stood in silence after that.

Tomlin looked uncertain for a moment. Then he seemed to arrive at a decision. "It's true we have little enough supplies to share. But we can still trade. For a goat, we will fill your skins with clean water from the rainwater tank on the house. And I'll throw in some food for the little ones. Not much, mind, just enough to take the edge off for this evening."

Mordat's face reddened. His young daughter, exhausted by the long march, sat limply on his shoulders. "Fine. Malia, give them Aleena." His wife's face fell, but she untied the goat from the others and pulled on the rope to make it go up to Tomlin. The man took the rope and then nodded to Pavel, who ran downhill and collected the waterskins.

While Pavel ran up to collect the water, they all stood silent. Tomlin noted the rough clothing of the strigas, the primitive stone daggers they kept tied to their drenched tunics. His interest was replaced with shame as he looked at the ragged group. He suppressed the feeling. It would not serve him well that night.

Soon enough, Pavel made his way down, burdened with over a dozen skins, which he threw over his shoulders. Under his arm, he held a large bread loaf pilfered from Torik's stores. He beamed at the strigas with all the innocence of youth. He was met with stony expressions.

"We better make our way down then." Tomlin nodded. The walk down the small hill took longer than it took to climb it. The soil was drenched and slippery, and they all took great care, for a single mistake could land them in the rushing waters below.

Once on the path, Tomlin raised his hand to make sure the strigas were listening. "I will go first. Karam and his son will walk last to make sure none of you fall. We have to stay in single file, as you can see. Walk where I walk, and you will be fine." He coughed and glanced at Karam. "Once on the other side you may take shelter by the mines. As long as the river didn't wash them away, there will be small huts there. You may stay there till the water subsides.

Karam opened his mouth to object but Tomlin interrupted him "You going digging anytime soon, Karam? No? Then shut your mouth." Pavel glanced at his father. His face went bright red, making its color nearly indistinguishable from his hair. Tomlin wondered briefly if the blush was from anger or shame.

Mordat nodded gravely and signaled to the other strigas that they should get going.

The path was barely wide enough for a grown man to walk through and merely two feet or so below it the water and the mud that had ravaged the town was rushing by. Here and there large pieces of debris were floating. Tomlin tried not to look in the water for fear he might see more than old walls or pieces of smashed furniture. The river cut into the town, pouring over the main street, the force of the current tearing down the houses on either side. Not everyone had been accounted for yet. The hope was another hill on the western side of the river might have sheltered more of the Heyne folk. Tomlin prayed that once the waters receded there would be more happy reunions than tears over lost loved ones. But it would do him no good to think on it now, when the mud of the path squelched beneath his feet and the ground felt no more solid than jelly.

Behind him followed a somber procession, with Mordat at the end. Tomlin felt a tinge of admiration for the man, who, carrying his daughter, watched over his entire tribe as it made its perilous journey. When Mordat had announced his intention to follow at the back, Tomlin said, "If one of them slips and falls you won't be able to do anything to help them."

Mordat looked at him with anger burning in his dark eyes. He struggled for control for a moment and then said, "Then at least I will bear witness to their end. I owe them all that much."

The rain had stopped but the wind was bitterly cold. Nobody talked, conserving their energy. Emila walked on, barely putting one leg in front of the other. She looked back, casting her eyes one last time at the Green Sister. "Look!" she called out in shock.


Up on the hill, Annie squinted as she looked towards the forest. She gasped. "There's more coming!" All those gathered were now pointing at the two shapes making their way up the hill. Miriat and Torik approached the edge quietly and strained their eyes in the dark. "That's Dola!" Miriat said.

"Which one?" Torik looked at her confused.

"Ours! And she looks like she's... Gods!" She ran, stumbling back down the path, Torik close behind her. She didn't need to say a word, as the horror on her face spoke volumes. Dola and Maladia called out to Miriat as she ran up to them.

"Wait, before you..." Dola tried to hide Salka behind her back, but Miriat was not to be deterred.

"Salka! She's alive! What's happen–" Miriat stopped abruptly as her hands touched her daughter's emaciated body.

Dola looked down, too ashamed to look Miriat in the eye. "She's alive. But she needs help. She needs rest and food, though gods know if she'll be able to keep it down."

Miriat barely listened. She put her arms around Salka and lifted her off Dola's shoulders.

"It's like holding a twig." Tears filled Miriat's eyes. "And her hands... What's happened to her hands?" She held Salka close to her chest. She felt a small shiver as something touched her shoulder.

"Miriat!" Torik said, in shock. He pointed, with a shaking finger, at the stigoi sitting next to Miriat.

"It's all right." Dola raised her hands. "It's Salka. It's still her, Miriat. She will do you no harm."

"I know that. Don't you think I know that?" Miriat said, and in that moment, she knew it to be true. She looked at Salka's stigoi, her daughter's shadow, which at that moment looked more like the daughter she'd known than the slight body in her arms, teetering on the brink of life.

"Mama?" Salka's eyelids fluttered. She saw her mother and tried to smile. "I'm sorry I left you."

"I know, baby, I know. Don't worry about that. I'm here. I'm with you now," Miriat said. She smiled, though she couldn't stop the tears falling down her cheeks.

Salka raised her hand and wiped a tear off Miriat's face. "I'm all right, Mama, really. Help me sit up."

Torik moved to help but Miriat warned him off with a look.

"Let me carry her," he said. "I have some food at the house. Water. Let me help. Please."

"I'll carry her." Miriat stood up, Salka in her arms. She staggered but gave Torik a look that kept him silent. She made her way up the hill, Dola and Maladia close after. The townsfolk moved aside so she could pass, more out of fear than respect, Miriat thought.

"I can hear the river, Mama," Salka said. "Show me the river." Miriat closed her eyes and nodded. She didn't trust herself to speak.

They moved to the edge, and Salka gestured for her mother to set her down. Miriat kneeled behind her daughter, so Salka could lean on her. Dola and Maladia stood behind them. The townsfolk watched in silence. They all felt they were witnessing something deserving of it.

"What's going on there?" Pavel looked up at the folk gathered on the hill. His father put a heavy hand on his shoulder and squinted. The moon shone bright, but even so, he had a difficulty discerning the shapes above them.

Suddenly his eyes widened in horror. Right above their heads, a dark shape loomed. In the night it could be almost mistaken for a human, but the shape itself flowed like the river.

"Treachery!" Karam screamed. "They sent their demons up the hill! They mean to kill us all!" He lunged at Mordat and started punching indiscriminately. Mordat turned away just in time to shield his child from the blows, trying to block Karam's punches with his forearm

"Father, no!" Pavel tried to pull his father away.

"What's going on?!" Tomlin screamed from ahead of them. The path was narrow, and he could not go around "Karam, stop it!"

"Stop this madness!" Tolan called out in alarm. "Nobody means your people any harm!"

"Liars!" Karam screamed. He punched Mordat again in the face. The striga stumbled backwards, dazed, and let go of his daughter. A moment swept by and she slipped into the dark water with a shriek.

"No!" Pavel didn't stop to think. He jumped straight in.

"Pavel!" Karam looked on in shock, suddenly sobered. "No! Son, come back!"

As the water rushed past them, the two children's heads disappeared underwater, only to appear moments later. Pavel was holding onto the little girl's body, but the rush of the water made it impossible for him to swim to the shore.

"What's happening there?" Maladia approached the edge of the hill. She looked down and gasped. "Someone's in the water!"

The townsfolk all rushed to see. A small woman made a strangled cry as she looked down. "My boy!"

"I'm sure it's not him, Alana," an old man comforted her. "It's too dark to see. I bet it's just a stigoi." He checked himself and glanced at Maladia fearfully to see if she'd heard him. Maladia stared back at him blankly.

"No, it's him! I see his red hair! Look! He's holding somebody... A child."

Down below the strigas attempted to throw a rope towards the boy, but each attempt failed. They watched helplessly as the children's heads disappeared and reappeared further down.

"The tree!" Mordat screamed. "If he can only get to it! Swim, boy! Swim!"

Pavel seemed to hear the cry, and he thrashed in the water, aiming for the lone tree some fifty yards down the river. The wide branches hung just above the water, skimming its surface. With a grunt, the boy managed to grasp one of them with his hand, but the effort of holding the striga girl's head above the water meant he couldn't lift himself up onto the tree.

"Let go of her!" Karam called out. "For gods' sake, boy. Just let her go!"

Mordat spun around and with a growl hurled himself at Karam, his fist connecting with the man's jaw. A loud crack and a yelp of pain and the big man was on the ground. Mordat pulled his elbow back, preparing for another strike, when a hand on his shoulder made him hesitate. "Our daughter is out there, dying. I need you now, husband."

Mordat turned around and looked into his wife's eyes. With an effort, he clasped her to his chest. He looked down at Karam, trying to control his voice.

"If she dies, so do you," Mordat said through gritted teeth. He stood up and looked to the water. "We have to do something." He looked around.

"We have some ropes. If we can make a raft and throw it towards them..." Tolan said.

"It'll be too late." Mordat pulled at his hair. "Tie a rope around me. I will grab some driftwood and you can pull us out."

"And how will you swim back with the two of them? You will all drown!" Rida piped in. Her words were hard but her blanched face showed she was as affected as the rest of them. Emila stood next to her mother and held her hand as they all looked towards the water and counted the seconds until the boy would lose his strength and let go.

Dran watched on from the edge. He had immediately sat down once they stopped walking. His face was bright red as he struggled to breathe. Kalina stood next to him, unseen, watching as his chest rose up in halting breaths. Her face was blank as she turned away.


Above, the noise and the shouting reached Salka's ears. Her eyes fluttered open. "Let me see." Her voice was no more than a whisper now and her chest rose and fell rapidly.

"Don't worry, my girl. There is nothing there to see. Just rest now." Miriat whispered, her hand resting on Salka's cheek.

"No. Let me see," Salka said. Her eyes flashed angrily. Miriat looked at Maladia and Dola, who approached her in silence and helped her bring Salka closer to the edge.

"They'll drown," Salka said. Beads of perspiration fell from her forehead as she struggled to lean forward to see better.

"Yes," Miriat said. There was no point in lying.

Salka shook her head. Her stigoi sat next to her, her face turned towards where the boy fought for two lives. Salka raised her hand and the stigoi clasped it in hers. As it did so, they both seemed to grow a little, or perhaps it only appeared so to Miriat as she watched her daughter through tear-filled eyes.

"A stigoi!" An old woman screamed from the crowd. "It's growing! Kill it!" Miriat recognized her as the one who had given Aurek a knife earlier. She made a move as if to approach her, but all of a sudden Torik stood between them. His anger seemed to pulsate just beneath his skin. A live thing, threatening to sweep away any that would dare make an attempt on his daughter's life. Too late in life, Torik became the man Miriat had hoped for.

Salka gasped and the old woman was instantly forgotten. "Hold me up," Salka said.

Dola approached them and offered her arm.

Salka squinted at where Pavel still struggled to hold onto the branches, though his grip was weakening.

Salka breathed in and lifted her hand in front of her. She felt for the tendrils of her power and sent them down into where the water battered the ground and what was left of the village. She felt for how the current ploughed the soil, for how it pulled out the rocks and all that stood in its path. She slipped her consciousness into it and reached for its strength. She staggered for a moment, as the power of it almost swept her up. But Miriat and Dola kept her upright. "There," Salka said. "I feel it."

She spread her fingers and channeled the water's strength to lift the ground around the tree so it rose up as the water rushed around the new obstacle. The human boy with the girl in his arms looked down in shock as the water that had moments ago pulled and torn at them, receded, and then trickled away.


The strigas on the path looked on in shock for just a moment before they sprung into action.

"Get the ropes!" Mordat screamed. "I don't know how long we have. Tie something to the end."

"Here." Kalina leaned far over the water and pulled out a plank drifting by. She almost fell in as it hit her hand. Mordat tied one of the ends of the rope to his waist, while Lesny tied the plank to the other.

"Throw it, Lesny." Mordat nodded.

Lesny bit his lip, judged the distance, and threw the plank with all his strength. It fell into the water with a sad splash.

"No matter," Mordat said. "Try again, now."

Lesny took a deep breath and, with a spin, threw the plank a second time. This time it hit the ground by the tree but slipped back into the water before Pavel had the chance to grab it.

"You were so close! Again, boy, do it again!" Karam said as he rose behind Lesny. He slurred the words, but his eyes were bright with hope.

This time, Lesny took a couple steps back up the narrow path and ran up to the edge, letting the momentum push the plank farther. This time it fell right by Pavel, who grabbed it with his free hand, still too scared to let go of the striga girl.

"Hold onto it, boy, we'll pull you out!"


High above the water, the townsfolk barely dared to breathe as the two children were pulled across the rushing water. Then the crowd erupted in laughter and happy tears as Pavel and his charge were pulled into the safety of their fathers' arms.

Miriat looked into her daughter's feverish eyes. "It's all right, baby. You can let go now."

Salka didn't seem to hear her. Her sight stretched far beyond the ground below. She felt the cool rush of water and slithered up its current. The pain of the trees as the water tore at their roots. The unexpected and unwelcome change of the water's route destroying the burrows and crushing the tunneled dens of the forest animals. She swam past the debris and the fallen trees. She paused for a moment as she encountered the drowned face of a boy she once knew. Salka's stigoi's hand moved across his pained face, smoothing its lines and closing the eyes. She turned away from Niev in sadness, once more investigating the river bed, looking for where its direction was changed.

*Ah.* She almost smiled.

It was there, the boulders and the trees, turned and moved. She gave the water a prod, not working against it, but persuading, coaxing it towards the boulders. Pushing, slowly pushing until they began to roll. Like a child's toy, they moved smoothly now, going back where they belonged, as the water began to flow into its old bed, the deep furrows it had made in the ground holding no more appeal. Salka thought she could almost feel the sigh of satisfaction as the river turned towards its old familiar path.

The townsfolk looked towards their town as the water began to recede. Some shouted and pointed, while others stood motionless, looking instead towards the young girl standing rigid by the edge of the hill.

Salka fell to her knees. Her stigoi retreated into the familiar shape beside her, spreading itself like a cloak over her bony shoulders. It struggled to bring a bit of warmth back into her rapidly cooling body.

"It's done," Salka said. She opened her eyes and smiled at her mother.

"No. No, it's bloody not," Miriat said through gritted teeth. "Maladia!"

"Yes." Maladia stepped forward, an uncertain look on her face.

"Save her," Miriat said. "With your shadow. With your other heart." She waved vaguely at Maladia's stigoi. "Save her." She looked fiercely at Maladia, daring her to refuse.

"I– I don't know how…" Maladia said. "And there's nothing for me to draw on. I could kill someone if I just tried to draw on the surroundings. I wouldn't know when to stop." She drew closer the two infants tied to her chest. "I can't risk hurting them."

"You have me," Miriat said. She rolled her shoulders and pulled Salka up towards her chest. "Take what you need from me. There's strength in me. Make your stigoi give it to my daughter."

"I could kill you," Maladia said.

"Then you better take care," Miriat said. She looked almost wild, as she stared at her daughter's fading eyes.

Maladia passed the two infants to Dola and knelt by Miriat. She hesitated, but one look from Miriat steeled her to the task. She exhaled, and as she did so, her stigoi grew and became more tangible, in some ways more solid than Maladia herself. It put one hand on Miriat's shoulder and one on Salka's diminishing shadow.

Maladia's stigoi lifted both its index fingers and then brought them down quickly. The little tap was felt as an earthquake by those gathered around them, as the shadowy tendrils enveloped Miriat's arm. The strength seemed to pour from her and into Salka's body.

Miriat felt her daughter's hearts, their slowing pulse, and urged her own body to fill them with strength. Torik exclaimed in horror as Miriat's body began losing its reserves, her fat and muscle burning away.

"You're killing her!" he screamed. "Here. Me too! Use me too!" He knelt by Miriat and plunged his right hand into the darkness of Maladia's stigoi, while holding Miriat with the other.

He felt a jolt of pleasure from the stigoi as it began to draw on him also. He fought revulsion as he looked at the pulsating surface of the stigoi's arm. Less like an arm now and more like a huge leech, with his and Miriat's lifeblood running down its black body.

He clasped Miriat closer to his chest as he felt his muscles weaken, and skin slacken.

"She saved my son." Karam's wife stepped forward. "Take what you need from me also."

"Alana! You can't let them touch you!" The old woman looked at her in disgust. "The shadow will pollute you!"

"Shut your mouth!" Alana said.

The old woman stepped back, an appalled look on her face.

"Here." Alana knelt by Torik and Miriat. "Let me help." She grasped Torik's wrist and let the black tendrils wrap themselves around her arm too.

# CHAPTER 47

Down below, the strigas all looked up. They all felt the pull of the power that separated the waters and could now see Salka's stigoi as it moved past them to correct the river's course.

"What's happening?" Emila asked.

Dran looked up from the spot where he had sat through the ordeal and gasped as he saw Salka's face, shining in the moonlight like a death mask. It was almost unrecognizable, except for the two women who held her up.

"Salka..." he said.

At hearing the name Mordat looked up sharply. He had taken his shirt and cloak off and wrapped up his daughter warm. "It was her then?"

A whisper ran through the crowd. They had all watched in awe as Salka's stigoi's outstretched arms reached into the water and, taut as bowstrings, moved gently till the river gradually ran dry. Salka's stigoi had now moved up to return to her as slow as spilt molasses while the strigas watched.

"I didn't know we could do that," Emila was the first to break the silence.

"Nobody *should* be able to..." Mordat said. Still, he looked at his daughter in his arms and the words stuck in his throat.

"Hey! Where are you going?" Lesny called out, as he watched Dran scrambling up the hill.

Dran ignored him.

"Hey! You're going to fall! You're too weak!" Lesny tried to go after him, but was stopped by Mordat's hand.

"Look there!" Mordat said.

Salka had fallen into her mother's arms. Above her stood Maladia, her hair flying wild above her head. Her stigoi loomed above them all, spreading out like a net to collect any strength offered.

"They're healing her," Trina was the first to understand. Through it all, she had stayed silent. Pride rang loud in her voice.

"So, Maladia's a stigoi after all!" somebody shouted from the crowd.

"I suppose she is," Trina laughed wildly. "By gods, it suits her."

"Not for long," Tolan said. "Look! She's drawing on Miriat's strength to heal that child. She will kill her. And die too, most like."

"No, she won't." Rida stepped forward. She took a couple deep breaths and stretched out her arms. Nothing happened. She closed her eyes and bit her lip. Her shadow shivered and spun, like floss on a spinning wheel, releasing the thinnest tendril, weak and pale, which slid and slithered up the hill, moving swiftly between the rocks and the roots.

Trina hesitated for just a moment. She looked up at her daughter and ran her fingers through her hair. And from where her hair ended, between her fingers flowed strands of darkness, racing to the ground and up the hill.

Emila stared at her mother with her mouth ajar. Tolan looked at his wife and smiled. He stood next to her and, his hand on her shoulder, he took a breath.

Lesny saw what they meant to do and looked to Mordat for direction. The older man had little to give. He watched the tiny face snuggled to his chest and nodded.

The remaining strigas stood in a line, each one taking a deep breath to free their stigois, which ran up the hill towards Maladia.

Kalina was the last one to join them. She looked at her calloused hands and bit her lip. She searched for her stigoi, but nothing happened. She stilled her breathing and listened to her other heart, weak and starved. If there was a door she could just push open inside her, she couldn't find it. She looked at the other strigas and, hesitantly, approached the dark stream of their stigois as they made their way up the hill. She knelt by it and reached out with her hand. As her fingertips touched the dark surface, she felt a current surge through her. She gasped. She leaned into it, and for the first time in her life, Kalina let go.

Dran gasped for breath as he saw the stigois flow past him. He looked up at Maladia's stigoi and smiled. He half ran, half crawled up the hill, hope gleaming in his eyes.

Up on the hill, Maladia opened her eyes and gasped in shock as she watched the faces of Miriat, Torik, and Alana shrink and shrivel. She tried to stop the flow but couldn't. Her eyes filled with tears as Alana sank to the ground, still holding fast to the stigoi's arm, her eyes fixed on Salka's face.

Then what felt like a wave hit Maladia, with her body and mind filling with the strength and love freely offered. Voices in her head struggled to be heard, their fragmented words like prayers.

*May she be all right...*

*Gods, I'm so sorry...*

*Will it hurt?*

*So sorry...*

*Take...*

The strength offered poured through her, overflowing. She felt for Salka's body, and painstakingly rebuilt the muscle and tissue, recreated the fat layers to fill out the sagging skin, ravaging the bodies of others to heal the young woman in Miriat's arms. And then, gradually, more hands touched the stream, reaching inside it. Maladia turned her head and opened her eyes wide, as one by one, the town folk knelt beside her and touched their fingers to the spreading pool of her stigoi.

Maladia laughed out loud and looked towards Salka. Carefully, lovingly, she gave back what was lost. Salka's skin closed over the open wounds of her palms. The branch-like scars on her arms pulled together, browned and lightened in turn, till they were no more than silver webs on her skin.

Maladia turned towards Miriat and felt the depth of the love offered. She poured some of it back towards Salka's mother and returned what she had plundered moments before.

Torik and Alana shivered, as their strength returned and blood once more flowed steadily through the ruin of their veins.

"That's enough…" Maladia said as the offered strength battered at her walls. "That's enough!" she screamed. The pain was now hard to bear. But what came in had to come out and she frantically searched for an outlet. Her stigoi smoothed the cracks and fixed what was broken, but still, the river or power flowed through her.

Then she felt a sharp tug as another's voice whispered in her mind. *Not enough. Not done. Not yet. Please…*

Something pulled at and redirected the healing flow, drawing it in, greedily tearing at it.

Maladia opened her eyes wide and looked down. She locked eyes with Dran, who watched her with a dreamy smile on his lips.

"Have it then," Maladia said. She lifted her arms and let it all out.

A piercing scream filled the air, startling the strigas and the humans alike into withdrawing.

Maladia fell to her knees, panting. She didn't take her eyes off Dran, who lay on the wet ground, writhing in pain. She watched him coldly, as those around her stirred back to life.


Miriat stroked her daughter's dark curls. Torik hovered over them uncertain, not daring to speak. Salka's chest rose and fell rhythmically, but her eyes stayed closed.

"Is she well? Did it work?" he asked finally.

Miriat didn't reply. She held Salka's immobile body close to her chest and stifled back a sob. She ran the tip of her finger across her daughter's cheek.

"Salka? Sweetling?" she whispered.

Salka opened her eyes and smiled.

# EPILOGUE

"This should keep," Torik said, trying out the new door he had installed on Miriat's hut. Miriat gave a curt nod, but there was a hint of a smile in the corners of her lips. Torik beamed at Salka. "I had some blue paint left in my shed. Maybe you and I can paint it later?"

"Salka has her own hut to worry about now, and other things besides. I'll do it," Miriat replied before Salka had the chance to. Torik seemed happy with that answer as well.

"There is plenty I still need help with if you can spare the time," Salka said, dropping the rabbit she'd retrieved from a trap that morning. "The post you reset the last time has shifted and I fear the next storm will tear a great big hole in the roof." Torik nodded and grinned. Though the last few months had been filled with little but hard work, as he spent every moment he could in the village, his face looked less tired and younger than when Salka first met him.

"Who's the other rabbit for?" Miriat asked in clipped tones, throwing a bunch of wood sorrel into the pot.

"You know who it's for, Mama," Salka sighed.

The air smelled of sweet sap as Salka walked towards a small hut a little way away from the other striga houses. A lot of new timber had been hauled to the village to rebuild what had been destroyed.

The Heyne townsfolk helped too, in payment for the strigas' help saving and rebuilding the town.

Salka noticed with some pleasure that the ground was once more hard beneath her feet, as the summer sun had dried the winter melt. The strigas she passed smiled and some stopped to ask for advice, though she suspected it was more to make her feel like a true leader than because they needed it.

Salka knocked on the wall of Emila's hut and waited until the tired face of her once-friend appeared from behind the curtain.

"May I come in?"

Emila looked away, as she always did now whenever Salka addressed her. "Yes, of course, Salka, it's kind of you to visit us." She accepted the rabbit Salka brought her with extravagant thanks, until Salka silenced her with a raised hand.

"How is he?" Salka looked towards the raised bench in the corner where Dran sat rocking back and forth. Salka walked forward and brushed a curl off his face. He looked at her for a moment, without recognition. Then he turned back to his feet and continued his unintelligible muttering. The same stolen energy which healed Dran's foot, seemed to have burned out the essence from him. There were many in the village who wanted him gone after that, and Emila too, once her treachery had come to light.

Salka used her newly gained authority to let them stay. It was the right thing to do. And what did the before matter anyway. They had the now to take care of.

"He's much the same," Emila said. "His mind's still gone."

"Take care of him. Maybe in time he'll come back."

Salka emerged from the hut and smiled broadly at Pavel, who was hauling grain for trade on the back of a tired-looking donkey. He and the other young humans became a not uncommon sight in the village once the passage from town had cleared up a bit. He came up to her with some new piece of gossip from the town as he often did now. She smiled as he chattered away, barely registering his words. She noticed his eyes would often wander to her shadow, guiltily, like she would be offended by it, though it pleased her beyond words to see nothing but eager interest reflected in them. Even though the older humans were still wary of the strigas, and were ever watchful for the signs of the monsters they were brought up to fear, Salka noticed that for the younger generation the striga shadows drew only awe and fascination.

And though it would be impossible to say that a friendship had blossomed between the humans of the Heyne Town and the striga tribe, a new truce and a trading partnership had emerged, which, even if it did not warm the hearts, at least filled some bellies.

As Pavel chattered away Salka looked above the tall fence to where the pines met the clouded sky and leaned into the comfort of the warm breeze and the friendly words spoken.


And where the forest met the field, the Hope Tree still grew, with the wooden markers tied to its branches still swaying in the wind, though none of them were new.

# ACKNOWLEDGMENTS

This book is in your hands thanks to the support I've received from so many people. I'm grateful for the opportunity to thank them here.

My husband Cameron, for all his love, support, and patience whenever I ditch him to go writing. For understanding how important writing is to me, even before I had anything to show for it. Couldn't have done this without you. You make me a better person and have contributed more to this book than you think.

My best friend, Kasia Szafranowska, who means more to me than she can ever know. Through all the years I've known her she's always cheered me on, supported me and offered guidance and advice whenever I needed it.

My writing buddies, the very talented Nadia Idle and Rachael Twumasi-Corson, whom I'm so privileged to work with and learn from. This book would have taken a lot longer to write without their camaraderie and friendship.

My parents, my grandma Lonia, and the rest of my family. You have all had a part in shaping me into who I am today. I love you all so much and I'm grateful to have you all in my life.

My English teacher, Urszula Siuta. This book is the culmination of a journey she's helped to set me on.

My secondary school literature teacher, Anna Kramek-Klicka, for expanding my horizons and supporting my love of English literature even when it had absolutely zero to do with the curriculum I was supposed to be learning from.

My very kind and enthusiastic agent, John Baker, who believed in my writing and worked tirelessly to land me a deal. Also, Sarah McDonnell and everyone else at Bell Lomax Moreton.

My editor, Eleanor Teasdale, for falling in love with *The Second Bell* and providing the guidance I needed to make it shine.

The Angry Robot team: Gemma Creffield, for her editorial notes and for helping to spread the word about my book with Sam McQueen, whose humorous tweets never fail to brighten up the day. The Angry Robot designer, Glen Wilkins, for creating a cover I completely fell in love with, and for his patience with all my notes and suggestions.

The Transpatial Tavern video chat group for both the lighthearted banter and a sense of community which every writer needs. You guys are amazing.

And finally, thank you, reader, for picking up this book. I hope you enjoyed it. It means a lot to me.

# Fancy some more magical fantasy?

## Try the John W. Campbell Award-winning Under the Pendulum Sun by Jeannette Ng

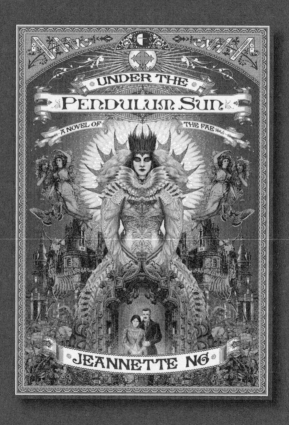

## Read the first few chapters here!

# CHAPTER 1
## *The Quiet in the Port*

Great and ancient empires, Mahomedan and Heathen, have received a shock by the prowess of British arms, nerved and strengthened by GOD, which has broken down strong, and hitherto invulnerable barriers; and so a way has been opened for His blessed Gospel to pass from here to the remotest bounds of reality.

Thus, Palestine is now accessible; and Englishmen may travel freely through the length and breadth of the Holy Land. The enlarged, and still enlarging, boundaries of our dominions in India, open new fields of labour for the Lord's servants. China, its forbidding gates forced open by war, calls out to the faithful.

But it is the Faelands that arrest our attention. Arcadia's vast unknown, which has been for many ages closed against us and the Divine Word, is at last made clear and knowable. And, as Britain has had the high and singular honour, in the wonderful providence of GOD, the Lord of Hosts, of breaking down that barrier, it is but apposite that she should have the honour of being the first to carry in the balm of the blessed Gospel.

Rev William E Matheson, "Appeal on Behalf of Arcadia", NEWS OF THE WORLD, 5th December 1843

My brother and I grew up dreaming of new worlds.

Our father had owned a paltry library of books and a subscription to the most fashionable periodicals, all of which we gleefully devoured. We would linger by the gate, impatient for the post that would bring new sustenance for our hungry imaginations. Bored of waiting, we told each other stories of what *could* be. I remember my brother, Laon, finding one of our tin soldiers at the bottom of his pocket. The red paint was barely worn and it looked up at me with a long-suffering expression. I snatched it from Laon's hand, declaring it the Duke of Wellington, and ran off claiming that the two of us would adventure together. Like Lord Byron or Marco Polo.

We invented whole new worlds for our soldiers to explore: Gaaldine, Exina, Alcona, Zamorna. From our father's books we learnt of pilgrims and missionaries and explorers, and so we wrote of grand journeys, long and winding. As we read of the discovery of the Americas, of the distant Orient, and of strange Arcadia we added similar places to our ever more intricate maps. We mimicked the newspapers and periodicals we read, writing new ones for our tin soldiers. In the tiniest, tiniest writing, we detailed their exploits, the politics of their parliaments, and the scandals of their socialites.

But for all our stories, our imaginations were small and provincial. For the talk of tropics and deserts, our childish fictions filled them with the same oaks and aspens that grew in our garden. We built on their landscape, exotic buildings that were just our little   whitewashed church in Birdforth in disguise. We rained down on strange soil the same Yorkshire rain as that which drenched our skins and drove us inside, peeling off our clothes, housebound by the weather and desperate for diversion.

As such, I could never have imagined Arcadia.

I was familiar with all the tales, mind. The first explorers had spun overwrought stories upon their return: *Until I laid eyes upon the Faelands, I was blind, and now I see. I have never seen colour, nor grandeur, nor wonder, until I saw the shores of Arcadia.* Later travellers were more prosaic, but still offered no adequate description. There were few maps and fewer landscapes available, and almost all of them had been denounced by one explorer or another as fraudulent.

For all the many contradictory theories I had read on the relationship between our world and that of the fae, I was no more enlightened. It was said to be underground, but not. It overlaid our own, but not. It was another place, but not.

All I do know was this: Our ship, *The Quiet*, sailed in circles on the North Sea for six whole weeks. On the dawn of the first day of the seventh week, my wavering compass informed me that we were heading straight back towards smog-shrouded London.

Nervously, I clutched my compass. My brother had given it to me before he left for Arcadia to become a missionary. He was among the first to be tasked to bring the Word of God to the Fair Folk. He had been there three years now and had been nothing but terse in his correspondence. I tried to swallow the worry that consumed me, but it knotted around my heart.

That was when I caught my first glimpse of the Faelands.

Impossibly white cliffs rose from the white sea foam. For a moment my mind feared it to be Dover, that I had simply returned to those mundane cliffs of chalk and stone, that no foreign land awaited me.

Yet those cliffs were too white, too stark. They could not be Dover.

Behind them I expected the rolling hills of home. But instead the landscape was jagged and jutting knife-sharp from the sea. It seemed cobbled together, each part eerily familiar but set against something other. I recognised the leering profile of a hill, the knuckle-like crest of a mountain. Yet as wind and wave shifted the shapes, it all seemed different again and my strained eyes watered.

*The Quiet* glided gull-like into a wide, wide river. Unfamiliar structures sprawled against the green grey mass of the land in arching, crumbling lines. Squinting, I made out the spined turrets, barbed roofs and oddly leaning walls. For a moment I thought the town to be an endless dragon coiled around the edge of the harbour, huffing smoke from its distended nostrils. It shimmered, the shingled roofs seeming scale-like, and then it *shifted*.

I blinked, and buildings were back to where I remembered

them. There was no dragon made of shifting structures. Just a town of crowded streets.

The ship heaved under our feet like an unruly stallion. A shout broke out among the sailors in words I didn't understand. They started busying. As they clambered up and down the ratlines and hauled rope this way and that, they muttered invocations under their breath. I wanted to chide them for their superstition but we were sailing to Arcadia and none of it made any sense.

I tried to stay out of the way as the sailors blasphemously crossed themselves in the name of salt, sea and soil.

An unnatural wind curled around the sail, whipping it back and forth. It fluttered full and then deflated with each breath of the wind. *The Quiet* became anything but as the timber groaned. The cabin boy flung his arms around the prow and cooed at it.

It was a long while before the ship was tamed and brought to shore.

And then I was simply there, stepping unsteadily from the ship into the shamble of a docks. Twisting streets full of seeming people reminded me of crowded London.

The ground was a shock to my feet, and I staggered. My carpet bag and trunk joined me on the docks. I fumbled for my documents and scanned the milling crowd for my guide. I tried not to notice the oddities of each figure – the strange colours and the wings and the horns. There would be time aplenty for the wonder of Arcadia once my bags had been unpacked and I had found my brother.

"Miss Catherine Helstone, I presume? The missionary's sister?"

With an upturned nose, round chin and soft, brown eyes, the woman I turned to meet was perhaps one of the least ethereal people I'd ever met. She was shorter than me. But as her skirts hung long and limp, without a murmur of wave or curve, her figure seemed tall and lank. She dressed in sombre, mortal colours, her gown being a muddy shade of navy blue and her shawl more grey than white.

A smile spread across her freckled cheeks as I nodded.

"I thought I recognised you," she said. "You look just like your brother."

"I do?" Though Laon and I shared the same dark hair and strong nose, few remarked on our resemblance. Features that were handsome on a man were becoming on a woman's frame.

"I'm Ariel Davenport, as I'm sure you know. Your guide."

"I am very pleased to finally meet you," I said. We had exchanged a handful of letters through the Missionary Society in preparation of my journey.

She shook my hand vigorously between her two clasped ones and swooped in two sharp kisses. Her smile getting wider, she added, "Though I'm not the real one."

"I'm... I'm not sure I follow."

"I'm not the real Ariel Davenport, you see." There was an unpleasant edge to her laugh; it was a touch too brittle. "I'm her changeling."

"Her changeling?" Many of the intermediaries between the fae and humans were said to be changelings. One of Captain Cook's botanists was said to have learnt of their fae origins upon arrival to Arcadia and was conscripted to their cause. Despite such accounts, changelings never seemed quite real to me. But then, given how sheltered I had been, the French were never quite real. "So you were raised as her–"

Ariel Davenport gave an exasperated sigh and rolled her eyes at my ignorance. "She was a human child, I was a fairy-made simulacrum of a human child. We traded places. I grew up there and she grew up here."

"What became of her?" I asked.

"That's not for me to tell." She gave me a disarmingly lopsided smile and in an impeccably proper accent, added, "And it's hardly polite to ask."

"I- I'm sorry," I stuttered. I dropped my gaze. Our nanny, Tessie, used to keep a pair of steel scissors by our beds to ward off faerie abductors. In restlessness and boredom, I once said to Laon that we should close the scissors, so that they no longer formed the sign of the cross, and invite in the fae. He was horrified. And so I never suggested it again.

"Regardless, now I'm here again. Because I'm useful to them and I understand you humans," said Miss Davenport. "Speaking of which, I am most remiss in my duties. I should hardly keep you talking here all day." She waved for an expectant-looking porter to hoist up my trunk onto his shoulders. His sallow skin glinted green as it caught the sunlight.


Miss Davenport hummed tunelessly as she led our way to the rounded carriage. I tried not to stare at the flaring gills of the porter as he heaved my trunk and bags onto the carriage. He lashed them with rope to a wizened stem that jutted from the middle of the roof.

"How far to Gethsemane?" I asked, an ominous shudder passing through me as I said the name.

"That what the missionary called the shambles?" said the coachman.

"Yes, I believe so," I said. "It is where Reverend Laon Helstone resides. Though I believe his predecessor did the naming."

The coachman grunted, turning his attention from me.

"You've not answered me," I pressed. Perhaps it was simply that Laon's predecessor was overly enamoured with winning the martyr's crown. After all, what other reason has one to name a building after the garden in which Christ spent his final hours before his Crucifixion? "How far to Gethsemane?"

He tutted to himself, the space between his brows folding like an accordion. "Two revelations and an epiphany? No, there has to be a shortcut... Two painful memories and a daydr–"

"Sixteen miles," interrupted Miss Davenport. "It is sixteen miles away. We'll arrive well before dark."

I nodded uncertainly.

"He says that for the tourists," she added, glaring at the muttering coachman.

As I alighted, a cacophony of bells chimed midday.

Hand still resting on the carriage door, I turned and looked up.

My breath caught, heart bursting with expectation. I had read so much of the pendulum sun of the Faelands. Foolishly, I half-expected to see it waver in the sky before rushing east again, like my own pendant did in my experimenting hands when I was trying to comprehend the very idea.

It did not, of course.

The sun was significantly larger than the one that had been a constant of my life. But it seemed otherwise the same, stinging my eyes as I squinted at it.

"It doesn't move *that* fast," said Miss Davenport. "You won't see much by just looking up. Even at midday."

I looked back down, white spots swimming in my eyes from the brightness. I pressed my own cold fingers to my closed eyes. I knew I wouldn't see anything, of course. Arcadian days were as long as earthly ones.

Still, the temptation had been too much.

"Sorry. I should know better," I murmured, shuffling into the carriage and sitting myself on the dappled upholstery. I even knew that I was at the very edges of the Faelands and that many of the oddities of the sun's pendulum-like trajectory would not be discernible here.

"Your brother also did that when he first got here," she said.

I smiled. For all the distance that had come between us, I felt closer to him again.

Laon and I were inseparable from the second I returned from the Clergy Daughters' School after the death of our sister, Agnes. I was seven and a half when I was bidden to press my lips on the cold, dead skin of her corpse. I tried not to think of the coffin laid out on the table. Of how the corpse seemed like a stranger wearing my sister's clothes, of how hollow the promise of other worlds seemed then. I laced my own fingers, not thinking of the warm hands of my brother holding mine when we stood watching the soil swallow up the coffin.

"It's not very far, Gethsemane," said Miss Davenport, interrupting my reverie. "But it's outside of Sesame, you know, the port town. Not many people go beyond the borders of that. Almost all the other missionaries we've had set up in Sesame or one of the other ports. Things are rather more earthly there, you know. Though perhaps it doesn't matter. You do not seem alarmed by the carriage."

I glanced about the bare, woody interior of the carriage and calfskin upholstery, which was scored by a disconcerting pattern of scrape marks.

"The seats are a little lumpy?" I ventured, resetting myself on the stubborn cushion.

"Ah, yes. The fabric is…. We are but borrowing the skin from the cows."

"What?" I was understandably incredulous.

"It's my fault, really," she said, sheepishly, scratching her upturned nose. "The artisans had no idea what a carriage was so I had to describe it to them. I did so incorrectly, or rather in ways that weren't correctly understood. I try not to make that sort of mistake, but I was in a hurry and old fishbrains out there has a very specific mind. And more used to making animals. Point is that I forgot to mention that the cow was dead when you made seats out of their skin, so here we–"

"How is he?" I interrupted. I almost dared not ask. The thought clasped a cold hand around my throat. The allegedly living upholstery under me roiled; the carriage rumbled and I felt sick to the core. I had kept my worries in check for a very, very long time and now, and seeing the possibility of a reprieve, it was all the harder to endure. "Laon. My brother… the Reverend, I mean."

Miss Davenport shrugged. "I don't really know how to answer that. He's as I've always known him. Alive and healthy, I suppose, you care about that." She frowned, her high forehead furrowing.

"I- Yes, I do. Very much." My fingers hurting with how hard I was holding myself, I forced myself to loosen my hands. I would be seeing him soon enough.

"Why! Pleasantries are a lot harder than I remember them to be." Miss Davenport giggled behind her glove, a piercing twitter of a noise. "He's very well. Better than the mission, truth be told. Which I probably shouldn't say, but it's not easy to be a missionary around these parts. He's conducting services no one comes to, begging to gain access to the rest of the Faelands and asking them questions about their–" She cleared her throat and continued in a deep, ponderous tone, "cosmological and metaphysical importance."

I attempted a laugh, but faltered. "That doesn't sound like him."

"That is rather the point," she retorted. "That's where the humour comes from."

After a silence, Miss Davenport filled the empty space of the carriage with amiable, effortless chatter. She described to me the properties of the pendulum sun and the fish moon. Much of what she said was familiar to me from my reading, but it was good to be distracted by her voice. Too long have I spent alone with my own thoughts aboard *The Quiet*.

I found myself staring and studying her mannerisms more than her words, trying to detect her fae origins. At first glance she seemed as human as me with that scatter of freckles and lopsided smile. Still, she had that awkwardness I heard rumoured of changelings, a certain deficiency in their simulation of humanity. Tessie once told me to stop my tantrum and to behave so as to prove myself not a changeling.

"You could look outside, if you want, Miss Helstone. The window does open."

After excessive fumbling, I unlatched the window and leaned out. Mist closed around the spiny sprawl that was Sesame, like layers of gauzy curtains. We were alone on the road as it stretched into dense fog. Frowning, I could make out the hunched canopies of bearded trees. Above us, a cloud-bruised sky was heavy with rain.

"The weather isn't always like this," said Miss Davenport. "But at least you'll feel at home. You could pretend that it's moors behind the fog. It'll chase away all those feelings of homesickness you feel."

"I'm not homesick."

"Not yet."

Her eyes darted to the window and she hesitated, her gregariousness stemmed by some unspoken emotion. Studying her gloved hands, in a voice quite quiet and quite different to her earlier demeanour, she said, "I was raised in London. Spitalfields."

I waited, unwilling to intrude upon her vulnerability. I realised after a moment that I was holding my breath. I tried not to stare, but glancing over at the now silent Miss Davenport and her features, I noticed there was something odd about her, though if this was to do with something unsettled rather than unsettling about her aspect, I could not say.

She seemed to gather herself as she smoothed her skirts and disguised the brushing away of tears as the tucking of stray locks behind her ears.

"I'm not crying," she said, quietly. "I can't. This is just a force of habit."

"I've only been to London once," I said.

"It's rather splendid," she enthused, animation returning to her face. "There's no place quite like it. Even here. Sort of."

It was impossible to tell if the clouds burst open or if we drove into the storm, but at the first droplets of rain splattering into the carriage Miss Davenport urged me to close the window. The rain was sickeningly warm against my hand. Before I could marvel at the sheer strangeness of hot rain, a gasp of wind chilled the splashed raindrop.

Our vehicle slowed to a squelching walk, mired by the mud underfoot. Our coachman clambered from his seat on the roof to lead his horse by hand.

It was some hours before the rain lightened enough that I could again open the window to look out. An admittedly futile effort, given how my eyes failed utterly at penetrating the murky, roiling fog. Half curious, I clicked open the compass. I had expected to see its needle spinning indecisively but it pointed more or less ahead.

So there was *a* North.

The fog was a shroud, seeming to muffle everything beyond the ghoulishly yellow lamplight. There was a curious emptiness as many of the natural sounds of birds or the rustling of trees that I so often took for granted were simply absent. I told myself this was no different than any other isolating storm, that the silence was but a mundane illusion cast by the wind and rain tormenting the carriage.

Unearthly shadows shifted in the swirling eddies. Harsh lines pushed against the sky, implying severe cliffs and narrow valleys. Hulking shapes darted behind one another and I tried not to give them faces but, unbidden, my imagination began filling in the grey landscape before me. Half-remembered etchings from *The Voyages of Captain James Cook* and exotic phantasms from *Sketches of a New World* populated the space.

And so in the thick swirling eddies of the fog, I found ethereal sylph faces staring out at me and picked out gnome forms playing, imagining their gait like that of a strutting Lancashire moonie.

"There, you can see it now!" Miss Davenport's voice summoned me from my reverie as she pointed out my brother's home to me.

I blinked. At her voice, the fog parted like a curtain.

Laon had always referred to it in his few letters as his lodgings. Despite the name, I had not imagined anything particularly grandiose.

But the house defied such expectations as it coalesced from the sheets of rain before me. It was more castle than manor, a knot of spires and flying buttresses atop a jagged hill. Stone leaned against stone in a bizarre edifice, with nothing but scorn to the very concept of aesthetic consistency and structural purpose. Though silent and lonely, it was far too skeletal to be termed picturesque.

The vast edifice disappeared again behind dense fog and foliage.

"Gethsemane," I murmured.

The gatehouse was flanked by two angular towers of dark grey stone, overlooking what appeared to be an endless chasm.

We stopped. There was no whisper of footsteps, no voices, no sound but for a loud undrawing of heavy iron bolts. I saw how overgrown the walls were, veiled in moss and nightshade. At the rattling of chains the portcullis gave way and we progressed ever so slowly under it. Further gates creaked open and we were delivered into a courtyard.

When I finally stepped out of the carriage, I looked back to see the shattered outline of the embattled walls and I could not shake the sense of unease that welled up inside me.

Of all the places to grant him, why had the fae chosen this one?

# CHAPTER 2
## *The Sister in the Tower*

There may indeed be countless worlds revolving around countless suns, as Lady Cavendish described in her poems. These wandering worlds may indeed be hidden from us due to the brightness of their stars.

But Arcadia is not one of those worlds.

The Faelands do not possess a sun in the way we would understand a sun to be. The cycle of a sun rising from the east and setting in the west is a sight wholly alien to this place for it does not orbit a burning star.

If you would imagine a bright lantern hanging at the end of a long cord. Then imagine that it swings as a pendulum over a surface, bringing each part in turn into its light.

That surface is Arcadia and that lantern is their sun. Thus at the edges of the Faelands, the sun reaches the pinnacle of its upswing before falling back the way it came. The equilibrium position of the pendulum sun is near the centre of the Faelands, directly above the city of Pivot. There, it is almost never night, as the sun is always close enough to impart at least a hazy twilight of illumination.

Thus, periods of light and dark – I hesitate at using the word "day" – are very different along the length of the Faelands, depending on where under the swing of the pendulum sun one is. For those in the city of Pivot would experience two periods of light and relative darkness for every one experienced at the far reaches. Those in between would experience a long "day" followed by a short "day."

This makes the reckoning of days in Arcadia rather complex, to say the least. It has been proposed that regardless of periods of light and dark experienced by those beneath the pendulum sun, one should term one full oscillation a "day." Inconsistent adoption of this has only caused further confusion.

The Faelands do possess something approximating seasons. As their year progresses, the arc of the pendulum sun grows smaller, but the duration of the oscillation, as with any pendulum, is independent of the arc and thus remains constant. The edges of the Faelands thus have less heat and light, giving them a recognisable winter.

The sun is also, I am reliably told, literally a lantern.

Adriaen Huygens, On the Horological Nature of the
Faelands Skies, as translated by Sir Thomas
Rhymer & Coppelius Warner, 1839

A wide, maw-like arch and worn steps led me into the keep. A red door opened into darkness.

"We seem to have caught them rather unprepared," said Miss Davenport dryly as she strode over to the far side of the room and pulled open the thick dust-coloured drapes. A stark, surprising light pierced in, through the startled moths and dancing dust.

Partially panelled in dark woods and edged by lacy balconies, the foyer was a grand affair. Ornate pendants of painted wood dripped from the intersection of each arched rib, holding up the ceiling. The tight weave of the elegant curves reminded me of a birdcage.

Gloomy faced lords and ladies stared out at me from rows of portraits in mismatched frames. Though long-faced and vacant-eyed, they seemed so very human. Threadbare tapestries and faded carpets amassed from several lifetimes cloaked many of the surfaces.

This was a storied dwelling, its vast history written in a language I only half understood, though the seams of where ancient masonry met newer brickwork were visible even to my eyes. The patchwork of different styles alluded to a long succession of prior owners, each with their own eccentricities of taste. Each mark in the mortar, each old window placed into older walls, each revision and addition to the stone told of some greater past.

A short goblinoid being with speckled, silver birch skin introduced himself as Mr Benjamin Goodfellow. He bowed low and awkward.

"I- I was not expecting you so soon," he said haltingly, squinting at me through his wire-framed spectacles. "The Reverend is away."

"Laon is away?" I tried to suppress a flash of worry, remembering the letters I had received. "I thought–"

"Away-away," he said, nodding. "Very away. Away for so long. Back soon. And we does what we must. We does what we cans. Does and the doings. The tower room is always ready for guests." He paused in his mutterings, face crumbling in thought. "You are the sister, are you not?"

"I am," I said. "But where is Laon?"

"Away?" he said, voice lilting upwards.

"Do you not know where he is?"

"The tower room," he said resolutely. I was confused for a moment before I realised he had just ignored my question. "Yes, the sister in the tower. And the changeling in the green quarters. Yes, yes. That makes sense. I will lead you to it."

"Then I thank you for your pains, Mr Goodfellow."

"Mr Benjamin, if you please." His accent assumed the affectations of the Oxford voice. "Just as the Reverend named me."

Miss Davenport was by my side, curtsying at the creature. "Charmed, Mr Benjamin."

He brightened at her display and so I mirrored her action. Miss

Davenport gave me a solicitous smile and wink, though I was not certain entirely what she meant by them.

"You should get settled, Miss Helstone," said Miss Davenport. "Or at least see your room. I'll pay the coachman, take care of the luggage and see you at dinner. I can't wait for dinner. I am very hungry."

Tucking my carpet bag under his arm, Mr Benjamin led the way to the tower room. He gave his history as we walked. He identified himself as a gnome, which I understood from Paracelsus to mean an elemental of the earth. He had been the first and only convert of the prior missionary in residence, Reverend Jacob Roche.

"The Reverend always said Mr Benjamin seemed the littlest of the biblical brothers," he said. "Little name for little gnome."

"Do you mean Roche or my brother?" I asked.

"The first but not the last."

There was also, apparently, a housekeeper somewhere in the castle, whom Mr Benjamin termed "the Salamander."

As we wound through the keep, I felt as though we were coiling back in time, through the layers of the castle's history. The comparatively modern foyer joined onto a corridor lined in dark flock paper that was the height of fashion just under a hundred years ago. The lush floral designs in dark green and gold gave way to tapestries hung over crisp walls and then finally a spiral staircase of worn, naked stone.

At the top of that tight twist was a single wooden door. Once unlocked, I stooped into the chamber.

"Here is room," announced Mr Benjamin brightly. "Use water, throw out of window after."

I thanked the gnome as he set down my carpet bag. He bowed ornately, dragging a gnarled hand into the ground as he did so.

As he turned to leave, he started as though remembering something important. In the most solemn tones he told me, "Almost almost forgot. Remember, no walking down the silver corridor when it's dark. No looking behind the emerald curtain. No staring portraits in the eye. No eating things without salt. And no trusting the Salamander."

And then he was gone, the door bolting shut before I could ask him how I might recognise the Salamander, what food he had thought I would be encountering or, rather more practically, when I could expect dinner.

The room was round. All the furniture, from wardrobe to bookcase to bureau, curved with the wall. A window had been cut into the thick, ancient stone, but very little light filtered in through the lattice of lead and glass. A number of cushions made the recess into a window seat. Slivers of light from the knife-thin arrow slits cut through the shadows of the room.

A narrow door with an oversized knocker stood opposite me. Three pairs of brass eyes looked out at me from the foliage-wreathed face that held the heavy ring in its mouth. It was green with age but for where the hand would rest on the ring. There the brass had been polished by wear to a gleaming brightness. It reminded me of a hagoday, the enormous knockers affixed on cathedral doors that used to grant sanctuary to any who touched them.

Wondering what part of the castle I was in and what purpose this round room could have served, I unlatched the door. It opened silently.

The rush of cold air engulfed me; colder hands clawed at my heart. Hands still gripping the knocker, I shrieked and threw myself backwards. I was glad that I had not unthinkingly stepped through.

The door led to nothing but thin air. Perhaps there had once been a balcony or even a bridge of sorts. For all of Mr Benjamin's warnings, he had not thought to warn me of this particular danger.

Heart still thundering, I bolted the door with shaking hands.


It was a moment before my breathing settled and I was able to stagger to my feet.

I poured myself some lukewarm water from a pitcher on the sideboard and washed myself in the basin. Finally, I could lick my lips and not taste a shadow of the sea.

The majority of my belongings were still downstairs. But my writing case was in the carpet bag and so was a change of clothes, which I made use of. The gown was not clean per se after my seven weeks on *The Quiet*. But it and my last clean chemise were still a welcome reprieve from my woollen travelling dress.

The wardrobe was latched shut with a pair of interlocking wooden hands. I approached it to throw my carpet bag inside, but it was not empty as I expected. My hands found buttery soft wool, rippling silk, and velvet as thick and luscious as ermine. As I examined the wealth of stiff dresses, a flurry of moths spiralled out from the depths.

Some of the long trailing dresses seemed to be as old as the castle, belonging in a world of tapestries and paladins and courtly romance. A few of them I recognised as being no more than sixty or so years old; I had cut up similar brocade gowns when I had briefly been a companion to Miss Lousia March. The gowns had mouldered in their attic for decades but as the fashion began to favour again thick, rich fabrics over light muslins, they had raided the splendour of the past. They were things of such impractical beauty and it had saddened me to tear them apart even if it was to remake them for new use.

Of the dresses, only one bore any resemblance to recent fashions and it was ivory in shade. Wide necked and layered in lace, it reminded me of the etchings of the queen's wedding dress and the subsequent efforts to imitate it in the seven years since.

Opening my writing case, I found the letter from the London Missionary Society. Sitting on the bed, I read it again, though I had already committed its contents to memory. The preamble was mostly concerned with assurances that for all the numerical success of the Catholics in other lands, it was but built on a rotten foundation of formalism and thus we should not envy their cause.

After a barbed allusion to the work of the Society for Missions to Africa and the East, Rev Joseph Hale echoed my concerns for my brother. After two years of near silence, I had written to the Society asking after Laon. The Reverend had few answers for me and though he never outright stated what he thought had happened in the Faelands, his worry was evident in his circling of the issue, apologising for not having sufficiently prepared Laon for his post and making dark reference to others who had perished.

It also included a request that I recover the journals and notes of the previous missionary, Rev Jacob Roche.

In youth, I had shared Laon's restlessness. University had only nourished and nurtured his ambitions, but education had stifled mine. I had been taught to tame my wild impulses and desires that had agitated me to pain. I had folded it with my soul and learnt to drink contentment like you would a poison. Drop by drop, day by day. Until it became tolerable.

Laon disdained tranquillity. He could not learn my glacial stillness, for all that I had tried to teach him. When I had just turned nineteen and had no position of my own, I watched as he chafed under the surplice of priesthood. His parishioners desired a mild-mannered curate, but he had the soul of a soldier, a statesman and an orator. He longed for all that lay beyond the petty concerns of his parish. He grew sullen and silent, withdrawing into himself.

It was a long winter, that year.

In spring, light had returned to Laon's eyes: He was to be a missionary.

I hated his epiphany. Selfishly, I had thought myself abandoned. I spared not a heartbeat for those that languished in the grim empires without word of the Redeemer. All I knew was that he would leave behind the scenes and skies of our shared childhood and, in seeking adventure beyond my reach, he would sever himself from me. Festering full of fear and envy, I took up a position as a lady's companion and later, a governess.

It wasn't until I opened his first letter home, all smelling of sugar and sulphur, that I discovered that he been sent to Arcadia. His letters were infrequent at best and spoke little of his life here. I had assumed he thought such details would agitate me and reawaken that buried wanderlust.

But my brother had apparently been just as worryingly terse to the mission society. After the extent of his silence became evident to me, I began planning my own journey. In a flurry of letters, I somehow managed to convince the London Missionary Society that though it may be unorthodox for an unmarried woman to travel abroad, I should follow my brother. I had never thought myself particularly persuasive in writing, but I must have been superlatively so for them buy my passage on *The Quiet*.

And so, here I was: clutching the compass he had left behind, knot tightening within my heart, under the light of a pendulum sun

Take a look at our other brilliant
fantasy-esque novels at
angryrobotbooks.com

**ANGRY ROBOT**

We are Angry Robot

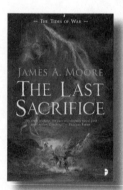

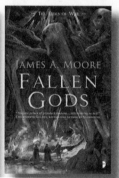

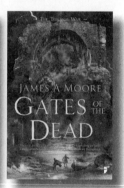

angryrobotbooks.com

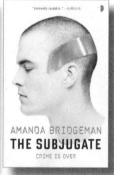